Douglas Schofield was raised and ed
degrees in History and Law. Over the p
trial lawyer in British Columbia, Bern
those years, he has prosecuted and de
sexual assault and other serious crim
Assistant Solicitor General in th

Succession is his second novel

By the same author

Flight Risks

*To Edie
with my best wishes!
Douglas Schofield*

SUCCESSION

DOUGLAS SCHOFIELD

miwk

Succession

This edition first published May 2012 by Miwk Publishing Ltd.
Miwk Publishing, 12 Marbles Way, Tadworth, Surrey KT20 5LW

ISBN 978-1-908630-28-5

Copyright © Douglas Schofield 2012

The rights of Douglas Schofield to be identified as the author of this work have been asserted in accordance with the Copyright, Designs and Patents Act 1988

All rights reserved. No part of this publication may be reproduced, stored in or introduced into a retrieval system, or transmitted, in any form, or by any means (electronic, mechanical, photocopying, recording or otherwise) without the prior written permission of the publisher. Any person who does any unauthorised act in relation to this publication may be liable to criminal prosecution and civil claim for damages.

A CIP catalogue record for this book is available from the British Library.

Cover and book design by Robert Hammond.

Typeset in Times New Roman.

Printed & bound in the UK by the MPG Books Group, Bodmin and King's Lynn

Paper stock used is natural, recyclable and made from wood grown in sustainable forests. The manufacturing processes conform to environmental regulations.

This book is sold subject to the condition that it shall be not, by way of trade or otherwise, be lent, re-sold, hired out, or otherwise circulated without the publisher's prior consent in any form of binding or cover other than that in which it is published and without a similar condition including this condition being imposed on the subsequent purchaser.

www.miwkpublishing.com
This product was lovingly Miwk made.

Dedicated to my indomitable mother
Rosemary Jackson
Survivor of the Battle of Britain
A royal lady in her own right

Acknowledgements

I first conceived this story in the mid-1990's, while I was living in British Columbia. A television documentary on the life of George III made a fleeting reference to Hannah Lightfoot, the so-called "Fair Quaker" who – the narrator alleged – George had secretly married eighteen months before he ascended the throne. On further research, I discovered that the story of George and Hannah's clandestine marriage, if it was mentioned at all, was dismissed by most historians as mischievous myth-making.

That may be so, but the potential consequences of such a union led me to imagine the story you are about to read.

A number of people have earned my undying gratitude for their help, suggestions and encouragement in bringing this story to publication. My longtime friend and colleague Robin McMillan deserves special mention, not only for his erudition, but also for his piquant sense of humor and perceptive insights into human nature. And no words can express the depth of my gratitude to Patrol Officer David Conte of the City of Bayonne Police Department, who went to extraordinary lengths to ensure that several critical scenes set in Bayonne are geographically accurate. As well, my heartfelt thanks go to Dirk Crokaert, manager of the Montague on the Gardens Hotel in London, for his cheerful assistance in reconstructing, at least in my mind's eye, his hotel as it was in 1997 – and for allowing me to christen the Montague's fictional hotel manager with his name.

There are many others to thank, almost too numerous to count: In the Cayman Islands, attorneys David Dinner and William Helfrecht, former Deputy Solicitor General Vicki Ellis, and court reporters Carol Rouse and Karen Myren. In Florida, Larry and Maria Fernandez, and Dr. Greg Hoeksema. In California, Jayne Wayne. In Holland, Dr. Tamer Tadros. In London, Mustafa, Everett, Anja, Daniella and all the amazing staff at the Montague Hotel, as well as our dear friends Martin and Sue Griffiths and their three astonishing children. Last, but by no means least, those stalwart gentlemen at Miwk Publishing, Matthew West and Robert Hammond.

I apologize in advance to any whose names I have inadvertently overlooked. I am truly grateful to you all.

Finally, above all and always, my love, my devotion and my thanks go to my dear wife Melody, whose joyful smile never fades, and whose faith in me never flags.

"Uneasy lies the head that wears a crown."

- Wm. Shakespeare, *Henry IV,* Part II, Act III, Scene I

Richmond, England
1759

In a thunder of hooves and flying gravel, a chaise carriage raced through the deepening night. The driver, riding postillion astride the lead horse, thrashed the animal's flanks, urging more speed.

Behind him, on the prow of the speeding carriage, a mahogany window blind dropped. A man's bewigged head appeared. The pale face below the wig was middle-aged, its thin features sharp as chert.

John Stuart, the Third Earl of Bute, scanned the blackness ahead. His bloodless lips were pursed with anger... but his sweating forehead and staring eyes betrayed fear.

A milestone slid past, gleaming in the moonlight. It bore a black-painted number: *12*.

Reluctantly, he settled back onto his seat. He plucked a lace handkerchief from the sleeve of his silk coat. He dabbed his brow. His normally crisp and devious mind was in a chaotic tumble.

One dread thought kept surfacing:

The King will have me hanged.

The carriage tore through the night.

An hour passed.

Flickering lights appeared on the road ahead.

The carriage slowed. It swung through an imposing stonework gateway. On both sides, inlaid terracotta medallions displayed an identical legend:

Marble Hill House

The carriage swept up a graveled drive, its verges marked by flaming torches. It swayed to a stop before an imposing Palladian villa. The horses pawed and snorted, the foam at their mouths flecked with blood. The driver leapt to the ground. He scurried to open the carriage.

Too late...

Bute erupted from the mud-spattered conveyance, straightened his coat, and strode across the flagged porch.

The huge front door swung inward. A manservant appeared, lantern aloft. His eyes widened at the sight of the great man moving toward him with awful purpose.

"My Lord!"

"The Prince, man! Where is he?"

"In the ballroom, My Lord! If you'll kindly follow–!"

Bute shouldered past him.

The ballroom was a flickering, candle-lit fantasy.

Courtiers congregated near an immense table laden with food and drink. Bewigged gentlemen in embroidered frock coats and knee-length breeches sported rented swords that most had no earthly idea how to use. Women wearing *mantua* dresses, heavy with silver weave and whalebone hoops, flirted with the men and passed coded messages to each other with their flicking fans. Musicians played. A low hum of conversation floated through the room, punctuated by tinkling female laughter and the occasional baritone guffaw.

One young couple was the obvious centre of attention. The male, barely out of his teens, had a soft face, girlish mouth and oddly protruding eyes. He was richly clad in emerald brocade. At his side stood a gorgeous young woman. She appeared to be a few years older than her companion. She had arresting liquid eyes and, unlike most of the women around her, a flawless complexion.

She was wearing a stunning wedding gown.

Several paces away, two men stood apart, conversing quietly. One was attired in the utilitarian choir habit of an Anglican minister. The other, tall and thin, cut an austere figure in the conservative dress favored by men who were well accustomed to the exercise of power.

The clergyman's name was James Wilmot. His companion was William Pitt, Secretary of State and *de facto* First Minister to the King. Wilmot had no inkling that just three hours earlier he had unwittingly helped this consummate politician perpetrate a brilliant piece of mischief upon their beloved Sovereign.

Beloved by Reverend Wilmot, perhaps… but not by William Pitt. The Chief Minister most cordially and unreservedly despised the current Monarch. Pitt consoled himself with the certain knowledge that the old man's health was declining. It was his fervent hope that the King's grandson and Royal heir, standing not thirty feet away, would one day prove to be a more well-disposed and malleable replacement.

A commotion disturbed the back of the room. Pitt and Wilmot turned to look just as Lord Bute rushed into view, two steps ahead of his frightened escort. His Lordship's steps faltered, then stopped. He stood rooted, taking in the scene before him. His gaze fell on the smiling young couple, busily engaged in conversation. His eyes flickered over the woman's gown.

Lord Bute looked positively appalled.

William Pitt's lips twisted into a smirk.

The young Prince noticed the lull in conversation. He spied Bute. He held up one hand. The music stopped.

"Ah. Our Lord Bute…"

Bute bowed, straightened.

"Your Royal Highness."

Prince George addressed the room. "As my Lords and Ladies will see, our Groom of the Stole has graced us with his presence." Puzzled murmurs, followed by a desultory scattering of clapped hands. The Prince continued, fixing his bulbous gaze on Bute. "Or, should I say, our Groom of the Stool! You are welcome here, sir, but I assure you – we no longer require assistance in our privy closet!"

After a moment of shocked silence, a nervous titter rippled through the assembly.

"But despair not!" the Prince continued. He swept an arm, encompassing the assemblage. "Champagne flows, and our lovely ladies imbibe! Perhaps one of them will require your assistance with her *bourdaloue*!"

A few scattered females gasped at this reference to the trusty urinary appliance – its use compelled by the vast, archaic dresses that imprisoned them – but most remained cautiously expressionless. They waited warily, their eyes on the Prince.

His face broke into a wide grin.

General laughter followed.

The Earl's face reddened. "Thank you, Sire. But I must crave an immediate word in private!"

The Prince's mirthful expression evaporated. "Not this night, sir!"

Bute's hand dipped inside his coat. He produced an envelope, sealed with red wax.

"Sire... I bring a letter. From the King!"

"Thank you. I shall give it my full attention on the morrow."

"Your Highness! The night is not spent! It is not too late!" There was a distinct note of panic in Bute's tone.

The room fell silent.

The Prince's gaze slowly swept over his watching guests. All eyes were suddenly averted.

All but Pitt's. The Prince of Wales and the Secretary of State exchanged a long and significant look.

The Prince's lips tightened. He addressed Bute. "Fie, sir! You are impertinent!" he replied tightly. "Moreover, you are wrong." He extended an arm to encircle the young woman's waist. "My bride and I have only these thirty minutes past descended from our apartments. Our gracious guests have accepted my apologies for our... tardiness. And so, you see, you are indeed unquestionably and irrevocably... too late."

The crowd tittered.

The young woman blushed and pressed closer to her Prince.

Lord Bute's dignity crumbled. "Sire, please! I beg you! His Majesty requires–!"

"I'm sure my dear grandfather has more pressing matters weighing upon him. Our war with the French, for example? Enough!" The Prince pointedly turned his back on the Earl. "Music!" he called.

Bemused musicians fumbled with their instruments, then broke into a lively cotillion. Couples formed up to dance.

The Prince gestured to a servant. "Please provide Lord Bute with a cup of punch, and see to his driver." He took his bride's hand and led her away to join the dance.

For an offended second or two, Bute stared at his Royal patron's firmly turned back. Then he stalked over to Pitt.

"God's blood, Mister Pitt!" Bute's face was mottled with pique and humiliation. "How could you countenance such folly?"

Pitt regarded the Earl with a cool eye. "The Prince would have his lady," he stated blandly.

Bute glared into Pitt's expressionless face. "You play your infernal politics at risk to the Realm, sir! The future King of England… married to a commoner? Lunacy!"

Pitt turned to watch the dance. The young woman's face sparkled with happiness. With each turn of the contredanse, her eyes sought out the Prince's. As Pitt watched, the Prince twirled the girl away from the dancing couples and swept her mischievously toward an archway. Beyond lay a dimly lit staircase, leading upward.

"Mark my words!" Bute declared, his voice choked with emotion. "England will pay dearly for this night!"

**Bayonne, New Jersey
1997**

1

The alarm clock destroyed her sleep.

At first, the sound was just a new element in her dream. Finally, after a few seconds of swirling dreamscape confusion, the insistent noise registered. She groaned. She reached out, her hand probing for the source of the annoying jangle. Her groping fingers ended the torment.

The dream melted away like spun candy, leaving just a filament of memory floating through her consciousness. It was something about her father and Eddie, aboard *Miss Penny*.

Then it was gone.

She rolled over and stared at the window. Outside, the world was black as a tomb.

Hell! What time is it?

She switched on her bedside light and checked the clock.

5:02?

Then she remembered…

The funeral.

Damn that Rita!

She sat up, blinking away sleep. She glanced at the empty pillow next to her. Her stomach knotted. She stamped down the accompanying thought. She swung her legs over the edge of the mattress. Her feet found the carpet. She rose, naked, and slipped into her robe.

She padded out of the bedroom into the small sitting room of her apartment, snatched up the remote and switched on the television. The coverage was well underway. For a few seconds, she stared dully at the screen. Then she plodded to the kitchen and switched on the coffee maker. She leaned on the counter, staring at the flickering screen in the sitting room, waiting for Mr. Coffee to sputter his way to a full pot.

Even in the semi-darkness, even half-awake with her luxurious dark hair in disarray, Emma Parks was a startling beauty. Her exquisite, classical features and Elizabeth Taylor eyes – violet with mysterious flecks of indigo – had dazzled more than a few ardent suitors. One mesmerized journalist, writing a Sunday feature about inner city emergency rooms, had succumbed to shameless purple prose. He'd described Emma as 'a stunning porcelain beauty, completely out of place in the gritty ER world of emaciated addicts, thumped-out hookers and gut-shot gang bangers'. That passage had offended her deeply. Worse, it had earned some bitter glances and acid comments from several female coworkers.

In the final decade of the twentieth century, medicine was supposed to be a meritocracy. And mostly it was. Outcomes counted. Pretty faces didn't.

At least, that was the theory.

The reality was that hospitals were no different from small towns. A few poisonous lies spread by the gossip machine could wreck the reputation of any good-looking, ambitious female resident.

No matter how dedicated.

No matter how competent.

Emma filled a mug with coffee and drifted back into the sitting room. She thumbed the remote, flicking from channel to channel. They were all broadcasting live... ABC, CBS, NBC, Fox, CNN... even E!, the cable entertainment channel.

Emma wasn't surprised. No one was a bigger celebrity than this woman – especially in death.

Princess Diana's coffin, affixed to its gun carriage and awash in arrangements of white lilies and tulips, was passing Wellington Arch, escorted by an honor party of Welsh Guards. Security helicopters thumped overhead. A vast crowd lined The Mall. Here and there, a fussing baby cried. Some mourners wept as the carriage passed, some applauded, but most stood frozen in somber silence. Diana's two young sons, accompanied by their Royal father, grandfather and uncle, walked with studied dignity behind the coffin. Behind them, five hundred civilians, representatives of the dozens of charities Diana had patronized during her life – many in wheelchairs – followed in respectful procession.

The running commentary from the U.S. network anchors irritated her. It was mawkish and at times nauseating. After a few minutes, Emma switched to the BBC simulcast on C-SPAN and returned to the kitchen to refill her mug.

As she resumed her seat, her eyes were drawn to a pair of photographs in a diptych frame sitting next to her television. In one photo, a handsome man in his thirties, wearing full boxing gear, grinned with pride as Emma, aged about ten, faced off against him, gloves up, in a classic boxing stance. In the other, the same man faced the camera from the afterdeck of a lobsterman's workboat. His face wore a crooked half-smile. The boat's name and homeport were embossed on the stern:

Miss Penny
Port Clyde Maine

Emma sighed an apology to the photographs. "I know, Dad," she said out loud. "You don't have to say it."

It was Rita Gomez's fault she was sitting here. Ever since Princess Diana's car crash in that Paris tunnel, Rita's every free moment had been spent in tear-filled genuflections before the high altar of CNN.

"Oh, Emma!" she'd sobbed in her faint Spanish accent. "That beautiful, lovely, fine lady! Those poor boys!"

They'd been sitting in the staff lunchroom, with the old television in the corner permanently tuned to the news cycle's latest Never-Ending-Story. A handful of hospital staffers sat around, hanging on some overwrought correspondent's every word:

"On Sunday night, Prince Charles brought the body of Diana, Princess of Wales, home to a nation convulsed with grief. Prime Minister Tony Blair said–"

For Emma, the whole affair had begun to grate. She'd turned on her friend. "Yes, it's terrible that she died so young! And I'm sorry for her sons! But young women die every day and leave children behind! Why this emotion for someone we've never met? This isn't grief, Rita… it's beyond grief! It's some kind of mass hysteria!"

"How can you say that? At a time like this! That poor wounded woman!"

"Wounded?"

"Yes! By that horrible man, that Charles! And by her terrible life!"

"Terrible life!" Emma snapped. "What the hell did she know about a terrible life?" Emma stood up. Heads turned. "She wasn't *our* 'People's Princess'! We threw that Family out of this country two hundred years ago and now you're acting like somebody shot the President! Do you know how weird that is?"

Disapproving stares followed her to the door.

Now, five days later, here she was, sipping coffee and watching Diana's casket wind its way toward Westminster Abbey… and, somehow, unable to look away.

Somehow, against the grain of Emma's firmly held opinions, she was drawn to this spectacle.

She glanced at the clock.

Time to hit the shower.

Emma leaned in her bedroom doorway, drying her hair, watching the memorial service. But when Elton John began his saccharine paean of goodbye, with its lamely re-jigged lyrics, and when Emma actually felt a lump rising in her throat, she knew she'd had enough.

It was a car accident, dammit! You see worse every day!

She killed the TV.

Back in the bathroom, Emma quickly brushed her hair and popped in new set of disposable contacts. She checked the box. Four pairs left. She made a mental note to refill the prescription.

On the counter below the mirror, cosmetic containers sat in a neat row, precisely arranged with labels facing out. Each label bore the same logo: *Matis-Paris*.

Emma didn't touch them.

She ducked into the bedroom to get dressed.

Emma dropped her keys and clip-on ID on the kitchen counter and opened her apartment door. A newspaper lay on the threshold. She scooped it up and stepped back into the kitchen. She glanced at the front page. Every column inch was devoted to Princess Diana.

She flipped through the sections, sliding out advertising flyers and dropping them into her recycle bin.

She stopped suddenly. She stared in puzzlement at the front of the paper's fourth section. In the middle of the page was a photograph of a thirty-something couple, arms around each other's waist, standing on the vast lawn of an oceanfront mansion. The woman was Macy's catalogue pretty, with perfect teeth – the quintessential all-American blonde. The man was Ivy League handsome, his only distracting feature a somewhat inelegant comb-over of thinning dark hair. The headline read:

CONWAY HEIRESS TO WED PHYSICIAN - Social World Abuzz.

Emma felt her face go hot. She ripped the page from the newspaper, grabbed her keys and ID and stormed out of her apartment.

Princess Diana was forgotten.

2

On Sunday, September 6th, 1609, Captain Henry Hudson conducted a religious service aboard his ship, *Half Moon*, as it lay at anchor in what today's world knows as Rockaway Inlet, off Long Island. After the day's lesson, five Europeans set out in the ship's boat to explore uncharted waters to the west and north. The survey party skirted Coney Island and Gravesend Bay, and penetrated Verrazano Narrows. After clearing the northeast corner of Staten Island, they bore west. They entered what appeared to be a narrow river, although it was actually a tidal strait. In years to come it would be named "Kill Van Kull", a Middle Dutch phrase that means "channel from the pass". To their starboard, on the north side of the Kill, lay a sandy alluvial peninsula. Robert Juet, a Dutch crewman on the ship's boat, would later record in his journal that these lands were "as pleasant with grass and flowers and goodly trees as ever they had seen, and very sweet smells came from them."

On Saturday, September 6th, 1997 – three hundred and eighty-eight years to the day later – Emma Parks wheeled her dented Toyota Corolla across that same peninsula. Its landscape was no longer idyllic, and far from sweet smelling. The verdant lands that had so enthralled the Dutch explorer were no more. Over the intervening centuries, unceasing building, paving and terraforming had changed the lands first known to Dutch settlers as Konstapel's Hoeck, and later as Bergen Neck, into the rock-solid, proudly blue-collar City of Bayonne, New Jersey, population 60,000, give or take.

The climbing sun shone through a thin layer of cloud. It cast a pinkish glow over the Bayonne Medical Center's upper floors as Emma drove into the hospital's new multi-storey parking garage. The facility had only been open for a few months, but was already a source of recurring complaints from hospital staffers who, like the public, were now forced to pay for parking. Emma took her receipt, found a space on the ground floor, and marched across Avenue E to the hospital. She was in a grim mood and it showed. In the physicians' locker room, she shrugged into her lab coat and clipped on her ID. As she was about to leave, morbid curiosity overcame her. She extracted the newspaper article from her pocket.

*"**Newport, Rhode Island.** Randolph Conway, heir to the vast Grenier-Conway fortune, has announced the engagement of his daughter, celebrity socialite and reality show headliner, Caroline Conway, to–"*

The locker room door flew open and Nurse Rita Gomez, small and urgent, burst into the room.

"Emma! Bad one coming!"

Emma shoved the article back into her pocket. "What is it?"

"Head-on, on 185!"

"Head-on? That's got a median!"

"Some drunk in a pickup crossed that grass stretch up by the Linden crossroad!"

Emma started moving. "And I suppose we got the drunk!"

"No. The other guy."

The two women rushed into the corridor just as an ambulance gurney sped past, pushed at a quick trot by a paramedic. A second EMT scurried along beside the stretcher, hand-bagging oxygen to an unconscious young Hispanic male.

"Did you watch the funeral?" Rita asked as they rushed along in the paramedics' wake.

"As much as I could stand."

Rita grunted.

The gurney blasted through swinging doors into a crash room with Emma and Rita close behind.

An emergency team swung into action, tugging on gowns and aprons and caps, and snapping on gloves. They transferred the patient to the table and cut away his clothes.

The man's chest was a deformed mess.

Emma started the examination. Her eyes cut to the paramedic who'd been pushing the gurney. "Talk to me!"

"Airbag failed. Steering wheel collapsed. We had to pry him off the column."

"Tough going on the airway!" added his partner.

The patient's skin was gray. And that smell... Emma knew that smell. A sickening memory reared its head. She fought it off.

This guy was teetering at death's door.

Time! Please, God, just give me some time!

She bent close to the patient and raised her voice. "What's your name?" No response. She pressed her finger against the orbital bone of his eye.

No reaction.

"Where's Ted?" Emma barked.

"Right here!" A heavyset radiologist in a lab coat appeared at her side, still gowning up.

"I need X trauma protocol." Emma looked at Rita. "Intubate him!" She pointed at a junior resident, a nervous-looking male. "You! Help her! Learn something!"

While Emma listened to the patient's chest, the radiologist swung the flexible arm of a portable x-ray machine into position.

"Isn't Grant on today?" Emma asked. "Where the hell is he? We need a surgeon!"

"I phoned!" an older nurse answered.

The radiologist used the collimator lamp to site the x-ray field. "Step back!" he ordered. The team retreated for one zap, then another.

Rita finished the intubation and got oxygen flowing.

Emma checked the heart and BP monitor.

"Ted! I need that film yesterday!"

"Time travel is my specialty." The radiologist clipped an x-ray to a light box. Emma craned to study it while she moved her stethoscope across the man's disfigured chest.

"Pressure?"

"Sixty-five systolic, falling," the older nurse answered.

"He's bleeding! Where?"

"Here's the pelvic." The radiologist jammed another x-ray onto the light box.

Emma stared at it. "Nothing. Rita... I need a chest tube!"

"What size?"

"Yellow! Somebody call upstairs! Tell them we need a surgeon, any surgeon! We're losing this guy!"

The older nurse went for a wall phone while Rita broke out a chest tube tray.

Emma felt for landmarks. As she prepared to stab the trocar between the patient's ribs, the heart monitor's beeping faltered... the line flattened...

The alarm went crazy.

Emma blanched. She stared at the monitor, willing it to start. The line stayed flat. "Defib!" Rita moved fast and handed her the paddles. Emma hesitated. She stared at the x-ray. "Where's that damned bleed?"

"Maybe his heart!" the radiologist suggested. He slid an ultrasound probe across the patient's sternum. "Look!" He tapped the screen. "There's a tear in the heart muscle!"

Emma glared at the image on the monitor. "Shit! It's leaking under the pericardium, squeezing his heart!" She handed the paddles back to Rita. "Pericentisis!" Emma's face was tight, but her voice was calm.

The radiologist looked at her. "Have you ever done one?"

"I've assisted."

"Emma...?

Rita didn't just look uncertain – she looked terrified.

"Get me the tray, Rita!"

Rita didn't argue. The tray appeared. Emma picked up a syringe with a lethal-looking oversized needle. With one eye on the ultrasound monitor, she slid the needle into the patient's damaged chest. The room went still. Everyone watched the monitor as the needle penetrated the outer lining of the heart. Carefully, Emma drew the needle back, leaving a thin catheter in place.

Blood flowed into the barrel of the syringe.

A long second passed. The heart monitor beeped... beeped again... then restarted at a steady rate.

Emma checked the blood level in the syringe. "Twenty cc's."

A male voice came from behind her. "Ten more and he'd have been dead."

Everyone turned as Dr. George Grant entered the room, masked and gowned. He edged Emma aside and checked the patient, then the monitors. "Okay. Get him up to surgery!"

Team members pitched in, readying the transfer.

Emma stripped off her mask and gloves.

"Good job, Emma." Grant released his mask.

"You prick!"

Startled team members froze.

"I'm sorry! I was stuck in the elevator!"

"Not that, you bastard!" Emma yanked the newspaper article out of her pocket. "This!" She held up the torn page.

Grant's expression changed. He lowered his voice. "Emma... I've been meaning to–"

He didn't see the punch coming.

Emma nailed him on the jaw. Grant staggered, tripped over his own feet and fell against a utility cart. Instruments clattered to the floor.

The team members gaped.

Emma advanced on Grant as he climbed to his feet. He backed against the wall. He flinched as she slammed the article against his chest.

"Meaning to tell me what?" Emma's eyes filled. "That you've been using me?"

"It's not... like that! I never intended–!"

"Don't even try!" Emma stepped back. The page of newsprint fluttered to the floor. Emma wiped a tear with the back of her hand. "I feel sorry for your little rich bitch!"

She wheeled and marched out of the room.

3

Dr. George Grant sat alone at a table in a far corner of the hospital cafeteria. Most of the tables were occupied, but those closest to him were empty.

He suspected he knew why.

A half-eaten sticky bun sat on a plate at his elbow. He pushed it aside and sipped his latte. He grimaced as the warm liquid hit the split flesh on the inside of his lip. His fingers touched his mouth. The skin was pulped and swollen. He looked sharply around to see if anyone was watching him. One nurse, two tables away, had her eyes locked right on him. She turned away, grinning. She passed a remark to her companions. One of them shot a glance, saw him looking and turned away.

Grant kept his expression neutral, but inside he was seething.

Yes, he'd enjoyed his dalliance with Emma Parks. After all, she was sensationally beautiful and she'd looked damned fine on his arm the few times they'd stepped out. She was good in bed, maybe a bit conventional, a bit tentative – and later a bit clinical (clinical was a turnoff, but he knew that came with the territory when you dated a doctor) – but that amazing face of hers, looking up at him from the pillow, had made up for the deficiencies.

So, yes, Emma had been worth it. And it hadn't actually taken much effort. Working opposite rotations had given him the freedom he'd needed to stay fully engaged in the Caroline campaign while still getting a classy bit of crumpet, as the Brits called it, from young Dr. Parks.

And, no, he hadn't told her everything. He certainly hadn't told her that the last thing he wanted was a two-doctor marriage. They always went the same way – the woman took time off to have kids, then to raise the kids, all the while growing thicker in waist and thigh, while the husband worked his butt off so they could have a five-bedroom house on some suburban hill, juggling his practice, his wife, his kids and an endless string of community events.

Fucking boring.

Not that Emma had ever hinted she was looking for such a life, but with that blue-collar background of hers, it just had to be her goal. No question.

Who needed that shit? Not Mrs. Grant's little boy.

Caroline was a different thing altogether. She might not be the knockout Emma was, but she came with a lifestyle package that was a hell of a lot more stimulating – champagne-soaked parties, finger-snap service, Lears and Gulfstreams, and red carpet premieres in Toronto, Cannes and Venice. His interludes of exposure to his fiancée's glitzy world had been addictive. He had no inclination – zero! – to walk away from that. It had taken a lot of maneuvering to get where he was now. The pre-nup agreement Caroline's father insisted he sign had even included a few "golden opportunities", as Grant's surprised lawyer had gleefully pointed out.

The game was definitely worth the candle.

Hell, he thought, Emma had just been a diversion. He hadn't even been formally engaged when he was seeing her. Although he had to admit he'd cut it pretty close.

But now, the little bitch had made him look like a jerk.

He might have been willing to weather the humiliation if he'd been able to accept the position he'd been offered at the Boston Medical Center. But for some bizarre reason, Caroline liked it that he worked part-time at a community hospital, "helping the underprivileged" as she liked to put it. Maybe it appealed to some weird sense of *noblesse oblige* that Daddy had inculcated in her. She seemed to enjoy bragging to her friends – soon to be, he hoped, *their* friends – that her George was a selfless surgeon who would rather work among the poor than exploit his skills in a grubby pursuit of fame and wealth. Anyway, she'd said, we don't need to worry about money.

Caroline had insisted he didn't need a full-time position at a university hospital or prestige medical centre just to please her or to fit into her world. "My friends will respect you more," she'd said. "They are all pretty socially conscious."

Sure they are, he thought. It's pretty easy to be socially conscious when your parents are worth billions and you're coasting through life on a bottomless trust fund.

But, bottom line, he hadn't wanted to upset Caroline during this critical period, so he'd gritted his teeth and gone with the flow.

So, what to do about Emma? He didn't want to have to face her every day of his working life. She'd be a constant reminder to him, and to all her friends on the crash teams, of just what a crumb he'd been.

He could rearrange his work. Maybe increase his teaching hours, and find another low-end hospital to keep up the community service façade.

But why should he rearrange *his* life?

Maybe she should rearrange hers.

He thought about that.

4

Emma passed the ER nursing station, moving fast. Behind the counter, a nurse spoke quickly into a phone and then held the receiver aloft. "Dr. Parks! Call for you!"

"Take a message!" Emma kept walking.

"It's from London!"

Emma stopped. "As in... England?"

The nurse nodded.

Emma retraced her steps. The nurse passed her the receiver. She put it to her ear.

"Hello?"

"Hello! Might I be speaking to Miss Parks? Miss Emma Parks?" The voice was male, with a distinct English accent.

"This is Dr. Parks. Who's calling please?"

"Yes, of course. Dr. Parks! My name is Tannahill. Kenneth Tannahill. Thank you for taking my call."

"You're welcome. How can I–?"

"I'm a journalist."

"A journalist?"

"Yes. With the London *Herald*."

"Okay..." Emma was puzzled.

"I'd like to talk to you about that Meissen vase you presented on 'Antique Marketplace'."

" 'Vawze'? Oh... my vase! Sorry, it's not for sale."

A few feet away, the nurse busied herself with paperwork, obviously trying to listen.

"No, no, you don't understand! I don't want to buy it! I have important information about its provenance."

Emma's eyes narrowed. "What do you mean?"

"I'll explain when I see you."

Now Emma's alarm bells went off. "What do you mean?"

"I'll be in Newark tonight. May I call you at home?"

"Wait a minute! You're traveling from London to talk to me about a vase?"

"Yes."

Rita appeared at the far end of the corridor, moving fast. She was heading straight for Emma.

"May I call you?" the man on the phone repeated.

Silence.

"Dr. Parks?"

Emma was watching Rita. Her friend's face wore a worried expression. "Um... I suppose."

"Excellent! Until later, then... Goodbye, doctor."

"Bye. Wait a minute! You don't have my number!"

The man had disconnected.

Totally confused, Emma passed the receiver back to the nurse, who gave her a quizzical look.

"Emma!"

Rita arrived at her side.

"What's wrong?"

"The Chief's looking for you! He wants you in his office, stat!"

"What about?"

"I think... that little incident this morning."

Emma's expression hardened. "I don't need this." She headed for the elevator.

Five minutes after she reached the second floor, the phone call from the journalist was forgotten.

The Jaguar XJ6 saloon sped along the M4 motorway. Sprawling housing estates, interspersed with undersized woodland afterthoughts, slid past on either side of the car. Kenneth Tannahill sat alone in the rear seat. He pressed a dial code on his mobile – his 'cell phone' as the Americans strangely insisted on naming the device. He waited. After three rings, the other party answered.

"I've made contact," Tannahill said. "We'll meet tomorrow."

He listened.

"That depends." He allowed a second to pass. "I've been reconsidering my... remuneration package."

He listened.

"Yes. But that was then. This is now."

He listened to the expected question.

"Two million."

He gazed calmly out the window, waiting.

Seconds ticked.

"Thank you," he said finally. "I'll call you after the meeting."

He disconnected and slipped his mobile into his pocket.

Kenneth Tannahill was middle-aged, owlish and rotund. He had looked like this – at least, the owlish and rotund part – since he was ten years old.

Because of his appearance, for most of his forty-four years people had routinely underestimated him.

Their mistake.

When people underestimated you... when they looked you over and quickly labeled you as a harmless mediocrity, they let their guard down. Prejudgment was a dependable human failing, and it had made Kenneth Tannahill one of the London *Herald's* most successful reporters.

"You're a Tannahill, and a Tannahill is nobody's fool," his father had always said. "Never forget that, Kenneth."

This one certainly isn't, he thought. He allowed himself a small smile of satisfaction as he settled back in his seat.

Ahead, an exit sign read: *Heathrow (Terminals 1, 2, 3) Uxbridge A408*. The chauffeur flicked the turn indicator.

5

Dr. Ellington Rutledge, Pembroke Hospital's CEO, was a huge bear of a man with a head of thick black hair and a permanent five o'clock shadow. He sat behind a broad desk that looked two sizes too small for him. Although he was now primarily an administrator, he still dressed in a lab coat. He'd had it fitted by a professional tailor, but it still seemed to strain at the seams.

At this moment, Rutledge was absorbing the contents of a thin file that lay open in front of him. The folder was framed between two huge hands that had once been the terror of every opposing football team's offensive line. His teammates' nickname for him had been 'Bearpaw'.

At Med school, the Profs had been blunt. They'd said he'd never make a surgeon with hands like that. They'd been wrong. Over the years, Ellington Rutledge's two big hands had saved hundreds of lives.

Rutledge had already read this file, and a second reading was not making him any more comfortable.

There was a knock on his door.

"Come!" he called.

The door opened and surgical resident Emma Parks stepped in.

"I heard you wanted to see me." Her tone was neutral. If she was apprehensive, she wasn't showing it.

"Emma! Come in." Rutledge waved at a chair.

As Emma approached his desk and settled into a guest chair, Rutledge felt a watery sensation in his knees. Emma Parks was one of those effortless beauties with the unnerving capacity to excite teenaged giddiness in grown men – and intense envy in women. Ellington Rutledge had been married for eighteen years, and he'd never once cheated on his wife. But there was just something about this young woman that made a man think about…

He banished the thought with an involuntary cough.

"Sir, if this is about this morning…" Emma began.

It was. But Rutledge wasn't ready to deal with that yet. He deflected her with a question.

"How's that ER rotation going?"

That took her off guard. "Fine, I guess." She paused. "Actually, better than fine."

"'Better than fine'?"

"I like the adrenaline." Her smile had a predictable effect on Rutledge. He felt his groin muscles tighten.

He managed a measured reply. "I know what you mean. It's a bit addictive, isn't it?"

Emma nodded. "Am I here to discuss the rotation?"

"No, Emma. I wish you were. There's been a complaint."

"A complaint?"

"Yes." Rutledge paused. "I understand you saved a life today."

Emma stared. "And someone... complained?"

"Not about that. If the patient's family had their way, they'd erect a monument to you. That was fine work." He shifted in his seat. "The complaint relates to what happened next."

"You mean, when I decked George Grant."

For a millisecond, Rutledge savored a mental image of Grant being knocked on his ass by Emma Parks. He struggled to suppress a smile.

"Yes. I'm sorry."

"I'm not."

Rutledge blinked. "Oh."

"Who complained?" Emma asked. "The patient was unconscious. And the team members are all my friends."

Rutledge sat quietly, waiting.

Emma looked at him. "Grant?"

Rutledge nodded once.

"You've got to be kidding!"

"Not kidding. Dr. Grant has filed a formal written complaint against you."

Emma was momentarily speechless.

"He states that you assaulted him in front of other staff members," Rutledge continued. "I take it you admit that?"

"Yes. And he knows why! But I'll bet he didn't mention that in his complaint, did he?"

"He says, and I quote—" Rutledge read from the file "—'the respondent's actions were calculated to lower the complainant in the esteem of his professional colleagues and associates, thereby irreparably damaging the complainant's reputation within the institution. The complainant says that the respondent's unprofessional conduct should attract condign punishment, not short of dismissal from employment'."

"Bastard!" Emma breathed the word more to herself than to Rutledge.

He looked at her. She was staring at the page he'd been reading from, her eyes glistening with pain, disbelief... and something else.

Something he had never seen in Dr. Emma Parks.

Vulnerability.

Rutledge didn't know where to look. To give her a few seconds to recover, he pretended to search for something in a drawer.

"*Condign* punishment?" Emma blurted. "Where did he get that? This isn't the eighteenth century!"

"It is an odd choice of words. But don't worry about that part. The complainant has no say in the final disposition. Grant lifted most of the wording from the H.R. Manual. I spoke with our attorney. He says Grant has an arguable case. Unprovoked assault is a criminal offence and it can be grounds for a finding of gross misconduct."

"Unprovoked?"

Rutledge nodded.

"Do you know why I slugged him?"

"I think I can guess." Rutledge slid a hand under the file folder and produced a creased section of newsprint. It was the article Emma had torn from the newspaper. "I didn't tell Rita Gomez why I wanted to see you, but she's a smart lady. She brought me this. She said you and George Grant have been dating."

"Until two weeks ago. He ended it. He wouldn't explain why." She nodded at the article. "Then I saw that."

Rutledge sighed. "Emma, let's pretend for a minute I'm not your Chief Officer. Let's say I'm just... an old friend. Okay?"

She looked at him warily. "Okay."

"What was the attraction?"

Emma's mouth opened, then closed. She didn't answer.

"Didn't you notice anything about Grant that worried you?"

Emma bit her lip.

"For example," Rutledge continued, "the fact that he has no friends?"

Emma took a deep breath. "I thought, you know... the work... the hours."

"Okay. We all understand that. What about this: do you want to have children one day?"

"Yes."

"Do you see in George Grant the qualities you would want in your children?"

Silence.

Rutledge watched Emma's eyes. He saw the hint of recognition. She'd thought these thoughts. And she'd suppressed them.

"Emma, I've read your personnel file. You haven't listed a next of kin. The only name you provided was that of an attorney. I looked her up on the State Bar list. You're both about the same age, so I'm guessing... a friend from school, or college?"

"College."

"The H.R. Department's notes from your initial interview state that you lost your family when you were young."

Emma dropped her head as memories crowded in. "I don't see–"

"I'm not asking what happened, Emma. But would I be right in guessing that you've had to rely on your own resources since you were quite young?"

"Yes."

"You've worked very hard to get to where you are today."

"Yes."

"Would I also be right in suggesting that because of that you never really had much time for... personal relationships."

"You mean, romantic relationships?"

"Yes."

Silence hung in the air between them.

Finally Emma sat back. She looked at him with wounded eyes.

"I was naïve, wasn't I?"

"Don't blame yourself. I've known George Grant for a long time, and I know what he is. He uses people."

"I should have introduced him to Jan – my friend, the attorney. She's good at sizing people up."

"Why didn't you?"

"I guess... I knew. Something told me he was a mistake, but I didn't want to hear that from her."

"Instead, you had to read it in the newspaper."

"Yeah." Emma swallowed. "What happens now?"

"Unfortunately, the Board gets uptight when staff members bring their dramas to work." He grimaced an apology. "Those are the Chairman's words, not mine. So now you and I both have a problem. As much as I hate to do this, Grant's complaint forces me to put the whole disciplinary procedure into motion. I want you to stop by Della's desk on your way out. She'll give you a copy of the formal complaint and a copy of Grant's statement. I'll need your written response on my desk by Wednesday." He paused. "I want you to take the next three days off."

"But why? I can still–!"

His lifted hand stopped her protest. "No 'buts', Emma. I've arranged coverage for you. You're not being suspended. You're on full pay. I just want you to take some time for yourself. I don't need a distracted physician treating patients."

He pushed back and rose from his chair, signaling that their meeting was over.

Emma stood. "Thank you, sir. I think." She headed for the door.

"Emma…"

Rutledge saw her wipe an eye as she turned back to face him. He spoke gently. "May I offer some advice?"

She nodded.

"Use your time off to work on your statement. Tell it straight – how long you and Grant were intimate, any–" he looked vaguely embarrassed "–you know, promises he made… and when he made them."

Emma's face flushed.

"I know that probably makes you cringe."

"It does!"

"Try to swallow your pride. Explain your emotional state when you came to work today, and the pressures you were under in the crash room. Remember, despite those pressures, you saved a young man's life. That counts for a lot. If we… if *you* handle this right, the only person coming out of that hearing looking like an ass will be George Grant." He paused. "You're going to be a damned good surgeon, Emma. Better than Grant. I won't be permitted to sit on the discipline panel because technically I'm the investigator, but I want you to know I'll do everything I can for you."

"I'm grateful, sir. Thank you."

Emma left.

The door closed.

Rutledge sat down.

He put his head in his hands.

Mentally, he was squirming. He was supposed to be objective.

Even-handed.

Impartial.

The fact was… he was jealous of George Grant for sleeping with Emma Parks. And he was furious at the slimy creep for hurting her.

I'm a damned fool, he thought.

Rutledge sat very still for several seconds. Finally, he gave up trying to sort through all his competing thoughts and urges. He lifted his phone.

"Della, did Dr. Parks pick up her copy of Grant's statement?" He listened. "Okay. I want the name of every staff member who was in the crash room at the time of the incident. Once you've got that, we'll start setting up interviews. Thanks."

He hung up.

He closed his eyes. Men really shouldn't be placed in charge of smart, beautiful women. At least, not until they're over seventy.

Maybe not even then.

6

The pistol range was in a sub-basement, three levels below the street. It was small – just two shooting lanes – but otherwise it was a modern facility in every respect. Its fluorescent fixtures were fitted with parabolic lenses that concentrated the light on a horizontal plane and reduced the wall glare. It had positive exhaust to evacuate the lead dust, baffled ricochet control, and bullet traps and backstops constructed of core-filled concrete blocks with sacrificial cladding.

It was a damned fine little range and Carl Juneau was having a damned fine little session.

Juneau was in his thirties, tall, lean, and dark-eyed. His ear protectors framed an angular and strikingly handsome face. His light brown complexion hinted at mixed race antecedents.

He quick-fired nine shots downrange. He pressed a button. The pulley system zipped the paper target up the lane toward him.

He studied it with satisfaction.

Behind him, an elevator door opened, revealing Henry Leggatt, a precise, wiry man in his late thirties. His style of dress exuded a distinct impression of a metro-male. He blocked the door of the lift with a polished bespoke shoe.

"Carl!"

Juneau turned. He pushed one ear protector aside.

"He wants to see us." Leggatt's cut glass accent was pure public school.

Juneau packed up. He snapped a full clip into his Sig P220, holstered it inside his jacket and strolled to the elevator.

As the door slid shut, Leggatt glanced back at the target hanging directly in front of Juneau's firing position. Nine perforations formed a close pattern in the 5X kill zone.

The office was on the top floor of Canary Wharf tower. On two sides, broad windows looked out over London's urban sprawl. The room itself was furnished in a hodge-podge of Regency and Victorian antiques. The only modern appliances in immediate evidence were a wall-mounted television – tuned at this moment to the endless coverage of Princess Diana's funeral – and a high-tech treadmill upon which Victor Dawson, the office's sole occupant, was determinedly pacing.

Dawson was in his sixties. In decades past, he might have been described as attractive – in a rugged, Celtic sort of way – but today the man's unblinking eyes, with their dark pouches sagging below, lent a soulless aspect to his appearance. Dawson was not unaware of the impression he had on others, and had never been reticent to exaggerate the effect when it suited him. One unsettled business rival had been heard to state that Victor Dawson reminded him of Calabrian mafia Don.

It was well known that the man had not been referring to Dawson's physical appearance alone.

The jowled cheeks below the dark pouches were flushed with exertion, but Dawson's stride was measured and unfaltering. A damp triangle crept down his sweatshirt. His treadmill was positioned to face west, looking out over the city. Brilliant crepuscular rays streaked across the sky – parallel columns of sunlit air, separated by clouds – forming a spectacular backdrop to the London skyline. As Dawson strode, his eyes drank in the sight.

Victor Dawson might not be the master of all he surveyed, but he exercised power that few in this Western capital could equal. He controlled a media empire that spanned the globe, and he was a billionaire many times over.

Juneau and Leggatt entered the office. They crossed the room to the treadmill.

"The Parks project is in motion," Dawson announced without turning his head. "Tannahill left a few hours ago."

Dawson's accent revealed his North Wales background. He'd never tried to hide his early life of poverty in Gwynedd, or change his distinctive manner of speech. In fact, he took a certain perverse pleasure in inflicting his regional accent upon the Pretty People, as he called them. Their arch conversations sickened him. Their smug uselessness offended him.

Consistently out-donating them at every charity function pleased him.

Dawson's eyes cut to Leggatt. "Did you find a photographer?"

"Clive has one, sir."

"Clive has long-lens surveillance spooks! I want a professional."

"Clive has identified a portrait specialist. He says the man is available on short notice."

Dawson stopped the treadmill and stepped off. He slung a towel around his neck and strode to his desk.

It was not an ordinary desk. Ordinary desks were for ordinary men. In the long and meticulous development of Dawson's considerable self-regard, he had never once considered himself an ordinary man. One reason he'd been able to consistently outwit his rivals, he believed, was because the fools spent their working lives lounging in comfortable chairs.

Dawson anchored his feet on a pair of footprints etched into the special gel flooring in front of his two-meter-wide, leather-inlaid Georgian standing desk. He mopped his face with one end of his towel.

"Call the hanger. Tell them we leave for Teterboro tomorrow morning. Wheels up at seven."

"Yes sir," Leggatt replied.

"Mr. Juneau?"

"My team will be ready, sir."

"Good." Dawson lifted a clipped bundle of paperwork from a tray near his elbow. "Thank you, gentlemen."

Juneau and Leggatt turned for the door.

"Henry..."

"Yes sir?"

"You spoke to Bernard?"

"I did. He's cancelled all programming after six tonight. They've put together a nice appreciation... file footage of Diana... classical music... everything you suggested."

"They weren't suggestions, Henry. They were requirements. And make sure he leaves Charles Windsor out. I don't want that man's face on my network!"

"I told him, sir."

Juneau and Leggatt exchanged a look as they left the room.

7

The big man reversed his car into a slot on the second row. It was the only one parked with its nose facing out, but he doubted the woman would notice. The empty stall directly across from his position gave him a clear view of the target's car.

He checked the plate number again.

UVJ44F.

Definitely the right car.

Garden State, the plate bragged. What garden? He hadn't seen any in this town.

He sat low in his seat, waiting.

An hour passed.

She was late. Maybe she was catching up on paperwork.

Then he saw her.

His eyes tracked her movement as she walked toward her car.

He raised his camera. The mechanism whined as he shot a quick sequence.

He watched her dig in her bag, searching for keys. That struck him as negligent – not having her keys out and ready. After all, this was America. He recalled a statistic: every two minutes, somewhere in the United States, a woman is raped.

What a primitive country, he thought.

He zoomed in and snapped off another series. The lighting in the parking garage gave the woman's skin an almost spectral look – like some weird Hollywood special effect.

The expression on her face intrigued him.

Thin-lipped.

Angry.

Almost... hostile.

Was she reliving an argument? Or imagining one?

One thing was certain: Dr. Emma Parks was not a happy woman tonight. But even unhappy, the woman was, well... quite spectacular.

Yes, indeed. A real find.

Good thing rape's not my thing, he thought darkly.

The woman unlocked her car and slid behind the wheel. The man clipped a filter over his camera's lens – one designed to cut through lighting glare and window glass.

He checked through the viewfinder. The back of the woman's head came into sharp focus. He waited while she reversed her car out of the stall.

As soon as he could make out her face through the side window, he resumed his camera work. He kept shooting until the Corolla disappeared from view.

Then he started his engine.

Emma wheeled through the streets of Bayonne, driving on automatic pilot.

Father… mother… brother

Her disturbing interview with Rutledge had dredged up *those* memories. One by one, they'd escaped from the secure place where she kept them locked away. One by one, they had burned their way through her consciousness.

She knew what would come next.

An ash cloud of depression that sometimes took hours to dissipate.

I'm alone…

The hard cruelty of that fact never left her.

Emma had never bought into the one-size-fits-all theory that grief was a "journey" that had to be worked through in some prescribed way. She considered some aspects of counseling industry – with its bereavement gurus, obsession with "journaling", and standardized conventions on the so-called "stages of grief" – to be a contemptible fraud. She'd read the literature. Most studies showed that people who underwent bereavement counseling emerged from grief at exactly the same pace as people who did not.

But, for all that, Emma's mother had unquestionably needed some kind of professional help. In the ten years she'd survived after the loss of her husband and son, Penny Parks had never really emerged from grief. Because of this, Emma's personal reaction to the loss of her father and brother had been forced on her by urgent necessity. Within a few months of the disaster, she'd begun to realize that her mother would never come out of it. So Emma took a conscious decision… one she knew would be essential for their joint survival. One night, lying in her narrow bed, she had mentally wrapped her anguish in heavy canvas and stowed the bundle in the darkest corner of her memory bank.

At the age of twelve, by an act of pure will, Emma Parks had transformed herself into an adult.

Looking back, Emma often wondered how she'd done it. She had plowed on determinedly through her teens and into her twenties. She had worked after-school jobs even before she was old enough to be legally hired. She had eschewed any meaningful social life. She had studied deep into the night, navigated her own way through high school and college and medical school, and consistently aced her exams.

She had done it. She had gone the distance. She was an MD. She loved the work, and she'd never be poor again.

I did it all, and I did it alone.

And now this!

She made a right off Avenue E, spied an open parking space near her apartment building and pulled in.

She remained in the car with the engine running. She closed her eyes and took several deep breaths. Her lips tightened. She nodded, as if she was giving herself a direct order – which she was – shut off the engine and stepped out onto the sidewalk.

She locked her car and then strolled up to Broadway, turned south and headed for the Big Apple.

The street named Broadway in Bayonne, New Jersey, might not compete with the Broadways of New York City and Chicago, but the Big Apple Bar and Restaurant boasted a pretty reliable following. Framed players' jerseys lined the dark paneled walls, and team pennants vied with brewery banners above the immense rectangular bar. The Big Apple offered just the right mix of pro sports on its screens, and amateur entertainment at the bar, to satisfy the steady stream of off-shift cops, paramedics and emergency room denizens who made up a good proportion of its clientele.

Tonight, however, the bar was practically empty. Apart from a few scattered patrons talking animatedly over pitchers of beer, and three guys watching baseball replays on a wall-mounted screen, there wasn't much going on.

Emma and Rita sat in the friendly gloom near one corner of the bar.

"Kinda dead for a Saturday night, Lou," Rita ventured, as the bartender set a Corona with a wedge of lime in front of her.

"Yeah," he replied. "Maybe folks are depressed about Princess Diana."

Rita glanced at Emma, but her friend's expression didn't change. Emma's mind was obviously somewhere else. Rita squeezed the lime into her Corona. She watched the bartender select a bottle from the multi-hued forest of glass on the bar's center island and free-pour clear liquid over ice. The label on the bottle said *Moscow Signature Cristall*. Lou dropped a twist in the glass and set the drink on a napkin in front of Emma.

Rita looked offended. "What's that stuff, like five bucks a shot?" Before the bartender could reply, she snapped, "Separate tabs, Lou!"

"I'm a local. Lou gives me a loyalty discount." Emma's voice was toneless. She wasn't inviting banter. Rita didn't take the hint.

"Hey! What about me? I'm loyal!"

The bartender's only response was a raised, mocking eyebrow.

"And I'm just as good looking!" Rita insisted.

Silence.

"Okay... almost! I'm cute, aren't I? Cute's good, right?"

A middle-aged man with a pockmarked face took a seat at the other end of the bar.

Lou grinned. "Yeah, Rita. Cute's good. You're cute as a button." He moved off to serve the new customer.

Rita stared glumly after him. "I look like a button?"

"He meant a belly button," said a voice from behind them. A fashionably dressed blonde dropped a massive purse on the bar. "Look alive, ladies," she declared as she claimed the stool next to Emma. "Super-Jan is in the building!"

The girls' half-smiled greetings carried the faint weariness of long familiarity.

"So... how was your day?" Jan began, then noticed her friends' expressions and added, "Hey, it's just a social convention. You don't have to answer."

"Okay, we won't," Rita replied. "How was yours?"

"A disaster."

Bartender Lou returned. "Hey Jan!"

"Lou, my darling! My savior! My parched soul awaits your restoring elixir!"

"The usual?"

"Yes, please. But double it!"

"Bad day at court, huh?" He iced a martini glass.

"Let us just say our client took the stand, against Paul's advice and against my advice. The prosecutor spent the next three hours removing his arms and legs." She embarked on an excavation of her purse, depositing the detritus on the bar. "It's supposed to be a trial, but it's more like a guilty plea in slow motion." She located cigarettes and a lighter. She looked at Emma and added incongruously, "I should have taken my Dad's advice."

Jan Chernoff was an attorney. She and Emma had roomed together as college undergrads. What had begun as a symbiotic relationship had matured over the years into an odd but enduring friendship. Jan, a quirky, slightly overweight extrovert with a healthy appetite for male company, had been more than happy to have Emma around as a hunk-magnet. Emma, gorgeous but introverted, never quite comfortable with her undeniable power to attract, had been just as happy to have Jan around to run interference.

Lou set a huge martini in front of Jan. She immediately lifted it to her lips and downed a slug.

Rita goggled. "What is that? A quadruple?"

"I drink to forget," Jan replied evenly. She slid a cigarette from the pack. As she flicked her lighter, she noticed the look on Emma's face. "Oh. Right. Sorry." She laid the cigarette and lighter aside. A second passed, then she added quietly. "I'm sorry, Emma. I haven't had a chance to check the paper."

Rita called out. "Lou, we need a copy of today's *Journal*. Any chance?"

"Think so." He rifled through a recycle bin under the bar and came up with a few newspapers. The top copy was drink-stained. "Sorry. They're a bit beat up."

Emma shuffled through the pile. She found a clean copy of the article. She slid it over to Jan.

Jan stared at the photo, then read the caption. "Christ, what an asshole," she breathed.

She took a long sip from her drink and read the text.

Emma watched her friend's face.

At the other end of the bar, the man with the pockmarked face sat nursing a whiskey. He watched the three women from under hooded lids.

Jan looked up from the page. "You guys know anything about Caroline Conway?"

"Rhode Island Princess," Rita volunteered. "Flunked out of Yale. Always in the celeb mags with that stupid grin on her face." She paused, thinking. "Didn't she elope with some rocker when she was, like, seventeen, and her father got it annulled?"

"That's right." Jan looked at Emma.

Emma shrugged. "Sorry. I don't read *People*."

"Let me put it this way... God's-Gift-To-Surgery has sentenced himself to connubial hell. He has no fucking idea!"

"Maybe," Rita said. "But he's screwing with Emma's career."

"Well, he can try. But he'll have to get past me. I'm coming with you, Em."

"Where?"

"To the discipline hearing."

"Is that smart? They'll think–!"

"They'll think you're just exercising your rights! This is America, Emma! Everyone gets an attorney."

"I'm not denying I slugged him!"

"The assault's not important. Even to him. I'm guessing it's the humiliation he can't stand. He wants you gone so he doesn't have to look at you every day."

"Then he should be the one to leave!" Rita snapped. "Because if he forces Emma out, the rest of us will make his life a living hell!"

Down the bar, the pockmarked man watched and listened.

"Don't worry. I'll barbecue him."

"Grill or spit?" Rita asked.

Emma gave Jan a look of mock gratitude. "I'm sure the Board will find the spectacle riveting."

"Emma, I just want to help!"

Emma sighed. "I know. And I'm grateful. I'm just not sure unleashing Super-Jan on poor little George is the best strategy." She sipped her drink. She remembered something. She looked vaguely at her friend. "What were you saying about your Dad? Something about him giving you advice?"

"Mmm? Oh... he wanted me to go into corporate. 'Stay out of that courtroom shit', he always said. Get a nice position as in-house counsel at some multi-national... parsing contracts... negotiating mergers. Basically, one of those jobs where lawyers sit with checklists, ticking boxes, and fly all over the world taking meetings. Big money, low stress."

"Low stress?" Rita piped in. "Doesn't sound like it."

"His point was, it's only money... it's not life and death."

Silence.

"Sometimes money *is* the difference between life and death," Emma said in a small voice.

The girls looked at her. Jan swallowed. "Oh, crap! I'm sorry, Em! I wasn't thinking about, you know..."

"Yeah. I know." Emma squeezed Jan's hand. "It's just me." She drained her glass and slid off the stool.

"You're going?"

"Yeah."

"We just got here!" Rita bleated.

"Sorry. All this... with Grant. Then getting suspended."

"You're not suspended!" Rita blurted.

"Not officially, but it still feels like it. I'm stressed out. I need to go home."

"Call me at the office on Monday," Jan ordered. "We'll have lunch."

"Sure."

"Promise?"

"Promise. You've convinced me. I need a lawyer." She smiled wryly. "And I've always enjoyed a barbeque party." She picked up her bag. "Later, guys..."

Jan and Rita watched her go, then returned to their drinks.

"Fuck!" Jan muttered.

"What?"

"That girl could have any man! She could *use* any man!"

Rita nodded. "Yeah. But she never does."

"And she never has! Then she picks the *one* bastard who uses her!" Jan picked up her giant drink and took a big swallow.

They didn't notice the pockmarked man slip off his stool, drop money on the bar and leave.

Outside, the man followed Emma to the corner of 19th Street. He stood watching as she walked quickly toward her apartment building. He thumbed a button on a cell phone.

"She's coming," he said.

8

Emma entered her apartment block, one of an identical pair of 40's-era twelve-unit buildings near the intersection of 19th and Avenue E.

She didn't notice the big man standing in deep shadow under the awning of the funeral home across the street. He photographed her as she traversed the sidewalk and entered the building. After the door swung shut behind her, he moved along the sidewalk and shot more photos through the inset glass in the front door while she collected her mail in the foyer.

Emma unlocked the inner door and walked past the elevator, heading for the stairs. The elevator was small and cramped – a nine square foot afterthought installed decades after the building's construction. To Emma, it felt like riding in a vertical coffin and she hated it. She mounted the stairs to the top floor, unlocked her apartment, entered, and bolted the door.

She turned... and froze.

It struck her immediately.

A foreign odor.

Her nostrils flared. It was faint, but definitely there.

A male scent.

She flicked on every light switch within reach and stepped into her sitting room. There was no one there. The room looked undisturbed.

Her eyes narrowed with suspicion. Grant still had a key. She called out. "If you're in here, George, I'll have you arrested!"

Silence.

Emma's jaw tightened. She marched into her bedroom.

There was no one there. Bed, dresser, closet... everything was as she'd left it.

Puzzled, she checked the bathroom.

Nothing.

Methodically, she went room to room, checking her belongings.

All was as it should be.

She lifted her head, checking the air. Whatever that smell was, it had now dissipated.

She strode back to the sitting room and drew the drapes. Before they had closed completely, she noticed headlights on the street below. She peered out in time to see a car pull away from the curb and drive away.

She didn't recognize the car, but that wasn't unusual on this street.

She wheeled and surveyed the room. Her eyes drifted to an exquisite antique porcelain vase sitting in the centre of her small drop-leaf dining table. The vase held a single pastel-pink English Heritage rose.

She suddenly recalled the strange telephone call from the English journalist.

She moved to the table. The rose was drooping. Emma touched it. Petals fell. Unbidden, a syrupy lyric played through her mind.

"Goodbye England's rose..."

Emma lifted the vase and carried it to the kitchen. She removed the spent rose. She held it in her hand for a moment, then, with a twinge of regret, she dropped it into the trash.

She rinsed the vase and dried it gently with a soft cloth. She turned it in her hands. She had always enjoyed looking at it. Across one side, bordered in gold filigree, was a vividly-painted scene of a man in 18th century attire mounted on a horse in full stride.

Emma carried the vase to a sideboard next to the dining table. She opened a small glass-fronted display case and set it inside next to a framed photograph. In the photo, Emma and a bearded man stood together at a small, linen-covered table. The man wore a striped shirt and polka-dotted bow tie. Emma's vase sat on the table in front of them. She and the man both wore wide smiles.

As Emma closed the display case, her telephone rang. For some reason, she felt a frisson of apprehension.

She picked up and answered warily.

"Hello?"

"Dr. Parks?" A male voice.

"Speaking."

"Ken Tannahill here. We spoke earlier."

Emma's jaw clenched. "Tell me how you got this number."

"I'm an investigative reporter, Doctor."

"And you're investigating a vase?"

"Yes. In a sense, I am. I've just checked in at the Reardon. It's really crucial that we meet!"

"What could be crucial about a vase?"

"Your TV appraiser was unaware of certain underlying facts." Emma's eyes cut to the photograph next to the vase. "Believe me, I've–!"

"What underlying facts, Mr. Tannahill?"

"I could start with the true identity of Captain James Conrad Parks."

Emma was taken aback. "Are you talking about my great grandfather?"

"If he is the same James Conrad Parks who died at Sebago Lake, Maine, on the tenth day of October, 1928... Yes, I am."

Emma didn't respond. She was trying to decide how to deal with this intrusive Englishman.

Tannahill sensed indecision. He pressed. "The information I have is very important, Doctor! Important to you."

"You're talking in riddles, sir."

"Give me a chance to explain. Why don't you join me for breakfast? Shall we say, nine?"

Emma hesitated.

"Doctor?"

Emma let a second pass.

"Make it ten."

"Wonderful! Let's meet here at the hotel. I'll be in the Webster Room. I'm five nine, sandy hair... I'll be wearing a blue blazer and grey slacks. I'll watch for you."

Emma blinked. "You know what I look like?"

"Oh, yes! Until tomorrow, Doctor. Bye."

Tannahill disconnected quickly, as if he was afraid Emma would change her mind.

Emma stared at the receiver in her hand. She set it back in its cradle.

She was thoroughly confused.

"If he's the same James Conrad Parks who died at Sebago Lake, Maine, on the tenth day of October, 1928..."

Emma strode to her bedroom and dragged a chair over to the closet. She mounted it and rummaged through the clutter on the shelf above the hangers. She retrieved a worn leather-bound photo album. She stepped down and sat on the bed.

She leafed through the album, searching. She stopped at a wrinkled manila envelope that was pasted onto a page. She opened it and pulled out a handful of black-and-white photographs. She flipped through them until she found the creased old photograph she was looking for. She extracted it from the pile.

In the photo, a grizzled old man wearing a pea jacket stood next to a teenaged boy on a dinghy dock. One of the old man's hands rested lightly on the boy's shoulder. They were each holding a bamboo fly rod.

Emma turned the picture over. On the back was a penciled, barely-legible scrawl:

Grandpa James & Gus
Sebago Lk. 1916

Emma stared at the words.

She returned to the sitting room. She kneeled in front of the television.

47

She opened a small cupboard. Inside was a neat row of VHS tapes. She ran a finger along their labels, selected a tape, and slid it into the TV's built-in cassette player. She sat on the coffee table and used the remote to fast-forward the tape. After a few attempts, she found the footage she was looking for. She let the tape roll.

On the screen, Emma stood with the same bow-tied man from the photograph in her display case. The man was speaking to the camera. His voice was tinged with excitement.

"–flawless example of hard paste porcelain from the Meissen manufactory in Germany…"

The man upended the vase. He pointed to an inscription on the bottom. The camera zoomed and focused. The hand-inscribed letters '*AR*' appeared in the centre of the screen.

"This proves that this vase was a Royal gift," the man continued. "These initials stand for 'Augustus Rex'. He was the King of Poland and the Elector of Saxony. He died in 1733."

Reverently, the appraiser set the vase upright. He turned to Emma.

"This is a very fine piece, Ms Parks! I would value it at eighteen to twenty thousand dollars." He paused significantly. "Of course, if its exact provenance were known, it could be worth quite a bit more."

Emma stopped the tape. She rewound it. She thumbed the Play button.

"Of course, if its exact provenance were known, it could be worth quite a bit more."

She stopped the tape.

Lost in thought, Emma drifted into the kitchen and made herself a sandwich. Then she sat on the sofa, eating slowly… and wondering what the hell was going on.

Forty minutes later, she got ready for bed. She went to the bathroom to brush her teeth. She reached for her toothbrush.

Her hand stopped in mid-reach.

Her eyes were locked on a small bottle of *Matis-Paris* eye-care gel.

The label was facing the wall.

Emma stared at the bottle, her brows knitted in concentration, trying to remember her actions in the bathroom this morning.

She hadn't used makeup.

She never wore makeup at work.

And she always left the labels facing out.

But when she'd come home…

That smell…

Emma sprang into action. She darted through the apartment, checking the locks on every window. She jammed a chair against the door to the outer corridor. She marched to the display cabinet and removed the vase and the photograph. She carried them to the bedroom. She dragged the chair back to the closet, stacked some thick books on it and climbed up. Reaching up, she removed an attic space access panel.

One by one, she set the vase, the framed picture and the old photograph album among rafters next to the access opening. She replaced the panel. Then she arranged spare pillows and an old quilt so the access panel could not be seen.

She closed her closet doors, pulled the chair back to its usual place and climbed into bed.

Emma lay for a long time, staring at the ceiling.

Wondering if she should be afraid.

9

Victor Dawson stood before a long mirror, combing damp hair. He wore trousers with knife-sharp creases and a snowy-white shirt. Nearby, a suit jacket and a selection of expensive silk ties waited on a valet stand.

It was six in the morning on September 7, 1997, and Dawson was about to make history.

There was a knock, and Carl Juneau entered. "The cars are ready, sir."

Juneau had an American accent.

"Thank you, Carl." Dawson nodded at the valet stand. "Which one?"

Juneau's eyes flicked to the stand and back to Dawson. "The red one, sir."

"My choice too." He selected the tie and threaded it under his collar. "Are you fully briefed?"

"Yes sir."

"The girl might need convincing."

"I understand."

"She's American."

"Yes sir."

Dawson caught Juneau's eye in the mirror as he finished knotting his tie. "Is that a problem?"

"Not for me, sir." His lips twisted slightly. "But it might be for you."

Dawson smiled to himself. There was a subtle side to this Yank that intrigued him. He plucked his suit jacket from the stand. "Let's go."

Twenty minutes later, a black Rolls Royce navigated through traffic, escorted by a brace of midnight blue Range Rovers, rolling front and rear. Carl Juneau sat up front in the Rolls with the chauffeur, wearing a discreet earpiece. Henry Leggatt rode with Dawson in the back.

Leggatt gazed out the window as their convoy eased past a crowd near Kensington Palace. People stood in groups, holding hands, hugging.

Leggatt gestured at the crowd. "Half six in the morning, and look at that!"

Dawson was engrossed in the small television mounted in the console in front of them, watching taped footage of Princess Diana's funeral. He glanced up. "It will go on for weeks. Or, months." On the TV screen, scenes from an aerial feed showed the final procession of funeral cars turning into the grounds of the Althorp estate. Dawson turned up the volume.

"This was the scene at the Althorp estate yesterday, bringing to a close an unprecedented week of mourning across the world. And, it must be said...

these shattering events may well continue to reverberate. Polling numbers are reflecting intense and widespread ill-feeling toward the Royal Family."

"Surely the funeral will help them recover," Leggatt ventured.

Dawson looked at his aide with a touch of pity. "They've enraged the public, Henry. It says something when the Royal Family's most popular member in centuries was a young woman who repeatedly criticized them." He smirked. "They can't help themselves. The Duke of Windsor was right."

"About what?"

"He said they have ice water in their veins."

Leggatt thought about that.

"You're smiling, Henry."

"Yes sir. I was just thinking…"

"Thinking what?"

"That people have probably said the same thing about you."

"I'm sure they have. Your father among them."

Leggatt went silent.

Outside, a young black woman stood in front of a mountain of floral tributes. Apparently inconsolable, she fell weeping into the arms of a police constable.

10

The Reardon Hotel in Jersey City was an American classic – a golden age monolith in the French Second Empire style, with a brick and glazed terra cotta exterior, arched lobby windows and a mansard roof. Inside, the vast lobby was a time warp of paranazzo marble walls, coffered ceilings and crystal chandeliers.

The finer architectural features of the Reardon were of no interest to the smooth-faced man waiting at the front desk. The man's professional name was Darius. At least, that was the name he provided to his clients.

At that moment, he was watching Kenneth Tannahill traverse the lobby. Tannahill moved fast on quick choppy steps. He wore a blue blazer and grey slacks. The watcher's pale eyes followed the reporter as he entered a wide doorway under an ornate sign:

The Webster Dining Room.

Darius slipped a lozenge into his mouth.

"Trying to quit, sir?"

Darius turned back to the desk clerk.

"What was that?"

The clerk nodded at the package in his hand. "Nico-Ban. I tried that stuff myself a few months back. You need a prescription for it here." He smiled resignedly. "I'm afraid it didn't take."

"Yes. It's difficult," Darius replied. "You need a prescription? It's over the counter in Oz."

"Oz?"

"Australia."

"Oh. Right."

Darius's accent sounded vaguely English, but somehow not. English, Australian, Kiwi, South African... the desk clerk, like most Americans, couldn't tell the difference.

The clerk tapped a few keys and studied his computer screen.

"I see we have a message for you, sir."

"A message?"

"Yes sir. It came by fax overnight." The man opened a filing drawer, shuffled through tabbed dividers and retrieved an envelope. He passed it to Darius.

Darius opened the envelope and removed a single sheet of paper. It took him exactly one second to read the short message.

The clerk placed a key card on the marble counter between them. "Room six-oh-four, Mr. Woodruff. Enjoy your stay, sir!"

"Thanks, mate." He pocketed the faxed note and the key card, and then dropped a twenty-dollar bill on the counter. "Have the bellman take my bag up."

"Of course, sir."

Darius strolled over to the Webster Dining Room. As he entered, a hostess was in the process of seating Tannahill next to a window. Darius plucked a menu off the entrance podium, scooped a stray section of newspaper off a vacant table, and seated himself next to a service alcove. He sat with his back to his target. He opened the newspaper and pretended to read while he watched Tannahill's reflection in a smoky decor mirror.

A waitress stopped at Tannahill's table. "May I start you with coffee, sir?"

"Yes. Thank you."

The waitress hurried to the service alcove near Darius's table.

Darius watched in the smoked glass as Tannahill lit a cigarette, then started impatiently tapping his fingers while he smoked.

In the service alcove next to Darius, Tannahill's waitress began filling a guest thermos flask with coffee. Suddenly, the restaurant was disturbed by a loud clink of glass, a splashing sound, and a muted cry. An elderly lady tried to stand up quickly to avoid spilled water. She nearly fell, but a man at a neighboring table caught her before she toppled.

Tannahill's waitress rushed over.

In the service alcove, the coffee flask intended for Tannahill sat open. Darius eyed it thoughtfully. He glanced at Tannahill in the smoked glass. The man was already lighting a second cigarette.

Darius's hand dipped into his pocket. It reappeared holding the Nico-Ban package. He glanced at the waitress. She was busy clearing the mess while the hostess chatted a mile a minute at the old lady, obviously trying to quell the excitement.

Darius squeezed four lozenges out of the package. He rose from his seat, stepped across to the service alcove and dropped them into the open thermos.

Then he stood there, next to the alcove, waiting until the waitress returned.

"Hi. I'm sitting right here–" he gestured at his table "–and I'm in a bit of a hurry. Do you think I could I get an order of rye toast and a cup of tea?"

"Of course, sir! I'll just be a half a sec!"

The waitress topped up the coffee thermos, twisted on the lid, and carried it to Tannahill's table. As she filled the journalist's cup, she asked, "Are you ready to order, sir?"

53

"Not yet. I'm waiting for someone."

The waitress nodded. She left to attend to Darius's order.

Darius pretended to be engrossed in his newspaper while he watched Tannahill empty three packets of sugar into his cup. The man sipped his coffee. He removed a pen and notebook from his pocket. He sipped more coffee. He checked his watch, sipped coffee, and lit another cigarette. A few minutes passed. He drained his cup, refilled it from the thermos, and dumped in more sugar. He sipped and checked his watch.

He was beginning to look decidedly nervous.

The waitress brought Darius his order. As he spread marmalade on his toast, he watched Tannahill take a mobile phone from a pocket and thumb a speed-dial button. But as he put the phone to his ear, his head jerked. He quickly disconnected the call and set the phone on the table. He rose and hurried toward the restaurant entrance.

Darius turned in his chair. A young woman had just entered.

Darius recognized her. None of the photographs had done her justice.

He went back to his toast.

11

Emma almost hadn't come. When she woke up this morning, the first thing she'd done was telephone the superintendent of her building. She'd asked to have her locks changed. The man hadn't argued. In fact, he hadn't asked a single question. He'd promised it would be done today, and said he'd leave the new keys in her mailbox.

After that call, Emma had sat with a cup of coffee and replayed in her mind everything that had happened. She was decidedly uneasy about meeting Tannahill. She'd come within an inch of calling Jan for advice. But in the end, curiosity had trumped judgment.

Now she watched a portly man in blazer and slacks move toward her on surprisingly energetic legs.

"Miss Parks? I mean… Doctor Parks?"

"Yes."

"I'm Ken Tannahill. Thank you for coming!" He offered his hand. Emma hesitated, then took it.

She let Tannahill lead her to his table.

She was about to sit when she noticed the cigarette burning in the ashtray. She remained standing, waiting. Tannahill saw where she was looking. He took the hint.

"Sorry." He hastily butted it.

They sat.

She didn't notice the man sitting a few tables away, watching their reflections in the decor mirror.

"May I see some identification?" Emma asked.

Tannahill was unfazed. "I thought you might ask."

His hand slipped inside his jacket. He passed her a Press ID card and a British passport. Emma checked the passport photo, glanced at the press card, then handed them back.

Their waitress appeared.

"Coffee, ma'am?"

"Please."

The waitress filled Emma's cup and then topped up Tannahill's. "Are you ready to order?"

Tannahill looked at Emma. "You haven't had a chance to look at the menu."

"It's all right. I know what I want."

Tannahill opened his menu. He gazed at it without interest. "I'll try your "Lexicographer's Special".

"Yes, sir. How would you like the eggs done?"

"Sunny side up, please."

"And... for the lady?"

"Wheat toast, please." Emma picked up a spoon. Her eyes scanned the table. "And I'd like some non-fat milk for my coffee if you have it."

"We do. I'll be right back." The waitress hurried off.

Tannahill stirred more sugar into his coffee.

Emma leaned forward. "Okay, Mr. Tannahill. Why–?"

"Please. I'm Ken. May I address you as Emma?"

"Yes. Now, why am I here?"

"You like to get right down to business, I see."

"I don't like mysteries... and I don't like it when people snoop through my home! Do you know anything about that?"

"Snoop? What do you mean?"

Emma studied Tannahill's face. The man looked genuinely confused.

"Someone went through my apartment yesterday!"

Tannahill looked unnerved. "Was anything taken?"

"No."

"Did you call the police?"

"No. I wasn't... sure."

"About what?"

"It's hard to explain. Never mind. Start talking!"

Tannahill blinked at her. He opened his notebook. "James Conrad Parks emigrated from England to the United States in 1889. We believe your vase came with him."

"Maybe. Probably. It came down to me through Dad's side of the family. But that's hardly earth-shattering news."

The waitress returned with a small pitcher of milk. Emma thanked her and poured some in her coffee. She stirred it in.

As she lifted her cup, Tannahill said, "I believe your parents are deceased."

Emma set down her cup. She could feel the flywheel of her emotions start to turn. Her eyes locked on his notebook. "How do you know that?" She leaned forward. "*Why* do you know that?"

"Newspaper archives... I read about the accident, and your mother's, ah..."

"You've been busy!"

"I'm sorry."

Emma felt the bile rise in her throat. "It wasn't a suicide!"

"What was it?"

"A mistake! With her pills! What business is this of yours? And what the hell's it got to do with my vase?"

"If you'll bear with me, it will become clear."

"It better, Mr. Tannahill! It better become clear! My best friend is an attorney!"

Tannahill didn't seem perturbed. He glanced at his notebook. "Medical school must have been very expensive."

"I had a scholarship! And a lot of crappy jobs!" Emma grabbed her bag and stood up. "Mr. Tannahill, I don't know what your game is, but I'm not listening to–!"

Tannahill looked up at her. "It's all about provenance, Emma."

"There's that word again!"

"Yes. An artifact's value is always affected by provenance."

Emma hovered, uncertain, then slowly subsided onto her seat.

"Chain of ownership," Tannahill continued, "as evidence of–" He coughed wetly, covering his mouth. "Excuse me." His face looked slightly flushed. He dabbed his brow with his napkin.

Emma noticed the man's oddly changing complexion.

"I'm talking about chain of ownership as evidence of authenticity," Tannahill continued. He coughed again. Then he changed the subject. "Was 'Parks' always your paternal family's surname? Do you know?"

"I don't understand."

"I'm thinking of a name change in the past, maybe due to an adoption? Were there any family stories about that?"

"No. I don't think so. I've never heard that. Is it important?"

"Just a question that came up in our research."

"*Our* research?" Emma cocked her head. "You said you work for the London *Herald*?"

"Yes."

"Isn't that one of the papers owned by that loud-mouthed billionaire? Lawson, or…?"

"Dawson. That's right. But this is–" Tannahill's body jerked violently. The blood drained from his face. He dropped the notebook and tugged at his collar.

Emma's eyes narrowed. Her training kicked in. She leaned closer, assessing. "Your color… and you're sweating!"

"Please, excuse me!" Tannahill replied. He tried to rise, then dropped back onto his chair. Patrons at nearby tables turned to look.

Emma jumped up and came around the table. She checked his pulse. "Your heart rate is elevated," she told him quietly. She tried to check his eyes. He pulled away from her and stood up.

"Please just give me a moment... I'll be right back!"

"What have you eaten this morning?"

"Nothing." He waved for her to sit. He walked away unsteadily. A few diners covertly watched him go, then returned to their meals. A man sitting alone, reading a newspaper, didn't seem to notice him at all.

Emma watched Tannahill until he disappeared into the restroom corridor. Her attention shifted to his coffee cup. She picked it up and smelled it, then sniffed her own cup. Her nose wrinkled. There was an odd scent, just below the coffee smell, a faint medicinal sub-note. She slid her cup to one side. She looked around for their waitress. She was nowhere in sight.

As she waited, her gaze fell on Tannahill's notebook. The corner of a photograph protruded from the back. The exposed part of the picture looked like a car's taillight.

Her car's taillight.

Emma glanced quickly at the restroom corridor. She slid the notebook across the table. She opened it.

There were several photographs.

Surveillance photos... of her.

Photos of her wheeling groceries to her car. Photos of her riding her ten-speed through Bayonne Park. Photos of her leaving the hospital at night. Photos of her standing at her apartment window.

One photo showed her standing in her bedroom, her back to the window... naked from the waist up.

Emma's nostrils flared with anger. She checked the restroom corridor again, then flipped through the notebook. She stopped to examine a page of neat handwriting.

Emma Augusta Parks   DOB 24 Aug 69   Rockport Maine   5'8" eyes blue(?)   hair auburn Univ. Conn Med School   Honors   Surgical Resident – Bayonne Medical Center   Bayonne, NJ   92 Toyota Corolla – Lic. UVJ44F

Emma's eyes burned. She jammed the notebook and the photographs into her bag. She stood up. She noticed Tannahill's cell phone. On an impulse, she picked it up. She thumbed buttons, cycling the display readout.

"Call Log"

"Dialed Numbers"

She scrolled through the log. Most numbers were just meaningless rows of digits, but she recognized her hospital's switchboard number and her number at home. Then she stopped.

The display read: *Dawson private.*

She dropped the cell phone in her bag and marched out of the restaurant.

Tannahill bent over the toilet. For the fourth time, he vomited explosively. He groaned. He couldn't understand what was wrong with him.

Maybe it's the smoking, he thought. I must, I must, I *must* cut down! That's it! It's the coffee and cigarettes! I need to live healthier! Cut down on everything. Exercise!

Getting more exercise was the last conscious thought Kenneth William Tannahill, 44, late of Pembridge Square, Notting Hill, London, ever had. Because at that instant, a smooth-faced man materialized in the cubicle behind him, seized him by the collar and fired two bullets into his brain.

Darius tucked the silenced pistol under his jacket. He jerked Tannahill's body upright and maneuvered it into a sitting position on the toilet. He searched the reporter's pockets. He removed a hotel room entry card.

He dragged the body out of the cubicle.

The door to a service cupboard stood open. Darius shoved the reporter's inert body inside. He closed the door and leaned heavily against it until the latch clicked.

A thin trail of blood led from the cubicle to the cupboard. He yanked paper towels from a dispenser and carefully wiped the floor.

He shoved the bloodstained toweling into the trash bin. He washed and dried his hands. He pulled extra paper from the dispenser and piled it on top of the stained toweling.

He stepped to the door. A thin knife projected from under the jamb, serving as a lock. He yanked it out, pocketed it and left the men's room.

He returned to the restaurant. He immediately noticed Emma's empty seat. He dropped a twenty next to his unfinished order of toast and strode out of the restaurant.

He followed signs to a stairway and took the steps two at a time. He crossed an elevated walkway to the hotel's parking arcade.

He arrived just in time to see Emma's car squealing away, heading for the exit ramp.

He turned on his heel and strode back into the hotel.

12

November 1981.

The family was broke.

Dad and a few of the others had been losing their catches to poachers. The thieves weren't just taking the lobsters. They were stealing the traps. Dad and some of his friends had formed an informal patrol, taking turns on the grounds, but they hadn't caught the bastards yet. They figured they were working at night, running without lights. Trouble was, only a few of the guys had radar.

Their mortgage payments were three months behind, and Mom was deep into one of her depressions. Winston Churchill had named his dark moods "the black dog". Penny Parks didn't have a name for hers. She just muttered, "the colors are gone", and sank like a stone.

A late-season storm had formed off Jacksonville. The disturbance never was assigned an official name. The National Weather Service designated it Subtropical Storm 3. It was crawling up the east coast, pushing mountainous seas, flooding seafront towns, and setting its crosshairs on Maine.

Dad was overwhelmed. He was worried about Mom, but he was also worried about his catch. He took Eddie and they went out on *Miss Penny* to pull the traps. Mom and Emma watched them leave and then Mom shut herself in her room. Years later, she told Emma she'd known she'd never see her husband or son again.

She'd been right.

Dad had left it too late. The weather went downhill and got very crazy, very fast. Somebody must have been dozing at Marine Radio, but there never was a proper investigation. The Coast Guard man who came to the house told Mom that Dad and Eddie had been heading for port. He said they would have made it if they hadn't responded to the Mayday. Howie Burkell and his deckhand were in trouble.

Howie was Dad's best friend.

So Dad and Eddie reversed course and went to the rescue.

The storm never did make landfall in Maine. A high-pressure area nudged it northeast, toward Nova Scotia, and it eventually dissipated over Canada. The only thing that did come ashore – along with twelve hours of gigantic waves, flying spume, sheets of rain and a whale carcass – was Emma's father's body.

Emma found him.

When Dad went missing, Mom just went to bed and turned her face to the wall. So Emma hiked alone out to the breakwater. She stood there for hours, alternately wiping away tears and scanning the ocean with her Dad's old binoculars.

Praying that *Miss Penny's* radio was out.

Praying she'd see *Miss Penny* chugging over the horizon, heading home.

At dusk, she'd given up.

But as she made her slow way back, she spotted something in the now quiet waters below.

A lifejacket, supporting a body.

The body was face down, but Emma knew...

She shrieked. She scrambled down the treacherous riprap slope, over the slick broken rock, falling, gashing her leg, calling, whimpering... and dying inside.

She threw herself straight into the cold, debris-clogged water, grabbed the life jacket and swam it and its heavy burden back to the rocks. She turned the body over.

She screamed at her Dad to wake up.

She struggled to get him out of the water. He was too heavy. Moaning with despair, she started mouth-to-mouth.

When they found her, she was lying next to her father, half in, half out of the water, blue with hypothermia, still desperately trying to breathe life into his long-dead corpse.

They lifted her gently and carried her up the slope.

Ten minutes after she left the Reardon, the memories were hitting like shrapnel. Emma pulled over. She took deep breaths.

After a few minutes, she drove home.

She retrieved the new keys from her mailbox. Before she entered her apartment, she dialed '9-1' on her cell. She kept her thumb on the '1', ready to press it, and unlocked the door. She sniffed the air suspiciously. She checked every room.

Everything was in place.

She grabbed her telephone directory, thumbed through it, found the listing for the Reardon Hotel and dialed the number.

"Reardon Hotel. How may I direct your call?"

"Mr. Tannahill's room please."

"Thank you. One moment please..."

Darius wore gloves. He worked methodically. He started with the journalist's briefcase. He replaced each article exactly as he'd found it. Next he searched the man's suitcase, one garment at a time. He felt along the suitcase's linings. Nothing.

Inch by inch, he searched the entire suite. He removed and replaced every drawer in the bureau and the nightstands, checking under and behind them. He took the bed apart and checked the entire frame, then put it back together and re-made the bed.

He found the envelope taped to the back of a framed print hanging in the short corridor between the bedroom and the bathroom. He removed it and replaced the picture, making sure he left it hanging perfectly straight.

The envelope was sealed. A typed label bore a single word: *PARKS*

He used a pocketknife to slit it open. He extracted a multi-paged document. He read the short title at the top of the first page.

Emma Augusta Parks, MD
Born 24 August 1969

The room's telephone started ringing.

Darius folded the document and slipped it into an inside pocket of his jacket. He placed the envelope on the desk in the bedroom, in plain view, beside the ringing telephone.

He exited the room and strolled to the elevator.

He could still hear the phone ringing when the elevator doors slid open.

Emma disconnected. She dialed again. A sleepy voice answered.

"Yeah?"

"Jan! What's wrong? Are you sick?"

"No. Late night." Her voice was gravelly. "Jury sat right into yesterday. Judge wouldn't let them break deliberations. They came in just before midnight. Then we went to the Apple to lick our wounds."

"I need your advice!"

"What's wrong?"

"There's some kind of scam going on, and I'm the target!"

"Grant again?"

"No! Listen, can I come over? It'll take some time to explain."

"Uh… sure. Give me an hour. And bring some Starbucks."

"Thanks. See you then."

An immaculately groomed man, sleek in a three-button suit and a perfectly knotted silk tie, finished washing his hands. He stepped to the towel dispenser. He stabbed at it with a dripping hand.

No towels.

The man's lips compressed with irritation. He stepped to the door and threw it open. A uniformed Hispanic woman was just emerging from the lady's room. She wore a nametag.

"You, there! There are no towels in here!"

The woman stopped. "Oh, sorry! I get Mister–"

The man huffed impatiently. He showed her his wet hands. "No! You do it, please! Now!"

The woman shrugged. She eased nervously past the man, entered the men's room and extracted a set of keys from her pocket. She unlocked the cover of the paper towel dispenser.

"You expect your guests to dry their hands with toilet paper?" the man asked irritably.

"Sorry, sir. Just be a second…"

She removed the spent roll from the dispenser. She unlocked the door to the service cupboard.

As she reached in, she glanced down.

She jumped back with a yelp.

She ran shrieking into the corridor.

The indignant man peered into the cupboard. He swallowed convulsively.

A man's body was jammed under the bottom shelf, his legs pushed into a fetal position.

His head was lying in a pool of blood.

13

Emma switched on her computer. She ran an Internet search. She scanned the first entries.

Kenneth Tannahill... *'Modernization of the Monarchy'... prize-winning five-part series... London Herald...*

Kenneth Tannahill... *Royals reporter extraordinaire... When Ken Tannahill listens, everybody talks...!*

She scrolled through page after page of hits. Almost every entry related to an article about the British Royal Family.

This man needs therapy, she thought.

She searched through her bag and found Tannahill's cell phone. She cycled through the Call Log. She pressed 'Call' and put the phone to her ear. The first ring was interrupted by a humming sound, then a relay click.

She heard a distant ring.

The Dassault Falcon 900EX was streaking west at thirty-six thousand feet. The ride was smooth as glass and the cabin was quiet. Carl Juneau sat in a wide leather club seat, facing aft, reading a dog-eared paperback. Across the aisle, Henry Leggatt was playing chess on his laptop. Victor Dawson was perched at a small mid-cabin conference table, tearing off faxes as they curled out of a printer.

Further aft, Denny Nowak, Dwight Wickham and Baz Cooper, three members of Juneau's security team, lounged on soft divans, wearing earphones and watching a film. Wickham and Cooper were big fit men with cropped hair. Nowak was older, shorter, and shaggier.

Dawson's satellite phone rang. He checked the caller ID. He answered quickly.

"Ken?"

A female voice answered. "Is this Victor Dawson?"

Dawson was wary. "Who is this?"

"Guess! I met your creepy Mr. Tannahill this morning!"

"Dr. Parks?"

"I want to know why you're crawling through my life!"

"That will be explained, I promise you. Why are you using Ken Tannahill's phone?"

"Ask *him*! I don't know what you people are up to, Dawson, but my next stop is the police!"

Emma's final words were shouted. Juneau and Leggatt both heard the voice, but not the words. They looked up.

"Hello? Hello? Damn!" Dawson disconnected. "She rang off!"

"Who was it, sir?" Juneau asked.

"The girl! Emma Parks!" He looked at them. "She had Tannahill's phone. Something's gone wrong!"

Juneau moved to the conference table. He eased the satellite phone out of Dawson's hand.

"What are you doing?"

"Calling Clive. He's supposed to be watching her."

The room was a mish-mash of floral wallpaper, worn out Axminster carpets and shabby furniture. The heavily marked antique desk and the guest chairs were from different periods and different styles. The bookshelves lining two walls sagged with age. In one corner, an electric heater sat at an angle on the hearth of a small marble fireplace. A single tall window overlooked a flagstone terrace.

By any standards, much less Royal standards, Alan Boswell's office would have been an embarrassment. But this part of the Palace wasn't on any public tour. In fact, Boswell's office was out of bounds to almost everyone who worked at the Palace except certain select members of the Royalty Protection Branch.

And the Queen herself, of course.

Alan Fitzroy Boswell, C.V.O., was sitting behind the desk, deep in thought. He was in his early fifties, and trim for his age. He wore a tailored shirt, gemstone cufflinks, a striped tie, and a neatly-trimmed beard.

His desk phone rang. He picked up.

"Boswell." He listened. "Yes, I did. 'Dawson'... usual spelling... Dassault Falcon... that's the one. Flight plan?" He listened. He checked his watch. "Thank you. Keep me advised."

Emma's fingers drummed on the surveillance photos lying next to her keyboard. Her eyes were fixed to the screen in front of her.

She felt a sudden prickling sensation on the back of her neck.

They're monitoring me...

She shut down her computer. Then she crawled under her desk and disconnected the cable connection from the wall.

Tannahill's phone rang. She snatched it off the desk and checked the display.

65

It was Dawson.

Emma switched off the phone. She dropped it into her bag, along with the surveillance photos.

She left her apartment and headed down the stairs.

She didn't hear the elevator open behind her.

Darius stepped out of the elevator. He checked the hallway. Clear. He moved silently to Emma Parks' apartment door.

He listened. No sound.

He tried the door. Locked.

Soundlessly, he picked the lock.

He stepped inside.

He pulled his gun and walked through the apartment.

She wasn't there.

He'd seen her car on the street outside. He went to a window and looked down. Her car was still there.

Then he saw her.

Emma Parks was walking west up 19th Street toward Broadway.

Darius moved fast.

Emma hadn't seen the dark blue Mercedes parked two spaces behind her car. And she didn't notice the man following her along the sidewalk.

She reached Broadway and entered the business premises on the corner. The sign on the door read: *Networking Cafe.*

Darius followed her in.

Emma bought a chit from the cashier and went to a computer station.

Darius bought a coffee. He settled into a soft seat in a corner, picked up a magazine and pretended to read while he watched Emma.

Emma logged on. She continued her Internet search.

Kenneth Tannahill... *exclusive interview with Princess Diana... 'fragile, bewildered and tragic figure'... full transcript available on...*

Emma typed "London Herald" in the search field and clicked the mouse. She clicked on the first hit.

A tabloid-style homepage appeared on the screen. A headline screamed at her:

COLD HEARTED ROYALS! *Public Slow To Forgive.*

She clicked through a few links.

Our Board... Our Chairman... Victor Dawson... world's fourth largest media conglomerate... third satellite launched June 15th by ESA...

Emma typed 'Victor Dawson' into the search field.

Victor Dawson... *the Welsh-born press baron who backed the failed Antarctic odyssey said in a public statement...*

*Glitterati, Hollywood stars, converge on **Victor Dawson's** Clairmont Estate for 'weekend of summer drinks'*

*... **Dawson** ruled in breach the PCC Code of Practice...*

*... in an apology to the Royal Family, **Victor Dawson** stated...*

Emma switched on Tannahill's cell phone. It beeped at her. The display read: *7 missed calls.* She dialed a number from memory.

"Reardon Hotel. How may I–?"

"Kenneth Tannahill's room, please."

"Um... I'm sorry? You asked for... Mr. Tannahill?"

"Yes!" Emma replied impatiently. "He's a guest!"

She heard a click, then a ring.

Police detectives wearing latex gloves moved carefully about Tannahill's hotel room. A uniformed Bureau of Criminal Investigation officer methodically dusted for prints.

The phone rang once... twice. A detective held up a hand to quiet the room. He lifted the receiver.

"Yeah?"

"Mr. Tannahill?" A female voice.

"Who's calling, please?"

"Sorry! I must have the wrong room."

"This is Mr. Tannahill's room. Who's calling please?"

The woman had already hung up.

The detective turned to a young cop. "Mancini! Go down to the switchboard and see if they have any record of the number that just called this room!"

Emma hadn't expected an American accent.

What the hell is going on?

She checked her watch. Time to head over to Jan's.

Tannahill's phone beeped at her. The display read: *8missed calls.*

She packed up, left the cafe, and headed back down 19th for her car.

She didn't notice Darius gliding along thirty feet behind her.

Tannahill's phone was still in her hand. Just as she reached her car, it rang.

She looked at the display. It was Dawson. She wavered... then thumbed the Talk button.

"Hello Dawson!"

"Dr. Parks!"

"Why are you calling me?"

Emma unlocked her car.

"To protect you! You may be in danger!"

"Protect me? You don't even know me!"

Emma got into the car and slammed the door.

"Actually, Doctor, I know you very well! I'll explain later, but right now, you're in danger!"

"So are you!" Emma put her key in the ignition. The engine shuddered, hesitated, then caught. "You're in danger of arrest! New Jersey has an Anti-Stalking Law!"

"Doctor! Emma! Please listen! I've just learned that Kenneth Tannahill has been murdered! We think you'll be next!"

Emma sat stock still in her seat, trying to process what she had just heard.

"I saw him this morning!"

"It happened right after you left! Believe me! Please!"

Emma finally noticed Darius. His image appeared in her side view mirror. It was the man's odd gait that caught her attention. He was walking purposely toward her, holding one arm awkwardly behind his leg.

"I see your man following me, Dawson! Call him off!"

"What man?"

In the mirror, Darius's trailing arm moved clear.

He was holding a silenced pistol.

"He's got a gun!"

Dawson's voice roared at her. "Emma! Get out of there!"

Darius raised the pistol.

"Oh God!" Emma yelled. She dropped the phone, jammed the car into gear and stomped on the gas pedal.

As her car lurched away from the curb, its rear window exploded. Bullets burned past Emma's neck. A slug nicked one of the knuckles of her right hand on the steering wheel before shattering her dash. Another exited through her windshield. Emma shrieked as she accelerated away.

In her rear view mirror, she had a glimpse of Darius sprinting toward a parked Mercedes.

Moaning with fright, Emma wrenched the wheel. She slid through the corner at Avenue E, tires squealing, and roared away heading south.

14

Dawson shouted into the phone. "Emma!" No answer. He stabbed a button on a console. The sound of screeching tires exploded from a bulkhead speaker.

He unplugged the sat phone handset from the fax machine and thrust it at Juneau. "Someone's trying to kill her!"

Juneau plugged the phone into a jack on his seat. "Dr. Parks? Pick up the phone!" No answer. The sound of a screaming car engine blasted out of the bulkhead speaker.

"She's red-lining," Juneau said to no one in particular. The other security team members were moving forward, drawn by the commotion. Juneau looked at Wickham. "Tannahill's phone! Is it one of our phones?"

Wickham nodded. Juneau stabbed a finger at Leggatt's laptop. Wickham grabbed it. "What's the number?" he asked. Juneau flashed him the sat phone's call display. Wickham scribbled the number on his palm. He turned back to the computer. "I'll try DX One!" His fingers flew over the keyboard. Data filled the monitor. "No good, Carl! It's over the Med!"

A low moan of fear filled the cabin.

"Keep looking!" Dawson barked.

Juneau yelled into the phone. "Dr. Parks!"

Wickham kept typing, peering at the screen, typing again. Finally, he looked up at Dawson.

"None of ours are in position, sir! The closest is over Ontario!"

"Where's Nightshade?" Dawson barked.

Wickham hesitated. His eyes shifted to Juneau, then back to Dawson. "That was an experiment, sir. Are you sure?"

"Yes!"

"The NSA–!"

"–won't react in time!"

"They'll have a record–"

"–of us trying to save her life! Do it!"

Wickham jumped up and darted to the forward bulkhead. He opened a storage locker. He retrieved a knapsack.

"What's Nightshade?" Leggatt asked.

No one answered.

Wickham slammed back into his seat. He opened the knapsack and pulled out an odd-looking device that looked like a cigarette lighter. He plugged it into a port on the laptop. A dialogue box popped up on the monitor.

"What is that?" Leggatt asked.

"Universal serial bus," Wickham muttered as he worked.

"A what?"

"The latest in peripherals. They're not on the market yet. This one has a special little program our IT boys wrote." Wickham clicked on the box, typed quickly and stabbed the Enter key.

Juneau called into the phone. "Dr. Parks! Emma!" He kept his eyes on the monitor. Seconds ticked by as the sounds of straining vehicle engine vibrated through the cabin.

Suddenly, an image materialized. It hovered over the American eastern seaboard, then zoomed into an ever-shrinking field of view. The image focused on the grid of a city... and then locked onto a moving, blinking beacon on the streets of Bayonne, New Jersey.

Leggatt left his seat and leaned in to look at the monitor, crowding Wickham. "Whose satellite is that?"

"The NSA's," Wickham answered. "Move! You're blocking Carl's view!"

"You're hacking an NSA satellite?"

"Sit down, Henry!" Dawson barked.

Leggatt dropped into his seat. He looked at Dawson, appalled. Dawson returned a level stare. "Wake up, Henry! You think only governments get to do this? How do you think media companies survive?"

Emma blasted past the Maidenform headquarters and through the intersection at 17th while her mind shrieked at her.

No police cars! Where are the damned police?

Emma had run the amber and beaten the Mercedes through the light. Her pursuer was blocked by cross traffic, but not for long.

I need to get off this street!

She checked her mirror just as the Mercedes ran the red and accelerated after her.

Emma panicked. She swerved around a car, passing on the right and nearly clipping off its off-side mirror. A horn blared the driver's outrage, then blared again as the Mercedes shot past it and closed on Emma's bumper. The road began a hard curve to the right, reducing her visibility ahead. Suddenly a Volkswagen Beetle materialized from her right. It was halfway into her lane before it jerked to a panicky stop. Her tires moaned on the pavement as she swerved to miss it. In her mirror, she saw the Mercedes clip the front of the Beetle, sending a chunk of its front bumper spinning off through space.

Emma knew they were coming up fast on the blind corner at Linnet Street.

She spotted the Citgo sign on her right, warning her that the turn was coming up. She made a quick decision. Her heart was in her throat as she squealed through a hard left, burned across the oncoming lane and shot into the underpass below Route 169. More horns blared.

As she had hoped, the Mercedes overshot and disappeared from her mirror. Her pursuer would have to loop around the diner at the south end of Broadway to resume the chase. She had maybe thirty seconds to disappear. She pulled a quick right onto Orient Street, raced down three blocks, smoked a left into Silver Street and looked for a place to hide.

I need the police!

She remembered the cell phone. She could call 911. She slowed and swung into an open space under a tree behind a beaten up old Lincoln. She reached between her legs and groped on the floor for the phone. She found it and sat up.

The porch of the house nearest to her car was festooned with flags and Uncle Sam figures. Sitting on a lawn chair among all the plastic patriotism was a thickset man wearing jeans and a grubby undershirt. He rose to his feet. He leaned over the railing and eyed Emma and her shot-up car. Abruptly, he wheeled and ducked into the house.

She was about follow him, knock on the door and ask for help when she heard her name shouted through the phone. She put it to her ear.

"Dawson?"

A different voice answered, talking fast. "No, Emma! My name is Carl Juneau. I work for Mr. Dawson. I'm going to help you!"

"How the hell can you help me? Some maniac just shot up my car! I'm hiding out on a back street. You can help me by calling the police!"

"Emma, I want you to do exactly as I say!"

At that second, she caught movement in her mirror. The Mercedes was crossing the intersection behind her. She heard a loud squeal of rubber as the car suddenly reversed and swung onto Silver Street.

Emma yelled, "Oh God! He's found me!" She slammed her car into gear and fled.

As she blew the stop sign onto East 5th, the Mercedes closed in at high speed, screeched into position and rammed her car from behind.

"Oh God! He's ramming me!"

She dropped the phone onto her lap and slammed her foot to the floor. The Corolla's engine whined as the little car flew along with the Mercedes two feet off its rear bumper. The two cars sped along a long, looping two-lane road bordering a vast tank farm. They flew past a marina. A sign warned about a sharp right turn: *15 MPH.*

Emma knew that road would feed her onto Route 169, a major road that ran north along the train tracks for the entire length of the Bayonne peninsula. With luck, she'd find a traffic cop. She went for it, sliding through the turn at nearly 50 mph, tires howling, sending a strolling woman and her leashed dog sprinting for their lives.

Juneau gripped the phone. He stared at the laptop. He could see the target beacon flickering along a highway. "Dwight, can this thing give us a real time overlay?"

Wickham's fingers flew over the keyboard. The image on the laptop monitor flickered, vanished, and then reappeared, now displaying traffic flow in real time.

Juneau spoke into the phone. "Emma?" No answer. He yelled. "Emma! Emma!"

Her voice answered. She sounded ready to weep. "He's right behind me!"

"I know."

"How do you–?"

"I want you to back off your speed!"

"Are you crazy? He'll–!"

"Let him get close! When his bumper touches, hit your emergency brake hard!"

"What?"

"Emma, listen–!"

"I'm on a highway!"

"Emma, you have to do what I say because it's the only way you're going to live through this! Do you understand?"

"Oh, Jesus! Yes!"

"What's that next intersection?"

"What?" Emma burbled. "Uh… 22nd! How do you–?"

"Blow that light, and then do it! When you hit your emergency brake, crank your wheel to the left! His car will push you into a one-eighty. You will not lose control! As soon as your car is facing the other way, release the brake and go! You got all that?

"I think so!"

"Okay. Drop the phone! Both hands on the wheel!"

Emma dropped the phone. Ahead, the light turned amber. She flew through the intersection with the Mercedes ten feet behind her. She touched her brakes. The pursuing Mercedes closed in.

CRASH!

Emma yanked up on her emergency brake and swung the wheel. Her car yawed left. The Mercedes shoved her rear end through the turn and shot past. Its wheels locked up in a cloud of blue smoke.

Emma's car rocked to a stop, straddling the northbound lanes, facing south. She released the brake and accelerated back the way she had come. Horns blared as northbound cars swerved to avoid her. To her rear, the Mercedes spun left, crossed the median, spraying gravel, and swung into the southbound lanes. It roared after her.

Emma swerved west through the intersection into 22nd Street, heading back into the city. She grabbed the phone.

"It worked! But he's still following me!"

"Forget him, Emma! Turn right on Prospect!"

"How can you see that?"

"Never mind! Make the turn!"

Emma turned.

"I want you to concentrate on my voice! I'm going to help you get rid of this guy. Now step on it!"

The Mercedes rounded the corner behind her. Its front end lifted as the driver buried the accelerator.

He's coming after me, fast!" Emma's voice trembled from the bulkhead speaker. "What do I do now?"

"Just a minute…" Juneau studied the monitor.

"I don't have a minute!" Emma shouted.

Juneau covered the mouthpiece. "I need kinetics!"

Wickham tapped keys. On the monitor, a window opened and expanded. Kinetic graphics appeared, showing traffic speeds. Juneau concentrated on the image, calculating.

"Emma, four blocks ahead of you is a school…"

"Lincoln School!"

"Make a right there and head for the traffic light on 169."

"Okay. And then?"

"After you take that corner, I want you to floor it!"

"What?"

"Trust me."

Emma hesitated. She checked her mirror. The Mercedes was closing fast. She squealed around the corner at the school.

Ahead, cross-traffic whipped past at the intersection with Route 169.

The Mercedes screamed through the corner behind her.

Emma floored the accelerator. The Corolla surged… then sputtered.

"Now, Emma!"

"My car! It's…!"

Weeping with fear, she stabbed her foot at the accelerator. The engine hesitated, then came back to life. She watched her speedometer climb slowly past fifty… fifty-five…

Juneau's voice jarred her nerves. "Faster, Emma!"

"The light! It's red!"

"Blow the light, Emma! Trust me!"

Emma dropped the phone and went for it.

Her car rocketed out of the side street into the throughway, missing a garbage truck by inches.

Tires screeched.

Horns blared.

The Corolla blasted across four lanes, milliseconds ahead of cross-traffic, and swerved left onto the northbound shoulder of the highway.

As Emma streaked across the final lane…

BOOM!

A Tropicana tractor trailer unit, wheels locked and sliding, jackknifed and slammed into the Mercedes, ripping the car in half, sending the pieces spinning in a shriek of tearing metal. In horrifying slow motion, the trailer tipped, fell on its side, pulling the tractor with it, and – still sliding – spilled thousands of cartons of fruit juice across the highway.

A chain reaction created a multi-car pile-up, as juice sprayed in all directions.

Emma stopped her car. She tried to shut off her engine but couldn't because her whole body was shaking.

Finally, she got her door open and stepped out. The intersection behind her was an obstacle course of smashed, dripping vehicles. She counted four wrecks, not including the Mercedes and the freightliner. She heard yelling. She started walking back to the scene.

"Emma! Emma!"

Juneau's voice was distant and tinny, coming from the cell phone that was still in her hand. She put it to her ear.

"Thank you," she said dully.

"Emma, I hear voices. Are you out of your car?"

"Yes… I… Oh God, you wouldn't believe what happened!"

"Get back in your car!"

"W-What? I'm a doctor. I should–"

"If you stay there, you'll be a dead doctor! Now, Emma, please!"

"What about the police? I have to wait for the police!"

Juneau looked at Dawson. The billionaire shook his head.

Juneau spoke carefully into the phone. "No, Emma. You're not safe! Do you know where Tait Street is in Jersey City?" Juneau was watching Dawson as he spoke. Dawson nodded.

"Yes, but…"

"Go to 676 Tait! There's a shop called 'Clairmont'. Park your car in the alley! Knock on the rear door. You'll be met."

"This is perfect!" Dawson blurted.

Juneau looked at his boss. A shadow crossed his mind.

He actually looks pleased.

Emma was confused. She got back in her car. She stared woodenly ahead, trying to gather her wits. Movement in her side view mirror caught her eye. An agitated man was running toward her car.

Emma spoke into the phone. "I can't leave here! I could be arrested!"

Carl Juneau's voice in her ear was quiet and patient. "Emma, if this is what we think it is, the police can't protect you. For your own safety, you must do as I ask!"

The running man skidded to a stop at Emma's window. He pounded on the roof of her car, shouting. "You crazy bitch! What the hell were you doing?"

In her mirror, she saw another two men running in her direction.

"I heard that, Emma! Go now, while you still can! And don't speed! You can't afford to be stopped for a ticket."

As the man reached for her door handle, Emma locked the door. Rattled, she slammed the Corolla into gear and pulled away, spraying gravel.

Behind her, the angry men yelled obscenities. One fumbled in a pocket, pulled out a pen and wrote something on his hand.

"You'd better be right!" she said into the phone. "They've got my license number!" She paused. "Where the hell are you, anyway?"

"In an aircraft."

"What?"

"We're over Newfoundland. We'll be there soon."

"Sure you are! Do you think I'm an idiot?" She disconnected and dropped the phone on the passenger seat.

For a few seconds Emma considered turning back. Then a thought crossed her mind.

Dawson got me into this. Now he can get me out.

She drove north on Route 169, staying exactly on the speed limit.

The long, low building covered an acre of ground on the outskirts of Norfolk, Virginia. Its three-foot-thick foundation slab sat on tungsten steel pilings that extended forty feet down into the sand, clay and marl of the coastal plain. Its walls were foot-thick, windowless sandwiches of poured concrete and mesh wire grid, raised on the site using the tilt-up construction technique first employed during the building boom of the 1950's. The entire complex was painted a monotonous shade of beige known to the French as *écru*, which literally means "unbleached".

No markings – no signs in any language – invited public attention or revealed the building's purpose. Any curious citizen searching the records at the Virginia Tax Assessor's office would learn that the building belonged to "Candliss Longstaff Inc.", a Delaware company. Further inquiries, should they be undertaken, would lead from one blind alley to another, and another, and eventually… nowhere.

This was because Candliss Longstaff Inc. did not exist.

The building belonged to the National Security Agency, the primary signals intelligence agency of the United States Government. Inside its walls, stretched along the entire length of one long, half-lit room, lay two back-to-back rows of computer bays. A faint sound of fingers tapping keyboards floated above the quiet hiss of air handlers. In each bay sat a trained operative – two long rows of human heads, bent over two long rows of glowing screens, while across the globe secret listening posts and swarms of satellites intercepted… and processed… and analyzed.

From time to time, a printer would hum to life.

Fifty seconds after Dwight Wickham hacked into Nightshade, three computers in this room had wailed out an alarm.

Five minutes after Wickham hacked into Nightshade, a tense NSA supervisor stood over an operative at an activated monitor as the man's fingers flew across a keyboard.

The supervisor pointed at a flashing icon moving across the screen. "What are they using for that beacon?"

"I'm working on that now, Ma'am" the operative replied. He kept typing.

15

Emma parked her car in a narrow, garbage-strewn alley. She got out and looked around. She started walking. After less than a minute of searching, she found a red door set into a featureless wall. A small sign on the door read: "Clairmont Antiques".

Emma knocked. The door opened instantly.

The pockmarked man from the bar was standing there. Emma stared at his face, trying to remember where she'd seen it before.

The man was holding a cell phone to his ear. He spoke into it. "She just arrived."

He had an English accent.

The man extended a calming hand to guide Emma through the doorway. Suddenly, two big men appeared out of the darkened hallway beyond. Emma stumbled backward, instantly wary, ready to run.

Both men nodded to her politely. One said, "Excuse us." They brushed past and walked out into the alley.

Still on the phone, the pockmarked man ushered Emma in.

"Yes sir. Rely on it!" He disconnected. He smiled at her. "I'm Clive. You're safe here."

He closed and locked the door, then guided Emma along a corridor. They passed a storage room and entered the sales area of the shop. It was filled to the ceiling with wondrous curios and antiques.

Emma looked around uncertainly. "Okay… So what's this all about?"

"Mr. Dawson will explain."

"When?"

"When he arrives. He won't be long."

"I need to make some phone calls."

"No calls. I'm terribly sorry."

Emma stared at him. "My car's sitting out there with the window shot out! I've just left the scene of an accident! I've got a lot of explaining to do! And so does Mr. Dawson! We need to talk to the police!"

Clive nodded at a security monitor behind a service counter. "Your car will be taken care of."

Emma looked. On the screen, she could see the two big men loading Emma's car on a flatbed.

"You're taking my car?"

"Just securing it. It's for the best."

"For the best?"

"Mr. Dawson will explain." He looked her in the eye. "Dr. Parks, believe me… it's in *your* best interests to wait for Mr. Dawson."

The man seemed resolute. Emma heaved an exasperated sigh. She wandered away from him, looking vaguely at the antiques on display. He moved with her, positioning himself discreetly between Emma and the shop's front entrance leading to the street.

Emma spotted a collection of vases. She studied them closely. Her eyes narrowed with suspicion. She turned to the man. "I want to know why you're not calling the police!"

Just then, a bell jingled.

A customer entered the store.

Clive whispered to Emma. "Come!" His tone was urgent. She allowed him to herd her into an office behind the service counter.

The room was large, but sparsely furnished with a desk and chair, filing cabinets, a sofa and an old console TV. Incongruously, one corner appeared to be set up for professional photography, with lights and silver umbrella reflectors.

Clive held the door for Emma, then followed her in. He snatched a cordless phone off the desk. He held out a hand.

"Your bag."

"What?"

"Your bag, please. It will be returned to you, intact."

"I don't see—"

The man's expression was uncompromising. Emma handed over her bag.

"Thank you. Please make yourself comfortable."

He left, taking her bag and the cordless receiver with him. The door clicked solidly behind him.

Emma rushed to the door.

It was locked.

There was a single window, covered by an old-fashioned blind. Emma pushed it aside.

The window was secured with steel bars.

She surveyed the room. She spotted a CCTV monitor on the desk. Its screen was dark. She stepped over to examine it. She touched a switch. Immediately, the screen went live. There was no audio, but she could see Clive talking to the customer.

Emma lowered herself onto the chair to watch. Clive appeared to be extolling a porcelain piece that had been made to look like a wicker basket, pointing out various arcane features. He appeared as confident as her bow-tied appraiser friend on "Antique Marketplace".

Emma's eyes burned with suspicion.

An ambulance stood with its rear doors ajar. Darius sat on a gurney in the back while a paramedic treated a gash on his forehead.

Outside, while gawking citizens watched rescue workers using jaws-of-life to peel the roof off a crushed sedan, a female officer popped the trunk of a police cruiser. She leaned in and lifted out a box. The printing on the box read, "Alcotest Roadside Screening". She slammed the trunk and walked toward the ambulance.

The ambulance doors were closed. She was sure they'd been open a moment ago.

She pulled them open.

The paramedic's body lay on the floor, its neck bent at an impossible angle.

The smooth-faced patient was gone.

Emma fidgeted on the office sofa, holding a coffee mug. Clive sat nearby, sipping a soda. On the old console TV, a daytime talk show host was busy offering up some saccharine homily.

Emma turned to Clive. "How long do you plan on keeping me a prisoner?"

Before he could answer, there was a thump of feet outside the door, and then a knock.

"Not long," Clive replied.

He got up and unlocked the door.

Dawson barreled in, trailed by Leggatt, then Juneau's men, and finally Juneau, holding Emma's bag.

Emma stood up as Dawson strode directly over to her.

"Mr. Dawson, I presume!" She made no attempt to hide her hostility.

Dawson gave an old-fashioned bow. "Your servant. This is my assistant, Henry Leggatt."

Leggatt nodded. "Doctor Parks…"

"And my security chief, Carl Juneau."

Emma shifted her confused gaze to Juneau. She found herself looking up into a strong, curiously pleasing, and – at this moment – faintly embarrassed face.

Emma held out her hand. "So, that was you, Mr. Juneau. I want to thank you again for saving my life."

"It was my honor, Ma'am."

Emma swung back on Dawson. "Now I want an explanation! What the hell is going on?"

"Everything can be explained later, Doctor. But for your own safety, you must come with us now!"

"Come with you? Where?"

Juneau interceded. He spoke softly. "We believe you're in serious danger."

"I know that, Mr. Juneau! A man tried to kill me! Why aren't we going to the police?"

Juneau was apologetic. "Ma'am... Emma... Please come with us now. I promise we'll explain later."

As he spoke, Nowak and Cooper eased into position behind her. Something in Juneau's expression told Emma that her compliance was non-negotiable.

Emma allowed herself to be escorted out of the office and down the passageway to the rear entrance. When they emerged from the building, she saw an identical pair of gray minivans waiting in the alley. Juneau's men escorted her toward the lead van.

The reasoning part of Emma's mind was in turmoil.

She elected to go with her instincts.

She bolted.

Juneau watched impassively as she sprinted away down the alley. He sighed. He nodded to Nowak.

Nowak trotted silently after her.

Juneau turned to Dawson. "You go ahead, sir. We'll catch up."

"All right, Carl. Please be careful."

"We always are, sir."

"I meant... don't break the china!"

"We won't, sir."

Dawson and Leggatt stepped into the lead van.

Cooper got behind the wheel of the second van. Juneau and Wickham climbed in the back.

Emma stumbled out of the alley into a side street. Half a block to her right was a main avenue. She ran toward it. Reaching it, she saw a few people waiting at a bus stop.

She raced toward them.

With a squeal of rubber, a van mounted the sidewalk, cutting her off. The bus stop people scattered. The van's side door slid open with a bang.

Nowak materialized behind Emma. His arm snaked around her neck.

Something crunched in his fist. His hand clamped over her mouth and nose.

Emma thought she smelled maple syrup.

The world went black.

Thick arms lifted Emma into the van. The door slid shut. The van backed off the sidewalk and sped away.

Emma lay across a seat, unconscious. Juneau looked down on her. He pushed back one of her eyelids. He glared at Nowak, furious. "What the hell did you use?"

Nowak opened his fist, revealing the crushed remnants of a small, mesh-covered glass vial.

"Alsik?"

"You want maybe to fight her all the way to the airport?" Nowak's accent was Eastern European.

Juneau snorted his disgust. Gently, he shifted Emma to an upright position. He opened Emma's mouth.

"What are you doing?" Cooper asked.

"Making sure she doesn't swallow her tongue!"

"The boss isn't going to like this!"

"She'll be okay," Juneau said. "But she won't be too happy when she wakes up."

Darius crossed the elevated walkway to the parking arcade, carrying his bag. There was a bandage on his forehead.

He stopped and looked around. The lot was full of cars.

He picked one.

Thirty-five minutes later, a nondescript family sedan pulled onto the shoulder of the highway just outside the perimeter fence at Teterboro Airport. Darius kept the engine running while he used binoculars to scan the scene beyond the fence.

A jet waited on an apron outside a small hanger, its stairs down and its turbines idling. A gray minivan sat parked and empty nearby. As Darius watched, an identical minivan appeared from behind the hanger. It rolled up to the aircraft's stairway. As soon as it stopped, its side door slid open and a tall man stepped out, carrying an unconscious woman. Effortlessly, the man mounted the steps two at a time.

Three other men emerged from the van and followed. As the last of their number boarded, the steps retracted, the door swung shut, and the jet immediately began to taxi.

Minutes later, it tore down the runway, stood on its tail and took off.

Darius kept watching until Dawson's plane disappeared from view.

London

16

Maple syrup…
1984.

The family had been flat broke when her father and brother died, and since then not much had improved.

Yes, they'd managed to hold on to the house, but only because Emma's father had kept up his dues at the Co-op. The group life policy had paid off the mortgage, but they still needed to eat.

Penny Parks was barely employable. The sympathetic owner of local mini-mart tried her out as a cashier, but after a year of her moods and frequent sick days, he'd given up and sent her home with three months pay. After that, they'd survived on Penny's string of seasonal jobs – mainly housemaid positions at various B&B's – and the extra money Emma brought in from babysitting.

Emma started her first summer job the year she turned fourteen. In Maine, children under sixteen who wanted to work had to apply for a work permit. The process and its paperwork required several steps. Since her mother was too disorganized to assist, Emma prepared and filed the application herself.

Early in July 1984, she started bussing tables at a coffee shop out on Route 73. The café was a long way from home, and the doors opened at six a.m., so every morning Emma got up with the sun and rode her bicycle to work.

Two weeks after she started, she got into a brawl.

There were three of them – ragged looking men with long greasy hair, dressed in tee shirts, stained jeans and ball caps. They stunk of fish, sweat and marijuana. Emma had watched them drive up in an old white pickup, its body rocking on worn-out suspension, its box full of wood lath lobster traps. They parked around the back, banged in through the side door, and flopped into a booth.

Carla took the table. She was the café's oldest waitress. She'd been around the block, she looked it, and she knew she looked it. She told Emma later she'd sniffed trouble brewing and figured she'd save the younger girls from the boorish comments and general aggravation.

It turned out she'd been right about the trouble, but not about who would start it.

Carla dropped three menus on the table.

"Can I get you boys something to drink?"

"Yah. I'd could go for a–" one of the men began.

The pickup's driver interrupted.

"Ya got all-day breakfast here?"

"Sure do. It's on the back of the menu."

"You got waffles?"

"Yes."

"We want... like, two each! No... three!" The other men nodded. "Butter 'n maple syrup. Lotsa maple syrup."

"Coming up. What to drink?"

"Beer. Bud'll do." More nods.

"Beer and waffles." Carla looked at them one by one. "That's what you want?"

"Yes, ma'am!" one piped in. "Breakfast 'cause we just got up... 'n beer 'cause it's afternoon." Guffaws all around.

Carla shook her head and put in the order. Fifteen minutes later, the three were wolfing down waffles and slugging back beer between bouts of lewd wisecracks and rough laughter.

They were still annoying the staff and irritating the other customers when Emma's shift ended.

She hung up her apron and slipped out the back through the kitchen. She unlocked her bike and walked it past the men's pickup. She was about to ride away when something caught her eye. One of the lobster traps in the back of the truck was sticking out over the tailgate, and its owner ID tag was hanging by a single rivet.

There was something under the tag. Something familiar.

Emma moved closer and pushed the tag to one side. Someone had used a woodburning stylus to etch three letters into the lath. The letters were still legible: ***APJ***

Augustus Parks Jr.

Wooden lobster traps can weigh over fifty pounds, so the handful of knowledgeable people in the restaurant were pretty amazed when Emma barged back in carrying the trap, raised it over her head and slammed it down on the table where the men were sitting. Dishes smashed, glasses shattered, and waffles and syrup spattered across the men's shirts.

In a millisecond, the entire café went deathly quiet.

The men at the table just sat there like stunned clods. Then the pickup's driver roared out "WHAT THE FUCK!" and started to get up. Before he could straighten his legs, Emma shoved him. Her bold move took him by surprise. He toppled, sprawling sideways across the banquette seat.

Emma jammed one hand into her pocket. She pulled it out and threw a handful of ID tags at the other two men.

"How did you bastards get my father's traps?" she shouted.

There was a frozen moment. Then all three men scrambled out of the booth. The driver, his face twisted with rage, grabbed Emma and gave her a vicious shove. She flew against the counter and spun to the floor.

The men ran out of the restaurant, piled into the truck and drove off in spray of gravel.

Emma had memorized their license number. Her boss phoned the State Police, and the truck was stopped an hour later outside Boothbay Harbor. A later search of the driver's home yielded a rich trove of illegal drugs, forged inshore lobster licenses and stolen traps, including several more that had belonged to Emma's father.

Emma ended up with two cracked ribs and two hours in a witness box.

The three creeps ended up with prison sentences.

None of this brought Emma's dad and brother back. But it felt damned good, all the same.

17

Emma awakened slowly. It seemed to take forever to pull her shattered mind and aching body into a semblance of working order.

There was an odd taste in the back of her throat. It reminded her of maple syrup.

She opened her eyes. She was lying fully clothed on a divan. Her eyes moved, taking in her surroundings.

A plane?

Juneau sat a few feet away, reading a book. Nearby, Dawson and Leggatt were leaning over a backgammon board, sipping drinks and conversing in low tones.

Emma lay there, straining to hear.

As if by some sixth sense, Juneau noticed she was awake. He moved to her side. She tried to rise. He gently pressed her back.

"Easy… easy… Stay flat."

"What the hell did you give me?"

"Alsik. It's a derivative of benzoic acid. And a few other things…"

"I know what that is! Are you completely insane?"

"I'm sorry. It wasn't planned. You're going to feel groggy for a while."

She propped herself up to look out a window. It was pitch black outside. She flopped back, fighting nausea.

Dawson and Leggatt approached. Emma glared up at Dawson.

"Where are you taking me?"

"London."

"London!" Emma tried to sit up. The color drained from her face. She swayed. Juneau supported her, easing her back. He passed her an airsick bag.

She rolled sideways and vomited.

Juneau handed her some tissues. Emma wiped her mouth. She looked at him. "That man in the Mercedes…"

"Not one of us."

"How do I know that? You could have staged the whole thing!"

"We didn't."

Emma studied his face. "Who was he then?"

"We're not sure."

"And now he's dead we'll never know, is that it?"

"He's not dead."

"He has to be! His car was torn in half!"

"He survived. He left the scene."

"He walked away?"

"Yes," Dawson replied gravely. "Right after he killed an ambulance attendant."

Emma's eyes darted from face to face. "Why was he trying to kill me?"

Dawson replied. "Best guess? After the Diana debacle, certain elements within the British government have decided they can't afford to leave you alive. You're a… loose end."

Emma gaped at him. "Loose end? What the fuck are you talking about?" Her body jerked. "Damn!" She vomited, more violently this time.

Finally, she flopped back. She lay there, exhausted and tearful.

Juneau shot a look at Dawson. "She needs rest."

Dawson nodded and returned to his seat.

Juneau unfolded a blanket and gently covered Emma's shuddering form.

A late model Jaguar threaded through London traffic. Alan Boswell was at the wheel, speaking on a mobile telephone.

"What time did it take off?" He listened. He checked his watch. "Thank you." He disconnected.

He slowed his car, signaled, and swung left. He crossed a sidewalk and drove into an alley. The Jag rumbled over cobblestones, crossed another sidewalk, made another left, and merged back into traffic.

Boswell thumbed a button on his phone.

"This is Alan. Has Her Majesty retired?" A pause. "I understand that. But tell her I need an audience. I'll be there in five minutes." He disconnected.

The Jag shot out of The Strand into Trafalgar Square.

Juneau helped Emma to a sitting position, then reached for his jacket. The dog-eared paperback he'd been reading earlier dropped out of a pocket. Emma picked it up. She read the title aloud. "*Assassination in America…*" She looked accusingly at Juneau. "Interesting reading, Mr. Juneau."

He took the book from her hand. "It's about President Kennedy. And some missing frames from the Zapruder film."

"A kidnapper *and* a conspiracy theorist! What will they think of next?"

He just smiled and offered his arm. Emma ignored him. She stood, took a step, swayed, and nearly toppled.

Juneau caught her.

She resigned herself to his help. He picked up her bag. She teetered up the aisle, leaning on Juneau, and allowed him to help her to a divan. He settled next to her.

Nowak, wearing a distinctly sheepish expression, brought her some ice water in a crystal glass.

Dawson emerged from the flight deck. He settled into the seat facing Emma. She fixed him with a groggy, hostile stare.

"I understand your anger," Dawson said quietly. "I'll explain everything when you're feeling better." He paused. "I need you to trust me."

"Trust you? You abducted me!" She snatched her bag from Juneau. She dug inside and yanked out the surveillance photos. She tossed them on Dawson's lap.

Dawson glanced through them. He grimaced at the last one. He looked up, his expression apologetic.

"How long have you been watching me?" Emma demanded.

"Since we found you."

"Found me?"

"Yes."

"When was that?"

"Three years ago."

Emma didn't even try to hide her shock. When she finally spoke, the words came out slowly.

"Why shouldn't I believe that that entire car chase thing was staged by you?"

"Because it wasn't. You have my word."

"*Your* word!"

Dawson ignored the insult. "Do you want to live, Miss Parks?"

"It's Dr. Parks."

"Of course. Dr. Parks."

"Yes. I want to live."

"Well, then. Here you are… alive."

Emma sipped water, watching him.

"Where is it, by the way?" he asked.

"What?"

"The vase."

"In a safe place."

He smiled. "Very good." He checked his watch. "We land in fifty minutes."

"And me without a passport! That should be exciting."

Dawson didn't react.

Emma sighed. "Guess I'd better make myself presentable. Where's the

Ladies Room?"

"I'll show you," Juneau offered. He helped her stand. He escorted her aft. Dawson watched them go. Juneau had his arm around her.

I'll need to watch that, he thought.

Dawn was a thread of brightening sky when Dawson's jet turned onto final at London City Airport. It touched down on the numbers and taxied to a hanger. Dawson's Rolls Royce and the two escort vehicles stood waiting.

The aircraft's main door opened. As the stairs deployed, an official vehicle pulled up. A uniformed immigration officer stepped out of the car. He stood and stretched his back. He glanced up. He saw Emma watching him through a window.

"Doctor?"

Emma turned. Carl Juneau was kneeling next to her, below the immigration officer's line of sight.

"You could tell him you're here against your will. You'd be interviewed, you'd tell your story, and we'd all be detained. I'm sure the police would really enjoy arresting a controversial billionaire. But if you do that, I suspect you'll be dead within twenty-four hours." Juneau delivered this assessment in a perfectly neutral tone. He rose and walked away.

Emma looked out the window. The immigration officer was mounting the steps.

Her mind was racing.

The officer ducked aboard and moved forward into the main cabin with an air of long familiarity. He nodded respectfully to Dawson. "Good morning, sir."

"Morning, Paul. Thank you for being so prompt."

The officer settled at the conference table. Juneau passed him a bundle of passports.

Emma's eyes focused on the bundle.

The officer opened passports one by one, looked at each individual... stamped the passport... and set it aside.

Emma watched, torn by indecision.

Finally, there were only two passports left. The officer opened a red one, glanced at Juneau, stamped it and set it aside.

The last passport was dark blue. It was accompanied by a landing card.

The officer opened it. He stared at it.

Emma watched him, confused.

The officer looked across at Emma. He studied her face... the passport...

her face…

Emma opened her mouth to speak.

The officer flashed her a quick smile. He stamped the passport and then the card.

Emma blinked in astonishment.

The officer handed the pile of passports back to Juneau, picked up the landing card, and rose from his seat. "Gentlemen–" a nod to Emma "–and Miss. Thank you all."

"Thank you, Paul," Dawson said.

The officer disembarked.

Emma sat there, stunned.

The Rolls moved off, escorted fore and aft by the Range Rovers. Emma sat in the rear of the Rolls between Dawson and Leggatt. Juneau occupied a jump seat, facing them.

As they drove away, Emma saw the immigration officer standing by his vehicle, watching.

The convoy crossed the Connaught Bridge and joined Victoria Dock Road. Juneau shuffled through passports. He handed one to Leggatt. It had a red cover. Leggatt checked it, then slipped it into an inside pocket. Juneau then passed two passports to Dawson… first a red one, then a blue one.

Emma snatched the blue passport out of Dawson's fingers. She glared defiantly at him. He watched her, amused.

She checked the cover. It was a U.S. passport. She flipped it open to the photo page.

Her brows knitted. It was her picture. But not her name.

Patricia Anne Loewen

Maryland, U.S.A.

Emma looked at Dawson, shocked and angry. "You planned this!"

"Not the way it turned out," Dawson replied calmly. "The passport was just a back-up measure… to get you into Britain undetected if there was a leak."

"A leak?"

"But now we need it to keep you alive," Juneau interjected.

His soothing tone irritated her. "That's my hospital ID picture! How did you get that?"

"One of your hospital's admin clerks had money problems," he answered simply. "Clive helped her out."

"It's a false passport! And you've just used it to get me into this country! Now you've involved me in *two* criminal offences! I'm probably wanted for leaving the scene of the accident in Bayonne... and now this! You'd better have a fucking good reason!"

Dawson tut-tutted. "Language, language! All will be explained. Let's just get you to a safe place first."

"Where? Some twelfth century dungeon?"

The billionaire smiled. "Not exactly, my dear..."

For long minutes, they rode in silence. Eventually, the convoy eased past Kensington Palace. Emma looked out at the heaps of floral tributes and children's crayoned messages of love. Even at this hour, people were standing in groups, holding hands.

"They embalmed her ten hours after the accident," Dawson said.

Emma swung her head. Dawson was watching her face.

"Makes you wonder, doesn't it?" he added quietly.

18

The escort car turned off the main road and entered into a porte-cochère driveway. The Rolls and the trailing vehicle followed. Car doors swung open. Everyone got out. Emma found herself facing an imposing front entrance bracketed by ornate planters displaying flawlessly sculpted shrubs.

They entered a grand foyer. Emma gazed around, taking in the opulence. Her world swayed.

Leggatt, standing closest, caught her before she fell.

Dawson noticed. "You must be exhausted, Doctor! We have a room ready. Henry will take you."

Emma stared at him through bleary eyes. "A room ready? How nice to be expected."

Leggatt steered Emma toward a sweeping marble staircase. She allowed him to hold her arm as they started to climb. She glanced back. Dawson and Juneau were already in deep conversation.

The staircase was lined with masterly paintings. Leggatt gestured at a prominent example.

"The Earl of Solway."

The painting's subject, resplendent in eighteenth century finery, gazed haughtily down upon her.

" 'Solway' sounds Scottish. I thought Dawson was Welsh."

"Oh, he's not Mr. Dawson's ancestor." Leggatt's tone was droll. "He bought the painting at an auction."

They reached a landing. Leggatt guided Emma along a carpeted hallway to an open door. He ushered her into a huge bedroom with a canopied bed. Thick drapes shut out the morning sun.

Chic women's outfits were laid out across the back of a plush sofa.

"We took the liberty of ordering some clothing for you." He laid a palm on a large antique wardrobe. "You'll find more in here."

Emma felt her knees start to sag. She dropped onto the edge of the bed. "For an abduction that wasn't planned, you seem to have thought of everything," she said wearily.

Leggatt pointed at a door. "Your private bathroom is there. I'll leave you to get some rest." He turned to leave, then stopped. "Oh, I'm sorry. Mr. Tannahill's mobile."

She looked at him dumbly. "Mobile?"

"His cell phone." He looked apologetic as he held out a hand. "I need to retrieve it."

Emma reached into her bag. She handed him the phone.

He gave a small bow and exited, closing the door.

After a second, the lock clicked.

Emma looked around. There was a telephone on the bedside table. She lifted the receiver. The line was dead.

Exhausted and beyond caring, she stretched out on the bed and instantly fell asleep.

As Leggatt descended the staircase, he thumbed the power button on Tannahill's phone. The display glowed. One by one, he checked through the readout cycles in the call log.

Missed Calls…

Received Calls…

Dialed Numbers…

He compared each number to a checklist in his mind.

Satisfied, he slipped the phone into his pocket.

In a darkened computer bay in Norfolk, Virginia, an alarm sounded. A dozing operative jerked in his chair. He gaped at his screen. He picked up his phone.

Fifteen minutes later, his supervisor walked swiftly along the line of bays toward a glassed-in office. The sheet of paper in her hand was dense with printed data.

She opened the glass door without knocking.

The Unit Section Head looked up from his paperwork. He took in the expression on the supervisor's face.

"What?"

"Who do you know at MI-5?"

The Section Head thought for a second. "Guy named Boswell. He and I destroyed a bottle of Petrus one night." He smiled, enjoying the memory.

"Isn't that stuff pretty expensive?"

"Eight hundred per, back then. A lot more now."

"Who paid?"

The Section Head's smile faded.

"You paid?"

"Yeah." He looked rueful. "I lost the toss."

"Good!"

"Good? My wife nearly killed me!"

"Good because now the guy owes you. That cell phone went active. We got a fix."

"Where is it?"

"In London."

19

The quiet snick of the lock awoke her.

She stirred. For a second, she was disoriented. Then she remembered.

Alert and afraid, Emma opened her eyes.

Her bedroom door swung silently inward.

She lay absolutely still, watching from under lidded eyes.

A uniformed maid entered, carrying a tray. The door swung shut behind her. Emma heard the lock re-engage. The maid set the tray on a bedside table. She moved to the window. She tugged at the drapes.

Light flooded the room.

Emma sat up. For the first time, she realized she was in the bed, under the covers…

Naked.

She pulled up the sheet.

The maid offered a bright smile. "Good afternoon, Miss."

Emma looked at her dumbly, then at the tray on the table beside her.

"Mr. Leggatt thought you might like some refreshment."

"Where are my clothes?"

The maid poured tea, still smiling. "We've sent them out to be laundered, Miss. But you've lots to wear!" She set down the teapot and tripped over to the sofa. She fussed over the outfits, tugging and straightening.

Emma sipped tea, watching.

After a few moments, the maid moved toward the door. She pointed to a velvet rope.

"If you require anything, Miss, just pull that."

Emma stared at the woman.

Am I in some period drama?

The maid tapped on the door. It opened. She disappeared into the corridor. The door shut. The lock clicked.

A bathrobe lay across the bottom of the bed. Emma rose and slipped it on. She strolled to the wardrobe. She opened it. Her eyes widened. There were at least a dozen outfits hanging inside.

She checked the sizes. Her eyebrows arched.

She opened drawers. One was filled with gorgeous sweaters, another with stylish shoes – both flats and heels – and another with delicate underwear.

She selected a shoe at random and tried it on. It fit perfectly.

She picked up a bra and checked the size. She blinked. She sat on the bed, still holding the bra, her lips compressed.

After a moment, she rose and selected one of the outfits arrayed on the back of the sofa. She stepped to a mirror and held it against herself.

Not bad...

She studied her image in the mirror. A pallid face stared back. She dropped the outfit on the bed and entered the bathroom.

She stopped in her tracks.

The bathroom is a spotless sanctuary of marble and gold.

Emma stepped across to the ancient tub. She moved carefully, as if she were traversing a museum exhibit. She tried a tap. Water spilled. Encouraged, she adjusted the taps until the temperature felt right.

A row of bottles on the countertop caught her eye. It took her shocked mind a full three seconds to react. She stepped to the counter.

A collection of *Matis Paris* cosmetics sat in a perfect line, arranged in the same order as in Emma's own bathroom in Bayonne. She picked up a bottle of *Matis-Paris* eye care gel. Her hand trembled as she looked at it. She set it down quickly and opened the cabinet over the sink. The shelves were bare except for five items.

The toothbrush and toothpaste were her preferred brand, and the hairbrush matched the one she used at home.

But what really unnerved her were the two remaining items: a package of disposable contact lenses and a pair of eyeglasses lying in an open case.

She removed her contacts. She picked up the eyeglasses. She tried them on.

She sat on the edge of the tub, deep in thought.

Emma stood at the mirror. She was wearing one of the new outfits. Her hair was dry, her makeup perfect.

She checked the clock by the bed, and then reset her watch to U.K. time.

There was a small TV near the sofa. She switched it on and surfed channels until she found a news program. She sat on the arm of the sofa to watch. Taped highlights from Princess Diana's funeral played on the screen behind a slickly groomed male presenter.

"Several Members of Parliament have called for a public inquiry into Princess Diana's death. The clamor is cutting across party lines, as MP's–"

A knock. The lock clicked and the door opened a crack.

"Doctor Parks?" It was Carl Juneau.

"Yes?"

"May I come in?"

"Yes." Emma killed the TV. She stood and faced Juneau as he entered. He took a few steps and then stopped. She noticed his eyes flicker over her appraisingly.

She noticed the appreciative look.

She was in no mood for that.

"I hope you're feeling better," he ventured cautiously.

"Should I be?" she snapped.

He looked genuinely apologetic. "They're ready for you now."

"That's what we say to our O.R. patients!"

Juneau looked at her uncertainly, apparently tongue-tied.

Emma pointed at the wardrobe and its array of half-open drawers. "Every one of those outfits is my size! Every pair of shoes! Every sweater! Every *bra*!" She stepped forward and seized him by the sleeve. She pulled him to the bathroom. She pointed an angry finger at the *Matis Paris* products. "That's the brand I use!" She snatched the eyeglasses and their case off the counter. She tapped a finger on the embossed printing on the case. "That's my optometrist in Newark!" She put on the glasses. The fit was perfect. "These are the same frames as the ones I picked last year!" She thrust her face at him. "Do you know how creepy this is?"

"I'm sorry. I–"

She slapped him. Hard.

She wound up to hit him again. He gently blocked her arm. "Listen! Doctor... Emma! I'm sorry, but it's not me!"

"Then who is it? And *why* is it?"

"Mr. Dawson will explain."

"I'm sick of hearing that!" She pushed past him, strode across the bedroom and grabbed her bag. "Fucking right he'll explain!" She stormed out of the room.

Juneau caught up with her in the corridor.

"Does this mean you're feeling better?"

Emma shot a look at him. "I liked you better when you were saving my life."

She marched down the stairs, trailed by Juneau. His face wore an expression of stifled amusement.

In the foyer, just inside the front door, Leggatt was in conversation with a tall, black-haired man wearing a long greatcoat. The man looks like an oversized Cossack.

Baz Cooper was hovering watchfully nearby.

The tall man's eyes locked on Emma. He stopped speaking in mid-sentence.

Emma strode over. She ignored the visitor and addressed Leggatt. "Where's Dawson?"

The tall man seemed fascinated by Emma, looking her up and down, then openly studying her face. Juneau eyed him.

"He'll join us in the front salon in a few minutes," Leggatt replied.

Emma turned to Juneau. "Show me!"

Juneau guided her across the foyer, through a set of double doors, along a carpeted corridor and into a richly furnished salon. A slide projector sat on a small table, its lens aimed at a screen hanging from a bookcase.

"Please make yourself comfortable," Juneau said. "I'll be right back."

He backed out the door, closing it behind him.

The lock clicked.

Emma stared after him, her anger mounting.

Juneau reappeared at Henry Leggatt's side just as the front door closed behind the tall man.

"Constable Andrew Devlin," Leggatt answered, before Juneau could ask. Dawson's aide looked irked. "He's with the Royalty Protection Unit. He wanted a private word with Mr. Dawson. I told him to make an appointment."

"He seemed to take his time getting that message."

"He was insistent, but for some reason he changed his tune after you and Dr. Parks appeared."

Juneau turned to Cooper. "You see any ID?"

Cooper shook his head.

"It's all right," Leggatt offered. "I know him. He transferred to the Palace when I was working there." He pulled a mobile phone out of his pocket and passed it to Juneau. "Tannahill's phone. I retrieved it from our guest. I'll find Mr. Dawson."

He hurried off.

20

Emma wandered the salon, examining artwork and antiques.

The lock clicked and Juneau entered. "Mr. Dawson will be here in a moment."

Emma eyed him.

"Who was that man by the door?"

"Someone to see Mr. Dawson."

"He seemed more interested in seeing me."

"Well… Ma'am, I'd guess that's because you're easier to look at."

"Can we drop the 'Ma'am' crap? The down-home routine doesn't work on me, Mr. Juneau! And you don't sound like a Texan."

"I'm not. Montana, born and raised."

"Montana…" Emma's eyes scanned his face.

Juneau smiled. "You want to ask, don't you? My mother was full-blooded Siksika." He smiled resignedly at Emma's blank look. "Blackfoot Indian," he explained.

"Oh? How fascinating. But I wasn't thinking about that."

"Then what?"

"You carry a British passport."

"My Dad was English. It's a long story…"

"Of course! They always are! Dad left when I was three… I have abandonment issues… Kidnapping is my only solace, my cry for help!"

Juneau's expression hardened. "He died when I was eight."

"Oh. Sorry."

Emma didn't look sorry. She continued her bad-tempered circumnavigation of the room, looking at paintings, touching antiques, examining the impressive liquor display. She arrived at a collection of vases, locked behind glass. Several pieces were similar to hers.

She turned back to Juneau. Her eyes flashed. "Kidnapping. Forgery. Seriously, Carl, how can you work for this man?"

"You're upset. I get it. But we did save your life."

"Oh, excuse me for being such an ingrate! I'm generally pretty low maintenance, but I guess being drugged and abducted tends to bring out the bitch in me!" Her voice went up. "I'm perfectly aware that you and your muckraker boss and his poodle saved my life! I'm in no danger of forgetting that, since you all keep reminding me. Thank you from the bottom of my heart! Now if somebody would just tell me why the hell my life needed saving in the first place, maybe I'd be a bit more understanding!"

At that instant, Victor Dawson bustled into the room, trailed by Henry Leggatt. "The muckraker and his poodle will be pleased to answer your questions!" He stopped in his tracks, smiling with admiration. "Emma! You look refreshed! And – may I say? – quite ravishing!"

Emma was too agitated to correct the man's fumbling attempt at familiarity. She stared at him as if he was a large insect.

Dawson breezed on. "Supper will be ready soon. Would you care for a drink? Henry!"

"I'm not sure I should. I mean, so soon after unplanned anesthesia!" She shot a look at Juneau.

"You're fine now," Juneau said evenly.

"Well, thank you, Dr. Juneau! I feel so assured!"

Juneau looked like she'd slapped him again. Emma felt a twinge of remorse.

Get hold of yourself, girl! You're here now, so just shut up and listen!

"Perhaps a vodka?" Dawson pressed.

Emma sighed. "Fine."

Leggatt opened the well-stocked liquor cabinet. As Emma watched, he filled a crystal glass with ice, selected a bottle and poured. The label on the bottle read *Moscow Signature Cristall*.

My brand. Of course. Why am I not surprised?

She stifled the impulse to make a sardonic remark.

Dawson guided her to a silk-embroidered wing chair. Leggatt carried the drink to her on a tray. She received it with a wintry smile.

Leggatt dimmed the lights and switched on the slide projector. The machine hummed into life and the screen lit up with a white glare. Leggatt activated the projector's remote. The slide magazine clicked and cycled.

A picture appeared on the screen.

It was a photograph of an eighteenth century painting. The subject was a pink-faced middle-aged man, resplendent in Royal regalia. He had oddly bulbous eyes.

"King George III," Dawson announced. "He came to the throne in 1760, at the age of twenty-two. As a king, he's remembered for two things: losing the American colonies, and losing his mind. You've heard of Mad Old King George?"

Emma leaned forward in her seat, perplexed. Dawson motored on.

"Ten months after George took the throne, he married Charlotte of Mecklinburg-Strelitz, a German princess… Henry?"

The slide changed. Another painting. This one showed a thick-lipped, vaguely simian-looking woman with sleepy eyes. She was also attired in formal dress.

"Queen Charlotte... Horace Walpole described her as 'small, lean and not well made'." Dawson chuckled. "Like most royal marriages, this was an arranged match. Despite the Princess's rather unprepossessing looks, George managed to sire fifteen children with her. The current Royal Family is descended from that union."

Emma sipped her vodka. She was getting impatient.

Dawson settled on a chair, still talking. "But there was a problem with this marriage, Emma. When George married Charlotte, he failed to mention one rather important little fact." He paused for effect. "He was already married."

It took Emma a second.

"What?"

Dawson looked her in the eye. "I said: *He was already married.* Henry?"

A photograph of an ancient document appeared on the screen.

"I'll ask Henry to explain."

Leggatt took up the commentary. "Dr. Parks, this is an original parish marriage record. On April 17th, 1759, eighteen months before he took the throne, Prince George married his mistress. The bride was a lapsed Quaker. Her name was Hannah Lightfoot."

Emma stared at the screen in puzzlement.

"As you may have noticed," Leggatt continued, "I stressed that this is an *original* record. That is important because a century later, in 1866, a woman who called herself 'Princess Lavinia of Cumberland' offered a separate record of this marriage as evidence in a much-publicized court case. It was a probate action in which the woman falsely claimed to be a member of the Royal Family. The marriage record and other documents she presented to the court were proven to be forgeries and the presiding Judge ordered them confiscated. After that finding, any claim that George III had entered into an undisclosed marriage prior to his union with Princess Charlotte was dismissed as pure fantasy."

Dawson interjected. "We'll come back to this document later. Next slide, Henry!"

Emma's interest was flagging. Her eyes wandered. She caught Juneau watching her.

Leggatt clicked to the next slide – a painting of a melancholy woman with dark hair and dark eyes.

"This painting is held in the National Trust collection at Knole Park, in Kent," Dawson said. "It was painted by Sir Joshua Reynolds, the famous eighteenth century portrait painter. The National Trust catalogue identifies this woman as Hannah Lightfoot, but the catalogue is wrong. A few years ago, Kenneth Tannahill gained access to the papers of a man named Phillip Metcalfe. Metcalfe was the executor of Sir Joshua Reynolds' estate. He died in 1818, and some of his private papers are now in the hands of a private collector. Ken found a handwritten catalogue, dated two years before Joshua Reynolds' death, which identifies the woman in this painting as Lady Annabelle Griffiths. There are, in fact, no known paintings of Hannah Lightfoot."

"She was a commoner," Leggatt added. "A draper's assistant. That may account for it."

"If she married a Prince, as you say," Emma ventured, "there must have been a painting done of her."

"Nothing definitive has ever turned up," Dawson replied. "So we don't really know what she looked like."

Emma expelled a breath. "Listen, this is all very interesting, but you're talking about a secret wedding that took place two hundred years ago! What's that got to do with a man trying to kill me?"

"It's coming."

"Really? Okay, I'll play along." She sipped her drink. "This wedding… How could the Prince of Wales marry without the King finding out?"

Dawson replied. "Prince George came of age in 1756, so he had his own household, separate from the King's. Hannah was quite a bit older than George – twenty-eight in 1759, to the Prince's nineteen. He was completely infatuated with her. He arranged to marry her in a chapel at Kew Green, with just a few select witnesses present, all of whom were sworn to secrecy. The Prince's primary advisor at the time was a man named John Stuart, the Earl of Bute. Bute was very close to the King, so the Prince deliberately kept him in the dark. Once the deed was done it couldn't be undone, even by the King. After the ceremony, they held a reception at Marble Hill, a country house in Richmond owned by the Countess of Suffolk. There was a bit of humorous mischief in this, because the Countess was a former mistress of the old King. When Bute found out, he crashed the party and attempted to dissuade the Prince from… ah, consummating the union. He was unsuccessful."

"Did they have children?"

"We'll come to that. Henry, take us back to the document, please."

The parish marriage record reappeared. Dawson rose from his seat and walked to the screen. "Emma, Ken Tannahill found this original parish record when he was researching a different story. It was in the Public Records Office, where its forged counterpart can be seen among old Court archives. The difference is... this is a *genuine* record. It had been deliberately misfiled, probably by some clerk with a pungent sense of humor."

"I don't follow."

Dawson grinned. "This document was tucked in among the official papers relating to the passage through Parliament of the Royal Marriages Act of 1772. That statute was drafted at George III's request. It prohibited a member of the Royal Family from marrying without the express consent of the monarch."

"Are you saying George III made it unlawful to do what he had done himself?"

"Delicious, isn't it? Apparently he was angry at his younger brother Henry, who had married a commoner without telling him." Dawson looked genuinely pleased with the irony.

Despite herself, Emma was now intrigued. "So, back in 1759 it was perfectly lawful for Prince George to marry Hannah without getting the old King's permission."

"That's right."

"When did he marry Princess Charlotte?"

"In 1761."

"Okay. But he was a prince..." Emma was thinking out loud. "It's not like he had no influence. He probably had his fling with Hannah, then just arranged for a quiet divorce and married the Princess."

"At that time, Doctor," Leggatt interposed, "a divorce required an Act of Parliament. Even for a prince."

"And no such Act was ever passed," Dawson finished.

"Hmmh," Emma muttered. She studied her drink, trying to work out where this was going. It had to be connected to her vase.

Dawson's voice broke into her reverie. "Ken Tannahill first brought this project to me six years ago. He had sniffed out the outlines of the Hannah Lightfoot story from various second- and third-hand sources – mostly snippets from letters published in obscure periodicals a century after the fact. He wanted my permission to keep digging. Frankly, I thought he was off his head. But he'd always delivered in the past, so I agreed." Dawson resumed his seat. "Then two things happened. First, we got our hands on George's personal diaries for the years 1753 until 1770. No historian has ever seen those."

Emma's head came up.

"How?" she asked.

"Eh?"

Emma looked Dawson in the eye. "How did you get your hands on a king's personal diaries?"

Dawson and Leggatt exchanged a quick glance.

"November 20, 1992," Dawson began. "Does that date mean anything to you?"

"No."

"There was a fire at Windsor Castle. It burned for fifteen hours."

Emma nodded slowly. "I remember. It was on TV."

"Two of the companies that were hired to do the restoration work belong to me."

Emma processed that. "So. You stole them."

"Borrowed. Copied and returned."

Emma was unmoved. "Let's see…" She counted off on her fingers. "Kidnapping… forged passports… stealing from the Royal Family. Interesting hobbies for a newspaperman."

"Please! 'Media Baron' sounds so much more impressive." Dawson smiled, unabashed. "And don't forget satellite hacking."

"Satellite hacking?"

"Yes. I'm sure it's some kind of offence. But it saved you from an assassin."

Emma sighed. "There you go again."

21

The man moved fluidly along the sidewalk. He was carrying a long sports bag.

He stopped and looked around. There was no one in sight.

He scaled the wall. He dropped silently on the other side. He pulled on gloves. He ghosted across the rear garden of the darkened mansion.

He picked the lock on a garden-level door.

He entered and closed the door behind him.

Seconds later, he emerged from a second floor window onto the lowest landing of a fire escape. He released the first storey extension and lowered it slowly and carefully to the ground below.

Leaving it in place, he turned, slung the sports bag across his shoulders, and started climbing.

He reached the roof.

He kneeled, opened the bag, and removed a long case.

The case bore the insignia of one of the Queen's Household Regiments. The zipper was wired shut and sealed with lead. A crest that looked like a coat-of-arms was stamped into the lead.

He cut the wire and unzipped the case.

He removed a silenced, night-scoped L96 British military sniper rifle.

He checked the mechanism with an expert's touch.

He moved to the front of the roof and took cover behind an ornamental parapet. He looked over the edge, scanning the scene below.

He brought the weapon up.

He put one pale eye to the scope.

Dawson waved a hand at the parish record on the screen. "In his diary, Prince George devoted several pages to his courtship of Hannah Lightfoot – how he first saw her in a shop, how he arranged through a helpful Lady in Waiting to meet her, and how he eventually came to arrange their clandestine marriage. I won't bore you with the details, but he was fully aware that he was in breach of Royal convention, although not in breach of any law, and his diary sets out the agonies he suffered as duty chafed against desire. He described the wedding as 'a scrambling shabby business, regrettable but unavoidable'. One of the official witnesses at the ceremony was William Pitt." Dawson rose and returned to the screen. He pointed. "That is Pitt's signature. We have an enlargement." The slide changed. An ornate but perfectly legible signature filled the screen:

Wm. Pitt

Dawson watched Emma's face as she studied the screen. "Next slide please, Henry."

Another slide. Another painting. A bewigged man kneeling before an aging, cold-eyed monarch.

"William Pitt was George II's Chief Minister. Pitt hated the old King. He knew he'd be furious over his grandson's marriage to a commoner. We think Pitt encouraged the ceremony in order to curry favor with the heir apparent." A pause. "You asked about children."

"Yes."

"As George himself put it in his diary, he kept Hannah 'in the secret recesses of Hampton, where I tasted the bliss of purest love'." Dawson began to pace, warming to his subject. "And yes, there was a child. Hannah bore the Prince one child, a son. He was born a year after the wedding. They named him George Augustus Guelph. 'Guelph' was the Prince's seldom-used surname. But when George took the throne, he abandoned Hannah and his son. He simply married Princess Charlotte and pretended Hannah didn't exist."

Emma was having trouble hiding her impatience. "Very sad, but he wouldn't be the first king to turn his back on a wife. So how does my vase fit in? Was it a wedding present?"

"Yes, it was. From the Prince to Hannah, actually. It was part of a set."

"Okaaay…! So my vase is some kind of missing link!" Emma waved at the antique pieces lining the room. "And, let me guess… you need it to complete your damned collection!"

"No, Emma…"

"I told Tannahill the vase is not for sale, but I've changed my mind! But I want a lot of money, Dawson! At least… a million! Pounds, not dollars!"

Dawson stopped pacing.

"And I want your jet to fly me home!"

Darius steadied the rifle, sighting on the mansion directly across the corner of the green. The angle could have been better, but it would have to serve. He cancelled the low-light reticle illumination as the target zone moved from unlighted rooms to lighted rooms. The image in the scope settled on an illuminated gap between the drapes in a ground floor room.

The woman was visible.

Dawson was pacing, crossing and re-crossing in front of her.

He waited.

Dawson stopped pacing. But he was standing right in front of the gap, blocking the shot.

Darius slipped his finger through the trigger guard.

He waited.

Dawson turned, gazing out into the night. He was still talking.

After a few seconds, he turned back, facing the woman.

His body edged clear of the gap.

Now the woman was talking. She looked angry.

Darius put slight pressure on the trigger.

The laser rangefinder engaged.

The mil-dot reticle settled between the woman's breasts…

The targeting dot was pale blue… almost invisible.

Juneau almost missed it.

With a yell, he launched himself at Emma, diving through space, toppling her chair.

The faint tinkle of breaking glass… the slug slicing across his back… the thud as it punched a hole in the floor behind them… It all seemed simultaneous.

At 3200 feet per second, it pretty much was.

Juneau's momentum slammed Emma to the floor.

More breaking glass…

A sequence of slugs walked a pattern across the floor toward them.

Juneau rolled Emma's body out of the way.

More shots. Display cases shattered. Vases exploded.

Juneau seized Emma and dragged her, half-senseless from her collision with the floor, into the hallway.

He turned back. Leggatt was scrambling backward, crab-like, out of the line of fire. Dawson was crawling for the door. A slug hit the floor next to his leg. He scrambled for his life, reaching for Juneau. The next shot blasted the heel off his shoe. Juneau grabbed him by the back of his shirt and yanked him into the hallway.

Juneau pulled his gun. He ducked his head back into the salon. Leggatt was lying flat against the wall in the far front corner.

"Stay there!" Juneau shouted.

Leggatt nodded, terrified.

Juneau barked into his wrist mike. "Shooter! Across the Crescent! Looks like Number 149, on the roof!"

He turned. Dawson was getting to his feet. Juneau scooped up Emma. He carried her as he herded Dawson into an alcove off the corridor.

"Sit down!" he ordered.

Dawson sat. Juneau gently set Emma down and leaned her against

Dawson. She was conscious, but dazed. Juneau kneeled in front of her. "Did I hurt you?"

Emma smiled wanly. "I think I'm okay."

They could hear raised voices and running feet elsewhere in the house. Juneau keyed his radio.

"The boss and Dr. Parks are in the southeast corridor alcove. I want someone here, now!"

He handed his gun to Dawson. "Protect her!"

He raced back down the hallway toward the salon.

A bloodstain was spreading down the back of his shirt.

When Juneau reappeared, Dawson was helping Emma to her feet. Juneau had Leggatt with him. The man looked completely shattered.

Cooper, Wickham and Nowak arrived together, all packing lethal looking MP-5's. Juneau retrieved his automatic from Dawson, then looked around. "Where's McGinnis?"

"Here, sir!" A young man in workman's clothes was hurrying toward them carrying a pump action shotgun.

"Where were you?"

"In the garage."

"Give your shotgun to the lady."

The young man passed it to Emma.

"Know how to use that?" Juneau asked her.

Emma nodded.

"Figured you would." He turned back to McGinnis.

"Take Cooper's weapon and assemble all the staff in one place, away from windows! Cut all the outside lights, and stay close to Mr. Dawson and the lady! Baz, grab some night goggles and a carbine! Cover us from the roof!" He pointed to Nowak and Wickham. "You two come with me!"

Emma interjected. "Carl, you're bleeding! Let me–"

"Not now, Doc! Stay with McGinnis!"

On the rooftop, Darius methodically collected spent shell casings.

He was disappointed. But not discouraged. That security man was fast. He'd have to sharpen his game.

Across the green, the outside lights went out.

Here they come, he thought.

He smiled to himself. This should be interesting.

He melted into the darkness.

Juneau, Wickham and Nowak raced across the Crescent. Juneau and Wickham rushed down one side of Number 149; Nowak took the other.

Juneau and Wickham found the deployed fire escape.

Juneau keyed his radio.

"Baz? You in place?"

"Yes sir! Roof looks clear."

"Wickham's going up! Cover him!"

Wickham mounted the fire escape.

Juneau heard a noise. He moved to the back corner of the building.

A silenced shot blasted past his ear.

He ducked back, holding fire, his eyes boring into the night.

He heard the sound of running feet, then… silence.

He crept quickly through the rear garden. He found Nowak on the ground, struggling to sit up.

"Denny! You hit?"

"Gun barrel!" Nowak groaned and flopped back.

Juneau whispered into his mike. "Nowak's down! He's in the back garden! Somebody help him. I'm going after this bastard!"

Juneau scaled the rear garden wall and dropped into the roadway behind.

A hundred yards away, a male figure carrying a sports bag disappeared between buildings. Juneau sprinted after him.

22

Juneau reached a corner. A cobbled passage led into a set of upscale residential mews. A row of iron bollards blocked vehicle traffic from entering the complex from this side.

He crept forward.

A silenced shot whined off a bollard next to his leg.

Juneau moved low and fast through the gate and ducked behind a parked car. His eyes swept the paved courtyard. It was silent and empty.

Then he heard a sound… fabric on stone. He tracked the sound. Across the courtyard, a pitch-black vertical strip marked a gap between buildings. He circled toward it, dropped to the ground and peered in, weapon ready.

The gap was just wide enough for a man's body to pass.

A hundred feet away, a high wall blocked entrance into the gap from the lighted street beyond.

He saw a sports bag disappear over the top of the wall.

Juneau jumped up, holstered his weapon and squeezed into the passage. Seconds later, he dropped off the wall onto a busy sidewalk. A middle-aged woman stopped in her tracks, and then started to back away. He smiled. She hurried off, looking offended.

Juneau checked the street both ways. A sign bearing the British Rail logo read: *Victoria Station*. An arrow pointed south.

He set off in that direction.

Ahead, a pair of Bentleys stood at the curb, doors open. Elegantly dressed, half-drunk Sloane Rangers spilled laughing across the sidewalk, heading for a cellar nightclub.

Juneau loped past the throng of carousers as they stumbled down the steps to the club entrance. He didn't notice Darius standing in the stairwell, waiting. Darius moved back up the steps and trailed Juneau from a distance.

Juneau jogged, slowing as he passed strolling couples, speeding up when the sidewalk was clear ahead.

A pub sign read: *The Cromwell*. A few dozen patrons crowded the sidewalk, smoking and swilling beer. Juneau gave them the once-over, then stepped into the street to pass around them.

Behind him, Darius matched Juneau's pace, holding his pistol between the sports bag and his leg.

Juneau stopped. The sidewalk ahead was empty.

Somehow, he knew.

He turned slowly and began retracing his steps. His eyes raked the crowd of punters. He entered the pub. It was a noisy, packed scene. He eased against one wall, found a clear spot on a padded bench, and sat down.

His eyes probed the forest of legs and torsos.

He spotted the sports bag.

He rose slowly.

At the end of the bar, Darius raised a full pint to his lips.

The two men's eyes locked.

Juneau shouldered through the crowd, jostling tipplers. Pints slopped. A red-faced bruiser wearing an Arsenal tee shirt grabbed his arm.

"Hey, mate! What'r ya think yer–!"

Juneau turned. Conversations ended in mid-sentence.

The look on Juneau's face shut the man up. He released his arm. Other patrons spotted his bloody back.

They moved away.

BANG!

The door to the restroom corridor shuddered on its hinges.

Juneau ran. He pounded into the corridor and slammed through the Men's Room door, his gun out. There was a man at a urinal. Similar clothes, similar build. Juneau grabbed his shoulder.

The man yelped. "Hey! What the hell are ya–!"

Then he saw the gun. He pissed down the front of his pants.

"Sorry!" Juneau mumbled. He dodged back into the corridor and shouldered into the Women's Room.

Two young women decked out in short skirts and fuck-me pumps cowered next to the sinks under a thick drift of smoke. One held a burning joint in her fingers.

They stared bug-eyed at Juneau's face... then at his gun.

Both women pointed to an open window.

Juneau nodded his thanks, checked both ways out the window, and then bailed out through it. He raced out of the alley.

Across the road was the giant edifice of Victoria Station. The sidewalks and concourses were teeming with hurrying pedestrians. Juneau sprinted across the road. He ducked low, scanning through the crowd.

He spotted the sports bag heading for the Underground station.

He ran.

Ahead of him, Darius vaulted a turnstile, pushed passengers aside, and slid down the slope between escalator rails. Juneau plunged after him, following the trail of sprawled humanity.

He saw Darius disappear into a pedestrian tunnel. He glanced around, and ducked into a different tunnel.

Moments later, Darius walked briskly along a tunnel toward a platform. Thirty feet ahead, Carl Juneau stepped into view. Darius stopped. Juneau smiled. His hand slipped inside his jacket. He walked purposefully forward.

Two steps from Darius, red lettering on a door read: *Emergency Exit Caution! Alarm Will Sound*! Darius threw himself against the crash bar and disappeared.

Immediately, a klaxon sounded.

Juneau sprinted to the door. Behind it, a concrete staircase led upward. He raced up after his prey.

He erupted through a door and found himself on the main floor of the train station. The klaxon was louder here. A red light flashed above the unmarked door where he had just exited.

Fifty feet away, a pair of uniformed policemen spotted him. They started pushing through the confused throng that was surging for the exits.

Juneau saw Darius moving across the concourse. He headed after him. A policeman yelled. "You sir! Stop!"

Juneau ignored him and kept going. He emerged from the station onto the bus platform. He worked his way into the open, his eyes scanning… searching…

Darius was gone.

Juneau glanced behind him as the two policemen stumbled out of the building. He ducked out of sight between a pair of standing buses. The policemen ran off in the wrong direction.

With a hiss of releasing brakes, a double-decker started moving. Juneau stepped back into the pulsating crowd on the platform.

The bus pulled away. It slowed and turned into traffic. Juneau glanced up.

Darius was sitting on the top deck, watching him.

He gave Juneau a little wave.

The bus disappeared into traffic.

23

They were in the dining room. Its walls were paneled in some dark exotic wood, inlaid with Spanish leather. The long table that dominated the room seated thirty. The heavy drapes over the windows were tightly closed. Wickham and Cooper stood guard. Staff members sat in a group, whispering nervously. Emma's maid seemed to be the most frightened. An older lady held her hand.

Emma was tending Nowak while Dawson and Leggatt hovered nearby. Nowak was conscious. Emma shone a penlight into his eyes. "You'll be fine, but tell me if you start to feel sleepy. That's important."

"Thanks." He looked at her sheepishly. "I'm sorry for using the Alsik, Lady. Boss gave me hell."

"Mr. Dawson?"

"No. Mr. Juneau."

"Oh."

Wickham pressed his earpiece, listened, then left the room. He reappeared with Juneau.

Juneau walked directly to Emma. "The man who tried to kill you in Bayonne… describe him."

"Late thirties, early forties, thin face, clean shaven. That's all I saw."

Juneau nodded.

Wickham handed Juneau a small object. "I found this on the roof."

It was a lead seal. Juneau turned it over in his fingers. There was a stamped crest on the reverse. "I've seen this somewhere."

While he studied the crest, Emma pushed him onto a chair. The back of his shirt was soaked with blood.

"Shirt off!" Emma ordered.

As he unbuttoned his shirt, Juneau caught Leggatt's eye. "That cop who came to the door…?"

"Devlin."

"What exactly did he want with Mr. Dawson?"

Emma gently peeled back Juneau's shirt.

"He wouldn't say. But I can guess. Everyone who worked at the Palace has some Diana story to sell. The tabloids are in a bidding war."

A trough of raw flesh glistened across Juneau's shoulders. Blood flowed.

"This needs a hospital," Emma pronounced.

"No hospitals!"

"It needs sutures!"

"Do what you can."

Emma snorted. "Warriors!" She turned to Leggatt. "Is there a first aid kit?"

Leggatt looked blank. Wickham answered for him.

"There's one in the kitchen."

"Show me!" Emma tapped Juneau on the head. "Don't you move!"

Emma and Wickham left the room.

Juneau looked at Dawson, who had taken a seat across the table from him. "We've got to get her away from here, sir."

He watched Dawson's eyes.

"Clairmont?"

Juneau nodded slowly. "Good. We'll need to leave early. Three a.m. Convoy to the office, then the chopper."

"I'll call the pilot," Leggatt offered. He was still looking pale. He hurried off.

Juneau watched him go.

Then he watched Dawson, who was now calmly lighting a cigar.

He was beginning to wonder who could be trusted.

Emma poked through the first aid box – sterile dressings, tape, bandage scissors, surgical gloves... not much else.

"This is it? Any antiseptic?"

Dwight Wickham shrugged.

"There's contact lens cleaner in my bathroom. I can use that."

"I'll send somebody up."

"Where's the spice cabinet?"

"I think it's that one." Wickham pointed.

Emma opened the cabinet, scanned the array of bottles and grabbed one. She turned back to Wickham. "We need a few other things. I'll make a list. And I have to go back to the salon."

"I don't know. The boss might not–"

"Your boss is my patient, so right now I'm his boss!" Emma handed him the first aid kit. "And our sniper friend is gone!" She marched out of the kitchen.

The salon was a shattered mess, but the liquor cabinet was intact. Emma scanned the contents. She selected an ornate, jewel-studded bottle. The label read: *Louis XIII de Remy Martin*.

Ten minutes later, a makeshift surgical suite was ready on the dining table. A slender candle burned in a silver holder. Laid out next to it were needle-nosed pliers, a sewing kit, a metal mixing bowl, contact lens cleaning solution, and the Louis XIII cognac.

Blood still oozed from Juneau's wound.

Emma stirred a solution in a drinking glass. She handed it to him. "Drink!"

"What is it?"

"Shut up and drink it!"

He tossed it down. He made a face. "Jeez! What the hell was that?"

"Cayenne pepper. It'll stop the bleeding."

Within seconds, the bleeding stopped. Dawson and Leggatt looked on in disbelief.

Emma opened the cognac bottle. She poured several ounces into the bowl.

"I'm sure there was some nice inexpensive Hennessey you could have used," Dawson muttered.

Emma ignited the cognac with the candle. A gorgeous blue flame leapt upward, dancing and flickering. "Don't you think Carl's worth the good stuff, Victor? After all, he did just save *your* life too!"

"I suppose you'll keep reminding me of that."

"I believe I will."

Emma used the pliers to hold the needle over the flame. When it was red-hot, she bent it into a "U".

She set the needle aside. She tugged on the surgical gloves from the first aid kit. She inspected Juneau's back. She picked up the bottle of contact solution and squirted it over and around the wound.

Juneau sucked in a breath as the solution started bubbling.

Emma threaded the needle. "This is going to hurt."

"I know. Do it."

Emma started closing the wound. Juneau flinched, gritted his teeth, shut his eyes, and sat perfectly still.

Emma shook her head, impressed.

She tied off the last suture, dressed the wound and trimmed the tape ends.

"That should hold you."

Juneau stood up. Cooper passed him a clean shirt. He slipped it on and turned to Emma.

"Thanks, Doc. I owe you."

"Guess I owe you back."

Their eyes met for one liquid moment.

Emma felt suddenly self-conscious. "We're not finished." She collected extra wound dressings, a roll of tape and the bandage scissors in a small pile. "You'll need these to change the dressing."

"You keep them, Doc." He smiled crookedly. "Looks like we'll be spending a few more days together."

Emma looked at him, shrugged resignedly, and dropped the supplies in her bag.

Juneau's blood-soaked jacket was hanging on a chair. He held it up to the light. There was a jagged rent across the back.

"Close one, boss," Wickham said.

"Maybe you should have it bronzed," Emma suggested.

"Very funny." Juneau emptied the jacket's pockets – wallet, keys, extra clip for his automatic, and a paperback book.

"What are you reading now?" Emma plucked the book from his hand. She checked the title: *Lord Chesterfield's Letters To His Son.*

"Not exactly a bodice-ripper," Emma commented.

"I'm catching up on the Classics. I missed out at West Point."

"West Point? Aren't you full of surprises?" She sniffed. "Chesterfield's hardly a Classic. He was a cynical old male chauvinist."

"Maybe. But he knew exactly how to address women."

"Oh?"

Juneau nodded solemnly. "He said plain looking women should always be flattered for their beauty. Ugly women and beautiful women should be praised for their intelligence."

Emma watched his face. Waiting.

He was silent.

She took the bait. "Okay... what am I?"

Juneau grinned. "Well, let's see... I'd say you're extremely–" he chewed his lip, making a show of deep thought "–smart!"

The images on the computer monitor were in black-and-white, but there was no mistaking the lead vehicle. The stop-action sequence showed Emma's car streaking through a red light with a dark-colored Mercedes in hot pursuit.

"That's Emma's car!" Rita Gomez blurted. "What the hell is she doing?"

The next frame showed a close-up of Emma's face through her windshield. A face contorted with terror.

Rita gasped.

The picture cycled, then froze again. Darius's face appeared behind the wheel of the Mercedes.

Cold and expressionless.

Rita and Jan were standing in front of a computer monitor on the second floor of the Bayonne Police Headquarters. They were surrounded by a clutter of document storage boxes, half-open file drawers and clipboards hanging haphazardly from every available section of wall. The overwhelming impression was one of overworked detectives struggling to keep up.

To Jan's right stood Lieutenant Jim Barstow, the detective who had answered Emma's telephone call to Kenneth Tannahill's hotel room. Barstow's exasperated expression lent strong support to the general atmosphere of understaffed tension.

Standing on Barstow's right were Dr. George Grant and his attorney, Edward Gottlieb. The lawyer was a bespectacled man whose face wore the pinched expression of a permanently sour disposition.

"How did you get those pictures?" Jan asked.

"From our Traffic Unit. They're trying out a new speed camera."

"Speed camera?"

"Invented by a Dutch guy. It uses radar. A speeding car trips a sensor and the camera starts snapping high-res photos." He tapped the screen. "That Mercedes was stolen. Do any of you recognize this man?"

Rita and Jan shook their heads. Rita flicked a suspicious glance at Grant.

"A moment," Gottlieb said. He pulled Grant away from the group. They conferred in whispers. After a few seconds, they returned.

"My client has never seen this man before."

Barstow nodded. He had obviously expected that answer. He opened a drawer and pulled out a clear plastic exhibit bag. Sealed inside was a white 8½ x 12 envelope. "Yesterday, an English newspaper reporter was murdered in a men's room at the Reardon in Jersey City. We found this in his hotel room." He let them read the word on the label.

PARKS

Rita blurted the obvious. "That's Emma's name!"

"Yes."

"What was in the envelope?" Jan asked.

"It was empty."

"Then that word could mean anything!" Jan retorted. "How can you say that relates to Emma?"

"Because your friend was seen with the dead man just before he was killed."

"You're saying Emma's a suspect?" Jan looked shocked.

"No. What I *am* saying is this–" Barstow counted off on his fingers. "Dr. Parks had a meeting with this Brit reporter. Right after their meeting, the man was murdered – shot twice in the head. Two hours later, your friend was driving like a maniac, fleeing from this man–" he nodded at the monitor "– and based on various reports we've received, he shot up her car, pursued her for several miles, and at one point rammed her from behind. The chase finally ended with the worst traffic pileup we've had in years."

"And just where were you police when all this was happening?" Grant's attorney asked sharply.

"At a residence fire at 45th and JFK Boulevard. We had injured firefighters and a big traffic problem." He turned back to Jan and Rita. "Dr. Parks left the accident scene. Witnesses say she drove north on 169. Thirty minutes later, the man from the Mercedes murdered a paramedic who was treating him and disappeared."

Rita let out a moan of despair. She collapsed onto a chair.

"Wait a minute! What time was this accident?" Jan asked.

"Twelve fifty-one p.m."

"Emma called me! It was in the morning. She thought she was being targeted in some scam! She was coming over to tell me about it, but she never showed up."

"A scam?" Barstow was thoughtful. "There is one more thing," he added slowly. "Late yesterday afternoon, Jersey City P.D. had a report of what looked like an abduction. Some people at a bus stop on Tait Street saw a woman matching Dr. Parks' description being forced into a van." He fixed hard eyes on Grant. "Would you know anything about that, sir?"

"What? I'm a respected surgeon!" Grant protested. He ignored his attorney's warning hand signal. "You can't seriously believe I had anything to do with Emma's disappearance!"

"At this point, sir, I don't know what to believe. But you wouldn't be the first surgeon to dispose of an inconvenient girlfriend."

Gottlieb blustered. "That's uncalled for, Lieutenant!"

"Maybe. But according to every witness we've interviewed, the only person who had any motive to harm Dr. Parks is your client." Barstow turned to Rita and Jan. "Okay. Ms. Chernoff... Ms. Gomez... you ladies can go."

"Lieutenant–?" Jan began.

Barstow cut her off. "I'll send officers to take your statements." The detective's eyes told her not her argue.

Jan got the message. She touched Rita on the shoulder. "Let's go, Rita."

They left.

Barstow turned to Grant, ignoring Gottlieb. "I have some questions about your relationship with Dr. Parks."

"My client has nothing to say," Gottlieb snarked.

"Really?" Barstow picked up a folder from his desk. "He had a lot to say in this complaint he filed against her at the hospital. I thought he might care to explain the background. I'm also curious to know why the Feds are sniffing around this case."

"The Feds?" Gottlieb looked alarmed. "What Feds?"

"The NSA *and* the FBI." Barstow looked accusingly at Grant. "Exactly who or what are you, Doctor?"

24

Dawson's staff members dozed on haphazard cushions and mattresses. Emma lay on a sofa, covered with a blanket. Juneau woke her gently.

"We're ready."

He helped her to her feet.

She looked at him curiously. "You've gained weight."

"Kevlar." He held up a bulletproof vest. "Here's yours."

"You're kidding!"

"This isn't my kidding face."

Emma stared at the vest, then down at her wrinkled outfit. "Couldn't you get a color that matched?"

He smiled. "Sorry."

Emma sighed. "Okay. Show me."

Juneau helped her into the vest.

"Carl…"

"Mmmh?" He continued snugging the straps.

"I want to know why we're avoiding the police." She dropped her voice. "The staff must be wondering that as well."

"They're loyal. Dawson pays very well. He asked them to remain quiet for now, and they will." He dug his hand in a pocket and brought out the lead seal Wickham had found on the roof. "I checked this on the Internet. That's the insignia of one of the Queen's Household Regiments. The question is: was it dropped by accident… or left there deliberately?"

Emma felt her shoulders tighten. "How is this going to end? I just want to go home, Carl. I want my life back!"

"I don't blame you."

"But I'm not, am I? Going home."

"I can't protect you there." Juneau looked genuinely unhappy.

Emma's mouth formed a faint smile. "*You* can't protect me?"

Juneau looked uncomfortable. "We can't…"

"I need to get word to my friends."

"We'll figure something out."

He led her to the front foyer. The Rolls and both Rovers were waiting outside, engines running. Juneau and his men hustled Emma, Dawson and Leggatt into the back of the Rolls. Juneau took the wheel, with Wickham beside him. Nowak and McGinnis took the lead Rover; Cooper took the rear.

The convoy pulled away. Juneau drove fast, wearing an earpiece, eyes scanning, checking mirrors, checking side streets.

Emma sat on the floor in the rear compartment, crammed between Dawson and Leggatt. Eventually, they reached Dawson's Canary Wharf office tower. The three vehicles plunged down a ramp into the underground parking. They squealed to a stop, nose-to-tail, next to a pair of open elevators. Juneau and Wickham escorted Emma and Dawson into one lift while the others filed into the next one. As the door slid shut, Emma noticed that Cooper was carrying two large suitcases.

The elevator rose silently. It opened on the top floor. With Juneau leading the way, they climbed a short flight of stairs and emerged on the roof. The other group followed seconds later.

A Bell 407 helicopter stood waiting, its turbines whining. Two solidly-built men Emma hadn't seen before were standing guard. One of them nodded to Juneau and slid back the chopper's door. Everyone boarded.

The helicopter lifted off, dipped its nose and accelerated westward.

They soon left the city behind. Below, farms, manor houses and scattered villages slid past as they arrowed across a mist-covered countryside.

Emma was tightly strapped in between Juneau and Wickham. Her entire body thrummed with exhaustion. After several minutes, she succumbed. She leaned her head on Juneau's shoulder and closed her eyes. She felt him shift his position to make her more comfortable.

Defined thoughts soon blurred at the margins, lost cohesion, and launched Emma's half-dozing consciousness down inchoate pathways… straight into a black pit of memory.

The physical storehouse of emotive memory might be tangled and knotted and riddled with imperfections. It might play endless tricks, as the experts claim. But for Emma Parks, certain memories remained crystalline and intact. One was that day in November 1981 when she had found her father's body. Another was the day three years later when she'd confronted three lobster poachers in the diner where she worked.

There was one other…

25

November 1991.

For a first year Med student to cut classes and drive to Maine two weeks before Thanksgiving break wasn't exactly the wisest choice, but Emma did it anyway. November 17th would be the tenth anniversary of her father's death, and she knew she'd better be there for her mother. Emma was acutely aware that her long absences in recent years were due more to her reluctance to face her mother's unpredictable temperament than to scholastic commitments, so a certain burden of guilt had tipped the scales.

And, if she were entirely honest with herself, the vivid memory of her mother's exquisite apple pies had helped edge her toward her dutiful decision.

"Mom and apple pie" she'd thought ruefully – the quintessential American cliché.

Except that, in Emma's life, there was nothing typical about either the mother or the pie.

The widow Penny Parks was a tormented soul. It was only the absence of alternating hypomanic episodes that had deterred a final diagnosis of bi-polar disorder, but that molecule of hope did not deceive her daughter. Her mother had a long history of resistance to therapy, so Emma suspected that the broad-spectrum diagnosis "severe mood disorder, recurrent" was just a sop. As one psychologist had conceded, "Your mother is a difficult study".

One thing was certain: Penny Parks was a far cry from Norman Rockwell's vision of the all-American Mom.

On the other hand, it could not be denied that her mother's Northern Spy apple pies were a triumph of inspiration over depression. For a few weeks each year, the late apple harvest instilled just enough optimism in Penny's haunted soul to actually lift her mood. The genesis of this autumnal mood swing was a complete mystery. "We call it your Mom's annual euthymia attack," a frustrated therapist had told her. When Emma had looked up the word, she discovered "euthymia" simply meant "not sad". If "Penny's North'n S-pies", as her Mom had branded her pies, made the woman feel "not sad", that was fine with Emma.

Apparently, it was also fine with a lot of other people, because every November the nearby supermarkets bought every pie her mother could produce. And with good reason… Northern Spy apples were juicy and crisp, with a flavor perfectly balanced between sweet and tart. Under Penny Parks' expert touch, they were transformed into the most delectable, aromatic pies imaginable. The single Northern Spy tree in the back garden of the Parks old clapboard house could never have met the demand, but the owner of a family-farmed orchard six miles inland supplied Penny with all the raw material she needed.

If Emma had one enduring cheerful memory, it was the warm, comforting aroma of pies baking in her mother's oversized La Cornue oven.

At 3:40 p.m. on Saturday, November 16th, 1991, Emma opened the front door of the house where she grew up, dropped her travel bag on the floor, called out "Mom?" and walked into the kitchen…

And smelled nothing.

She found her mother in the garden, under the apple tree. There was a ladder against the tree, an upended basket, and a few dozen apples spilled across the ground.

Her mother's skin was still warm. But she wasn't breathing.

Emma screamed at her mother to wake up.

Numb with shock, she started CPR while dialing 911 on her cell.

There was no signal.

With a shriek of despair, she lifted her mother bodily off the ground and carried her into the house. She laid her on the floor next to the telephone, worked on her, made the call, and worked on her some more.

Desperately.

Ten years ago, men had come and lifted Emma away from her father's cold body.

Thirty-two minutes after Emma's 911 call, other men came and lifted her away from her mother's cold body.

Two weeks later, the County Medical Examiner mailed Emma a copy of the autopsy report. As Emma read the toxicology report, her logical mind was saying the ladder and the spilled apples meant the overdose was an accident.

But her instinctive mind wasn't so sure.

The worst of it was… she would never know.

They landed at dawn.

The sun broke the horizon just as the helicopter settled on a vast lawn. Downdraft from the rotors blasted the morning mist into racing loops and whorls.

Clairmont was a sprawling redbrick manorial home, garlanded in pale light.

They disembarked. As they walked toward the manor house, Emma could hear dogs barking. When they reached the porch, two Irish wolfhounds appeared, wheeling and bumping and snuffling like a pair of friendly oafs.

A sleek middle-aged butler opened the door and held it while they trooped in. He was a picture of vertical dignity. He was introduced to Emma by a single name: Cranbrook.

Two more servants appeared and were introduced: Dennis, a rough-edged older man, whom Emma judged by his appearance to be a grounds keeper, and Mrs. Pauley, a middle-aged lady wearing an apron and drying reddened hands with a small striped towel.

"Mr. Henry! How lovely to see you!"

Emma watched, surprised, as Mrs. Pauley took both of Leggatt's hands in hers. Dennis stood at her side, looking equally pleased.

Leggatt appeared genuinely touched.

"Janet… Dennis… You're both looking very well!"

Mrs. Pauley beamed.

"T'ank you, sor!" Dennis effused.

The door, which Cranbrook had closed, swung open again, filling the foyer with the whine of the helicopter taking off. Cooper stumbled in with the two suitcases.

"Dennis… Take the luggage to the Ranulph Room," Dawson commanded.

"Yes sor!" Dennis took up the suitcases and lugged them away.

Juneau helped Emma out of the Kevlar vest. While he released the catches, she craned her neck, gazing at her surroundings.

"This was once a Royal palace," Dawson offered with clear pride. "I've been careful to preserve everything just as it was."

Emma noticed Leggatt's lips compress.

Dawson turned away to have a word with Mrs. Pauley. Juneau leaned close to Emma. "In other words," he said, *soto voce*, "all the trappings of Royalty are available if you have the money."

His short exchange with Mrs. Pauley concluded, Dawson turned his attention to Leggatt. "The conference call, Henry!"

"I'll see to it, sir."

"Ten o'clock! No excuses!"

Leggatt strode off. Cranbrook and Mrs. Pauley exchanged a disapproving look. Dawson eyed them. He called out after Leggatt. "And no one leaves this property without Mr. Juneau's permission!" No reply. "Henry?"

Leggatt didn't break his stride. "I hear, sir."

Satisfied, Dawson turned to Emma. "Come please, Doctor."

Cranbrook led them deeper into the house. Juneau trailed the group. Ahead, Emma could hear faint sounds of shuffling commotion. Cranbrook held the door as they entered a cavernous room hung with rich tapestries and dominated by a forty-foot mahogany table inlaid with silver.

Six or eight uniformed servants were standing in a rough line against one wall, hands behind their backs, their eyes aglitter with interest.

Emma was momentarily taken aback. "Good morning," she offered.

The response of mixed male and female voices and accents sounded almost like a chorus. "Good morning, M'Lady." "Marning, Mum."

Emma was charmed. She wandered through the room, gazing up at the lofty, fan-vaulted ceiling. As she passed along the line of staff members, the men bowed, and the women…

Emma stopped.

Did that girl just curtsey?

The young woman flushed.

Emma suddenly realized that all the attention was on her.

Puzzled, she turned to Dawson, who was hovering near the doorway behind her. He grinned and then nodded to Cranbrook.

Cranbrook clapped his hands. "Thank you everyone!"

The servants shuffled out, some casting covert glances back at Emma.

When the door closed on the last servant, Emma confronted Dawson. "What the hell was that?"

"I'll show you to your room. We can chat on the way."

"You're always telling me later! Answer my question!"

"Please…"

Frustrated, Emma followed as he guided her to a staircase. Juneau followed them at a discreet distance. An upper landing led into a long hallway lined with striking works of sixteenth century art.

"I didn't finish what I was telling you in London," Dawson opened.

"I'd heard enough, thank you."

Dawson ignored the remark. "When George married Charlotte in 1761, his first wife Hannah and their little boy were banished to Wales. We don't know when or where Hannah died. Her grave has never been identified."

"Victor…!"

"Please, Emma, listen to me! Hannah's son was raised by an old couple – retired servants from the Palace. The boy grew up and eventually had children of his own."

They stopped at a door. A sign read: *Sir Ranulph Room.*

Emma faced him. "Look… here's how I see it! The sooner you get the vase, the sooner your trigger-happy competitor out there will turn his sights on you! And as you English would say, 'Bloody good luck to him'!"

"No, no, no! I told you it's not the vase! Don't you see?"

"See what?"

"You're George Guelph's direct descendant. The last of his line!"

"My name is Parks, Victor! PARKS! It was my father's name, it was my grandfather's name, it was my great-grandfather's name! It was our family name all the way back to I don't know when!"

"I can tell you when! That retired couple who raised George and Hannah's son... their names were Henry and Elizabeth Parks."

Emma stared at him.

"When Hannah died, the Earl of Bute took charge of the boy. He placed him with Henry and Elizabeth and ordered them to raise him as their grandson." He paused. "Your real name is Emma Augusta Guelph."

Emma kept staring.

"You are the sole legitimate heir to the British throne," Dawson added quietly.

Emma exploded. "You must be out of your mind!"

Dawson's expression didn't change. He held her with his eyes. A second passed.

Then another.

Emma went pale. "You're serious!"

Dawson reached past her and opened the door to the Sir Ranulph Room. "Your bedroom, My Lady. I hope it suits."

Emma entered in a daze. Dawson and Juneau followed her in.

The room was spacious and comfortable. It had been modernized with care, and only where necessary, leaving the scent and feel of ancient lives lived. Three bay windows looked out over the front grounds of the manor. Inset into one wall was a working fireplace, with kindling and logs carefully laid and waiting. A carved four-poster bed dominated one wall.

Lying open on the bed were the suitcases Cooper had carried in from the helicopter. A young maid was busily unpacking Emma's new clothes. As they entered, the girl straightened respectfully.

Emma looked at her vaguely before dropping onto a soft chair.

Dawson glanced at the girl. "Leave us, please."

"Yes sir." The maid faced Emma, curtseyed, and withdrew. Emma was too distracted to bat an eye.

When Emma finally spoke, her voice was small and far away.

"You'd need DNA to prove this."

"Yes. Just some hair from a brush. Easily done."

"From *my* hairbrush?" She flared. "You had someone steal–?"

"I'm sorry. We had to be sure."

Silence.

"You'd need DNA from…" Emma could barely bring herself to say it. "From… the Palace."

"The same."

"A hairbrush? How the hell–?"

"Buckingham Palace has over two hundred housekeepers. A small payment, delicately offered, was all that was required."

Emma noticed a disapproving look flash across Juneau's face.

He didn't know…

Emma turned her full attention on Juneau. "Is this all true?"

"Yes. Henry walked me through the evidence."

"Dammit, Carl! Why didn't you tell me?"

The question seemed to embarrass him. He glanced at Dawson. "It wasn't my place."

Emma's eyes moved back and forth between the two men. She spoke slowly. "Why was that man trying to kill me?"

"Somebody sent him," Dawson replied.

"Who would do that?"

"There are a lot of vested interests involved here, Emma. Your very existence… the evidence we've found… It makes you dangerous."

"The Queen would never–!"

"Of course she wouldn't! This is obviously a rogue action… probably run by one of those Palace 'grey suits' that Princess Diana despised."

"Victor, you're a powerful man! You could go to the Queen! She'd order an investigation!"

"I'm sure she would. But to get to her I have to go through those same grey suits. Who do I trust?" He paused. "And there's something else…"

"What?"

"It would mean telling the Queen… who you are."

Emma's eyes filled with sudden panic.

"There must be a paper I can sign? Some kind of renouncement? An… abdication?" The idea sounded ludicrous to her as soon as she said it.

"Judging by what's happened in the last two days, I doubt that would save your life."

"So what do we do?"

"I have a plan."

"What plan?"

"I'm still working on it. We'll discuss it. I promise. Right now, you should get some rest."

"I don't need rest! I need to make phone calls... my friends, the hospital!"

"What will you tell them, Emma? You can't tell them the truth, so what will you tell them?"

She stared at him. "That... that I... that I decided to take a vacation... and I'm... I'm fine and I'll see them soon."

"A vacation, without telling your employer? And you'll be home soon? When is 'soon'?"

"I have to tell them something! I disappeared! Rita and Jan will file a missing person report! Jan's a lawyer! I know her. She won't rest!"

"Best to let that happen."

"Just for now, Emma," Juneau added soothingly.

"We'll talk later," Dawson offered.

"Later, later! It's always LATER!"

"Before the end of the day. My word on it." He turned for the door.

"Wait a minute! If this is such a big secret, why did you tell your staff?"

"Just a little experiment. Amazing, wasn't it?" Dawson smiled, gave a little bow and left.

Juneau remained behind. "We need to talk about security," he said.

"Am I to be locked in again?" Emma asked.

"No. We're past that, aren't we?"

Emma sighed. "Yes, Carl. We're past that."

"We're bringing in extra men. We'll have someone on the main gate twenty-four hours a day, and before the day is over we'll have men patrolling the grounds. But please don't go outside without an escort."

"So... house arrest."

"I'd say we're all under house arrest until we can figure this out."

Emma took in a deep breath, and let it out slowly. "You've saved my life, Carl. Twice. But now I'm starting to wonder."

"Wonder what?"

"Whether you're good at your job, or I'm just lucky."

"A bit of both, I guess. I'll see you later."

He left her door partly ajar, as if to prove a point. What point, Emma wasn't sure. She was still a prisoner.

She moved to a window. She leaned in the embrasure, looking out. Her mind was a swarm of emotions. She had to force herself to focus.

Step by step, she retraced her path through the events of the last few days.

Comprehension came swiftly.

Comprehension of the implications if Dawson was right.... and comprehension of the danger he had placed her in, whether or not he was right.

So much for planning your life, girl…

There was movement on the drive below. A pair of vans rolled up to the main entrance.

Six hard looking men got out of the lead van. Their dress and demeanour instantly identified them as security types.

The occupants of the second van were markedly different – a slight, middle-aged man in need of a haircut, accompanied three young women.

Cooper appeared and led everyone into the house. Seconds later, Nowak and Wickham began unloading hard-shell cases from both vehicles.

Emma wondered if they were weapons.

There was a noise behind her. She turned as the maid entered. The girl stopped and curtseyed.

"Is there a bathtub?" Emma asked, before the girl could speak.

"Yes, M'Lady!" She disappeared through a door. Emma followed. She found the maid turning taps.

"Thank you. I can do that."

Nonplussed, the maid withdrew.

Emma locked the door.

On the counter, her cosmetics were laid out exactly as before. For some reason, this persistent little touch exasperated her. She found an empty drawer and dumped the bottles into it.

A few minutes later, Emma lay in a deep bath, staring into space, turning her situation over and over in her mind. She was still a prisoner. But now she wasn't just the bewildered captive of an eccentric British billionaire with a grudge against the Monarchy.

Now she was a prisoner of her own identity.

After a while, she could feel the steaming water beginning to drain her energy. She rose to her feet. Her legs felt rubbery. She stepped out of the tub, dried off and stumbled into the bedroom, wrapped in a towel.

The maid was waiting. Undergarments were laid out on the bed.

"I need to get dressed," Emma said.

"Yes, M'Lady…" The maid held up a pair of panties.

Emma stared. She spoke carefully, as if to child. "I can dress myself. I'll call you if I need you."

Wide-eyed, the maid curtseyed and left the room.

26

Emma wandered a broad hallway. She encountered a male servant. He bowed deeply. Emma suppressed an impulse to roll her eyes.

"The kitchen?" she asked.

"Of course, Mum!"

He led the way, beetling along, looking back to be sure she was following. They passed an open room. Emma glanced in. It appeared to be a small parlor or sitting room. Inside, the four people from the second van were unpacking equipment.

Her guide led her to a door. He held it for her, bowing. Emma entered a vast kitchen. Mrs. Pauley and three other staff members were busy with meal preparations.

Everyone stopped working.

Emma smiled. "Hello!" She spotted a full carafe on a coffee maker. She made a beeline for it. "Just what I'm looking for!"

Four sets of eyes watched as Emma opened the cupboard above the coffee maker, discovered only teacups, shrugged and filled one to the brim with coffee.

Mrs. Pauley bustled over. "We'll bring it to you, M'Lady!"

"That's okay. Do you have milk?" She tasted the coffee. She made a face. "It's salty!"

"For Mr. Dawson, M'Lady. It's how he likes it."

"Is he crazy?" Emma set the cup down. "Who could drink that?"

Mrs. Pauley's eyes twinkled.

"Do you have any whole beans, Mrs. Pauley?"

"We do." Mrs. Pauley opened a cupboard. She retrieved a canister filled with coffee beans and an electric grinder. Emma took them from her. "Let me…" She nodded at the coffee pot. "Can we get rid of that?"

"Yes, let's!" Mrs. Pauley happily emptied the carafe into a sink.

Emma plugged in the grinder. As she was filling it with beans, Cranbrook appeared at her elbow. He gave a quick bow. "May I assist, M'Lady?"

"Thank you, Cranbrook, but I'm not helpless."

"M'Lady. You must understand… these people have their duties." He leaned closer and lowered his voice. "Were Mr. Dawson to learn of this, he would not be pleased… *with them*." He let the message sink in. "Please permit me to bring your coffee to you."

Emma looked around at her wide-eyed audience.

"In a mug, if you have one," she replied slowly. "With non-fat milk."

"Of course, M'Lady." He edged her toward the door.

"Thank you, everyone!" Emma called. A chorus of "You're welcome, M'Lady's" followed them out the door.

"Perhaps you'd enjoy the East Conservatory?" Cranbrook suggested.

"Sorry. I forgot my compass."

"It will be my honor to escort you."

"Thank you. I'm sorry… it's Mr. Cranbrook, right?"

"Just 'Cranbrook' is fine, M'Lady."

The bright two-storey solarium was a thick tangle of foliage. Emma relaxed in a cane chair at a linen-covered table. Cranbrook appeared with a laden tray. He carefully set out cutlery, fresh fruit, and a porcelain mug. He poured coffee from a silver carafe.

Emma stared at the mug. It was a Royal Wedding commemorative piece with a gilt rim. It bore a picture of Charles and Diana.

Nice…

Emma stirred in milk. She tested the coffee. "Excellent. Thank you!"

"My pleasure, Mum."

He lingered, tidying the tray. Emma eyed him as she sipped. "The staff seems very fond of Mr. Leggatt," she ventured.

"Oh, yes. Master Henry spent his childhood here. This was once his family's estate."

As Emma shot him a questioning look, she noticed the door behind him open a few inches, then close.

"It's a difficult story. And, of course, not my place…"

"I understand."

Emma waited him out.

Cranbrook glanced back toward the door. "The old Earl – Master Henry's grandfather – lost his title. It was during the war. Then his father lost his money. He was a bit, ah… profligate, as they say. Eventually, he couldn't keep up the estate. Mr. Dawson…" He hesitated.

"Came to the rescue."

"In a manner of speaking."

"How did his grandfather lose his title?"

Behind Cranbrook, the door swung silently inward. Juneau entered. Emma saw him. He looked her in the eye and touched a finger to his lips.

"Treason, M'Lady," Cranbrook pronounced.

"Treason?"

The butler leaned closer. He lowered his voice. "He'd been spying for

Germany."

"No!"

"He was hanged at Pentonville Prison. You can read about it." Dignified though he appeared, Cranbrook delivered this final nugget with a certain proletarian satisfaction.

Emma blinked at him, speechless.

Cranbrook still hadn't noticed Juneau. He lifted the carafe. "May I?" Emma nodded distractedly. He topped up her coffee. "Master Henry isn't like his father. Not afraid of work. He was even employed by the Palace press office at one time. He was working there when Mr. Dawson offered him his current post."

"Mr. Dawson bought his family's estate, and Henry still agreed to work for him?"

Juneau interrupted, making a pretence of entering. "There you are, Doctor!"

If Cranbrook was startled, he gave no outward sign of it. "Is there anything else, M'Lady?" he asked carefully.

"Not right now. Thank you."

The butler bowed and hastily withdrew.

"Good for you," Juneau smiled. "M'Lady."

"Meaning?"

"I've never heard him talk that much before."

"Maybe he was dazzled in the presence of Royalty."

Juneau didn't reply. He just stood looking at her, with his hands clasped behind his back, wearing a faintly admiring smile.

What's he looking at?

Emma rose from her chair. She moved to the edge of the tiled patio. Juneau followed. She examined a metal sign wired to the trunk of a tree, reading aloud. "Acacia *farnesiana*, Sweet Acacia, tropical America."

She turned to Juneau.

"Did you know all this about Henry and Victor?"

"Just the outlines. I thought I should keep my nose out of it."

Emma studied the sign on another tree. "Griffiths Ash, southeast Asia… I don't get it. Why would Henry work for Dawson?"

"Have to wonder."

Emma moved to another tree. She read the sign. She picked a leaf and crushed it between her fingers. She sniffed. "Mmmm. Smell that!"

Juneau took her hand and held it near his face, inhaling. He smiled at her. "Very nice."

There is a frozen moment.

"It's called 'Backhousia *citriodora*'," Emma said. She waited. A second passed. Another. "May I have my hand back?"

"Sorry." He released her fingers.

She looked at him, smiling. "You're a bit jumpy, Carl."

"Never." He checked his watch, too quickly. "Dawson wants you to meet him in the library."

"Is that where I die?"

"Sorry?"

"You know… Colonel Mustard, with the candlestick, in the library…"

"I wish our mystery was that easy to solve. Shall we go?"

They started walking.

"I'm guessing you haven't spent much time with females." Emma ventured.

He kept his eyes straight ahead. "Females, yes. Ladies… no."

They emerged into the corridor.

"Carl, if I can lighten up, you can lighten up."

"I will. As soon as I stop the bastard who's trying to kill you."

"Thank you."

"You're welcome."

"I really need to make those calls. My friends will go to the police."

"They already have."

Emma stopped walking.

"How do you know?"

"I checked Interpol. You're listed as a missing person."

"Christ!"

Juneau looked around. The door to the small salon Emma had passed earlier was still open. The people from the second van were busy inside. Juneau eased her to the opposite wall. He looked straight into her eyes.

"This whole thing… this shooter. Nothing adds up. I'd take you out of here tomorrow if I thought you'd be safe. But you can't just resurface in your old life. Not now. We don't know where this is coming from."

Emma bowed her head. She knew he was right.

"What's Dawson's plan? Do you know?"

"Think about it… what does that man live for?"

Hell! I should have guessed…

"Publicity!"

"He thinks it will protect you."

"And sell newspapers."

"Yes. And sell newspapers."

Emma sensed movement. She glanced across the hallway. One of the women from the second van was standing in the doorway. Behind her, the long-haired man was fiddling with a camera. A strobe flashed.

The woman's eyes were fixed on Emma.

She looked utterly fascinated.

27

The library was a warm sanctuary of dark wood and leather-bound volumes. A huge native-stone fireplace dominated one wall.

Juneau stayed near the door as Emma moved deeper into the room. She lifted her eyes. Full bookshelves reached a dozen feet to a mezzanine walkway, then a dozen more to a vaulted ceiling.

"There are over thirty thousand volumes in this collection." Emma turned toward the voice. Leggatt was sitting at a worktable in a corner. "Many are first editions," he continued. This is one of the finest private libraries in the country."

"I'm impressed."

"Mr. Dawson will be here in a moment."

Emma's gaze was drawn to a coat-of-arms mounted over the fireplace. She studied the heraldic crest, momentarily puzzled.

"*Menin Aeide*," she read. "Heraldics are usually in Latin, not Greek."

"Let anger be your song," Leggatt translated.

"Strange motto for a coat-of-arms."

"Mr. Dawson is Welsh. They are known to harbor certain… historical resentments."

"*Menin Aeide* is the first line of The Iliad," Emma observed.

Leggatt looked at her with interest.

So did Juneau.

"I'm surprised you know that," Leggatt said slowly.

"Why?"

"Because, M'Lady, with the deepest respect… you're an American." As Emma's sharp look sliced the air between them, Leggatt hastily added, "And a most fortunate one, it appears. A classical education is still something of a requirement for Royalty."

Emma's eyes went cold. "Don't mock me, Henry. I didn't ask to come here."

Leggatt looked chastened. "I'm sorry. That wasn't meant the way it sounded."

"Oh? How was it meant?"

Leggatt didn't have an answer. Emma let him shrivel under her gaze for a second, then turned away to browse the stacks. Juneau glided silently across the room and stood next to her. "I've got to admit," he whispered, "I was a bit surprised myself."

"Oh shut up! You're not the only one who reads."

Juneau settled on a chair, watching her, amused.

Emma's wandering brought her to Leggatt's corner. There was a small collection of framed photos on a shelf next to his worktable. One picture caught her eye. The photograph was of a younger Leggatt, bare-chested, sinewy and clearly fit, wearing boxing gear.

"Is that you, Henry?"

"Yes. At Cambridge."

"They box at Cambridge?"

Leggatt seemed to bristle at the question. "Boxing has it roots in this country, Doctor. The first rules were drafted in 1743. They were based on fencing... thrust, parry, riposte. There was actually a time when the sport had... how can I put it? Style. Even a certain grace."

"My Dad boxed in the Navy. And for a while, after..." She trailed off, not wanting to follow where those words might lead.

Leggatt missed the signal. "I'm afraid, as with many things, your America ruined that fine sport. The English sent boxing across the Atlantic with rules, Doctor. *Rules*! But your countrymen preferred more grisly spectacles – barbaric brawling between cabbage-eared mongrels! After that, the sport was ruined."

Emma silently assessed him. She spoke gently. "Henry, your condition is becoming acute."

"What condition?"

"It's called Anti-Americanism."

Leggatt smiled wanly. "Must have been my upbringing. My apologies."

"No need to apologize. These infections are usually the result of insularity. I could write you a prescription. It might relieve some of the symptoms."

"Oh?" He played along. "What would you prescribe?"

"Cyanide."

Behind her, Juneau exploded with laughter.

At that second, Dawson hurried into the room. He had a large binder tucked under his arm. "Sorry to keep you waiting! I was on a conference call with my editors." He dropped the binder on Leggatt's work table. "I wanted you to see this, Emma."

He opened the binder to a tabbed page, revealing a printed, colored diagram of a family tree. A brightline path threaded through the complex entries, starting from...

George Guelph, Prince of Wales m. Hannah Lightfoot, April 17, 1759

... and winding down through seven generations.

Emma felt herself drawn involuntarily to the page. She stooped over it. Her finger traced the highlighted path, down to a final entry:

Emma Augusta Guelph (Parks), b. August 24, 1969.

She straightened.

She had a haunted look.

Gently, Dawson lifted Emma's nerveless hand from the page. He turned to a separate tab. "You should recognize these."

The new page displayed a pair of odd-looking bar graphs.

"DNA profiles." Emma said tonelessly.

"The top one is you. The bottom one is… a senior Royal. The genetic markers prove that you have a common ancestor."

Emma studied them. "What are these marks?" She pointed. "Here… and here."

Juneau got out of his chair and came over to look.

"I'm told those are mutations. Something to do with the 'ALAD gene'."

"ALAD mutations cause porphyria." She looked up. "I have porphyria?"

"You're the doctor, Emma. That disease is hereditary, isn't it?"

"Yes."

"Could someone just be a carrier? No symptoms?"

"Yes."

"Many medical historians think George III had porphyria. It would explain why he went mad."

Emma suddenly felt detached from her body.

God! What's next?

Dawson touched her arm. "Emma, we don't know who's trying to kill you, but there may be a way to protect you. I want to get your story out there – newspapers, television, Internet. They'll be afraid to touch you then!"

Emma could feel Juneau beside her. "That was always your plan, wasn't it, Victor? Even before the shooting started?"

Dawson shrugged. "I'm a publisher. I want to show you something. Henry, do you have that tape?"

Leggatt hadn't left his seat at the worktable. He opened a briefcase and removed a videocassette. A small television sat on a shelf behind him. It had a built-in video player. He fed the cassette into the slot. The screen lit up.

A news clip appeared. It showed the Queen and Prince Philip strolling outside the Palace, examining floral tributes that were piled high against fence railings.

A large crowd was looking on.

The quiet was unearthly.

A male announcer's voice cut in. "This is very unusual. There's no applause. That crowd actually seems hostile!"

A female voice responded in hushed tones. "Her Majesty looks very pale."

Suddenly, a man shouted out from the crowd: "ABOUT BLOODY TIME, TOO!"

The Queen's face remained set.

"Did you hear that?" The female announcer was shocked. "This may be the first time in Her Majesty's reign that she's faced so much animosity!"

"That's right, Connie. The Royal Family has seriously misjudged the public's deep affection for Diana. It's widely perceived that they treated her badly in life... and that now they've snubbed her in death."

"Her Majesty has scheduled a television address."

"It may be too late."

The tape ended.

"Their tears are crocodile tears," Dawson said. "And the public knows it. That family is just as dysfunctional as any other family... they just wear nicer clothes. A monarchy can only survive as long as people buy into the whole stupid thing, and no one's buying anymore. They're on their way out, and you and I were going to show them the door. I'm not saying it would have been easy – they've been squatting on that throne for centuries. But now, with these vicious attempts on your life... don't you see, Emma? We've got them!"

"*We've* got them? Victor, I don't really care if George III was my ancestor! I'm not playing Pretender to the Throne so you can sell newspapers!"

"They're pampered parasites, Emma! Not one of them has ever really worked... earned a real living! They cost this country over a hundred million pounds a year!"

"I should care? As Henry keeps reminding me, I'm an American!"

Leggatt blanched as Dawson shot him a look.

Dawson spoke slowly. "Well... not exactly an American."

"What do you mean?"

"The Act of Settlement. As a descendant of Electress Sophia of Hanover, you are–" He stopped. "It's complicated. Let's just say you're entitled to British citizenship."

"Gee. Thanks very much. The key word is 'entitled'."

"As such, there are no impediments to your claim."

"There's one! I'm not claiming! You're doing all the claiming!"

"You can't just walk away from your birthright."

"Damn right I can!" Emma paused, her mind racing. "Wait a minute! Let's say you succeed! Let's say the Queen abdicates, and I–!"

"She can't abdicate! She's not the Monarch! She was crowned in error. All she can do is pack her bags and retire to the country."

"Fine! Then what do you do with me? What if the country wanted me crowned? There'd still be a Monarchy."

"Never happen! You're an American."

"But you just said–!"

"I know what I said. But the British people would never accept a Yank on the throne." He smiled smugly.

Emma stared at him. She turned to Juneau. "Did we just go around in a circle?"

Juneau looked bemused. "Kind of…"

Emma swung back on Dawson. "So I'm just a weapon in your hands?"

"You could put it that way," he agreed blithely. "But you'll be a celebrity. You'll be able to sell your story for a lot of money."

"So your original plan was to just drop into my life and promise me fame and riches?"

"Yes. Understand this, Emma – I could have gone ahead without warning you. You have a right to privacy, but your ancestors don't. No one has a copyright on history. Sure, I could have run the complete story without naming you. But you and I both know that once it was out there, some obsessed reporter would have tracked you down. It would have been messy. I wanted to give you a chance to cooperate from the start. Maybe you would have told me to go to hell, but–"

"Good guess!"

"–that doesn't matter now, don't you see? The soft options are gone. Someone's been tracking our research. Someone wants you dead! Like it or not, the publicity I was planning is now your best protection!"

Emma stared at him.

She knew he was right.

She knew she had no choice.

It was just that the bastard seemed too damned pleased about it.

When she spoke again, her voice had a new edge. "Let me get this straight. Before, it was just a story about those useless parasites in the Palace and – hey, everybody! – did you know the whole family is illegitimate? But now in your corkscrew mind it's an even *bigger and better* story! They're not only illegitimate, ladies and gentlemen, they're ruthless killers! They hired a hit man to keep their dirty little secret! They're no better than the Mafia!"

"That about sums it."

"You must be thrilled."

"I am, actually."

"You really are an ocean-going asshole, Victor!"

"Come, come! That's no way for a Queen to talk."

28

The long-haired photographer and his female assistants from the second van were waiting. They were set up for a serious fashion shoot: strobes, cool lights, reflectors, two cameras – one on a tripod, makeup and wardrobe cabinets.

The photographer escorted Emma to a straight-backed chair. He said his name was Jean-Pierre. She decided it wouldn't be polite to ask why he had a French name and some kind of Brit north-country accent.

"M'Lady, if you would…?"

Emma sat.

Dawson had already disappeared, saying he had telephone calls to make. Juneau hovered near the doorway, watching the styling team swing into action – hair, eyeliner, lipstick, wardrobe selections. Working in coordination, they steadily transformed Emma from merely exquisite to…

Stunning.

Juneau never took his eyes off her. The women noticed. The one doing Emma's hair caught her eye in the mirror. She whispered, "You have an admirer."

Juneau detected the women's amused glances. He turned away, pretending great interest in a painting on the wall next to him.

Watching in the mirror, Emma caught herself smiling.

Stop it, you foolish girl!

Her smile didn't go away.

Cory McGinnis was bored.

He was standing watch at the main gate. He'd rather be working in the garage, tuning up one of Mr. Dawson's cars, but the boss was short of men so he'd assigned Cory to the security rotation.

He bent and picked up a rock. He winged it at a rook that was insulting him from a nearby tree branch, but he wasn't quick enough and the rook was too smart. It flew off, cawing abuse.

He heard the sound of an approaching vehicle. He turned.

It wasn't one vehicle. It was two police cars.

The convoy stopped. The lead vehicle's passenger door swung open. A tall man in his fifties stepped out. He was wearing a checked tweed blazer and slacks. He flashed a warrant card.

"Open the gate, son!"

"I'm sorry, sir. I have orders not to let–"

"We have a warrant. Open the gate... or we will! And you'll go into custody!" The officer pronounced each word clearly, his tone hard as steel.

"May I see the warrant, sir?"

"Do you own this property?"

"No."

"Then you don't see the warrant. Open the gate!"

McGinnis shrugged and walked toward the gate. He keyed his mike and spoke into it rapidly.

He unlocked the gate and swung it back.

The tall policeman returned to his car. The police convoy sped through the opening and into the long tree-lined drive.

An intense photo session was underway. The photographer was gently coaxing Emma along: pose... FLASH... pose... FLASH... She was actually getting into it. With each shot, she held herself more erect, looking more and more...

More what? Regal? What the hell are you doing, Emma Parks?

She knew Juneau was watching, and pretending not to. She glanced over at him.

He was pressing on his earpiece. He quickly left the room.

The photo shoot continued.

The police vehicles slid to a stop in front of the manor house. The tall policeman was out of the lead car before it stopped moving. Uniformed officers spilled out of the second vehicle.

Henry Leggatt emerged from the manor's front door. He stepped onto the broad porch. Behind him, Juneau blocked the open doorway. They watched the uniformed officers take up positions.

The tall policeman strode over. Leggatt moved forward to intercept him.

"My name is Henry Leggatt. I'm Mr. Dawson's assistant. How can I help you?"

"Superintendent Rice... London Met." The man flashed his warrant card. "We're here to speak with Mr. Dawson."

"Six of you? May I see your warrant card again, sir."

The man handed it over. Leggatt carefully compared the photograph to the man. He took a notebook from his pocket and made a show of writing down the officer's name and number.

He handed the card back to the officer, who was now showing signs of impatience.

"I must advise you that we have an arrest warrant for–" he opened his own notebook and showed a page to Leggatt "–this individual."

Leggatt's eyes widened. He turned to speak to Juneau.

Juneau was gone.

"I suppose you'd better come in," Leggatt said reluctantly.

The Superintendent waved at the lead car. A man wearing an Immigration Officer's uniform stepped out.

Leggatt paled.

The Immigration Officer and one of the uniformed policeman joined the Superintendent on the porch.

"Hello, Mr. Leggatt," the Immigration Officer said.

Leggatt nodded. "Paul…"

"Shall we?" the Superintendent said.

Leggatt led them inside.

Juneau reappeared in the parlor. He walked straight to Emma, who was standing among the reflectors. "Trouble! Come with me!"

"What trouble?"

Before he could answer, there were heavy footfalls in the hallway and Henry Leggatt appeared, followed by the Superintendent, the uniformed policeman and, finally, the Immigration Officer.

Emma recognized him instantly. He was the same Immigration Officer who had processed them when they'd landed at London City Airport.

An instant chill settled over the room.

The tall man scanned the tableau. His gaze settled instantly on Emma. He looked at the Immigration Officer. The man nodded. The Superintendent strode over. "Are you Emma Augusta Parks?"

Emma examined him coolly. "Yes. And you are?"

"Superintendent Arthur Rice… London Met." He flashed his warrant card.

Emma looked at Juneau, who was standing a few feet away. His stiff expression didn't tell her anything.

"Three days ago," Superintendent Rice stated, "you landed at Docklands Airport on Mr. Dawson's private aircraft. Am I correct?"

"Yes."

"Perhaps you remember Mr. Houghton, the Immigration Officer who cleared you?" Rice gestured at the officer, who removed his hat.

"Yes, I do. Hello again, sir."

Mr. Houghton nodded, swallowing. "Miss."

"As it happens," Rice continued, "Mr. Houghton is a very conscientious officer. He routinely checks the Interpol Website for fugitives, missing children, that sort of thing. Yesterday, he recognized your face. You are currently being sought by the U.S. authorities as a material witness."

"A material witness to what?"

"Murder."

Emma paled. "What?" She looked at Juneau. "You said 'missing person'!"

Juneau moved closer. He fixed Superintendent Rice with a suspicious look. "That's all it said. 'Missing Person'."

"Step away, sir!" Rice ordered.

The uniformed officers closed in. Rice placed a hand on Emma's arm. "Emma Parks, I hereby detain you on a provisional warrant pending your extradition to the United States of America. I also detain you for the offence of possession of a forged passport, contrary to section 5 of the Forgery and Counterfeiting Act 1981. You have the right to remain silent. Anything you do say may be taken down in writing and given in evidence. Do you understand?"

Emma blinked.

"Do you understand what I have just said to you?"

"Yes."

"You will have to come with us."

As Rice took Emma by the elbow, Dawson pounded into the room. He took in the scene. "I'm Victor Dawson, and this is my home," he announced. He spotted Rice's hand gripping Emma's arm. "What's going on here?"

Rice put on his game face. "I'm Superintendent Rice, with London Met. I'm detaining Emma Parks pending extradition to the United States. I also have good reason to believe that she entered the United Kingdom illegally. I suspect your hand in this, Mr. Dawson, and I intend to interview this woman very carefully."

Dawson bristled. "You dare to threaten me in my own home? I'll have your–!"

Juneau interrupted. "Where are you taking her?"

"London."

Dawson turned to Leggatt. "Get Thurlow on the phone!"

Leggatt hurried off.

Superintendent Rice's fingers were still gripping Emma's arm. He urged her forward. The uniformed officer ran interference, shouldering Dawson out of the doorway. As Rice passed the billionaire, he said, "Your solicitor can reach me at Scotland Yard."

Rice escorted Emma out of the building. The police vehicles had been turned around. They both sat waiting, their engines running. Rice placed Emma into the back seat of the lead car, shut the door, and settled in the front passenger seat. A uniformed officer was already behind the wheel.

The car's rear door jerked open. Rice twisted in his seat just in time to watch Juneau slip in next to Emma.

"You forgot something," Juneau said. He handed Emma her bag. Then he shut the door, remaining in the vehicle.

"What do you think you're playing at, sir?" Rice demanded.

"I'll be accompanying this lady."

"Get out of the car, sir, or you will be forcibly removed!"

"You can't extradite a *witness*, Rice! You know that and I know that. There is no extradition warrant, is there?"

Rice didn't answer.

"I notice you didn't bring a female officer to search your prisoner. So let's just say I'm here to make sure you respect the lady's rights."

Rice's eyes bored into Juneau's.

There was no compromise in Juneau's expression.

Rice blinked first. "It's Mr. Juneau, isn't it? Carl Juneau?"

"Yes."

"What exactly do you do for Mr. Dawson, sir?"

"If you know my name, you know what I do."

"Are you armed, Mr. Juneau?"

"Yes."

Rice held out his hand.

"My weapon is licensed."

I'm sure it is, Mr. Juneau… but the simple fact is this: you surrender your weapon or you get out of this car!"

Juneau unholstered his Sig, ejected the round in the chamber, pocketed it, and handed the gun to Rice.

"Now your bag please, Miss!"

Emma passed it to him. He searched it. He found the spare dressings… and the bandage scissors. He held them up, his look questioning.

"I'm a doctor. I was dressing… someone's injury."

"What kind of injury?"

Emma felt Juneau's fingers press on her leg. "One of the kitchen staff. She cut herself quite badly."

Rice tested the point of the scissors against his palm, shrugged and dropped them back in the bag. He handed it back to Emma. He turned to the driver. "Go!"

29

Dawson and Leggatt stood on the porch, watching the police convoy drive away. Dawson was seething. Leggatt looked at his employer, his expression reproachful.

"Shut up, Henry!"

"I said nothing, sir."

"You didn't need to! I want you to set up another conference call!"

"With whom, sir?"

"Every producer and editor I own!"

"That many time zones will require a series of calls."

"Fine. Get to it! But first get Jimmy Maas on the phone!" He turned and stormed back into the house.

Emma leaned against Juneau. She mouthed a question. "What are you doing?"

He squeezed her arm reassuringly and addressed Rice.

"Why London, Rice?"

The Superintendent didn't reply. He kept his eyes on the road ahead.

"Rice?"

"Orders from the Home Secretary. Your Mr. Dawson has something of a… reputation."

Juneau and Emma exchanged a look. Juneau leaned forward. "But it wasn't him you arrested."

The Superintendent ignored him.

"Tell us why you're really here!"

Rice remained silent.

"They're afraid, aren't they, Rice?"

A long second passed. Rice replied, "Clearly there are certain concerns, Mr. Juneau."

"And we both know what they would be, don't we?"

Rice didn't reply.

They rolled along in silence for another half-mile. As they neared a secondary road, Rice spoke to the driver. "Turn here!"

The police car slowed and turned. Juneau twisted to look out the rear window. The other police vehicle kept going.

Emma sensed rather than felt Juneau tense up.

"What are you doing?" Juneau demanded.

Rice turned in his seat. "Following orders." He smiled, showing discolored teeth.

Ahead, a claret-colored 1970's-vintage Rolls-Royce Phantom limousine sat in a roadside lay-by. The vehicle had no number plates. Its windows were darkly tinted.

The police car rolled to a stop exactly abreast of the Rolls. The limousine's driver's door opened. A tall man stepped out. He opened the rear door of the Rolls, then the rear door of the police car.

He stood waiting.

"Please get out, Miss Parks," Rice ordered. "You stay, Mr. Juneau."

Juneau held Emma's arm. "Don't!"

Rice twisted his body. Juneau's own pistol appeared between the seats, pointing at Juneau.

"Release the lady, Mr. Juneau!"

Juneau slowly eased his grip. His eyes stayed locked on the Superintendent's. "This is an innocent girl, Rice!"

"Now, Miss Parks! Please get out!"

Emma looked plaintively at Juneau. She moved to the door, her eyes never leaving his until the last second. She stepped out. She looked at the Rolls driver. She recognized him. He nodded. He shut the rear door of the police car and waited for her to get into the Rolls.

Hesitantly, she entered the rear compartment. The driver shut the door.

In the police car, Rice and Juneau were still staring at one another. For a split second, as the driver shut the limousine's door, Rice's eyes slid away.

Juneau's foot lashed out. He stomped the policeman's gun hand to the floor. Bone cracked. Rice grunted with pain. The gun slid from his grip. The police driver spun in his seat. Juneau snatched the gun off the floor and pistol-whipped him. The man slumped against the door, unconscious.

Rice lifted his eyes from his broken wrist to find himself staring into the muzzle of Juneau's gun.

Juneau pulled the handle on the police vehicle's door and then kicked it open. But as he emerged, the door slammed back at him. A male hand grabbed for his gun hand. He had a glimpse of a face.

Devlin.

The Palace cop who had showed up in the foyer of Dawson's London residence.

Juneau heaved back on the door with all his strength. Metal buckled. He exploded out of the car. Devlin went for him. Juneau slipped the man's first wild punch, grabbed him by the coat and bounced his face off the doorframe of the police car.

It was over in seconds.

Juneau stepped across Devlin's half-conscious form and ripped open the rear door of the Bentley. Inside, Emma was perched nervously on a broad leather seat. She looked up to see Juneau filling the doorway with his gun trained on the man on the plush jump seat facing her.

Alan Boswell was dressed in his usual tailored shirt and striped tie. He was talking on a cell phone. He seemed blithely unconcerned that a firearm was pointed directly at his head.

A flint-faced woman sitting on the neighboring jump seat was of a different view. Her hand shot out, grabbing for Juneau's gun hand. She wasn't fast enough. Juneau seized her by the hair with his spare hand and forced her face down into the plush fabric of the empty seat next to Emma. He pinned her with a knee.

His gun never wavered.

Boswell appeared unfazed by the quick violence. He continued with his telephone conversation, his eyes locked on Juneau. "Yes, they're with me now. Yes... Mr. Carl Juneau. Her, ah... bodyguard, I suppose... Yes, very able... Of course. I understand." He disconnected. He offered Juneau a friendly smile. "Welcome, Mr. Juneau. Please join us."

"Emma," Juneau said quietly, "how would you feel about walking back to Clairmont?"

"I could handle that."

"So hasty, Mr. Juneau! Please! Release my impulsive assistant and allow us a moment of your time."

Juneau studied the man. He made a decision. He yanked the woman upright and shoved her bodily back into her seat. She sat there, shocked, struggling for breath.

Juneau slipped onto the seat next to Emma. He left the door open. "Watch her, Emma." He kept his weapon pointed at Boswell. He eyed the man. "Let me guess... MI-5."

Boswell smiled. "Very astute! Alan Boswell." He glanced at the gun. "I won't offer my hand. My companion here is Ms. Conyers. She prefers to go by her surname."

The woman in question was using her fingertips to gingerly investigate a fabric burn on her nose and one cheek. She appeared to be in her mid-thirties. Her only acknowledgement of Boswell's offhanded introduction was a resentful nod.

There was a shuffling noise outside. Devlin appeared at the open doorway, a gash on his forehead and fire in his eyes, ready to resume hostilities.

"Stop there, Mr. Devlin!" Boswell ordered. "Please take the wheel and wait for my instructions."

Devlin scowled. His eyes focused on Juneau's firearm. "You're sure, sir?"

"I am, Mr. Devlin. Thank you."

Devlin stepped away. Gravel crunched under his boots and the driver's door opened. It thumped shut. Juneau's eyes followed the sound. An opaque screen obscured the driver from view.

"Mr. Devlin appears a bit the worse for wear. How is the Superintendent?"

"A broken wrist," Juneau replied evenly. "He'll live."

"Yes, well, you've been well trained, haven't you, Mr. Juneau. 1st Battalion, U.S. Army Rangers? And later, I understand, an exchange posting with 22 SAS?"

Juneau didn't answer.

"I shall take your silence as affirmation. Excellent! I'm sure we can all feel safe in your presence." He addressed Emma, looking directly into her eyes. "I have something to show you, Dr. Parks. Will you trust me, now that you have Mr. Juneau to protect you?"

Emma looked at Juneau. Her eyes asked the question.

A second passed.

He lowered the Sig and sat back. He held the gun ready on his lap.

Emma nodded to Boswell. "All right."

Boswell tapped on the privacy screen. It slid down two inches. "Proceed, please, Mr. Devlin."

The screen slid back into place. The Rolls started to move.

"Where are we going?" Emma asked.

"It's just a short drive."

"That's not an answer."

"I agree. Would you like some tea?" He indicated a thermos carafe secured on a service module to Emma's right. "We do have proper cups."

"I prefer coffee."

"Of course! My oversight. My apologies."

The Rolls moved at high speed along country roads, passing cars, ignoring traffic laws. The ride was smooth and quiet. Boswell and the sour-faced woman sat in silence, offering nothing. Juneau watched them, one finger on the trigger guard of his pistol.

Emma leaned close to him. "You never mentioned the SAS."

"You never asked."

"Right… I guess it was always all about me, wasn't it?" Her tone was sardonic.

He smiled faintly. "Looks like it still is."

The Rolls slowed, turned and stopped at a gatehouse. A uniformed policeman stepped into view. He had a muttered conversation with Devlin, and then stepped away. A metal traffic barrier swung aside. The Rolls passed through and accelerated away. It sped along a narrow driveway through ancient oaks and broad sweeps of groomed greensward.

Finally, they stopped. Devlin got out. He opened the door on Emma's side and held it while she and Boswell alighted. Juneau and Conyers exited from the other side. Devlin got back behind the wheel and moved the vehicle onto a hardstanding next to two other royal vehicles.

Emma found herself looking at a gleaming white manor house. The building seemed to float above its manicured surrounding lawns.

After a sweeping examination at their surroundings, Juneau holstered his Sig. He and Emma followed Boswell along a russet-colored gravel path that skirted around the end of the house. Conyers kept pace behind them. Only when they turned the final corner did Emma get a full sense of the building's sprawl. Her eye ran along a long colonnade, glazed in tall French windows.

"Very impressive," Juneau said. "But I believe the main entrance is on the other side."

"You know where you are, do you, Mr. Juneau?"

"Frogmore House. Windsor Great Park."

"Correct." Boswell led them to a heavy door. He swiped a security card. A lock released. He swung the door inward and stepped aside to allow them to enter. "Please…"

They entered, and Conyers re-secured the door. Boswell led them through a small antechamber. They came to another door, painted and edged in gilt. He ushered them through it. Emma's jaw dropped. They were in an eighteenth century drawing room, richly furnished and dominated by a gilt-bronze chandelier. They continued through two more wondrous rooms. Emma gazed about, drinking in the elegance. Finally, they reached a hallway, passed through a plain door, and made their way up a narrow creaking stairway, through a windowless gallery and through another door. Conyers closed the final door behind them, remaining outside.

The room where they now stood was small, cuboid, and bare of furniture. A single narrow window overlooked an expanse of lawn that ran down to a small lake. The floor of the room was uncarpeted, laid in an almost colorless hardwood of uncertain origin. To the left of the entry door, a swoop of damask curtain obscured an entire wall. To their right, another door stood slightly ajar, open only a few inches, offering no hint of what lay behind it.

Boswell slowly turned to face Emma.

Juneau's hand moved closer to his holster.

For a long ominous second, Boswell's eyes remained locked on Emma's. Then he took a step and, with a swoop, he pulled back the damask curtain.

Emma looked up, mystified.

Hanging before her was a magnificent original oil painting. The quality of the artwork was very different from the paintings Dawson had gloated over in his little slide show. The colors were vibrant; the execution exquisite. The work had a unique, almost photographic, clarity. The subject was an exquisitely beautiful woman wearing a satin gown.

There was something about the woman's face. Emma gazed at it in astonishment.

She could be my sister...

But there was something else.

She stepped closer.

It was the eyes.

Their shape...

And their color.

The painter had rendered them in liquid lilac.

Those are my eyes...

As this thought flashed through Emma's mind, she heard Juneau's intake of breath. She turned. Juneau looked at her... he looked at the painting... he looked back at Emma.

"Yes," Boswell said. "The eyes. Unmistakable, aren't they?"

Emma's attention slid back to the painting. Her gaze migrated lower. She moved closer.

"It was painted by Joshua Reynolds in 1759." Boswell offered. "The commission came from the Prince of Wales. The work has remained in the Royal collection since that time."

But Emma wasn't looking at the artist's signature. She was looking at a distinctive vase sitting on a small table in the painting.

"My vase!"

"I believe it is."

Emma looked at him, surprised.

Boswell smiled. "*Antique Marketplace* is quite popular on this side of the Atlantic as well. In fact, it's one of Her Majesty's favorites."

Emma raised a skeptical eyebrow. She turned back to the painting. She read aloud from a brass plate. " 'A Royal Lady'."

"The original title plate was removed."

"I suppose they were afraid."

From behind them came a woman's cultured voice: "There is some truth in that, my dear."

Emma and Juneau spun as Queen Elizabeth emerged from the neighboring room, accompanied by two burly Royalty Protection Officers and a trio of panting corgi dogs. She was dressed simply in a sweater and a tartan skirt.

"Your Majesty." Boswell bowed.

Emma and Juneau stood frozen.

The Protection Officers closed in on Juneau, positioning themselves between him and the Sovereign. In a deft movement, one of them disarmed him.

The Queen addressed Juneau. "Mr. Juneau, we would like a private word with our cousin. These gentlemen will take care of you."

Juneau had trouble finding his tongue. "Uh... Yes...Y-Your Majesty..."

The Queen moved back through the doorway. The corgis scampered after her. Emma hesitated, confused, her mind suddenly blank. "Your Majesty...?"

"Come, my dear. We have much to discuss. Alan...please join us."

"Yes, Your Majesty."

Boswell nodded politely to Juneau, then followed the Queen and Emma into the next room. He closed the door behind them.

30

Emma followed The Queen into a comfortable sitting room filled with dainty satinwood furnishings. Because it occupied a prime corner of the manor building, it afforded a ninety-degree panorama of lawns, gardens and lake waters.

Boswell whispered to Emma. "Don't speak to Her Majesty unless she speaks to you."

She and Boswell stood respectfully while the Queen settled on a floral-upholstered antique camelback sofa.

The Queen looked up at Emma, smiled, and patted the seat next to her.

Emma was taken by surprise. Uncertain, she sat.

"Why don't we have some tea?" the Queen suggested.

On cue, a liveried servant materialized, wheeling a trolley. On board were a cobalt-and-gold tea service, a plate of fruit scones and a kaleidoscope of petits fours.

The servant embarked on an elaborate service ritual, first for the Queen, then for Emma. Before Boswell was served, the Queen had had enough ceremony.

"Thank you, Michael," she said quietly.

"Yes, Mum..." The servant withdrew, leaving Boswell to fend for himself.

The Queen sipped from her cup. She gave a little sigh. "A perfect tonic for frayed nerves."

Emma decided she'd been given permission to drink. She sipped her tea. It's not coffee, but... not bad, she thought.

World-weary Royal eyes studied Emma. "How fortunate you are to have been spared the Georgian features. They were not an attractive family. You've heard of James Boswell?"

Emma looked in confusion at Boswell, then made the connection. "Oh... do you mean Dr. Johnson's biographer, Your Majesty?"

"Yes." The Queen looked at Boswell. "A distant relation of yours, I believe, Alan?"

"Yes, Mum," Boswell replied, puzzled.

"Very early in George III's reign," the Queen continued, "Mr. Boswell wrote, 'We have got a shabby kind of family to rule over us.' Mr. Boswell was often somewhat... plain speaking, but he was right." Her Majesty smiled gently. "You're very lovely, dear. You have Hannah's eyes."

Emma blinked. She didn't know what to say.

Boswell listened to this with an expression of growing amazement. He stirred his tea. It seemed his only role was to observe.

"Many people think we're remote. Isolated from the real world. Isolated from reality."

"The past few weeks may have changed that perception, Your Majesty," Emma said quietly.

"Perhaps." The Queen's mind seemed to drift. "I should be... with my grandsons."

"Your Majesty. I'm so very sorry. I never dreamed my life would intersect with yours! And at a time like this..." Mortified, Emma trailed off.

"It's not your fault, my dear." The Queen looked pointedly at Boswell. "From our knowledge of Mr. Dawson, one would guess the timing was deliberate."

Boswell grimaced. "I expect that is so, Your Majesty."

"Actually, I'm most grateful to Mr. Dawson for finding you, Emma," the Queen continued. "I've often wondered about the fate of your branch of our family."

"You knew we existed?"

"Yes."

"Your Majesty... may I speak?"

"Of course."

"Until two days ago, I was unaware of our... connection. But at this moment, I'm more preoccupied with just staying alive." Emma struggled to keep her voice calm. "There have been two attempts on my life."

"Two?" The Queen turned reproachful eyes on Boswell. "Alan only mentioned one."

Boswell looked chastened. "It was only this morning that we learned of the last evening's incident in Belgravia." He looked at Emma. "There was an earlier attempt?"

"In New Jersey. A man named Kenneth Tannahill called me at the hospital. He was a reporter working for Mr. Dawson. He asked to meet with me. He was very insistent."

The Queen sighed. "Mr. Tannahill is known to us."

"I met him at his hotel on Sunday, the day after... the funeral, Your Majesty. He was murdered shortly after our meeting."

"My goodness!"

"That may partly explain the material witness warrant that the Americans issued for you," Boswell added.

"I suppose. Later on the same the day, a man tried to kill me. He must be the same man who killed Mr. Tannahill. Carl Juneau saved my life."

"Tell me," The Queen invited gently.

Emma related the entire train of events in Bayonne, completing her narrative with her groggy awakening over the middle of the Atlantic.

"Alsik…" The Queen mused, looking at Boswell. "I've not heard of it."

"It was developed by the, ah… intelligence community." Boswell looked faintly embarrassed. "But not by us," he added hastily.

The Queen gave him a wintery look. "Of course. Not by us."

Boswell hurried for safer ground. "According to our information, Mr. Juneau also saved Dr. Parks from the second attempt on her life in London."

"A brave man." The Queen turned to Emma, her face taut with concern. "Emma, the Prime Minister and I have asked Mr. Boswell to take charge of your personal safety. He has promised that no effort will be spared. Alan?"

"My word on it, Your Majesty."

"Thank you!" Emma's voice was a whisper as she felt relief wash over her.

Silence settled over them like snow.

But Emma was acutely aware that there was an elephant in the room.

There's still the matter of Hannah… Her Majesty seems so calm.

The Queen broke the silence. "I'm told you're a Casualty Room physician."

Emma was taken off-guard. "Yes, Your Majesty."

"That must be very trying."

"It can be. Sometimes people die that… shouldn't."

Why did you say that? Diana died in a car crash!

"Tell me about your work."

"Your Majesty?"

"My dear, I am patron to hundreds of charities. I make dozens of official visits every year. I am told that my presence helps, and I accept that it does." Her Majesty paused. Clear intelligent eyes sought Emma's. "But there is one experience I am denied. Not since the War have I experienced the simple satisfaction of personally assisting another human being in need."

Emma felt a rush of understanding. She wanted to hug the lovely woman beside her. But her nerve failed her.

The Queen leaned closer and patted her hand.

"Tell me how it feels… to do your job."

Boswell didn't seem to know where to look. Without asking permission, he refilled his cup with tea.

Her Majesty didn't notice.

She was listening intently to Emma.

The Protection Officers guarded the closed door.

Juneau paced.

"How long have they been?" he asked.

One of the officers grinned. "Ten minutes longer than the last time you asked," he replied.

"Very funny."

The officer checked his watch. "One hour and forty-two minutes."

"And how many seconds?" Juneau snapped irritably.

"You asked, sir."

Juneau went back to pacing.

The Queen was thoughtful as she fed pieces of scone to her corgis. She turned to Emma. She addressed her carefully. "I wonder, dear... did Mr. Dawson mention Hannah Lightfoot's... problem?"

"Problem? No, Your Majesty."

"Of course, he wouldn't have. Quite a serious one, as it happens... Alan?"

Boswell rose from his seat and stepped to a nearby desk. He returned with a large unsealed envelope. He removed a single page. The Queen nodded to him. He passed it to Emma.

It was a photograph of an ancient document. Emma studied it.

"Can you decipher the writing? The old secretary hand can be difficult."

"Yes, I can, Your Majesty."

"Take a moment."

Emma read through the document. Every word. Twice.

"The date is rather important," Her Majesty suggested.

Emma had already noticed the date.

No wonder you're so calm...

Emma looked up. Her expression lightened.

"You seem relieved."

"I am, Your Majesty. I am!"

"Believe me, dear girl... You should be."

The Queen smiled.

Emma smiled back.

Two extraordinary women shared an extraordinary moment.

Boswell managed to look both bewildered and heartened at the same time.

Emma's smile faded as an intruding thought suddenly intervened. "Your Majesty, Mr. Dawson is planning a front page story about me!"

"As he would… He can be such a dreadful man." For a moment, The Queen was thoughtful. Then she patted Emma's hand. "Emma… would you mind? I'd like a few moments with Mr. Boswell."

"Oh? Of course!" Emma stood. "Thank you for seeing me, Your Majesty."

"I think it might be the other way around. Thank you for visiting. Mr. Boswell's task now is to defuse this situation and keep you safe. I want to discuss that with him." Her Majesty paused. "You might find it pleasant to visit the gardens. The autumn crocuses are in bloom."

"Thank you." Emma stayed rooted on her spot, looking uncertain.

Do I curtsey?

"No need for that, dear," the Queen said, reading her thoughts. "You're part of the family."

Emma smiled. Boswell escorted her to the door. He opened it and bowed.

"You know that's not necessary," Emma whispered.

"I believe it is, M'Lady. Her Majesty just waived long-standing court protocol. For you."

31

It was late in the afternoon when Emma emerged from the meeting.

Juneau was waiting, ragged with impatience. He took in the stunned expression on Emma's face. He held her by the shoulders.

"What's wrong?"

"Nothing." She smiled. "Absolutely nothing."

Conyers appeared to lead them out of the building. As they followed her out, Juneau whispered, "Emma?"

"Mmmh?"

"What just happened?"

"In a minute." Emma nodded toward Conyers, who was walking only a few paces ahead.

They emerged onto Frogmore's vast lawn. Juneau steered Emma toward a bench near the roadway. They sat. Conyers stood off at a discreet distance, watching them, expressionless.

"You just spent two hours with the Queen of England," Juneau said. "I want to know what happened!"

"It's a secret."

"A secret?"

"Yes. A *state* secret."

"After everything we've been through..." The man actually looked hurt. Emma tried to keep a straight face, but couldn't. He noticed. "Out with it!" he demanded.

She grinned, and told him everything.

When she finished, he was silent. Finally he spoke. "This changes a lot."

"It changes everything. Dawson's a fraud."

"Maybe. But Tannahill wasn't." He gazed out over the lawns, thinking.

Boswell emerged from the building. He spoke briefly with Conyers. At that moment, a motorcade rolled into view. Emma quickly stood, tugging Juneau by the sleeve. He took the hint and rose to his feet just as the Queen's car passed them.

The Queen waved.

Emma waved back.

Juneau just blinked.

As the motorcade rounded the building and disappeared from view, Boswell joined them. "M'Lady," he said quietly, "Her Majesty has asked me to move you into Buckingham Palace. We'd like you to remain there until we can complete our investigation."

"Buckingham Palace?" It was Emma's turn to blink. "Well, I suppose it's a step up from house arrest in Mr. Dawson's hideaway."

"It won't be house arrest, M'Lady. Her Majesty asked me to assign you a full security detail."

Emma touched Juneau's arm. "I already have one."

Juneau looked suddenly uncomfortable.

"Of course. And since Mr. Juneau has single-handedly kept you alive, Her Majesty predicted there might be some small attachment between you." Boswell smiled, clearly enjoying their apparent embarrassment. "However, Mr. Juneau is Mr. Dawson's employee, and you are now under the protection of Her Majesty's Government."

While Emma pondered the implications of that statement, Boswell continued, "Her Majesty has also asked you to dine with her this evening."

"Dinner with the Queen?" Her fingers plucked at her outfit. "In this?"

"Our car will take you to Clairmont to collect your personal effects. But there's no need to worry. The meal will be informal."

"Is anything informal in Buckingham Palace?"

"People do need to relax."

Emma looked uncertain.

"If you wish, Mr. Juneau may accompany you to dinner."

Emma didn't try to hide her relief. "I do wish."

"Unarmed, of course," Boswell added, turning to Juneau. "You will be required to leave your firearm with Palace security."

Juneau nodded distractedly. His mind was obviously engaged elsewhere.

The Silver Phantom rounded the building and rolled to a stop next to them. Devlin was behind the wheel. The split skin on his forehead had been bandaged, but the flesh around it was badly swollen and discolored. Juneau pretended not to notice the Constable's morose glare.

"Constable Devlin will drive you to Clairmont, and then to the Palace," Boswell said. He opened the passenger compartment door. "Her Majesty also requested Mr. Dawson's attendance this evening. He declined."

"He declined an invitation from The Queen?"

"Not surprising, considering his well-known views. I told him you were safe and offered to prove that fact over dinner at the Palace. He said he had no intention of putting his head in the lion's mouth – his words. He sends you his best wishes and said he will have your effects packed and ready."

Emma took his hand. "Thank you for everything."

"My duty, M'Lady. And, my pleasure."

Juneau shook Boswell's hand and they stepped into the Rolls. As they drove away, Emma looked out the window. Conyers was standing in the same place on the lawn. She had a cell phone to her ear. She favored Emma with a frosty smile.

The Rolls left Windsor Great Park and headed west. Emma and Juneau rode in thoughtful silence. After a while, Juneau felt Emma's eyes on him. He turned. His expression softened.

She leaned against him.

Sir?"

Boswell turned. Conyers was walking toward him.

"Central took a call for you from a man named Robert Sewell. He says he's with the NSA."

"I know him." Boswell patted his pockets, looking for his mobile phone.

"He wants you to call on a secure line. And he says you'll need a computer."

"I'll use our office at the Castle."

Windsor Castle could be seen above the tree line, a mile away.

"I'll get the car."

"Meet me there. It's a nice day. I could use the walk."

The Silver Phantom's headlights probed the falling darkness as it sped along a paved two-lane road bordered by thick hedges.

Without warning, the car slowed. It turned onto gravel.

Juneau's head came up. He peered out his window. They were driving past a line of earthmoving equipment.

"What's wrong?" Emma asked.

Juneau tapped on the security screen. No response.

The Rolls swung into a vast road works maintenance area, illuminated by a few widely-spaced yard lights. It came to a stop next to a black Range Rover.

"Carl!"

"Stay close!" He tugged on his door handle. The door wouldn't open.

"What's wrong?"

"The lock's disabled!"

They heard their driver's door open. Shoes crunched on gravel. Juneau's eyes tracked the sound.

Without warning, the door on Emma's side flew open.

Leggatt was standing there.

"Hello, Princess."

Emma looked up in surprise. "Henry? What are you—?"

Leggatt produced a heavy revolver from behind his back and pointed it at her. "Sorry about this."

Emma shrank against Juneau.

At that second, Juneau's door swung open and the muzzle of an automatic banged against his skull.

"Step out slowly!" Devlin ordered.

Leggatt aimed his revolver at Emma's head.

"Now, Carl! Or our little Princess dies!"

Juneau stepped out of the car. With a sneer of satisfaction Devlin shoved him hard against the trunk. He took his gun and his cell phone, and patted him down.

"Use the cuffs!" Leggatt barked.

Devlin pressed his gun against Juneau's head. "A bullet works better."

"Not yet! We'll need his help to move the slab."

Devlin snorted. He produced plastic handcuffs. He cuffed Juneau's wrists behind him, and then clubbed him with his gun barrel. Juneau grunted. His knees buckled. Devlin seized him by the coat, jeered "That's for before!" and shoved him bodily back into the rear seat.

Juneau sagged against Emma, blinking back the pain. Blood trickled out of his hairline and down his neck.

Emma's bag was on the seat between them. Her hand dipped inside, searching. She pulled something out and deftly slipped it into Juneau's nearest sleeve.

Her hand dipped back into the bag. Leggatt spotted the movement.

"What are you doing?"

"Looking for a bandage! He's bleeding!" She pulled out one of the dressings she'd kept after suturing Juneau's wound.

Juneau leaned his head back against the seat, groaning.

Leggatt held out a hand. "Give me that bag!"

Emma kept the bandage and held out her bag. He snatched it away.

Devlin slammed the door on Juneau's side and got back behind the wheel.

Emma twisted on the seat and knelt beside Juneau. Her searching fingers found the split skin on his scalp. She used the bandage to staunch the bleeding.

Leggatt leaned in the open door behind Emma, watching her work.

"So, Henry…" Emma hissed. "True colors."

"Haven't you learned by now, Doctor?"

"Learned what?"

"Never mistake niceness for weakness."

"In your case, I didn't even mistake niceness for niceness."

Leggatt slammed the door and got into the front. The security screen slid down. His face appeared.

"When your hero wakes up, I'm sure he'll want you to jump. Save your energy. We control the locks."

"Where are you taking us?"

Leggatt smiled. "To meet Hannah."

The security screen slid up.

32

A small light glowed red on the telephone set on the desk. Boswell sat with the receiver pressed to his ear and his eyes glued to the computer monitor. He clicked the mouse.

"Yes, I have it now."

On the screen, photographic images cycled in stop-action motion. The first sequence showed Emma hurrying across the elevated walkway to the Reardon Hotel's parking arcade, then jumped to Darius striding across the same walkway several cycles later. The next sequence was spectacular – Emma blasting across an intersection… her would-be assassin hot on her tail… the Mercedes being torn in half.

The voice of Robert Sewell, the NSA Section Head, came over the phone. "We managed to get a decent blow-up from the hotel's security camera. Here it comes."

On the screen, an image froze, then enlarged.

"Got it!" Boswell leaned closer, studying Darius's emotionless face.

"He's a freelancer. Goes by 'Darius'. Real name, DOB, nationality… nobody's sure. The French think he's a Brit."

"They would."

"The Germans think he's Russian. They like him for that string of hits on ex-Stasi agents who supposedly knew too much."

Boswell swiveled his chair, turning his back on the monitor. "I remember," he said quietly. He knew who was behind those hits, and it wasn't the Russians.

"The BKA has been after him for a year. They tracked him to an apartment in Munich, but it was clean when their team kicked it in. That was last week. They found a fax machine in a dumpster behind the building. It was in pieces, which they thought was odd, so they got their tech people to run a program on its memory chip."

"Fax machines have memory chips?"

"For the journal report function. Some brands only log outgoing transmission verification data, sometimes with a partial image of the first page, but this machine also held a list of the last thirty incoming faxes."

"With partial images?"

"No, just date, time and originating number." He paused. "Their lab people discovered that the journal product was encrypted, which really got their attention. We talked to our people in Berlin and they persuaded the Germans to send the chip over. We cracked it this morning."

Boswell straightened in his chair. "Did you get anything we can use?"

"Maybe. It had two incoming faxes from a number in London. A residence."

Boswell sat very still. He closed his eyes.

Waiting for it.

"It's one of those swank places off Belgrave Square. An address on–" Boswell could hear papers being shuffled "–Wilton Crescent. The property is registered to 'DX International Limited'. It's an Isle of Mann company. Do I need to say more?"

Boswell's eyes opened, betraying shock, but his voice remained calm. "No. I know the company."

"Thought you would."

"Thanks, Rob. You've done an amazing job... putting this together so quickly."

"All part of the friendly service. Of course, there's the little matter of one of your nationals screwing with our satellite. We'd appreciate your help on that."

"And you shall have it. I'll ring you back."

"Okay. And Alan...?"

"Yes?"

"The next bottle's on you."

Boswell managed a faint smile. "You'll have that too. My word on it."

Boswell replaced the receiver. He stared into space, his lips compressed, his jaw working. "Conyers!"

The woman appeared in the doorway.

"Get me Devlin!"

Conyers thumbed a code on her mobile. Seconds ticked. She looked at Boswell. "Voicemail."

He checked his watch. "Keep trying!"

He picked up the desk phone. "Connect me to the Protection Unit!"

Other vehicles gave way as the Silver Phantom slipped effortlessly through traffic, past the Duke of Wellington monument and into Grosvenor Place, paralleling the high, wire-topped wall surrounding Buckingham Palace Gardens.

The Rolls slowed. A gate swung open. They turned in.

Inside the car, Juneau sat slumped in his seat, his hair matted with blood. But his eyes were alert.

The security screen slid down.

Leggatt grinned insanely back at them.

Emma looked ahead. "Buckingham Palace. How original."

Their captor's grin evaporated. "A rear entrance," he growled. "You didn't expect to drive grandly up to the front gate, did you?"

Devlin keyed a remote attached to his sun visor. Emma twisted in her seat in time to see the gate behind them swinging shut. "No guards," she whispered to Juneau.

Leggatt heard. "This gate only controls a secure car park. Entry into the Palace is controlled by manned checkpoints."

They drove into a walled parking lot. The Rolls stopped near a steel gate.

Leggatt and Devlin got out quickly and pulled Emma and Juneau out of the car.

Devlin watched Juneau scan the trees above their heads. "If you're looking for cameras, mate, you're out of luck. They're playing a loop. Those fools in the security room are too busy bragging about shagging the housemaids to notice. Move!"

He tapped a code into a keypad mounted on the wall next to the gate. The lock clicked. Devlin pulled the gate open and Leggatt prodded them through the opening. They found themselves on a wooded path. Leggatt waved his gun.

"That way!"

They walked.

"Okay, Devlin, I'll bite." Juneau said. "That night you showed up on Wilton Crescent. Why did you want to see Dawson?"

"I didn't. I was seeing my brother."

"Who's your brother?"

No answer.

"Half brother," Leggatt muttered.

"You?"

"Our father was a serial womanizer."

"Whereas his sons are just serial killers," Emma interjected.

"Shut up and keep moving!"

A fork in the path led them to a windowless stone building that had been built flush with the rear wall of old Buckingham House. Devlin unlocked a door.

Juneau glanced to their left. Two hundred feet away, through the trees, a security checkpoint controlled a service entrance to the Palace.

Leggatt jammed his gun into Juneau's kidney. "Forget it!"

They entered the building. Three gigantic boilers filled the interior space, each surrounded by a forest of pipes. Devlin bolted the door behind them. He strode to the first boiler to their left and slipped into a space behind it. Leggatt herded Emma and Juneau after him.

When they rounded the boiler, Devlin had his weapon holstered and was unscrewing a pair of bolts that held a sheet metal plate fast against a section of concrete wall. Evenly-spaced holes marked where other bolts had been removed earlier. They sat in a small pile on the floor.

While Devlin worked, Leggatt kept one eye on Juneau and his revolver aimed at Emma's head.

Devlin dropped the final bolts on the pile. He lifted the panel to one side, revealing a five-foot high opening.

"Go!" Leggatt ordered. "The Princess first, then Andrew, then Carl!"

One by one, they stooped and entered. Inside, the ceiling resumed almost full height. Only Juneau had to bend slightly to continue. They passed along a short concrete-lined tunnel that descended at an angle before leveling out. At the far end, a steel door stood ajar. They passed through it. Devlin swung it shut. He tapped a code into a keypad.

An electronic lock closed with a thunk.

They were now standing in an ancient stone passageway. The chill, dead air was pungent with old dirt and damp stone. Dim lights encased in rusted frames glowed at wide intervals along the ceiling. Heavy-gauge piping from the boiler room behind them ran along one wall. Water dripped.

"The Duke of Buckingham built several underground passages," Leggatt said. "Conveniently, this one is still in use."

"What the hell are you doing, Henry?" Emma demanded.

"Finishing a job."

"What job?"

"I believe you Yanks call it a 'frame-up'."

"He plans to pin your murder – our murders – on the Palace."

"If a job's worth doing… but then, nobody asks Henry." He gestured. "Move!"

They started up the passage.

"Henry, I'm not the heir!"

"I'm sure the Queen told you that."

"It's true!"

"It makes no difference. After the way they treated Diana, the public won't believe them. They'll believe Dawson's shrieking tabloids. Next to him, Goebbels was a rank amateur."

"Henry–!"

"They'll believe what Dawson will tell them: that the Royals protected their dirty little secret for two hundred years, and then, when it was about to be exposed, they arranged to have you liquidated. It's not complicated. It's the way the world works."

"No one would believe that of the Queen!"

"Maybe not." His lip curled. "But there are other members of that family with a lot to lose."

"For God's sake, Henry!"

"Be quiet and walk!"

They kept moving, their footwear shuffling and catching on the uneven rock floor. But Emma wasn't letting up. "But why you? Why are *you* doing this?"

"Why? My family's peerage goes back fifteen generations! My ancestors rode with kings! My roots go deeper in this country's history than the Queen's! Her family ruined mine! Now I'll ruin hers!" He stared at her, pop-eyed, hatred streaming from his pores.

Emma stared at him. "My, you do have issues, don't you?"

Juneau looked at Devlin. "Okay. So why you?"

Leggatt answered for him. "Filial devotion!"

"And money…" Devlin added.

"Money? I must be missing something."

Leggatt intervened again. "Clairmont's worth millions, and soon enough it will be mine, free and clear."

"How does that work? Dawson owns it."

"My grandfather was no fool; he knew my father was an alcoholic. By the terms of his will, my father could only sell a life estate. Dawson took the deal because he was desperate to add a former Royal residence to his collection. Very soon, when he ceases to be useful, Dawson will have a nasty little accident and Clairmont will revert to me."

His barking laugh rang down the passage.

They arrived at an oaken door, low and heavy, set into the sidewall stonework. Devlin put his foot against it. It swung silently inward. He grinned at Leggatt like a proud child. "I oiled the hinges." He bent and entered the chamber beyond, then turned and pointed his gun at Juneau.

"You, Carl," Leggatt ordered. He grinned malevolently at Emma. "Then Your Royal Highness."

33

Juneau ducked and passed through the opening. Emma followed. She reached forward and squeezed his hand. He squeezed back twice. She held on and let him tow her through the low doorway.

They found themselves in a slate-floored room, starkly lit by two pre-positioned camp lanterns. Romanesque columns thrust upward to form tight groin vaults supporting the floor above. The walls were streaked with mildew. Limestone panels marked individual burial vaults, their memorial lettering indecipherable with age.

Leggatt entered behind them. "The original Buckingham House was built on the ruin of a medieval chapel erected by the Abbot of Westminster," he pronounced, as if he were some National Trust tour guide offering the next installment in a memorized spiel. He pointed toward one end of the room, where red blotches in a polygonal recess of rough stone appeared to be the remnants of a painted decoration. "That apsed mortuary feature means the chapel was actually an expansion of an earlier Saxon church. George and Charlotte bought this property in 1761 to use as a private retreat. Since then, only one Monarch ever used this crypt, and only a few royal intimates ever knew of its existence."

Emma looked at him. "What monarch?"

"My guess would be George III. What do you think?" He gestured. Devlin lifted a lantern and carried it forward. Leggatt nudged Emma and Juneau after him. Devlin set the lamp on the floor. Its watery light washed across a massive black marble slab, highlighting an indented cross.

A carved epitaph appeared below the cross:

HANNAH ELIZABETH GUELPH

Died 28 February A.D. 1770

Beloved Royal Lady

On the floor next to the slab lay two heavy iron bars.

As Emma stared in utter disbelief at the inscription, Juneau's fingers slipped into one sleeve of his jacket.

"George's diaries made interesting reading. Dawson and Tannahill found the marriage entries. That was all they wanted. I kept reading. Very boring, mind you – Mad King George had a very tedious mind. But some very interesting entries appeared in early 1770. I removed the pages. I like to think of them as a treasure map. They led us here." He turned cold eyes on Emma. "An anonymous tip will lead the police to an ancient grave under Buckingham

Palace. You'll be found with your famous ancestor. There's a certain delicious irony in that, don't you think?" He smiled malevolently. "Mr. Juneau can join you."

"You're insane!"

Leggatt's nostrils flared. "Oh, I wouldn't go that far, Princess. But, as you pointed out, I do have issues." He pointed his gun at her head. "Andrew! Remove his cuffs! He can help you with the slab."

"I don't know, Henry. This guy's fast. We should just kill him."

"You're just as fast! And I have a gun to his girlfriend's head! Do it!"

"You might be fast on your feet, but you're not too fast in the head, are you, Andrew?" Juneau goaded.

Devlin looked at him.

"Maybe no camera recorded us coming in here. And maybe you'll kill us and drive away. But only one of you will be in the clear."

"What do you mean?"

"Shut up, Carl!" Leggatt ordered.

Juneau ignored him, his eyes on Devlin. "Boswell watched you drive us off in one of the Queen's cars. And thanks to you, my blood is all over the rear seat. I made sure of that. So when we go missing, who do you think the police are going to come looking for? Not your brother here. No one knows you picked him up. So what's your story, Constable? What are you going to tell them?"

"That I... you and the lady were talking. You convinced her not to trust Boswell. You made me drop you off..." He trailed off, and looked dumbly at Leggatt. "Henry... he's right!"

"I've already thought it through!" Leggatt barked. "Don't worry. I have a solution. Just get to work on that slab!"

"What solution, Henry? Tell me!"

Leggatt let out an exasperated sigh. "This!"

A deafening roar shattered the silence of the crypt as Leggatt fired a bullet straight into his brother's chest. Devlin flew back against a column. He slid to the floor, his face frozen in agony and surprise.

Leggatt swung the revolver back on Emma. He yelled at Juneau. "How did you know?"

"That you planned to kill him? You *had* to be using him. He worked for the Royal Family. There was no other way."

"Your own brother?" Emma yelled.

"His mother was a whore!"

"Oh... that explains everything!"

Leggatt ignored her. "You didn't achieve anything, Carl! Now it will just look like you shot him just before you died!"

Juneau looked down at Devlin. "He's got to be dead first, Henry!"

Devlin groaned.

Leggatt swung his gun. He fired another slug into his brother.

Behind Juneau, Emma's bandage scissors dropped to the floor, followed by the plastic handcuffs. In a blur, Juneau snatched up Devlin's pistol, swung it up…

And held fire.

Leggatt had his arm around Emma's neck and the muzzle of his revolver pressed against her throat. The hot metal was burning her skin, but she didn't make a sound.

"Give it up, Henry." Juneau's voice was quiet, menacing.

Leggatt circled, dragging Emma toward the door. She resisted. He pushed the muzzle harder against her flesh.

Juneau tracked them with Devlin's gun.

Emma's eyes locked onto Juneau's, signaling.

His answering nod was almost imperceptible.

With a sudden heave, Emma hurled herself backward, smashing Leggatt's cranium into the low lintel above the doorway.

Leggatt's grip loosened. Emma dropped straight down out of the loop of his arm and rolled away. Leggatt tumbled backward through the door, firing wildly. Bullets whined off limestone. Juneau returned fire. His bullets splintered the hardwood frame of the door. Leggatt disappeared from view.

Juneau scrambled over to Emma. "I'm okay," she whispered.

Juneau dove for the doorway, pistol ready. Cautiously, he checked the passage.

Leggatt had vanished.

Juneau turned back. Emma was kneeling next to Devlin. Leggatt's brother lay still in a widening pool of blood, eyes staring. Emma made a quick examination, then rose slowly. She turned and walked to Juneau. She leaned into him, her face against his chest. He held her in a strong embrace.

"I thought you said you were low maintenance," he whispered.

"A woman will say anything to get her man."

He kissed her forehead. "We'd better get out of here."

He checked the passageway again. It was clear. Thirty feet to their right, ancient stone steps spiraled upward.

"Come on." Juneau started to lead Emma toward the steps. She tugged at his arm.

"That's the way out!" she whispered. She pointed back down the passageway.

"Devlin locked that door."

She remembered. She nodded. They hurried to the steps and started up them. At the top, they found another door. It was unlocked. It opened onto a corridor.

The corridor was carpeted and lined with artwork.

"Carl, we're inside the Palace!" Emma whispered.

"I know." He looked up, checking in both directions. "I don't see a surveillance camera. We need to find a camera!"

"Why?"

"So we don't get shot! We need to stand in front of it with our hands in the open until the security guys spot us and come running." He pointed at a far door. "That should lead to the central quadrangle. We can stand out in the open there."

They jogged toward the door. When they arrived, Emma reached for the exit bar. Juneau stopped her.

"We don't know where Henry went," he warned. "Let me check first."

He started to ease the door open. Emma held his arm.

"What?"

She kissed him on the mouth.

He grinned, tasting his lips. "M'Lady forgets. I'm a commoner."

"I know. So was Hannah. Mad impulse apparently runs in my family." She kissed him again.

Juneau touched Emma's cheek and then stepped through the door. He moved cautiously out onto the red gravel of the quadrangle.

Emma waited.

From behind her came a rustling sound. She turned.

The fist came from nowhere.

Leggatt clubbed her to the floor.

He stood above her. He cocked his revolver.

Outside, approaching footsteps crunched on gravel.

Leggatt turned toward the sound and raised his gun.

"Emma!" Juneau called.

Leggatt kicked the door open. Juneau saw him and reacted instantly, dodging left to put the door between him and the shooter.

BOOM! The slug knocked him to the ground.

Leggatt strode to Juneau's prone form. He pointed the revolver at his head. He pulled back the hammer.

SWOOSH!

A kick sent Leggatt's gun flying. He whirled. Emma was standing there.

"Pick on someone your own size!" she hissed.

Leggatt aimed a vicious backhand at Emma's head. She slipped under it, then reappeared in front of him, her rising fist a blur. She rocked him onto his heels with a hard punch to the mouth.

Leggatt staggered back. He blinked in shock. His tongue licked out. He tasted blood.

"You BITCH!" he yelled.

Emma's eyes burned. "You bitch... Your Highness!"

Leggatt grabbed for her. THUD! She nailed him with a straight jab. He backed away, touching the ridge above his eye.

His fingers came away bloody.

"Navy Dad taught you a few moves, I see."

With a growl, Leggatt attacked her. He swarmed her with jabs, hooks, crosscuts... Emma danced, weaving in and out, slipping his punches, forcing him to fan air...

Enraging him.

Just as she'd planned.

Three floors above the northern edge of quadrangle, The Queen was passing a window. Movement below caught her eye. She stopped. She stared. She called out.

"Patrick!"

A Protection Officer appeared at her side. His eyes followed his Sovereign's gaze. His jaw dropped. He urged The Queen away from the window. "Your Majesty, please!"

The Queen refused to move.

The Protection Officer barked urgent words into a wrist mike.

Emma landed a hard jab. "Where's that style, Henry?" He swung at her. She danced away, then reversed course, closed fast, and unleashed a murderous punch, opening a gash over his other eye. "Where's that grace, you little prick?"

A loud klaxon sounded... and kept sounding.

Leggatt swung a haymaker. Emma stepped under it and drove a fist into his stomach. "You're turning this into a brawl, Henry! You're fighting like an American!"

Blind with fury, Leggatt rushed her. Emma took a glancing punch on the cheek. She answered it with a lightning jab.

The klaxon kept sounding.

Leggatt moved back, bouncing on the balls of his feet, working his stance.

Emma taunted him. "Finally joining the fight, Henry?" Leggatt snarled at her, feinted, then launched a fast jab. It connected high on Emma's cheek. She staggered. Leggatt's lip curled. He closed in and let fly with a thundering cross punch, straight for her jaw…

Emma ducked and Leggatt fanned empty space. She replied with a hard punch, straight up and fast, rocking Leggatt onto his back foot.

Emma heard her Dad's voice in her head.

Finish him, Emma! Carl needs you!

On a torrent of adrenaline, Emma drove her attack home.

Two sets of doors flew open. Armed Protection officers and uniformed police poured into the quadrangle. Male voices yelled, "Don't move! Down! GET DOWN!"

Above, the Queen finally recognized Emma. She seized her protector's arm. "Patrick! That woman! She's ours! She's one of us!"

Patrick blinked in astonishment. "Your Majesty?"

"Stop them, Patrick! Don't let them hurt her!"

"Yes, Mum!"

Patrick spoke quickly into his mike.

A black helicopter erupted out of the night sky. The heavy thump of rotors bounced and echoed off the limestone walls of the quadrangle as it hovered in space directly above the fight. The chopper's NightSun searchlight lit up, bathing the scene in stark light.

Below, officers closed in on Emma and Leggatt, still yelling at them.

Emma threw a blistering punch.

Leggatt flew backward and went down in a spray of blood.

Officers stopped, astonished.

"Is that DOWN enough for you?" Emma yelled at them. She pointed at Carl's prone form. "He shot that man!" She sprinted for Juneau.

Behind her, Leggatt, his face a bleeding ruin, rolled to one side and snatched up the revolver Emma had kicked from his hand.

He aimed it at her retreating back.

From above came the crack of a rifle. Leggatt's head exploded. His body flopped onto the gravel and lay still.

Still running, Emma looked up. The chopper swooped lower, landing. A police sniper sat in the doorway.

Alan Boswell was standing behind him.

Officers ran to intercept Emma. Another was on his radio. He looked up and saw the Queen and the Protection Officer at the window. He listened, eyes wide. He turned and yelled. "Leave the woman!"

When Emma reached Juneau, two officers were already kneeling beside him. Emma shouldered between them. "I'm a doctor! Find a medical kit!"

One officer sprinted for the building. The other helped Emma roll Juneau out of his jacket. "A doctor?" he said, a note of awe in his voice. "I thought you were Muhammad Ali."

The other officer returned on the run with a first aid kit. Emma got to work, struggling to staunch the bleeding. Juneau was conscious. She saw him looking at her hands. Her knuckles were torn open.

"Sorry, my love. Imagine... Here we are in Buckingham Palace and they have no surgical gloves in their first aid kit!"

"You KO'd him! How did you do that?"

"My Dad helped me."

"He sure did."

Emma kept working. Tears spilled down her face. Juneau grunted as he reached up a hand to wipe them away. He managed a wan smile through his pain. "Remind me to never kidnap you again. You're right. It turns you into a real bitch."

"You just shut up, Carl Juneau!" Emma sobbed. She wiped her face on her sleeve. "Just shut up!"

"Yes, M'Lady."

Behind them, iron gates swung open. An ambulance raced into the quadrangle and slid to a stop. As paramedics rolled a gurney to Juneau's side, Boswell appeared behind Emma. Gently, he raised her to her feet. He nodded at the ambulance crew. "Let them do their work."

"I'm a doctor!"

"You can ride with him." He led her toward the ambulance.

As they walked, Emma looked down. "God, look at me! What would Her Majesty think?"

"Somehow, I don't think she'd mind at all." As he helped Emma up into the ambulance, he glanced up. The Queen was watching.

He bowed.

The drapes closed, and Her Majesty was gone.

34

In the early hours of the following day, Victor Dawson stood at his broad office windows. He'd left his lights off so he could enjoy the sight.

The skyline of London.

My city, he thought. My country.

He lit a cigar.

At that moment, forty storeys below his feet, a convoy of cube vans was exiting the underground parking into a wide alley. The side panels of each van bore a giant reproduction of the masthead of Dawson's flagship newspaper: *LONDON HERALD*.

Tires chirped on the dry pavement as the vans peeled off in different directions, following well-worn routes. Moving... stopping... moving on... in an ever-widening circle, dropping newspaper bundles on newsstand doorsteps, in tube station ticket lobbies, on service ramps at food markets and pharmacies.

Here and there, abroad on the dark sidewalks, straggling pedestrians stumbled homeward from all-night parties or reluctantly plodded toward early shifts in obscure workplaces.

Here and there, a passersby stopped, his attention arrested by the disturbing headline clearly visible on the top copy of a bound pile of newspapers:

ROYAL USURPERS!

Here and there, an impatient citizen opened a pocketknife and cut away the bindings.

Here and there, freed copies of newspapers passed from hand to hand.

Here and there, small crowds grew into large ones.

Just after dawn, a whey-faced Palace footman rushed along a lushly carpeted corridor, clutching a copy of the *Herald* in white-gloved hands.

The crisis had begun.

When Boswell arrived at the King George VII private hospital on Beaumont Street, the press scrum outside the main entrance was becoming a mob. Conyers had warned him, so he wasn't taken by surprise. He wheeled past the crowd of journalists and rubberneckers and parked on the street a few blocks away. He used his MI-5 identification to gain access to the hospital through a rear entrance.

When he passed through the final police check in the tight security screen around Carl Juneau's hospital room, he found the security man sitting up in an armchair with Emma perched on the arm next to him. Juneau had one arm in a sling, strapped immobile across his bandaged chest. Emma's fingers massaged the back of his neck while they watched a news broadcast on a wall-mounted television.

Boswell was carrying that morning's edition of the London *Herald*, with its four-inch headline. He laid the newspaper on Juneau's lap. At that moment, an enlarged photograph of the same front page was shimmering on the television screen behind a male and female news team. The male presenter was addressing his companion.

"Sarah, this must be one of the strangest Royals stories we've ever covered."

"Yes it is, Chris! And, it must be said, one that may be vastly more far-reaching than the death of Princess Diana!" The female anchor faced the camera. She tried to arrange her face – to hide her profound shock – but didn't quite manage it. "By now, most of you have heard about today's front page story in the London *Herald*. The country awoke this morning to controversial publisher Victor Dawson's astonishing allegation that, and I quote, 'the British Royal Family is illegitimate, and has no legal right to the throne'. He claims to have spent several years and over two million pounds researching this subject. He says, and I quote again: 'I can prove beyond a shadow of a doubt that the Windsors have no better claim to the throne than Dr. Who'."

That statement drew a barely suppressed laugh from the presenter's colleague. A flash of annoyance crossed the woman's face. She continued:

"Sasha Saunders, our Buckingham Palace correspondent, tells us that officials there have been close-mouthed, although their off-the-record comments suggest that they view this story as just another cynical attempt by a long-time critic of the Royal Family to boost his newspaper's circulation. Meanwhile, on the streets of London–"

The picture cut to a city street, showing a long queue of people waiting at a newsstand to buy a copy of the *Herald*.

"–speculation rages as to the identity of the individual Mr. Dawson claims is – in his words – 'the only true, lawful and legitimate heir to the throne of England'. The billionaire publisher says he will name that person on Friday night, on a special broadcast of his own network's highly-rated news analysis program, *Critical Maas*."

The picture cut back to the news desk. The female presenter turned to her companion. "Chris, this could be the hoax of the decade… or the beginning of a huge constitutional crisis!"

"Exactly right! But either way, it sounds like more trouble is on the way! Sources at Dawson Broadcasting have hinted that their boss will also reveal details of several behind-the-scenes attempts by Her Majesty's Government to suppress this story."

Emma thumbed a remote and muted the audio. "Victor's going on national television to accuse the Queen–" she looked at Boswell "–okay, accuse the *Government*, of trying to kill me!"

"You mean international television," Boswell responded. "He owns his own satellites."

"Maybe they did," Juneau said quietly.

"What?" Emma asked.

"Maybe Her Majesty's Government did try to kill you. Dawson is probably right to bring this out in the open." His eyes were on Boswell.

Boswell didn't blink. And he didn't respond. He changed the subject. "A gang of reporters is waiting downstairs."

"Why?" Emma pointed at the television. "They just said Dawson hasn't named me yet!"

"It's not that. One of the Palace coppers, or an ambulance attendant – we're not sure yet – tipped a reporter about a violent incident inside Buckingham Palace. Conyers says the story on the street is that a heroic young couple saved the Queen from some lunatic intruder. One additional leak from a member of the hospital staff was all it took, and now we've got a media encampment down there. They have no idea what the real story is, but that's no help right now."

"The doctor said I can be released tomorrow," Juneau said. "How are we supposed to get out of here?"

"I'm arranging for a helicopter. From the roof."

"Sounds familiar," Emma commented wryly. "Where are we going?" She smiled. "Back to Clairmont?"

"The Palace. You will both be honored guests of Her Majesty and Prince Philip."

"Honored guests, or honored prisoners?" Juneau asked.

"The traditional abode for honored prisoners is the Tower. So you may feel relieved. As it happens, both Her Majesty and the Prince are looking forward to hearing your first hand account of the latest incident."

"I would guess that Her Majesty has something more in mind than campfire tales," Emma suggested.

"She does. She anticipates Mr. Dawson's Friday night broadcast will result in private discussions."

"'Private', meaning…?"

"Meaning, between you and her."

Victor Dawson descended the main staircase at Wilton Crescent. Dwight Wickham was waiting in the foyer near the front door. Next to Wickham stood a short, precise-looking man wearing the uniform of a London police officer. His shoulder boards bore a crown above an Order of Bath Star and crossed tipstaves, identifying him as the Commissioner of the London Metropolitan Police.

Dawson walked over.

"Are you Mr. Victor Dawson?" the man asked.

"Yes. I'm sure you know that."

"A necessary formality, sir. My name is–"

"I know who you are, Commissioner! The question is, why are you here?"

The Commissioner glanced at Wickham. "May we speak in private, sir?"

"No."

The Commissioner's expression hardened. "Very well. In that case–" he reached into an inner pocket and produced a thick folded document "–I am instructed to advise you that your attendance is required before the House of Lords on the date and at the time endorsed on this Summons."

He proffered the document. Dawson took it.

"Instructed by whom?"

"Her Majesty the Queen."

"You mean, Her Majesty the Pretender to the Throne."

"I am not here to debate with you, Mr. Dawson. I am here to place that Summons in your hand, and I have done so."

Dawson unfolded the document. He scanned the first page. He looked up, perplexed. "The House of Lords? Why?"

"The Prime Minister has asked the Lords to convene a Peerage Review Committee. They have agreed."

"A Peerage Review? To do what?"

"To investigate, sir."

"God, it's like pulling teeth with you! To investigate what, man? Investigate what?"

The Commissioner's lip curled. "The Succession, sir. Good day to you."

He turned on his heel. Wickham moved to open the door. The Commissioner waved him off, opened the door himself and walked out.

35

Emma and Juneau were nestled on a floral sofa. Each was holding a glass of wine. Fifteen minutes earlier, a footman had escorted them from their guest apartment one floor below (with separate bedrooms – this was Her Majesty's residence, after all) to a sitting room in The Queen's private apartments, where Her Majesty, Prince Philip and Alan Boswell had awaited them. Showing not the slightest interest in ceremony, The Queen had offered them drinks, Philip had fetched them himself, and they'd been invited to sit.

Emma looked around. Apart from two paintings from the Dutch Golden Age – by Frans Hals and Johannes Vermeer, Her Majesty had quite matter-of-factly told them – the sitting room's furnishing and appurtenances could have been found in any well-to-do Londoner's flat. A few antiques, yes, but mainly it was a room with the look and feel of modernity and comfort.

Philip had been watching her. He settled on a soft chair next to The Queen and set his glass of whiskey on the table between them. "You look surprised by your surroundings, dear girl," he rumbled. "You didn't expect we actually lived in one of those marble and damask nightmare chambers the public tours visit, did you? Some of those French chairs would put your back out!"

Juneau was sitting very still, with one arm in a sling. He hadn't quite got used to his new status, or his new social friends.

Prince Philip sipped his whiskey, and added. "We eat boiled eggs, and brush our own teeth, and put our pants on one leg at a time, too, just like the rest of the population. Well, I do – the pants, I mean. Her Majesty–"

"Philip." The Queen spoke quietly.

"Of course, my dear…" He continued, still addressing Emma. "The point is, one has to attend to the ceremonial aspects, and sometimes wear rather ridiculous outfits, but like anyone else, we prefer to be comfortable."

Boswell interjected. "Apologies, Your Highnesses, but I think the broadcast is beginning." He nodded at a television set, which was already turned on, its sound muted. He looked at the Queen. "May I, Your Majesty?"

"Please."

Boswell picked up a remote and restored the audio. A dramatic musical background theme was playing. On the screen, television host James Maas, a man in his fifties, sharp-faced as a ferret, was already occupying one of a pair of soft chairs on an intimate set.

The camera pushed in, closing on Maas. He addressed his unseen audience. "Good evening, and welcome to a special edition of *Critical Maas*.

Tonight we'll be speaking with Mr. Victor Dawson. As most of you will certainly know, Mr. Dawson is the owner of this television network. And, unless you've spent the last twenty-four hours in the bottom of a coal mine, you will also know that Mr. Dawson has recently made the astounding claim that Queen Elizabeth II's title to her throne is, in his words, 'utterly void and without merit'. Mr. Dawson claims that the Queen's entire Royal lineage, all the way back to the eighteenth century, is based on a bigamous marriage. It would not be an exaggeration to say that such a proposition, if proven, could change the course of history in this country and, indeed, the Commonwealth."

Maas stopped speaking. For a seasoned television host, he looked singularly uneasy, as if gathering his nerve for the next step. He appeared to catch a signal from off-camera. He rose uncertainly from his chair. "So, without more ado, let's welcome Victor Dawson."

Dawson joined Maas on the set, all makeup and smiles. They shook hands. They settled into their respective seats.

"Welcome to the show, sir."

"Thank you. I'm pleased to be here."

"Mr. Dawson, I'm going to jump right into this. I understand you have quite a story to tell."

"Yes, I do. And, Jimmy, please call me Victor."

"I'd rather not, sir."

"Oh? As you wish." Dawson paused. "Before we begin, I should tell you that the ground rules have changed somewhat since you and I first spoke about this broadcast."

"In what way, sir?"

"This afternoon, the Commissioner of the Metropolitan Police served me with a paper… a Summons, in fact. Apparently, there is to be an official hearing into my… allegations."

"A hearing? What kind of a hearing, sir?"

"As I understand it, it will be conducted before the House of Lords."

Maas's eyebrows notched up. "I'm not sure I understand."

"Nor do I. I'm having my solicitors look into it."

"You mentioned 'ground rules'?"

"Yes. I had intended to speak freely on your show and lay out the evidence I rely upon. But in light of the pending proceedings, my solicitors have counseled against that approach. I will, however, provide you and your audience with one rather dramatic example of what I have discovered, and I will also name the woman – she is a woman, by the way – who is the only living person on this planet legally entitled to sit on the British throne."

It took Maas a long second to absorb all this. He took in a deep breath. "All right, sir. Shall we start with the evidence you mentioned?"

"Of course. This item may be described as both an object and a person. The object is a recording."

"And the person?"

"Queen Victoria."

"Queen Victoria?"

"I'll explain. One of my reporters, the late Kenneth Tannahill–"

"Late?" Maas looked alarmed.

Dawson's turned a grave face to the camera. "Ken Tannahill was brutally murdered in the United States four days ago."

"Murdered? My goodness!"

"Yes. But I'll come to that in a moment." Dawson's three seconds of apparent grief evaporated. He continued. "Seven years ago, in early 1990, Ken told me about the discovery of a collection of very old sound recordings. They were found on the Isle of Wight. It was the usual sort of story… a battered steamer trunk in an old lady's attic, she dies, the heirs start cleaning up the property so they can list it for sale, they find an attic-full of memorabilia. There were ninety-six cylinders in the trunk. Some of the labels suggested that Queen Victoria herself had recorded them. You may recall that during her reign Victoria spent a lot of time at Osborne House on the Isle of Wight."

"But she died in 1901! Recordings?"

"Sound recordings date back to the 1870's, Jimmy."

"Oh?" Maas was thoughtful. "You said 'cylinders'. Are you referring to those old wax cylinders that, I think, Edison invented?"

"The earliest ones were made of tinfoil. Wax wasn't used until years later." He returned to the story. "I arranged to buy the entire collection. But we couldn't play them. Then, a year or so later, we learned that a Swedish firm had perfected a laser technique that reads the grooves on the cylinder and transfers the sounds to a CD. So we did that. With all of them."

"And what did you hear?"

"I didn't listen to every one, but Ken Tannahill did. Most were fragments – amateur attempts at recording music, unidentifiable voices reciting poetry, that sort of thing – but to our surprise they included over an hour of recordings by Queen Victoria, dating from the 1870's to about 1890. These recordings were apparently intended for her children. It is unlikely they were meant to be heard outside the family. We have no idea how they found their way into that steamer trunk. Ken suspected the collection had come down to the deceased lady from a relative who had worked as a servant at Osborne House. The recordings by Queen Victoria form an amazing historical record, and I plan to donate the entire collection to the British Museum." He paused. "Well... not the entire collection. I'm holding one cylinder in safe custody. It was recorded in 1877, the year Victoria was declared Empress of India."

"Why are you retaining that one?"

"You and your audience will understand when you hear it. Your sound technician has a copy of the CD." Dawson nodded to someone off-camera. There was silence, then a crackling sound. "You are about to hear the voice of Queen Victoria," Dawson announced dramatically.

A reedy voice filled the airwaves.

"–and it has now pleased Providence to place your loving mother in this new and exalted station, but I say to you, my children, in 'Empress of India' may lie the only true and sovereign title in the lengthy list I bear. I had cause these many years gone to have the diaries of your great-grandfather, the King that was, brought up from Brunswick Tower. They placed me in the sorry knowledge of Grandfather's secret marriage to the commoner Hannah Lightfoot, a union lawfully made under God and never dissolved. Ten years past, when infamous forgeries were proffered in that Lavinia woman's legal case, on strong advice of my Ministers, I ordered the true and original parish record to be seized. But it was not to be found. My examiners aver that some unknown person had deliberately excised the page from the parish register. It may have been destroyed at Grandfather's behest. If not, I fear the price of his unholy deception will one day be visited upon our noble House."

The recording ended.

Maas gawped at Dawson. For once, the famous interviewer was at a loss for words.

Dawson spoke quietly. "Our competitors have howled for evidence, Jimmy. Be assured that this is just the beginning, as all will hear in due course." His face lightened. "Would this be a good time to introduce someone?"

Maas recovered his voice. "Who?"

"How about... the true heir to the throne?"

Maas was taken off-guard. He craned his neck, peering nervously off set. "She's here?"

"Not in person."

Dawson gestured behind them. A blown up photograph of Emma, taken during the photo shoot at Clairmont, suddenly materialized on a screen.

"My God!" Maas swallowed. "She's beautiful!"

"Yes, she is."

"Who is she?"

"Her name is Emma Augusta Parks. She is twenty-eight years old. She's a medical doctor, unmarried, and–" Dawson paused for dramatic effect "–she's an American."

Any vestige of professional detachment that James Maas had been clinging to now dissolved. All he could do was gape at Dawson. Finally he blurted, "You've got to be kidding!"

Dawson replied slowly and calmly. "Jimmy… I'm sitting here with you, in this studio, talking to millions of Britons about the Royal Family. Do you really think I came here to play a joke?"

"I'm sorry. But what you're implying–!" Maas's voice seemed to stick in his throat. He flapped an arm.

"I want all of Britain to know – I want all of the world to know – who this young woman is. Do you know why? Because it is my belief that someone in the British Government has been trying to kill her."

Maas goggled. "Trying to… trying to kill her? That's an extraordinary claim, sir!"

"A claim that is entirely justified. In the past four days, there have been two very professional attempts on this young lady's life. Fortunately, both attempts failed. But in a brutal prelude to the first attack, which took place in the United States, one of my star reporters, Kenneth Tannahill, was murdered. The second attempt on Dr. Parks' life took place here in London, on Monday night."

"This is unbelievable! Surely the police are investigating!"

"Not knowing who we could trust, we delayed reporting. I take full responsibility for that decision. Our primary concern was Dr. Parks' safety. We moved her to what we thought was a secure location – Clairmont, my country estate. But yesterday afternoon a phalanx of London Met police officers, led by an individual who identified himself as Superintendent Rice, arrived at Clairmont, arrested Dr. Parks and took her away. For all I know, this poor lady is now being held by the very people who have been trying to kill her!"

"Held?"

"Yes. Or dead." Dawson turned and looked straight into the camera. "The game is up, Your Majesty! I ask you to produce Emma Augusta Parks to the people of this country, alive and in good health!"

Dawson stood and, with a quick nod and a thank you, he turned and walked off the set. The rest of the country was left to stare at the renowned, the formidable, James W. Maas, interviewer extraordinaire – a man who had been known to make Prime Ministers squirm – sitting on his familiar seat looking utterly catatonic.

After several seconds of dead air, some unseen producer finally emerged from his own state of shock and the broadcast cut away to a commercial message.

The scene in the Palace sitting room was not much different from that on the studio set. Prince Philip was bent forward in his seat, his fingers gripping an empty whiskey glass, wearing an appalled expression. Juneau was still staring woodenly at the television screen. Boswell sat frozen in his chair, studying his hands.

Emma felt her face flush. Even knowing as much background as she did, and knowing Dawson's predilection for melodrama, she was stunned and embarrassed by the man's audacity.

"Damnation!" Philip croaked. He stood up abruptly. He looked at Emma. "Excuse me!" He stalked out of the room.

Unnerved, Emma looked at The Queen.

Her Majesty sipped from her wine glass, then set it down. She seemed almost supernaturally calm.

"Sometimes Philip needs to ventilate. Please don't be offended."

"I'm not offended, Your Majesty. I was on the verge of using much stronger language."

"I guessed that."

Emma heaved a sigh. "I suppose Your Majesty now has no choice."

The Queen raised a questioning eyebrow.

"You'll have to release me from my rat-infested dungeon."

The Queen smiled. "We shall give the order."

Boswell came to life. "With apologies, Mum. I have the document here with me. Would this be a proper time?"

"Yes. Please explain it to Emma."

Boswell retrieved a folded paper from his inside pocket. He turned to Emma. "M'Lady…"

"Please, Alan. 'Emma' will do."

"As you wish, M'Lady. The Prime Minister has asked me to formally serve this document upon you. Knowing you as I do, I am confident that a simple verbal request from Her Majesty would have sufficed, but the P.M. wanted every formal step to be documented."

He handed her a Summons. She opened it. She skimmed the arcane wording.

"I'm not sure I understand."

"You heard on the broadcast that Victor Dawson has been summoned to appear before the House of Lords. Actually, the hearing will take place before a special subcommittee of the House of Lords Privileges Committee. The Prime

Minister and the Committee have specifically asked that you be present when Mr. Dawson presents his evidence."

The Queen interceded. "Emma?"

"Yes, Your Majesty?"

"That is a formal Summons, but I will not countenance any attempt to force you to attend. If you would prefer to return to the United States, and if you wish Mr. Juneau to accompany you, that will be arranged. Mr. Boswell will also arrange personal security for you both here and in the United States. But I would consider it a very special favor to me if you would remain in England and attend the hearing."

"It will be my honor, Your Majesty. It may be the best way to put an end to this madness."

At twenty-eight minutes after seven on the morning of Friday, September 12th, Jan Chernoff's telephone rang. She was brushing her teeth. She ducked into the bedroom and grabbed the extension.

"Hmmh?"

"Jan? Jan Chernoff?"

She jerked the toothbrush out of her mouth. "Sorry... yes. This is Jan. Who's calling?"

"This is Jim Barstow at the police office."

Jan caught the note of lightness in the detective's tone. Her heart jumped. "You found her!"

"Well, not personally. But she's been found."

"Thank God!" Tears sprang from her eyes. "Is she all right?"

"Yes. I think she's fine."

Jan gulped. "You *think* she's fine? What do you mean? Where is she?"

"Let's see... it's seven twenty-nine."

Jan glanced at the clock by the bed. "Yeah. What's that got to do with–?"

"Turn on CNN, Jan. Headline News starts in one minute. And if you happen to talk to your friend Emma, please tell her I will need to interview her about the murder of that British reporter. At her Royal convenience, of course." He hung up.

Jan stood frozen in confusion. "Royal convenience?" She dropped the phone and dashed into the living room. She clicked on her TV – and nearly collapsed.

Emma's face was looking back at her.

"–this bizarre story from England..." the news anchor was saying. "A major crisis has erupted over the future of the British monarchy, and, remarkably, it all has to do with this young American physician, Dr. Emma Parks, who, according to this man–" Victor Dawson's face appeared on a split screen next to Emma's "–is the sole legitimate heir to the British throne. The man making this astounding claim is billionaire publisher Victor Dawson, owner of hundreds of newspapers and television stations worldwide, including several dozen in this country. Last night, Dawson appeared on a British network broadcast and told an astonished national audience…"

Dumbfounded, Jan dropped onto her sofa.

Her telephone rang again. She picked up, still staring at the television.

"Jan?" It was Rita.

"I know!" Jan said. "I'm watching it now!"

"She just called! She tried you too, but your line was busy!"

"I was talking to Jim Barstow! What did she say?"

"She's in Buckingham Palace! Jan, she's staying there!"

"She's staying with The Queen?"

"Yeah! They're like… friends or something!"

The story was still running on CNN. Jan's eyes stayed locked on Emma's picture. Her friend looked gorgeous. Her hair, her makeup… Emma hardly ever wore makeup! What the hell?

"Friends, huh?" Jan felt the attorney section of her brain kick into gear. "I wonder how long that'll last."

Rita prattled on, unheeding. "She just wanted to tell us she's fine. She asked me to talk to Dr. Rutledge. Try to get her a reprieve or something. She said she hopes to be home in a week or so."

On the screen, the news anchor had yielded to an animated woman with mousy hair and schlumpy clothes. The woman was talking a mile a minute. Her name appeared at the bottom of the screen:

Harriet McEwan Professor of History Georgetown Univ.

"Rita!"

"Yeah?"

"I think this is going to take more than a week," Jan said slowly. "Maybe I'd better go with you when you see Rutledge."

36

A huge crowd surged against steel barriers outside Westminster Hall. Competing placards and banners waved violently above the sea of heads:
TURF THE USURPERS!
REPUBLIC NOW!
QUEEN EMMA WE LOVE YOU!
OFF WITH 'ER HEAD!

Factions shouted insults. Police struggled to break up fistfights.

A three-car motor cavalcade arrived.

Emma sat with Juneau in the rear of the middle car. People cheered and jeered. A few broke past the police barriers and thumped on the body of the car. Officers waded in to push them back.

Juneau's arm was still in a sling. Emma clutched on to his good hand.

A gate swung open. The car passed into a courtyard.

An imposing hand-carved dais dominated the business end of the hearing room. The Royal coat-of-arms and a small portrait of The Queen hung on the paneled wall behind it. On the rear wall, above the packed pews of a small public gallery, hung an enormous enlargement of George Gower's famous Armada Portrait of Queen Elizabeth I.

Uniformed police officers were stationed just inside the public entrance and at each corner of the room.

Below the dais, a smartly-dressed woman in civilian attire sat at a stenograph machine. Halfway along the left side of the room, a bespectacled man in a three-piece pinstriped suit sat at a small desk. A blank notepad lay open in front of him.

Behind his desk, a curtain covered a section of wall.

A long table, where one might expect to see bewigged barristers engaged in whispered conferences, was positioned laterally across the room facing the dais. Victor Dawson sat alone at the right-hand end of the table, dressed in a dark business suit. The surface of the table in front of him and to either side was covered with papers and lever-arch binders. Directly in front of his position, on a small separate table, a slide projector pointed toward a large white screen affixed to the wall.

A door opened. An usher wearing a swallowtail coat, starched white shirt and black tie stepped into view. "Silence!" he ordered. "Please stand!"

Dawson rose from his seat. The low drone of chatter behind him faded as the occupants of the packed public gallery shuffled to their feet.

Three elderly men filed into the room. Each of them wore a dark business suit. Two of the men were white, both slightly portly. The third panel member was darker-skinned, perhaps of Anglo-Indian background, fine-featured and whippet-thin.

The three panel members took their seats on the dais. One of the white men appeared to be the Hearing Chairman. He remained standing while his colleagues settled onto their chairs on either side of him, and then he took his own seat. He addressed the room.

"Thank you. Please be seated."

The gallery rabble sat down. Dawson remained on his feet. The Chairman looked down at him. "You are Mr. Victor Dawson?"

"Yes, my Lord."

"You appear without counsel, sir?"

"I do, my Lord. No one has a better grasp of the evidence than I do."

"That is to be seen, sir," the Chairman replied thinly.

Dawson gestured at the empty stretch of table to his left. "I had expected Dr. Parks to be present. And, of course, a representative of the Queen."

"Yes. A few moments ago, we received a message from Buckingham Palace. Dr. Parks has been slightly delayed. She was in audience with Her Majesty." A swell of muttering riffled through the gallery. "She is now entering the building and will join us momentarily. In the meanwhile, there are matters that I believe we may fairly address in Dr. Parks' absence." The Chairman's eyes swept the gallery. He raised his voice. "First, let me say this: We realize that this case has aroused widespread interest and concern. Emotions are running high. That is understandable. Nevertheless, members of the public gallery should be warned that any person who, by noise or gesture, disrupts these proceedings *will* be expelled!"

The room went very still.

"Thank you. Second, this tribunal has received a letter from Her Majesty's solicitors. They advise that the Queen will not appear as a party to this hearing, either in person or by representative. Her Majesty has, however, sent an official observer." He turned his gaze on the bespectacled man sitting at the small desk. "I take it, sir, that you attend here in that capacity?"

The man stood respectfully. "Yes, my Lord. My name is Stanley Wisdom. As you have stated, I appear on behalf of Her Majesty. My role is solely to observe. I am however instructed to advise your Lordships that, in the event this matter proceeds to a hearing before the full Committee, the learned Solicitor General will appear on Her Majesty's behalf."

"Have you met Dr. Emma Parks, sir?"

"Yes I have, my Lord, and she is aware of my role."

"We understand that Her Majesty has charged you with one additional duty."

"Yes." He produced a document from an inside pocket and unfolded it. "Her Majesty has instructed me to state the following on her behalf…" He referred to the document. "One: that she does not dispute that Hannah Lightfoot was a real person. Two: that she does not dispute that Hannah Lightfoot was involved in an intimate relationship with her ancestor, King George III, which liaison commenced while he was the Prince of Wales." This statement elicited scattered intakes of breath in the gallery. "And, three: that she wishes this Tribunal to have sight of this painting from the Royal collection."

Mr. Wisdom signaled the usher, who was standing ready. The man reached up and pulled back the curtain behind Wisdom's desk.

Hanging there was the Queen's painting of Hannah Lightfoot.

The effect was dramatic. Panel members, no less than gallery members, craned to look at the painting as Mr. Wisdom continued. "Her Majesty arranged for this painting to be transported from Frogmore House, Windsor. According to original records in Her Majesty's possession, this is a portrait of Hannah Lightfoot. It was painted by Sir Joshua Reynolds, on a commission from the Prince of Wales, during the month of May, 1759. Her Majesty asks that the painting not itself be marked as a formal exhibit in these proceedings. She has, of course, no objection to a photograph being taken and so marked."

"Did Her Majesty offer a reason for producing the painting to this tribunal?"

"Yes, she did, my Lord." At that second, a police officer appeared at Wisdom's elbow. They had a whispered conversation. Wisdom nodded and turned back to the panel. "My Lord, I think Her Majesty's reason for sending the painting will shortly become self-evident. I'm told Dr. Parks' arrival has caused something of a stir in the outer precincts."

The main door opened and was held by a police officer.

Emma entered, carrying a manila envelope, with Carl Juneau following closely behind.

Emma paused to get her bearings. She looked around.

An audible gasp rippled through the gallery.

On the dais, three sets of eyes locked on Emma, shifted to the painting of Hannah, then back to Emma.

It took a moment for the Chairman to remember his manners.

"Dr. Parks, I believe?"

"Yes sir."

"Welcome! My name is Lord McHale. Sitting on my left is Lord Biggs, and this–" referring to the darker-complexioned gentleman "–is Lord Timmins. Please, make yourself comfortable."

"Thank you." Emma looked about uncertainly. The usher, apparently bewitched, stood gawking at her.

The Chairman glared down at the man. "Mr. Pennycuick?"

The Chairman's sharp tone jerked the usher out of his reverie. He escorted Emma to a seat at the long table. He held her chair for her. She smiled her thanks and sat.

Ignored by all, Juneau settled on a spare seat near Wisdom's desk.

The Chairman couldn't contain himself. "Dr. Parks, do forgive us! I think everyone here has been a bit taken aback."

"Flabbergasted might be a more accurate description," Lord Timmins interjected, polishing his glasses. He replaced them and looked at Emma with undisguised admiration.

"My Lord Timmins is correct," responded the Chairman. He gestured at the painting of Hannah Lightfoot. "Dr. Parks, have you ever seen this painting before?"

"Yes sir. I'm sorry... Yes, my Lord."

"Where was that?"

"At Frogmore House. In Windsor."

"And how did that come to pass?"

Emma hesitated. "Her Majesty sent a car for me."

A ripple went through the gallery.

"When was that?"

"Last week, on Tuesday."

Lord McHale paused. "Excuse me." He conferred with his colleagues. There was some animated discussion. When he turned back to Emma, he wore a frown. "Dr. Parks... afterwards – after your visit at Frogmore House – did anything unusual occur?"

"Yes. Mr. Dawson's personal assistant tried to kill me."

The gallery erupted. Police officers stiffened, alert for trouble. Usher Pennycuick's repeated calls for silence finally quieted the room. The Chairman seemed to have completely forgotten his earlier stern admonishment to the gallery. He waited for the noise to subside and then continued.

"Mr. Dawson has stated publicly that there were other attempts on your life. Is that true?"

"Yes. There were two earlier attempts... one here in London and, before that, one in the United States."

"And how is it, Doctor, that you are alive today to tell us about this?"

"Because on each of the first two occasions Mr. Carl Juneau saved my life." She nodded toward Juneau. "And on the third, a British officer shot my assailant."

There was another outbreak of jabbering from the gallery. Several people stood to get a look at Juneau. The Tribunal members didn't seem to notice the disorder. They had their heads together again, engaged in a tense discussion.

Suddenly, the Chairman rose to his feet.

The room went quiet.

"We will adjourn for ten minutes!" Without another word, the three panel members trooped from the room.

As soon as the door closed behind them, Dawson was out of his chair. He scurried over to Emma. "Dear Emma! When that Superintendent took you away, I thought you were dead!" He tried to hug her. She stiff-armed him.

"Bastard!" she hissed, as Juneau moved to her side.

Dawson smiled. "Say *Welsh* bastard… it sounds more English!"

Emma glared. "Don't try to shine me on, Victor! I'm sure you were pleased when that Superintendent took me away! It was just the excuse you needed to orchestrate that cheap accusation against the Queen on national TV!"

"I'm sorry you feel that way, Emma. And I'm sorry I got you into this." He waved his arm. "But now it's out there, and it has to be finished."

Emma's hand slipped into Juneau's. "Yes, Victor. It has to be finished. And it will be."

"Very good." His eyes slashed toward the dais. He lowered his voice. "They adjourned very quickly. Don't you wonder what they're doing?"

"Making phone calls," Juneau replied.

"I'm sure you're right, Carl. I find that interesting. Don't you?"

He strolled back to his seat.

The Tribunal reconvened.

Lord McHale addressed the room. "This Tribunal sits as a subcommittee of the Privileges Committee of the House of Lords. Let me repeat that. We are a *subcommittee* only! At the request of the Prime Minister, we have been convened to investigate certain well-publicized allegations made by Mr. Victor Dawson, through media outlets controlled by him, respecting the Royal Family and its antecedents. Our task is to determine whether evidence exists that would justify this matter being referred to the Privileges Committee sitting as a whole. My colleagues and I have conferred. In the circumstances, and having regard to the preliminary nature of these proceedings, we have agreed that for the protection of all concerned this hearing shall henceforth be conducted *in camera!*"

The gallery erupted with protests.

The Chairman raised his voice over the clamor. "For the benefit of those members of the press who are present, a transcript of this hearing will be kept and, in the event that the matter moves on to the next stage, a copy will be made available to you. In the meantime, and from this moment forward, there is a ban on publication of these proceedings." He looked hard at Dawson. "Since you, Mr. Dawson, will be the only member of the press in this room, I emphasize that this ban also applies to you. Do you understand?"

Dawson nodded.

"Say it aloud, please, Mr. Dawson! I want your response on the record!"

"Yes, my Lord. I understand. And I say for the benefit of all media representatives in this room that I am fully confident that this matter will go to a full and public hearing."

Lord McHale gave him a withering look. "Officers, clear the room! Dr. Parks, Mr. Dawson, Mr. Wisdom, Mr. Pennycuick, our lady transcriber–" he smiled down at the reporter "–and two police officers are to remain."

Juneau rose, looking uncertain. Emma went to him. She turned to face the Chairman. "Sir! My Lord!"

"Yes?"

"I ask that Mr. Juneau be allowed to stay!"

"Oh? All right. Just for the record – you are Carl Juneau? Dr. Parks' bodyguard?"

"Yes, My Lord. I was actually employed by–"

"–by Mr. Dawson. Yes, we know. Your resume has preceded you. You may remain, sir."

When the room was clear and the door finally shut, the Chairman addressed Emma.

"Dr. Parks?"

"Yes, My Lord?"

"These attempts on your life… Each of us on this panel was deeply shocked by your confirmation of these incidents. I expect you have been providing information to our police authorities?"

"Yes. And to the FBI. Mr. Dawson's reporter, Kenneth Tannahill, was murdered in the United States."

"Very well. My colleagues and I extend our heartfelt sympathy to you for your ordeal."

"Thank you."

"And, since we're sitting *in camera* now, we will dispense with formal terms of address."

"Thank you. The words 'My Lord' don't exactly come naturally to me."

The Chairman smiled. "We thought not."

37

Three hours later, a substantial proportion of the original gallery crowd was still milling about in the red-carpeted lobby. Police officers barred the door into the hearing room. A few journalists leaned in corners, talking on telephones.

Inside the hearing room, the high windows were growing dark. The panel members had removed their jackets and were presiding in shirtsleeves.

Emma occupied her original seat, with Juneau now sitting immediately to her right, between her and Dawson.

The slide projector was on. The stark glare reflecting from the screen spread a crazy-quilt pattern of light and shadow across the vaulted ceiling above. Dawson had already subjected the panel to the slide show he'd shown Emma in the salon at Wilton Crescent. A blow-up of her family tree was now projected on the screen, with its brightline path tracing down through six generations from George III to Emma.

Dawson was in full flow. The panel listened in grim silence. "George and Hannah's son, George Augustus Parks, died in July, 1821. He was buried in a concealed vault under the floor of Gryn'och Chapel, a small parish church near Carmarthen, in Wales. In 1995, one of my subsidiary companies secured the contract to renovate the church interior."

"And how was it, Mr. Dawson," the Chairman asked gruffly, "that one of your subsidiaries just happened to be looking for this type of work, in this part of Wales?"

"We already knew where to look, My Lord. As Mr. Tannahill's investigations had proceeded through the years, my...ah...former assistant, Henry Leggatt, who was working with him, became something of a master at genealogical investigation."

"I see."

"Mr. Tannahill had other assignments to deal with, so toward the end, Mr. Leggatt was carrying the bulk of the investigation."

"All the while plotting to kill Dr. Parks."

Dawson's face darkened. "Yes. So it appears. I want to make it clear that at no time did I have any inkling of his intentions."

"That is not being suggested, Mr. Dawson. Mr. Leggatt's activities are not directly relevant to our inquiry. They are a matter for the law enforcement authorities."

"Yes sir." Dawson thumbed the projector's remote control. On the screen, a photograph appeared, showing a slate-tiled floor in a church. Several large tiles had been lifted, revealing an excavated grave in the undercroft.

"This is the grave of George III's son, George Augustus Parks."

The picture changed again, now showing the inscription on a grave marker.

GEORGE AUGUSTUS PARKS
b. May 4 1761
d. July 16 1821
Put not thy Faith in Princes, but in the Lord thy God

"The epitaph chosen for Mr. Parks – or more likely, *by* him before death – is most telling," Dawson added. He waited while panel members read the inscription. "George Parks was buried in an airtight lead coffin. His remains were well enough preserved to support DNA testing. That testing has been done, and the results have been compared to samples taken from Dr. Parks, as well as samples obtained, ah… from the current Royal Family." Dawson ignored the sharp looks from the dais and pressed on. "The DNA testing confirms without a shadow of doubt that Emma Augusta Parks is descended from George III. You will find copies of the scientific reports in the binder I provided, under tabs eight, nine and ten."

Lord Biggs spoke. "You are not a lawyer, Mr. Dawson, but you must realize that it is one thing to demonstrate that a person is an heir in fact – for example, an heir by lineal descent – but it is quite another to demonstrate that a person is an heir *in law.*"

"I am well aware of that concept, sir. I have spent several years considering it."

"Then you will understand that, having regard to the unique nature of this case and to an intervening period of well over two centuries, your case faces certain formidable hurdles."

Dawson responded with a touch of condescension. "So it might appear to you, sir, but not to me."

Lord Biggs shot back. "*Legality* is not a concept to be taken lightly, Mr. Dawson!"

The Chairman looked at the clock on the wall. He intervened. "Thank you. It's been a long day. We will now rise. We'll resume sitting at ten o'clock tomorrow morning."

Emma jumped to her feet as the tribunal members rose. "Excuse me, sirs! My Lords! May I be heard?"

"You will be heard, Dr. Parks. But Mr. Dawson has not concluded his submissions. Naturally, we will want to hear from you as soon as he is finished.

Tomorrow morning, then…"

"But, sir, I have evidence that this claim is a fraud!"

"A fraud?" the Chairman muttered.

Dawson looked wildly at her. "What?"

Emma brandished the envelope she had carried into the room. A red wafer seal secured its flap.

The panel members settled back into their seats. The Chairman caught the usher's attention. "Mr. Pennycuick, if you would?"

The usher hurried to Emma. She gave him the envelope. He passed it up to Lord McHale.

"As you see, My Lord McHale, it's addressed to you," Emma stated. "Perhaps you recognize the impression on the seal?"

The Chairman studied it. "The Queen's personal arms." He broke the seal. He extracted an ancient document.

The other panel members rolled their chairs closer.

"What you are looking at," Emma continued, "is a certificate of marriage. I have a photocopy here, and one for Mr. Dawson." Juneau slid a sheet of paper along the table to Dawson. Emma continued. "With your permission, I would like to read the highlights aloud–

'By these Presents… witnesseth that… on this 11th day of December, in the Year of our Lord One thousand seven hundred and fifty-three… Isaac Axford, of bachelor state, and Hannah Lightfoot, maid and spinster, were wed in the presence of…'

–et cetera, et cetera… Hannah Lightfoot married a man named Isaac Axford in 1753, six years before her marriage to Prince George!"

The Chairman looked up from the document and peered at Emma over his reading glasses. "This appears to be an original."

"It is, my Lord."

"And Her Majesty entrusted it to you?"

"Yes, she did. Her Majesty and I preferred that I bring it to you personally, rather than provide it through her official observer." Emma looked over at the Queen's bespectacled agent, sitting quietly at his desk below the Reynolds painting. "I'm sorry, Mr. Wisdom."

"I understand completely," Wisdom replied, smiling.

"Extraordinary!" the Chairman muttered. "Do you know if Mrs.–" he consulted the document "–'Axford' obtained a divorce before marrying the Prince of Wales?"

"As I understand it, in those days a divorce required an Act of Parliament."

"You are correct." He removed his glasses. "Dr. Parks, historically there have been hundreds, if not thousands, of private Acts of Parliament passed. Would you like us to have the matter researched?"

"I already have, my Lord," Dawson said.

The Chairman turned to him, clearly startled.

Mr. Wisdom rose. "May I intercede, my Lord?"

"Of course."

"My information is that, two years ago, an employee of Mr. Dawson's company conducted a search of the journals of the House of Commons for the years 1753 to 1760, inclusive."

Lord McHale looked at Dawson. "Is that correct?"

"Yes."

"Did your employee locate any Private Act – or indeed, any Private Bill – touching on this matter?"

"No, my Lord. There was no record of a divorce."

"I see. Well… do you not see where that takes us, Mr. Dawson? The very marriage you rest your case upon was bigamous, and King George's later marriage to Princess Charlotte was *ipso facto* legitimate. And," he added pointedly, "it appears you knew this!"

Emma watched Dawson. The man was preternaturally calm.

Emma felt suddenly queasy.

Dawson rose from his seat. He walked around the end of the table and strolled to the slide projector. He carefully adjusted the slide tray.

Emma addressed the panel, her eyes still on Dawson. "Either Mr. Dawson was aware of this previous marriage, and suppressed it," she ventured uncertainly, "or his research is fatally flawed." She paused. "Either way, my family has no claim."

Dawson returned to his seat.

The Chairman addressed Dawson. "How do you respond to that?"

"It's a comforting fantasy, my Lord."

"A… fantasy?"

"Yes." Dawson activated the slide projector's remote. A new slide appeared on the screen. It was a photograph of another document – more particularly, a section of a page bearing quill writing in a clear and careful hand.

"This, my Lords, is part of an original document from the parish records of St. Giles Cripplegate. Let me read it aloud for you. It is very short so, unlike Dr. Parks, I shall read every word. I do so enjoy the quaint spelling–

'St. Giles Cripplegate – burialls 1756

Isaac Axford buryed the 31 daye Julye 1756 widowe Hannah Axford, born Lightfoot'

"Unfortunately, Mr. Axford's grave now lies under the foundations of a school for the handicapped. But this particular document is available for inspection in the Guildhall Library." He paused for effect. "It proves that Hannah Lightfoot was a widow in 1759 and that she was therefore free to marry."

Emma dropped onto her chair.

The room was utterly still.

Juneau squeezed Emma's hand. She turned and looked into his eyes. An unspoken message passed between them.

Emma stood. She waited until every eye was on her.

"My Lords, I'm renouncing!"

Dawson's body jerked. "Emma!" He got up and moved toward her.

Juneau blocked him.

Emma continued in a clear voice. "I'm renouncing any claim I have, or may appear to have, to the throne of England."

The Chairman regarded her carefully. "Why?"

"For one thing, I'm an American. Our constitution forbids me from accepting a foreign title."

Lord Timmins interceded. "Dr. Parks, *Sovereign* is rather more than a 'title'! And you must know that British citizenship could not be more automatic than in a case such as this! One would think, in the circumstances, that you would…" He stopped talking, clearly troubled by the implications of his analysis.

"My Lords, please! This really is unthinkable!"

Lord Timmins took off his glasses and rubbed his eyes. "Miss Parks… Doctor… after a long life in the law, I'm no longer certain that anything is unthinkable. And for you to 'renounce', as you put it, would have no effect on the rights of your children."

Lord Biggs spoke up. "She'd have to abdicate!"

Emma seized on the suggestion. "I can do that! Do I sign something?"

The Tribunal members looked at one another in consternation. Lord McHale finally responded.

"It's not that simple, Doctor. You can't abdicate until and unless you are found to be the lawful monarch. Let me explain…" He counted off on his fingers. "First, we must hear Mr. Dawson's evidence. Next, we must report to the full Committee of Privileges. Then, should the evidence be found sufficient, the Committee – which must include at least three Lords of Appeal – would hear the entire case anew. The process would be something like a hearing in your Supreme Court, with nine judges and legal counsel on both sides. If the

Committee should come to the opinion that you are indeed the rightful Sovereign, a full report of its findings would go to the Prime Minister, who would... then, I think–" he began to look uncertain "–I believe... be compelled to call the House of Commons into special session." He looked at his colleagues. "Wouldn't he?"

The three men had a whispered discussion. Finally, exasperated, the Chairman turned back to Emma.

"As you can see, we're not even sure of the process ourselves! There are no modern precedents. All we can say for certain is this: after a number of steps in the process, if you were found to be the true Sovereign, and were unwilling to take the throne, you would be required to execute an Instrument of Abdication, just as Edward VIII did in 1936. Are you familiar with that case?"

"He wanted to marry an American divorcee."

"That's right. But, you see, even your signature on that document would not be the end of it. Parliament would then be required to pass a Declaration of Abdication Act, just as it did in 1936." Lord Timmins tugged the Chairman's sleeve. They conferred. The Chairman nodded. "And finally, as Lord Timmins reminds me–"

"There's more?"

"Yes. Under a law known as the Statute of Westminster, some Commonwealth countries – not all – recognize the British monarch as their own Head of State. For the abdication to be complete, parallel Abdication Acts would need to be passed by each of those individual parliaments.

"How many countries?"

"Sixteen."

Emma blanched.

"So you see, young lady, like it or not, Mr. Dawson may have created a constitutional crisis of immense proportions."

"With respect, I didn't create the crisis. George III did."

Lord McHale turned a baleful eye on Dawson, who was sitting calmly, toying with a pen. The billionaire's facial expression was thick with satisfaction.

"Ten o'clock tomorrow!" the Chairman pronounced, and abruptly stood up.

Usher Pennycuick held the door as the three old men filed out.

Dawson sidled over to Emma and Juneau. He made an elaborate bow to Emma. "May I be the first to congratulate you, Your Highness, and the first to say: *Long live the Queen!*"

Emma turned on him angrily. "Why do you hate them, Victor?"

Dawson regarded her curiously. "Who?"

"The Royals! The old titles! You hate them, don't you? That's the only reason I'm in this mess!"

"Hardly a mess, dear lady! You're performing a great public service. You should award yourself a medal."

"Don't be facetious!"

"They're an anachronism, and they know it! Yet they continue to delude themselves that they're actually useful! They insult our intelligence. As a great man once said, the whole concept of a hereditary head of state is about as absurd as a hereditary mathematician!"

"Yes, I've read Thomas Paine! But he wrote those words when Kings actually ruled! This is today! Why do you care? For God's sake, you're one of the richest men on the planet!"

"So my newspapers tell me."

"You could buy and sell the Royal Family."

"Yes."

"They can't hurt you!"

"Not financially."

Emma's eyes bored in. "I thought so!"

"What do you mean?"

"What really pisses you off is that, rich as you are, The Queen has never given you a title or a medal, or even a piddling ribbon! Your editors call you a media *baron*, but that's just a silly expression, isn't it? You're not a member of the real nobility you pretend to despise! You're not a Lord or an Earl or a Viscount – you're not even a 'Sir'! You're just a no-class Welsh hustler–"

"Welsh 'savage' is the usual description."

"–who managed to leverage a few second-rate tabloids into a megafortune!"

"Demonstrating that this poor Welsh savage was smarter than anyone else."

"Bull!"

"What?"

"The self-made man myth! That's just a lie you tell yourself! You've told it so many times you probably believe it!"

Dawson blustered. "Do you have any idea what I had to overcome?"

"Yes, I do! I came from nothing too! But guess what? I worked! You were a small-time music promoter with two fraud convictions when one of your backwater bands had an accidental hit. They recorded that song two years before they ever met you! You had nothing to do with it! The only reason you're standing here today is because you sued them!"

"How do you know all this?"

"Research! You're not the only one who can do it."

"I'm worth over thirty billion pounds! *Pounds*, not dollars! You think that was an accident, Emma?"

"No. You're a determined man and you were lucky. Here you are, decades later, and you own newspapers and TV stations and satellites and God knows what else. Good for you!" Emma dropped her voice. "But you don't own a title do you, Victor? That's the one thing on this planet even you can't buy!"

"I haven't tried."

"Of course you have! You love to cultivate the image of the brash outsider who crashed the establishment's party. Always the outsider, always the challenger... but the fact is, they obsess you, don't they? The only thing you haven't done is offer Her Majesty a bribe!" Emma's violet gaze turned hot. Her eyes burned into him. "Have you ever considered that this destructive little game of yours could backfire?"

"Backfire?"

"Yes! And if it does – if I end up Queen–" Emma raised her voice "–don't expect to get a fucking title from me!"

She turned and stalked away.

An appreciative glint of suppressed amusement appeared on Carl Juneau's face. He glanced at Stanley Wisdom.

The Queen's observer wore a huge grin.

38

An official car delivered Emma and Juneau back to the Palace, where they spent a quiet night. The Queen and Prince Philip were spending time with their grandchildren, so they didn't see them.

Their assigned footman produced an extensive menu from the Palace kitchens. He told them they could order anything they wanted and, if they wished, the meal would be delivered straight to their sitting room. Realizing that this was a moment to be long remembered, they shared a superb Chateaubriand main course in front of the television, followed by a scrumptious chocolate and brandy dessert with some elaborate French name that went in one ear and out the other. At their footman's suggestion, they also ordered, and with quiet joy consumed, a bottle of 1983 Margaux - "rated 96 and above by the critics", their footman had cheerfully confided.

After an evening of talking and snuggling, they retired to their separate bedrooms, observing the unspoken protocol suggested by their room assignments. But it was a close run thing, because the deep kiss at their moment of parting made Emma's knees go weak and brought sudden, familiar heat to the intimate regions of her body.

The Chairman's backside had barely touched his chair when he fixed his eyes on Victor Dawson.

"Mr. Dawson!"

"Yes, sir?"

"Are you familiar with the Royal Marriages Act of 1772?"

"Yes, I am."

"And you, Doctor Parks?"

"I only know what Mr. Dawson told me. He said that after Prince George took the throne, he made it illegal for members of the Royal family to marry without his consent. I remember thinking that was a bit ironic, considering he'd done the same thing himself."

"Yes. After March 24th, 1772, if a member of the Royal family married without the express consent of the Sovereign – which was evidenced by a license issued by the Privy Council bearing the Great Seal – his or her offspring were deemed illegitimate for the purposes of the Act and had no right to succeed to the Crown."

"Is that law still in force?"

"Yes, it is."

Emma was thoughtful. "That would mean…"

"Exactly. You see where we are going. Even if Mr. Dawson is correct and your ancestor, George Augustus Parks, was the eldest son of George III, he would have required the King's permission to marry. By calculation, the boy had not yet reached his eleventh birthday when the Act came into force." The Chairman fixed laser eyes on Dawson. "What do you say, Mr. Dawson?"

"I say the Act does not apply."

Lord Biggs leaned forward. "And upon what, sir, do you base that rather bizarre statement?"

Dawson's face flushed. "Upon the facts, sir! Your Lordships give every appearance of astuteness, but you have clearly paid no attention to Dr. Parks' family tree."

The Chairman flared. "How could that document assist in this analysis, Mr. Dawson? Even if we accept your evidence of lineal descent as utterly flawless, as Lord Biggs has correctly said, you must still prove *lawful* descent. And in this case lawful descent evaporates after the first generation!"

"It does not, my Lord." He rose to his feet. "May I show you?"

"Please do!"

Dawson went to the slide projector, turned it on, and checked the slide tray.

Emma's family tree appeared on the screen…

~ GENEALOGICAL TABLE ~
EMMA AUGUSTA PARKS

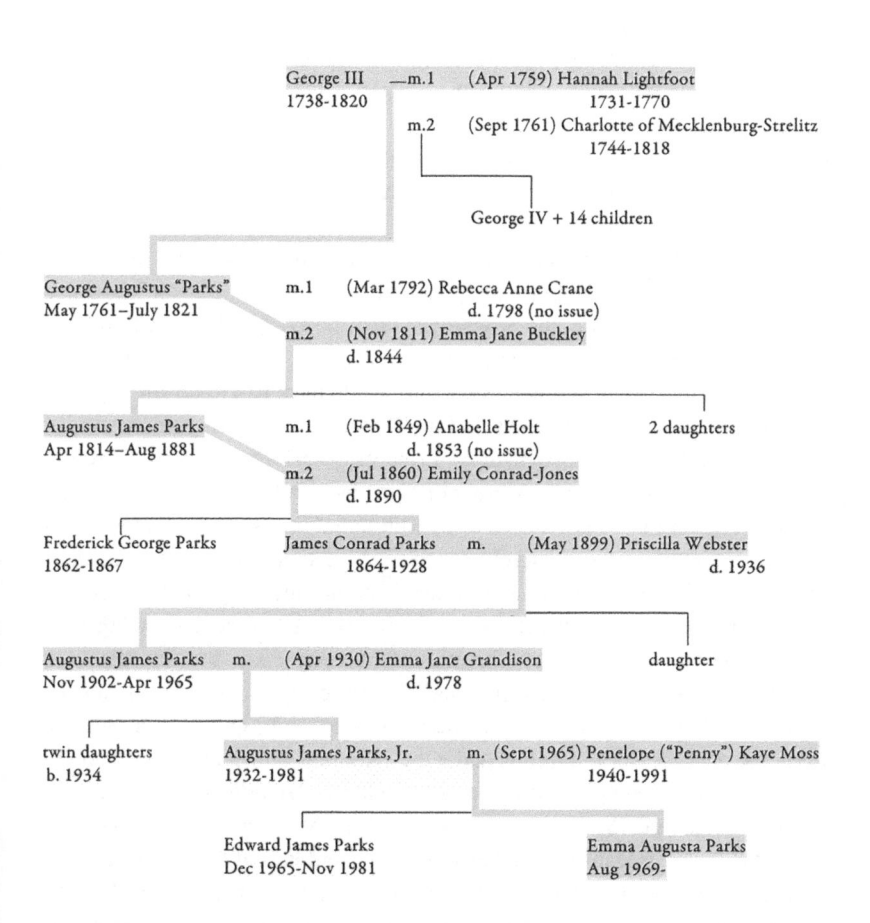

George III —m.1 (Apr 1759) Hannah Lightfoot
1738-1820   1731-1770
         m.2 (Sept 1761) Charlotte of Mecklenburg-Strelitz
                1744-1818

George IV + 14 children

George Augustus "Parks"   m.1   (Mar 1792) Rebecca Anne Crane
May 1761–July 1821   d. 1798 (no issue)
                          m.2   (Nov 1811) Emma Jane Buckley
                                 d. 1844

Augustus James Parks   m.1   (Feb 1849) Anabelle Holt   2 daughters
Apr 1814–Aug 1881   d. 1853 (no issue)
                       m.2   (Jul 1860) Emily Conrad-Jones
                              d. 1890

Frederick George Parks   James Conrad Parks   m.   (May 1899) Priscilla Webster
1862-1867   1864-1928   d. 1936

Augustus James Parks   m.   (Apr 1930) Emma Jane Grandison   daughter
Nov 1902-Apr 1965   d. 1978

twin daughters   Augustus James Parks, Jr.   m.   (Sept 1965) Penelope ("Penny") Kaye Moss
b. 1934   1932-1981   1940-1991

              Edward James Parks   Emma Augusta Parks
              Dec 1965-Nov 1981   Aug 1969-

205

Dawson returned to his place at the table, but remained standing. "If you examine this document again, you will see–"

"What I see, Mr. Dawson," Lord Biggs interjected, "is that George Augustus Parks married in 1792, presumably without George III's permission and again in 1811 – also, we must assume, without the King's permission!"

Dawson was unfazed. "Yes. His first wife died in 1798. They had no children. But his second wife, Emma Buckley, bore him a son – Dr. Parks' great-great grandfather, the second generation heir."

"I agree we can ignore the first marriage," Lord Biggs conceded. "But as I recall, George III died in 1820. Where is the evidence that George III gave George Augustus Parks formal permission to remarry in 1811?" Lord Biggs sat back. "Right there, your case falls away!"

"This marriage took place in November 1811."

"Yes, we see that."

"Ten months earlier, in January 1811, George III was declared insane and Parliament passed a statute granting the regency to his son, later known as George IV. Being insane, the Sovereign – that is, George III – had no legal capacity to grant or deny permission to marry."

"Then the Regent, acting in his stead, would have had to do so!"

"I have already established that the Regent was the illegitimate son of George III's bigamous marriage to Princess Charlotte. He was therefore incapable of exercising any sovereign power. Not only that, I took advice on this subject from three professors of constitutional law. I made no mention of the bigamous marriage. I merely asked each of them, separately, for their learned opinion on the issue you raise: could the Regent exercise the Sovereign's power under the Royal Marriages Act? All of them agreed that the Regent had no power to issue a permission to marry under the Act. It's all in your binders, gentlemen, but to summarize, all three opinions point out that the statute restricted the power to issue permission to, and I quote, 'His Majesty, his heirs, or successors, signified under the great seal, and declared in council'. Parliament may have given the Regency to George III's *illegitimate* son, later known as George IV, but the *true heir* when that happened was George Augustus Parks. Because his father was insane and lacked legal capacity, Mr. Parks, as the true heir, had the right to marry without permission. For the purposes of the statute, he *was* the Sovereign. Any argument to the contrary is pure smoke."

The room went quiet.

"Despite what you say, this could be a point of contention," Lord McHale said slowly, but it was obvious he was aware of how lame that sounded.

"That argument only covers the second generation," Lord Timmins ventured.

"As I said, my Lords, you need to examine the family tree carefully."

Every set of eyes in the room studied the document.

Lord Timmins was the first to react.

"My God! The man's right!"

Lord Biggs nodded slowly. He turned to look at Emma, seemingly through new eyes.

Lord McHale seemed puzzled. Lord Timmins leaned closer to him and explained quietly, pointing with a descending finger at particular entries on the family tree.

Emma was confused. Dawson noticed her expression. He addressed the panel.

"Perhaps I should spell it out, both for Dr. Parks' assistance, and so that the details appear in our transcriber's transcript."

Emma noted the warm smile Dawson flashed at "our" transcriber as he attempted in his usual slithering way to ingratiate himself. More than that, he seemed to be trying to insinuate himself onto the panel, as if he were a fourth member, or an expert consultant retained to assist them with difficult concepts.

"Yes. Go ahead." the Chairman replied, somewhat grumpily.

"As your Lordships have pointed out, technically each heir in Dr. Parks' line would have had to consent to the marriage of his primary offspring in order for any grandchildren to be deemed legitimate. Whether anyone would be required to adhere to this law if he wasn't even *aware* he was the heir to the throne will be a question for the lawyers. But that would only be an academic question because, as you see, the marriage of each intermediate heir all the way down to Dr. Parks' father took place *after* the death of his Sovereign parent.

"Returning to George Augustus Parks, George III's son by Hannah Lightfoot, as we noted, his first wife died without issue and he remarried, in November 1811, this time to a woman named Emma Jane Buckley."

"'Emma'," Lord Biggs commented, looking at Emma.

"Yes. Dr. Parks' forename will appear again later. George and Emma had a son, Augustus James Parks, born in 1814. They also had two daughters, one older, one younger, but as you know, under the rules of primogeniture their lines would be historically irrelevant unless the son's line failed."

"And we see that the son's line did not fail," Lord Timmins observed.

"Quite so, My Lord. Augustus James Parks lived to a ripe old age – for those times, at least. He died in 1881 at the age of sixty-seven. We know a bit more about his life than we do about his father's. The father, George Augustus

Parks, died in 1821. The son, Augustus James, married, first, Annabelle Holt in 1849. He was an Indian Army officer, posted to Hyderabad. His wife died of cholera in 1853. They had no children. Augustus remarried in 1860. His wife's maiden name was Emily Conrad-Jones. They had two sons. The eldest, whose name was Frederick, died in 1867 at the age of five. The younger son, James Conrad Parks, who was three when his brother died, survived and lived until 1928. In 1884, he emigrated to America. There, in 1899, he met and married Priscilla Webster. As mentioned, his father had died years earlier, in 1881."

"So," Lord Timmins interjected, "to this point, each primary male heir's date of marriage post-dated the death of his father."

"Correct, My Lord. And as you can see, the same phenomenon continued right through the twentieth century. James Conrad Parks' primary heir was another Augustus James Parks – Dr. Parks' grandfather – who married a lady named Emma Grandison in 1930, two years after his father's death, and his son – Dr. Parks' father, Augustus James Parks, Jr. – married Dr. Parks' mother in September 1965, five months after his father had passed away."

The Chairman turned to Emma. "Dr. Parks, forgive me, but we have been told that your father and older brother died in a tragic accident several years ago. Is that true?"

"Yes, My Lord."

"And your mother… is also deceased?"

"Yes."

"You have no other siblings?"

"No."

"I want to say that we're very sorry to hear… about your losses. It must have been very difficult for you."

"Thank you."

A silent moment of respect was called for, but Dawson wasn't waiting. "May I conclude?"

"If you must," the Chairman responded, an edge in his voice.

"The line of descent leading to Dr. Parks shows that each heir in each generation was *already the true Sovereign* when he married. The statute does not require a Sovereign to grant *himself* formal permission to marry. That means that each generation of offspring were legitimate under the law, and, if Dr. Parks were to marry tomorrow, her children would also be legitimate under the Royal Marriages Act."

For a few moments, the panel members were quiet as they absorbed the implications. Finally, Lord McHale asked, "Do you have any other evidence to offer, Mr. Dawson?"

"No, sir." Dawson self-importantly began gathering up his papers. "I look forward to receiving notice that this matter has been referred for hearing to the full Committee. Should it not be so referred, you may expect every shred of this evidence to appear in a special edition of every newspaper I own."

"That sounds very much like a threat, Mr. Dawson," the Chairman retorted. "Have you forgotten that we have banned publication of these proceedings?"

Dawson stepped around to his slide projector and switched it off. "It is a threat, sir. You gentlemen may have power to ban publication of proceedings, but you have no power to ban publication of historical facts." He retrieved his slide tray and returned to his place. "Those facts speak for themselves. As inconvenient as it may be to your Lordships, to Parliament, to the current residents of Buckingham Palace, or to this fine lady herself–" he bowed toward Emma "–Emma Augusta Guelph, also known as Emma Augusta Parks, *is* the lawful Queen of England!"

Pointedly ignoring the panel members' hostile gazes, Dawson proceeded to load his papers and binders into a large briefcase.

The panel members conferred. The Chairman turned to Emma. "Dr. Parks, it seems Mr. Dawson has taken it upon himself to declare this hearing at an end," he said, with a note of heat in his voice. "Is there anything you would like to say to us before we rise?"

"No, my Lord. I think you know my position on all of this."

"If this matter goes to full Committee, do you intend to be represented?" "No."

The Chairman grimaced. "I would expect, in the circumstances, the Government would appoint a senior barrister to argue the case on your behalf."

"You mean, against my wishes?"

"Yes." He was apologetic. "I'm afraid the subject matter of this case is so important that the wishes of one person, even – forgive me, those of a Queen – cannot take precedence."

"Now I understand how Her Majesty must feel."

"That's the problem, Doctor. 'Her Majesty' might be you." Emma's shoulders slumped. Juneau took her hand. The Chairman continued. "Whatever the outcome, I want to say that all of us sitting here have found you to be a remarkable young woman. You've been caught up in cataclysmic circumstances, none of your own making, and have handled yourself admirably. You may find it odd to hear us say this, but you have all the qualities of a very fine Monarch."

His colleagues' heads bobbed in agreement. Lord Timmins' enthusiasm made Emma wonder fleetingly if it was only her monarchical qualities the bright-eyed old fellow found most admirable.

"Thank you," Emma responded. "But I think, in the course of my lifetime, I might be more useful as a physician."

The Chairman nodded. "Quite so."

"We thank each of you for your assistance. And thank you for your attendance, Mr. Wisdom. These proceedings are now closed."

The panel rose. Emma and Juneau stood respectfully. Dawson, who had obviously decided the panel deserved no respect from him, remained conspicuously seated. The Chairman glanced coolly at him. Then, in unison, the three old men bowed deeply to Emma.

She stood there, unnerved, as they retired from the room.

Juneau started to lead Emma toward the door. She resisted. "I'm not ready to face a bunch of cameras. Isn't there another way out?"

"It'll be fine," he said. "Come."

They paused to shake hands with Stanley Wisdom. When they turned to leave, Dawson blocked their way.

"It's not over, Emma," he said quietly. "You know that, don't you?"

"It is for me, Victor. And if it's over for me, it's over for you."

"You don't understand."

"Understand what?"

"If you're found to be the rightful heir – and by that I mean, the lawful heir – it won't matter how many documents you sign. The current Royal family will still be illegitimate. Because of the Act of Settlement, a statute passed in 1701, Parliament will be forced to scavenge through the family tree of George III's great-grandmother, Sophia. She died in 1714. King George I was her son. So, the next in line after you, Queen Emma, could be anyone – a drunken count from Pomerania, or maybe a wife-beating Greek taxi driver. Whoever it is, it will make a wonderful mess!"

Stanley Wisdom was listening to all this. Dawson noticed his appalled expression. "Mr. Wisdom… Please convey that particle of information back to Her Majesty, with my compliments."

"Victor?"

"Yes, Carl."

"I've just resigned."

"I understand. But may I make a suggestion? You need to start educating yourself."

"About what?"

"Proper conduct for a Royal consort. No more breaking heads."

Emma had had enough. She tugged Juneau's sleeve. "C'mon, Carl!"

They pushed past Dawson. When they reached the door, it suddenly opened. Two men in suits entered. They both nodded carefully to Emma. One of them seemed to recognize Juneau. "Hello, Carl."

"William…" Juneau replied. "You look like you're on a mission."

"We are." He handed Juneau a business card. "Could you give me a ring later? We're going to need a statement."

"Sure."

"Excuse us." The men kept going.

Juneau held the door. Behind them, Emma heard the man named William ask, "Mr. Victor Dawson?"

"Yes," Dawson replied.

"Police officers, sir. My name is Detective Superintendent Mondale. This is Detective Inspector Sykes. We're with Special Branch. I'm sorry, but we'll have to ask you to come with us. We have a warrant for your arrest."

"Arrest? For what?"

"I'm afraid the Americans didn't take too kindly to your interference with their satellite. And we'd also like to speak with you about a certain theft from Her Majesty's archives."

"Show me this warrant!"

"Of course. There you are, sir. That's a copy for you."

After a moment of silence, Dawson erupted. "For God's sake, man! Do you think I don't know what you're doing?"

"What are we doing, sir?"

"You're here on orders from the Palace to disrupt these proceedings! Why else would you be here?"

"We've been advised that these proceedings have ended. Is that information incorrect?"

"No, but–!"

"We've had no contact from the Palace, sir. However, we *have* been contacted by the American FBI, the American NSA, the Commissioner of the Metropolitan Police, the Head of MI-5, and the head of the Royalty Protection Branch. Will you come with us, please?"

Emma and Juneau emerged from the hearing room. The lobby was empty. Every door was guarded by a policeman.

Emma glanced around. "Well, that's a relief. I thought we'd be mobbed by reporters." She looked suspiciously at Juneau.

He smiled.

She leaned into him. "Take me home," she whispered.

"Where's home?"

"Camden."

Juneau raises an eyebrow. "Camden?"

"Maine."

"Oh. Maine."

"The hospital where I was born is just down the road, in Rockland. I think I'd like to work there."

"It's kind of late. And you don't have a valid passport."

"No thanks to you. Okay. I'll settle for the nearest hotel."

"The Palace has a car waiting."

"I don't want to go to the Palace. I've fallen in love with a commoner and I want to run away with him."

"You'll need a disguise, Your Majesty. You know… to pass unnoticed among your loving subjects."

"Sunglasses should do it." Emma dug into her bag.

"It's raining."

"Oh. Well, a hat should work."

"You don't have one."

"What happened to all that legendary resourcefulness of yours? Couldn't you… you know… steal one from a cloakroom?"

"Okay. I'll find you a hat. But it's not going to be enough. You'll need a fake nose." He grinned. "And maybe some padding… back there–" he indicated with his eyes "–to give you a fat ass."

"I'll give you a fat lip! Will you please just shut up and abduct me?" She grabbed him and kissed him.

"One abduction coming up."

"And leave out the Alsik! I want to remember it this time!"

"Agreed."

He eased her toward a nearby door. A policeman touched his hat and opened the door. An empty corridor lay beyond. Without moving his lips, the policeman muttered to Juneau, "The hire car is waiting, sir. Third corridor on the right, door at the end." He winked.

As they set off, Emma gave him a sharp look. "I see you've been reading my mind."

"No. I've been reading mine."

39

The Montague on the Gardens Hotel, at 15 Montague Street in Bloomsbury, occupied a row of Georgian terraced homes on a short street just off Russell Square. It was an unobtrusively deluxe property, complete with a garden-facing conservatory, wooden deck, terrace, several dozen bedrooms, and eleven elegantly decorated private suites. The staff was warm, welcoming and utterly discreet.

In other words, it was ideal.

Emma and Juneau sat knee-to-knee amidst the potted greenery of a small bar overlooking the ornamental gardens. She was still marveling at how smoothly he had spirited her away, unnoticed by even a single alert Londoner, and smuggled her through a service entrance into the Montague's cocoon of tranquility.

They were the only patrons in the bar. It had not escaped Emma's attention that the door leading into the bar from the lobby had been discreetly closed and firmly locked within seconds of their entry. A tall and extremely handsome black waiter with a cultured British accent had just taken their orders. Emma's eyes followed the man as he slipped behind the polished bar to prepare their drinks.

"He recognized me and he didn't bat an eye."

"I had a word with the management," Juneau said.

She shifted her gaze to him. "I guessed. But how can you be sure someone won't tip off the press?"

"The manager is an old friend."

"What kind of an old friend?"

"The ex-Belgian para-commando, trained killer kind. His name is Dirk Janssens."

"What about the staff? Can we trust them?"

"Dirk threatened them."

"I doubt that."

He grinned. "We made a deal. They keep their mouths shut until we've checked out tomorrow. Then they're welcome to brag to the press, and Dirk can put up a brass plaque on the wall outside."

"A plaque?"

"Yeah. You know – 'Queen Emma slept here'."

"You mean: 'Queen Emma slept here with her bodyguard'."

"I'm in the adjoining suite."

Emma's face fell. "Oh."

"You're Royalty now, Emma. The delicacies must be observed."

"How very conventional of you, Carl. We might as well be back in the Palace."

He smiled. "We do have a connecting door."

"That's better." Her eyes twinkled.

"Dirk insisted. For your protection, of course."

"Of course."

"You should have more faith."

Emma's acute hearing picked up hushed voices. She turned. A pretty young dining room waitress was standing in an open doorway behind the bar, whispering to the waiter. She was staring at Emma with undisguised fascination. The waiter shushed her as he arranged their drinks on a serving tray.

"The staff won't be deceived." Emma said. She looked Juneau in the eye. "I mean, about the connecting door…"

"Mum's the word, as they say over here. I have Dirk's solemn promise."

"You men! You love to conspire!"

Juneau smiled. "You seem to be doing most of the conspiring."

"And what do the staff get in return for their silence?"

The waiter appeared at her elbow. He answered for Juneau. "Just your autograph, Mum," he said, as he set her drink in front of her. Emma looked up, startled. The man's dark eyes were dancing with amusement.

"I see." Emma replied slowly. She glanced over at the waitress. The young woman was still peering at her, apparently entranced. "And exactly how many copies will I be providing?"

"Sixty-one. We've arranged for some very nice stationery. It's on the desk in your suite."

"How thoughtful." Emma smiled. "Let me guess… along with the stationery, I will find a complete list of staff members' names."

"Yes, Mum."

"And which name is yours?"

"Rodney, Mum. Rodney Dangerfield."

Emma carefully studied the man's face. His expression was neutral.

"You're not pulling my leg."

"No, Mum. Regrettably, I'm not."

Emma looked at Juneau. He was grinning broadly. "Why does it feel like I'm in some bizarre foreign film?" she asked.

"Because you are." He paused. "We are." He looked at the waiter. "What do you think, Rodney? Have you ever heard of anything quite as bizarre as this?"

"Yes sir. The toe-curling antics of our current Royal Family would fit that description. Some of us believe the accession of Lady Emma, and–" he gave Juneau a significant look "–one would hope, her handsome and mysterious gentleman, would make for a distinct improvement." He made a careful bow to Emma and returned to the bar.

Emma shot a suspicious look at Juneau. "Did you and Rodney rehearse that?"

Juneau shook his head. "No."

Emma was thoughtful. She stroked the light brown skin on the back of Juneau's hand. "I think that little speech was meant to be understood on two levels."

"I suspect it was." Juneau replied evenly.

Emma was already in bed when the connecting door swung inward. Juneau slipped through the opening. The door snicked shut behind him.

He stood next to her bed, chest bare, with a towel around his hips. His arm sling was off and he was wearing a fresh dressing on his wound.

"You're supposed to kneel when you enter the Royal Chamber."

He smiled mischievously. "I will."

Emma nodded at the Sig Sauer pistol sticking out of the towel's improvised waistband.

"Do we really need that fashion accessory?"

"You never know."

"I thought Dirk was handling security."

"He is. He's sitting on a chair outside your door."

"He's... what?"

"He wants to make damned sure that nothing happens to a member of the Royal Family in his hotel."

"Does that mean we have to be quiet."

"Let's see how you do."

"What do you mean, how *I* do?"

He dropped the towel.

Emma sucked in a breath. Then she started to giggle.

"I'm not sure I like being mocked," Juneau observed quietly.

"You're not." Emma pulled back the covers. "Get in here!"

Juneau slipped in beside her. He slid the gun under a pillow.

Emma pressed her suddenly trembling body against Carl Juneau's long, dark form. Their kiss was soft and deep. When it ended, Emma's heart was pounding in her chest. "I think I just lost ten minutes off my life," she breathed.

Juneau swallowed, his throat working. "I think I lost twenty."

"You're already ten years older than me. Maybe we'd better stop."

"Hell, no! A short life and a glorious one…"

Emma rolled on top of him.

"Hey! Careful of my arm."

"I thought you were indestructible," she pouted.

"I am."

"Show me."

The next three hours were unbelievable.

Finally, Juneau flopped back onto his pillow. "I think I've just been Royally screwed," he moaned.

"Yes," Emma said, "and your Sovereign says you deserved it."

40

The entry was a breeze.

An imposing wrought-iron gate guarded the portal entrance into the private gardens of Montague Square. It was located almost in the center of the west side, a few doors south of the hotel. The gate's dozen or so coats of gleaming black enamel, floral accents and curlicues, and filigreed coats-of-arms were doubtless intended to convey dual impressions of aristocratic grandeur and implacable disapproval of idlers and trespassers. A coded electronic lock completed the gate's suite of deterrent features.

But appearances are usually deceiving, and they certainly were in this case.

It took him less than ten seconds to mount the ironwork, swing his legs over the impotently ceremonial pikestaff uprights and drop soundlessly onto the concrete driveway behind the gate.

He made his way into the gardens and worked his way north along a line of two-meter-high mixed shrubs and trees. His light steps on the fine gravel path were but a faint whisper on heavy night air.

He reached the rear of the hotel.

An opening appeared in the shrub line, revealing a narrow, mulch-covered passage. He followed it. It threaded between lilac and laurel bushes and terminated at a small iron gate. Behind it, bathed in the faint glow of a few lighted rooms on the floors above, was the top edge of a retaining wall. Beyond that – below ground level, facing onto a narrow sump between the retaining wall and the rear wall of the hotel – he spotted a row of darkened windows.

Rooms like that aren't rented to guests, he thought. They're used for back-of-house operations.

He tried the gate. It was locked. He climbed over it, flitted across to the top of the retaining wall and dropped down into the sump. He started trying windows. He wasn't surprised to find one that had been left unlatched. He slid it open and climbed through the opening. He found himself in a small shelf-lined pantry. A door led to what he judged to be a staff lunchroom. The next door opened onto a passage covered in threadbare carpet. He crept along the passage to a narrow staircase. From the worn condition of the risers, it was clearly a service stairway.

I couldn't have planned this better, he thought.

Silent as a panther, he made his way up to the ground floor, then mounted the next flight to the first floor.

He cracked the door and deployed one pale eye to scan the corridor. The first thing that attracted his notice was an empty straight-backed chair. It was sitting in the corridor right next to the entrance to a guest suite.

Someone had been stationed in that chair.

Guarding the room? Had to be… But where was he? Gone for a piss?

Or, maybe, something to eat.

He mused on his favorite topic – the abysmal negligence of others – as he scanned the ceiling. No security domes; no bullet camera installations.

No electronic security.

Maybe that was to be expected in a boutique hotel with a single-entrance lobby manned by a desk clerk and a concierge twenty-four hours a day. It also went with the fact that the establishment still handed out metal room keys, instead of one of the new plastic key cards.

It was all quite convenient.

He permitted himself a thin smile.

He remained in place, stilled his breathing and watched the corridor through the two-centimeter gap he had created.

All was silent.

He opened the door carefully and checked the corridor in the other direction. It was clear. He moved swiftly to the door next to the chair. He pressed his ear to it.

He could hear no sounds from within.

He produced a small tool from a pocket. He kneeled. Quickly and expertly, he picked the lock. He rose to his feet and entered the suite. He closed the door quietly behind him.

A short hallway led to a room beyond. From his position, he couldn't tell if it was a sitting room or a bedroom. It appeared to be faintly lit, probably due to outside light leaking around the edges of tightly-drawn drapes.

To his right, a windowless bathroom lay in pitch blackness.

He remained in place, motionless as a statue, listening for breathing.

There was no sound.

He flared his nostrils, testing the air.

His right hand dipped into an inside pocket of his jacket.

His final second of consciousness was marked by two simultaneous sensory events. First, the soft sound of a footfall in the bathroom doorway to his right…

And, next, the blurred image of a thin pale object arcing toward his forehead.

A soft scratching sound woke them. It came from the other side of the connecting door to Juneau's suite.

Emma clutched Juneau's arm.

"Did you hear that?" she whispered.

"It's probably Dirk." Juneau rose from the bed, scooped his towel off the floor and wrapped it around his midriff. He slid the gun out from under his pillow.

"Then why the gun?"

"In case it's not."

"Carl?" Emma's voice shook.

He spoke quietly. "I want you to go to the bathroom, put on one of the bathrobes hanging on the door, and get ready to run."

Emma rolled out of bed and scampered to the bathroom.

Twenty seconds later, Juneau came for her.

"Everything's okay. But you'd better see this." He pulled on the other bathrobe and led her back to the bedroom.

The connecting door now stood ajar. Juneau's suite was ablaze with light. A man stood just inside the adjoining bedroom. He was just above medium height, lean and fit, with chiseled features and thick dark hair that swept back from his forehead in a near-military cut. He was dressed in a crisp white shirt, open at the neck, and perfectly pressed slacks.

Emma immediately noticed two incongruous aspects of the man's appearance.

He was in his stocking feet.

And he was holding a cricket bat.

The man's eyes met Emma's. He looked embarrassed.

"Miss Parks... I mean... I'm sorry... My Lady! I apologize for this unseemly interruption."

He spoke with a faint accent that Emma couldn't quite place.

Juneau intervened. "Emma, this is the old friend I mentioned. Dirk Janssens. He manages the hotel."

"I guessed that. Please, Mr. Janssens... my name is Emma."

The manager sighed, clearly relieved. "Thank you. I'm Dirk." He displayed his hand, palm up. It was stained with what appeared to be blood. "I won't shake your hand."

Emma looked from his hand to the cricket bat. There was blood on the bat as well. Not much, but...

Dirk quickly set the bat aside, leaning it against the wall.

"Is someone hurt?" Emma asked.

Dirk's eyes took on a wintery look. He nodded in the direction of the main entrance to Juneau's suite. "I measured my swing, but he'll probably have a concussion."

He stepped aside so Juneau and Emma could enter. Twenty feet away, a man in a dark business suit lay sprawled on his back in the entrance hallway. Blood oozed from a long horizontal split in the middle of his forehead.

Emma looked at Juneau. "Is it the man who tried to kill me?"

"Take a look."

Cautiously, Emma moved closer. The others followed. She looked down at the unconscious man's face.

"That's not him!"

"I know," Juneau replied.

Emma knelt. She checked the man's pulse, felt his neck for swelling and checked for discoloration behind his ears.

"I need a flashlight."

"My mobile has a penlight," Dirk replied. He switched it on and passed it to Emma. She lifted the man's eyelids, one by one, and checked pupil response.

The man groaned.

"Looks like he's coming around," Dirk ventured.

Emma bent closer. "If you can hear me, sir, I want you to lie perfectly still," she ordered. She looked up at Dirk.

"Did you call an ambulance?"

"No."

"No?"

"I knew you were a doctor. We have a first aid kit at the front desk. Shall I send for it?"

"Not good enough. This man should be treated at a hospital!"

"Dirk and I thought we should discuss that first," Juneau said.

Emma stood up. "What's to discuss?"

"He broke in here, looking for us… or… for you," Juneau replied.

"You said the front desk listed both our rooms as vacant!"

"I think I know what happened," Dirk offered. "I spent half an hour sitting in a chair outside your door. Then I realized that was stupid. I was just telegraphing your room number to anyone who might be tracking you. So I set the chair outside Carl's door, and waited in here. Sure enough, here comes this guy."

Juneau glanced at the cricket bat. "I didn't know Belgians played cricket."

"It's a Flemish game." Dirk grinned. "The English stole it from us."

"So this man was here to kill us?" Emma asked.

Dirk shook his head. "I don't know. He's not armed. But he's not carrying

ID, and his clothes have no labels. The only things he had were a lock pick, and this…" He extracted a small camera from his shirt pocket. "It's one of those new digital designs."

"Maybe he's one of those… paparazzi," Emma ventured.

Juneau took the camera from Dirk and examined it. Comprehension dawned.

"I don't think so."

The man moaned. Emma kneeled down.

"Can you patch him up?" Juneau asked.

"I can suture his forehead, but if there's a subdural hematoma, he could die. He needs a CT scan."

Juneau turned to Dirk. "I guess you'd better ask the desk to call an ambulance. As soon as you've done that, I'll be making a call of my own."

Dirk went for the phone.

"Who are you going to call?" Emma asked Juneau.

"William Mondale. At Special Branch."

41

Emma and Juneau looked around Boswell's shambolic office, clearly surprised by its small size and general atmosphere of disorder.

He noticed their faces. "I have another office at Thames House."

"If you say so," Juneau replied. "I've been meaning to ask... I thought the Royal Family was supposed to be kept isolated from the Security Services."

"That convention changed after the Surveyor of the Queen's Pictures was exposed as a Soviet spy."

"Sir Anthony Blunt?"

Boswell nodded. "The infamous Fourth Man. But we didn't open a satellite office here in the Palace until 1989, when the Service was finally put on a statutory footing."

"And before that?"

"Let us just say we operated for eighty years on the basis that we did not exist." Boswell changed the subject. "You shouldn't have broken security yesterday."

"I left a message for you."

"Yes, but you conveniently forgot to tell me where you were."

"Apparently it was easy enough for someone to discover."

"So I understand. Your Special Branch friend called me."

"And?"

"Your intruder's name is Lothar Beck. He's Ex-DSIS – Danish intelligence. He went private about ten years ago. We've heard about him, but we've never come across him." He looked at Juneau. "Mondale agrees with your theory. It looks as if Dawson hired Beck hoping to acquire some, ah–" he glanced at Emma, obviously discomfited "–compromising pictures."

Emma was unfazed. "But Victor's in custody," she observed coolly.

"Mondale thinks Beck has been following you two since the hearing began. He must have been hired before Dawson's arrest."

" Mondale 'thinks'... or Mondale knows?" Juneau asked.

"Thinks. Beck's not talking. He'll probably plead guilty to burglary, serve his sentence and then make sure Dawson pays handsomely for his trouble." Boswell paused, tapping a pen. "But none of this helps us with our primary problem. Breaking security just makes our job harder. We're still not satisfied that Dr. Parks is safe."

Emma looked at him sharply. "Leggatt's dead, Alan!"

"The assassin who tried to kill you is still at large, and we don't know who hired him."

"So, you're sure the man was a professional," Juneau said.

"We are."

"But you're not sure it was Leggatt who hired him."

"Correct."

Juneau was thoughtful. He turned to Emma. "Do you remember what Leggatt said when he was marching us through that tunnel? It was right after I told you he was planning to pin our murders on the Palace."

Emma was thoughtful.

"He said something about a job being worth doing."

"Yes. Then he said: '*But nobody asks Henry*'. I wondered about it at the time, but then with all the chaos afterwards, it slipped my mind."

"Then who hired the killer?" Emma asked.

A long second passed.

"We're working on it," Boswell answered.

Juneau stared at Boswell. He'd replied to Emma's question a bit too dismissively.

Something wasn't right.

In a flash of movement, Juneau seized Boswell with his good arm and slammed him against the wall. "How about someone in this Palace?" he hissed at the struggling man. "Or, how about... MI-5?"

"Carl!" Emma cried.

"He's playing a double game, Emma!" Juneau's fingers tightened around Boswell's windpipe. The man's eyes bulged.

"Let him go, or you won't find out what the game is."

A second passed, then another. Juneau relaxed his grip. Boswell staggered back to his chair and dropped into it, gulping for breath. Emma strode over. She glared down at him without sympathy.

"Is Carl right, Alan?" she demanded. She bent closer. *"Is he?"*

Boswell seemed to cringe. "We only know who the killer is!" he croaked. "We don't know who's behind it. Give me a second, and I'll explain what we have." He waved vaguely at a pair of beat-up Second Empire chairs near to his desk.

They sat.

Boswell took a few seconds to recover. Then he told them about his communications with the NSA. He opened a drawer and removed prints of the freeze-frame photographs of Darius that the NSA had sent him. He laid the decoded printout of calls to the fax machine in Germany beside them.

"There's no doubt this man is a gun for hire. His professional name is

Darius. We don't know his real name. We don't even know his nationality."

"You mean, like the killer in *Day of the Jackal*?" Emma asked. "I thought that was fiction."

"It is, of course," Boswell replied, "but wittingly or not, it was based on fact. We've come across a few characters like that over the years. They appear, they disappear, they show up somewhere else, and we never identify them. Or we kill them, and we still can't identify them. No prints on file anywhere – at least, anywhere we can access. No photographs. I know of five open files like that, two of them dating from the sixties."

"Any idea where this Darius is now?"

"I had Conyers circulate the footage from the hotel in Jersey City. The Italians spotted him on some CCTV footage at Malpensa airport in Milan. He arrived there three days ago, on a flight from Paris. They're trying to track him."

"You'll need him alive."

"Yes, but it doesn't always work out that way."

"If he's out of the country, that should mean I'm off his menu," Emma suggested. "All the publicity Dawson stirred up must have worked."

"Maybe. But we need to know who hired him," Juneau replied. "Alan's right. You might be safe now, but we don't know for how long." He picked up the fax printout. He studied it. "Why are these marked entries in pairs?"

"The faxes were sent to the machine in Germany, using polled reception."

"What's that?" Emma asked.

"It's a function that allows you to collect a document from someone else's fax machine. The other person doesn't transmit it to you. He just leaves it for collection. You just dial his fax number and enter an agreed code, and his machine sends the document to your machine."

Juneau pointed at an entry on the printout. "This incoming is dated August 31st."

"Yes."

"That's the day Diana was killed."

"That's right."

Juneau passed the page to Boswell. "Look at the time of the call."

Boswell checked it. He gave Juneau a blank look.

"That call was made forty minutes after the official announcement of Diana's death," Juneau said. "What's that symbol next to the number? It looks like a 'W'."

"I don't know."

Juneau was quiet for a moment. "Was it a German-made machine… the one in the dumpster?"

"I think so."

"The German word for 'forwarded' is 'weitergeleitet'."

"You mean it might have been a forwarded call?"

"Yes. Forwarded from where? Didn't your people check?"

"Just a minute." Boswell picked up his phone and called Conyers. He explained what he wanted to know and told her he was waiting for an answer.

Ten minutes later she called back. Boswell made some notes, thanked her and hung up.

"It's a number registered to Victor Dawson. It has the same billing address as the number that was polled by the fax machine – Dawson's residence on Wilton Crescent."

"Show me the number."

Boswell handed over his notes.

"I know that number." Juneau dug into a pocket of his jacket and pulled out a cell phone. "This is Tannahill's mobile." He powered it up and thumbed buttons while he continued. "He had all of Dawson's numbers in his contact list. A few of them I didn't even have, but that's another story... There!" He showed the phone's display to Boswell and Emma. "The connection came from the satellite phone on Dawson's jet. It was forwarded through his home fax number."

"But could you send a fax to a machine, and have the same fax collected from that machine by another one, using polling?" Emma asked.

"A few brands can do that," Boswell replied.

"So, is the machine at Dawson's residence one of them?"

"Maybe we should find out," Juneau said quietly. He recapped what they'd learned. "Dawson had a fax machine on the plane that ran off the sat phone. Less than an hour after the official announcement that Diana had died, someone sent a fax from the plane to Dawson's Wilton Crescent house, and it looks like the machine in Germany retrieved it from there. So, the next question–"

"–is where was Dawson's jet when the call was made?" Emma finished.

Boswell phoned Conyers. He explained what he wanted.

This time it took half an hour.

Boswell set the phone back on its cradle. "LTCC records show Dawson's Falcon inbound from Paris."

"Special Branch arrested Dawson yesterday," Juneau said. "They were investigating the theft of George III's diaries, and I guess the NSA's complaint as well. Did you arrange that?"

"Yes."

"Is he still in custody?"

Boswell nodded.

"Has he made a statement to the investigators?"

"No. He won't answer any questions."

"How long can you hold him?"

"He'll probably be bailed this afternoon."

Juneau went quiet, lost in thought. Finally, he spoke.

"*Assassination in America...*"

Boswell looked blank. "What?"

"It's a book I was reading." He looked at Emma. "Do you remember that book?"

"You had it on the plane."

"It had a whole chapter to the law of treason." He turned back to Boswell. "Does the press know about Dawson's arrest?"

"Not yet. We've kept it quiet."

Juneau gestured at the computer on Boswell's desk. "Can you access British laws and statutes on that thing?"

42

The sixteen floors of the Paddington Green Police Station in central London were housed in a nondescript concrete office block. Before today, Juneau had been only vaguely aware of the building. He'd once been told it was the designated police station in London for lodging high security prisoners.

A uniformed Superintendent drove them to the Station in a small unmarked vehicle, with Boswell sitting beside in the front passenger seat and Juneau cramped in the back, half sprawled with his feet in the opposite foot well. As they swung into Edgware Road, the Superintendent spoke quietly into his radio.

"Disconnect now, please."

The officer made another left into Newcastle Place, a one-way lane that appeared to run the entire length of the rear side of Paddington Green Police Station.

Almost immediately after entering the lane, they edged left into a driveway entrance and came to a stop at an enclosed guard post. Ahead, a raised steel barrier blocked further progress onto a concrete ramp that ran up at a sharp angle to a blue metal gate. Behind the gate was a second guard post.

The Superintendent collected their IDs, stepped out of the car and spoke with the officer in the guard post. After several seconds, he got back behind the wheel. The steel barrier slowly lowered. The Superintendent waited for a traffic control light to change from red to green, and then drove them up the ramp. A siren sounded, and the blue metal gate swung open.

They rolled into a large enclosed yard and parked.

The Superintendent led them to a steel door, pushed a button and waited. A tinny voice conveyed through a small speaker issued a series of commands – "faces and IDs, one by one in front of the camera, gentlemen, please" – followed by a loud buzz as the door's lock disengaged. They passed through into a small foyer and found themselves facing another door. The door behind them swung shut, the lock re-engaged with a thunk and, after a few seconds of delay, the door in front of them buzzed and opened.

They made a brisk passage along a short corridor, through another door, and debouched into a concrete room. Straight ahead, a uniformed female officer sat at a glassed-in guard post, watching an array of CCTV screens. Behind her kiosk was a matte-finished stainless steel door. After more identification formalities, the woman pressed a button, a loud buzzer sounded, and the stainless steel door slid back. The Superintendent escorted Boswell and Juneau into the custody suite. The buzzer sounded again and the door shut behind them.

They were standing at one end of a long corridor. A row of cells lined the left side; the right side consisted of a solid wall with a single door situated about twenty feet from their position.

Directly in front of them, a Custody Sergeant sat behind a 1950s-vintage utilitarian desk. The Superintendent's rank and uniform did not seem to impress him, because he remained seated while he looked each of them up and down. Apparently satisfied that they deserved some show of respect, he rose from his battered chair.

"Sergeant Glynn, sirs… May I assume your attendance relates to our earlier visit from the MI-5 gentleman?"

"Yes," Boswell replied. "Mr. Welles works with me at D Branch." He showed the officer his MI-5 identification.

The Sergeant glanced at Juneau. "And this is the private gentleman who was mentioned?"

"Yes," the Superintendent replied. "Mr. Carl Juneau."

"Thank you. Now, before we proceed, I am obliged to ask certain questions." He faced the Superintendent. "Sir, do you confirm the instruction that there shall be no paper or electronic record of this contact with the prisoner?"

"I confirm that instruction, Sergeant."

"And do you confirm the instruction that, upon your arrival, we were to disconnect all cameras between the vehicle entrance and this corridor?"

"Yes… all except the feed to the satellite room. Was this instruction complied with?"

"It was. Finally, sir, do you confirm that the live feed to the satellite room is not to be recorded?"

"I do, Sergeant."

"Thank you, sir. The prisoner is waiting."

"Mr. Juneau…" The Superintendent escorted Juneau to the single door. "I'll wait here with the Sergeant. Mr. Boswell will observe from the satellite room." He opened the door and stepped away.

The space behind the door was a grim-looking interview room. It was furnished with a small table and two chairs. Juneau stepped in. The Superintendent closed the door behind him. A lock clicked.

Juneau glanced around. The room reminded him of a nineteenth century public toilet. The tiled walls were a bilious shade of institutional green. The unpainted concrete floor was liberally stained with evidence of police interrogations from earlier, less circumscribed times. The only apparent source of fresh air was a tiny vent in one corner of the ceiling.

Victor Dawson sat on the far side of a small table, facing the door. He stared at Juneau with a mixture of surprise and curiosity.

"Not exactly the surroundings you're used to, Victor," Juneau ventured. He pulled back the only other chair in the room and sat.

"I've survived worse," Dawson replied calmly.

"Maybe. But not recently."

"Why are you here, Carl?"

"Just for a talk."

Dawson eyed him suspiciously. "They wouldn't let you in here 'just for a talk'."

Juneau didn't respond.

"How's Emma?" Dawson asked.

"Do you care?"

"Of course. I've become very fond of her."

"The sentiment is not returned."

"Unrequited love is not new to me." Dawson's tragic tone contrasted sharply with the expression in the man's eyes – eyes that appeared to Juneau to be void of an inner life.

How could I have worked for this man?

"Why are you here, Carl?"

"Perhaps to complain about your prurient interests."

"Really? And what might they be?"

"Hiring some nasty little man to take photographs of Emma and me."

Dawson opened his mouth to respond.

"He gave you up," Juneau lied. "Don't waste your breath."

Dawson stared, then shrugged. "It's difficult to find good help these days." He leaned back. His mouth twisted. "But that's not really why you're here, is it?"

"No. I'm here because you have a problem."

"I have many problems. All are solvable."

"Not this one."

"I don't agree. I stole some diaries from a contemptible family of frauds and misfits and had them photocopied. I then used the diaries to prove that Emma is the true heir to the British throne. They wouldn't dare prosecute me for that."

"You're probably right." Juneau smiled at him. "But that's not your problem."

"What is it then?"

"Attempting to have your Sovereign killed."

"I didn't attempt to have anyone killed!"

"Of course you would say that." Juneau paused. "That particular offence carries the death penalty. Did you know that?"

"This country abolished the death penalty years ago."

"Yes, in 1969. It was abolished for every offence except one, Victor – *High Treason*. Anyone who kills, or attempts to kill, or conspires to kill the Sovereign… swings."

"Very interesting. But I didn't try to have Emma killed. So why are we having this conversation?"

"Because I know you're lying. You hired a man named Darius to kill her."

"How could anyone possibly prove that?"

"Quite easily."

Juneau carefully explained the telephone evidence. Dawson's face paled as he listened.

Juneau continued. "I called our friend Houghton at the City Airport Immigration office. He promised to pull the landing cards, but because your plane landed shortly after he heard about Princess Diana's death, he remembered the arrival and who was on board."

Dawson's body stiffened.

"There were only three people on the plane. The pilot, the co-pilot, and you."

Dawson's lips were a thin line. He said nothing.

Juneau smiled. "Sounds to me like you've boxed yourself in."

Seconds passed.

"It was all staged," Dawson finally replied. "I never intended to harm her."

"You might sell that story if the only attack on her was the one in New Jersey, but not after I describe what happened in Belgravia. You opened the gap in those curtains and then you stood back. The sighting laser was locked right on Emma's center of mass. The bullet that hit me was intended to take her out."

"Nobody could possibly believe I wanted Emma dead! She was more use to me alive! I just wanted her frightened, so she'd cooperate!"

"What about Tannahill?"

"For God's sake, Carl! I had nothing to do with his death! I needed him!"

"You really should stop lying, Victor."

"I'm not lying!"

"The night before we flew to the States, you sent a fax from your personal machine at the office to the Reardon Hotel in Jersey City. That's where Tannahill was killed."

"He was staying there! I sent him some final instructions for the meeting with Emma."

"No you didn't. Your message was for a guest named Woodruff, a.k.a. Darius – real name unknown. He used a fake Australian passport to book into the hotel the same morning Tannahill was killed, and he left the same day. His room bed was never slept in."

Dawson's expression hardened. He said nothing.

"Even if the prosecution accepted that you didn't want Emma injured, they will argue that you wanted to drive the point home by having your reporter killed. What a great way to convince her that the Royal Family would stop at nothing!" Juneau paused. "Or was it something else? Was there some other reason that made you decide to have Ken eliminated?"

Juneau watched Dawson's face.

"Blackmail," Dawson replied stonily. "Tannahill found out I'd hired Darius. He kept upping his price."

Juneau shook his head. He felt suddenly weary of this squalid little man. It was time to end this.

"Okay, let me spell it out for you. If you're right that Emma is the true Sovereign, and if the jury believes you were only trying to frighten her, then the best you can hope for is life imprisonment for criminal endangerment of a member of the Royal Family. But you'd better get in a quick guilty plea for conspiring to murder Tannahill."

"Why?"

"Because you could be facing extradition to the States, and New Jersey has the death penalty." Juneau let that sink in, then he added, "But it's more likely you won't be believed, so you'll get to stay here and hang."

Dawson took a moment to digest Juneau's words. Then he shrugged with obviously feigned bravado.

"It would never happen!"

"It would, and it will. The death sentence for High Treason isn't discretionary. It's automatic." He paused for effect. "And the gallows at Wandsworth Prison are still there, waiting just for you. I checked."

Dawson looked unwell. "You seem to be taking a lot of personal interest in all this!" he snapped.

"I am. And it gets better," Juneau added.

"What do you mean?"

"Only the Sovereign can commute a death sentence."

It took Dawson a second before the point sunk in. "You mean, if I was convicted, only Emma could stop me from being hanged?"

"That's right." Juneau's expression hardened. "The only person who can save your miserable life is the woman you tried to have killed. Twice."

Dawson blanched.

Juneau was starting to enjoy himself. "And then… there's this other thing."

"What other thing?" Dawson's voice squeaked.

"If you're convicted, all your property – and I mean all your personal property, and all your companies, and all your real estate – is automatically forfeited to the Crown. So you can forget about running your empire from behind bars."

"What the hell do you mean? This isn't the Middle Ages!"

"No. But the law of High Treason has remained intact since the Middle Ages, and all those ancient provisions still apply."

"How do you know all this?"

Juneau smiled. "I read."

"It can't be right!"

"It is. This is what we Yanks call a 'lose-lose', Victor. Even if you're wrong about Emma being the true heir to the throne, the chances are pretty good you'll still get life for attempted murder. But then your real problem will be a trial in New Jersey for Tannahill's murder." He paused. "On the other hand, if you're right about Emma – and all that evidence you dredged up sure supports you on this – then you'll hang and all your property will be forfeited to the Crown and Emma will become the world's next billionaire." Juneau smiled broadly. "Sounds like justice to me."

Dawson now looked genuinely afraid. He leaned forward.

"Who sent you in here?"

"No one. I asked to come."

"Why?"

"To help you make a deal. No prosecution for High Treason, and no extradition to America."

"What possible influence could you have?"

"With the British Government? None."

Dawson slapped a hand on the table. He sat back and crossed his arms.

"But… quite a lot with Queen Emma," Juneau added.

Juneau emerged from the interview room. The Superintendent escorted him to Boswell.

Juneau tore a piece of paper from a small note pad and handed it to Boswell. "The killer's new fax number. He had it memorized."

"I saw that." Boswell looked at the note. "Thirty-nine… that's the country code for Italy."

"What's the zero?"

"Italy still uses "0" for a trunk code. But these two numbers here are a city code."

"What city?"

43

Night.

The jet's fuselage was a featureless gray. It bore no markings, not even a registration number. The aircraft sat on the apron, boarding steps down, offside turbine spooling.

A brace of identical SUV's pulled up near the stairway. The lead vehicle's front passenger door swung open, and Boswell stepped onto the tarmac. He wore an open-necked shirt, sports jacket and faded slacks. He moved to the rear of the vehicle. The back hatch swung up. He pulled out two identical bags.

Three men dressed in casual clothes emerged from the second SUV. One lifted his vehicle's rear hatch.

A rear passenger door of the lead vehicle opened, and Carl Juneau stepped out. His injured arm was still in a sling.

Emma followed him out. She was holding a satchel.

Juneau turned, looking at her.

"What are you doing?"

"I'm coming."

Juneau's lips tightened. He placed his good hand on her shoulder.

"Careful with the merchandise," she warned. "I'm Royalty, remember?"

"You're Emma to me! And we're going after the man who tried to kill you!"

"That's why I'm coming! I'm tired of being a bystander in my own life."

"For God's sake, Emma, this man's extremely dangerous, and you could still be his target!"

"I'm getting pretty used to living dangerously – thanks to you."

"You can't come! You don't have a valid passport. The Italians will–!"

Emma held up a U.S. passport. "Our ambassador couldn't have been more helpful. He kept bowing to me. At one point, I thought he was going to kneel."

Juneau stared into Emma's eyes. She stared back, unblinking. He turned to Boswell, who was watching their exchange with ill-concealed amusement.

"Alan?"

Boswell's eyes twinkled. "You're asking me to order a member of the Royal Family to stay put?"

"Yes!"

"How can I?"

"You're MI-5! Put her on an Immigration hold!"

"The Home Secretary would never agree."

Juneau cursed. He turned back to Emma. "Dammit, girl! After everything that's happened, wouldn't it behoove you to play it safe? Just this once!"

"*Me* play it safe? Who dragged me into this exciting life? I don't remember kidnapping myself!" She paused. " 'Behoove'? Do you actually *think* in words like that?"

Juneau's cheeks puffed with exasperation. He turned on his heel and strode toward the plane. Emma hurried to catch up.

"I'll stay in the background," she offered, placating. "Besides. You might need a doctor."

"Why?"

"You said it yourself... the man's dangerous. Someone could get hurt."

"I can deal with that! It's what I do!"

"Maybe... but not with one arm in a sling."

It was 2:00 a.m. when they landed. A water taxi was waiting at a cordoned-off jetty behind Marco Polo Airport. The craft's throaty exhaust rumbled and burbled in the swells. Emma, Juneau, Boswell and the MI-5 snatch team boarded, ducked into the low cabin and took their seats.

The taxi's operator was swarthy and silent. He cast off lines. He idled the boat clear of its berth, swung the bow and buried the throttle. The engine opened up with a shudder and then a roar, and the acceleration threw Emma against Juneau's shoulder. He wrapped a protective arm around her.

A sign on a piling admonished: *"Max 7 Kts"*. They blew past it at four times that speed and thundered off into the channel.

They could see the lights of Venice on the horizon.

"Ever been to Venice?" Juneau asked.

"No," Emma replied. "I've heard it's amazing."

"It's hauntingly beautiful. It speaks to you." He brushed a wisp of hair away from her eyes. "I'm sorry."

"Why?"

"Because you're probably not going to see much of it."

The water taxi delivered them to Campo San Stae, in front of a church that faced the Grand Canal. Boswell went forward to speak with the operator, then ducked back into the cabin. He gestured at a narrow canal that ran inland along one side of the church.

"He says the tide's too high to take us up to the hotel's water door. The taxi won't fit under the first bridge. We'll have to walk."

Emma, Juneau and Boswell stepped ashore onto the Campo and waited for the team to unload their gear. Emma tilted her head back to gaze up at the church's theatrically baroque façade, dotted with statues of angels and cardinal virtues.

"Chiesa di San Stae," Boswell told her. "The Church of San Stae. Founded in the tenth century, but torn down in 1678 and rebuilt by the architect Giovanni Grassi. The original church faced west, but it was realigned so it would face the Grand Canal."

Emma smiled. "You're full of surprises, Alan. Were you studying history before the spies recruited you?"

"No, M'Lady." He tugged a small book out of his trouser pocket and held it up. "Just the Michelin guide on the flight over."

The unloading complete, Boswell led the group along Salizada San Stae, a wide pathway that arrowed inland from the east side of the church. They reached a narrow alleyway to the left – a passageway between buildings that was no more than a meter in width. Boswell switched on a penlight and pointed the beam at a small brass plate mounted high on the wall above the passageway's entrance.

Hotel Al Ponte Mocenigo

"Welcome to Snatch Central," he announced.

He led them along the slot between the buildings to a weathered wooden door. He pressed a small brass button on the wall. After a second, a lock clicked and they entered a small tiled foyer. An impeccably-dressed man with Asian facial features stood waiting. He nodded to Boswell, muttered a quiet "Buonanotte", handed over a packet of small envelopes, turned away and disappeared.

"These are your room keys," Boswell told them. He began passing out individual envelopes to the team members. "This inn was once a small part of a Venetian palace. It has ten rooms. I arranged through our Consulate to rent the entire property for five days. Room 9 is the largest, so we'll use that one for meetings." As the others tramped up the stairs, hauling their gear, he handed a single envelope to Emma. "Room 10 is the second largest room, but it's in the most secure location. I can put Mr. Juneau in the room next to you, M'Lady, or…"

"One room will do," Emma replied.

Boswell's eyes twinkled. "I thought it might."

The snatch team might have been exhausted, but they weren't there to sleep. At least, not yet. They quickly switched clothes and left to start the surveillance.

Juneau and Emma found their room. It smelled of ginger. It was richly decorated in red, and had a marble floor.

"The perfect boudoir for a scarlet woman," Emma observed.

"Oh, so you're the Red Queen? And here I was... thinking you were Alice!"

"Maybe I am." She touched his cheek. "And maybe you're not real. Maybe I stepped through the looking glass and this is all some weird dream."

"No dream," he said. He kissed her. His hands moved over her body. Her knees sagged. He caught her and helped her to the bed. "You're exhausted."

She sighed, nodded. "Can we adjourn the festivities..."

"Sure."

Juneau helped her out of her clothes and into bed. He started to undress. Emma was fast asleep before he finished.

He slipped into bed and wrapped her in his arms.

It was early afternoon when Emma awoke, but even at that hour, the room was dark. Juneau's side of the bed was empty and he wasn't in the bathroom. She got up and went to a window. She drew back the heavy drapes. Ornate ironwork barred the opening, and she found herself looking at the featureless limestone wall of a neighboring building three feet from where she stood.

She craned to look up, and was rewarded by the sight of a narrow strip of blue sky.

Emma bent her head to look down. All she could see was blank wall, and a bit of the paved bottom of the passageway in each direction.

Then she noticed movement.

From somewhere high on the opposite wall, a basket appeared, suspended from a thin rope. Sitting in the basket was a small dog. Emma watched, fascinated, as the basket descended to the floor of the passage.

The dog stepped out, trotted several feet down the passage, cocked his leg and peed against the wall, trotted back and stepped back into the basket.

The basket slowly rose until it, and its canine passenger, disappeared from view.

Emma laughed out loud.

Behind her, a lock snicked and the door opened. Juneau entered. He was wearing a thick bathrobe and carrying a tray laden with coffee and croissants.

"Not exactly a room with a view, is it?" Juneau said as he set the tray on a table in front of a small sofa.

"Maybe not, but you wouldn't believe what I just saw."

"Oh? What was that?"

Emma chuckled. "Tell you later... I hope that's not breakfast! I was hoping to try one of those famous sidewalk cafes on the Grand Canal."

"Can't happen."

"Why?"

"The last thing Boswell wants is some paparazzi reptile spotting us and our photo – especially *your* photo – showing up on the cover of some tabloid. Uncomfortable for us, and dangerous for the operation. He just laid down the law to me: we're are not allowed out of this hotel during daylight."

Emma thought about that. She grinned. "I guess we'll just have to make the best of it."

She launched herself at him.

"My arm! My arm!"

"Don't be a wimp!" She kissed him.

"How about some coffee first?"

"That doesn't sound like you. Last night you were ready to jump my–!"

"They found him," he said quietly.

Emma stared. "Darius?"

Juneau nodded.

Emma dropped onto the sofa. "How? We just got here!"

Juneau sat beside her. "Before we left London, Boswell's people hacked into the Italian phone system." He filled their coffee cups. "They set up on that cell number Dawson gave us. They couldn't intercept calls, but they had no problem tracking usage. They told Alan that almost every call came from the area around Piazzle Roma, where the buses and taxis come over from the mainland. Early this morning, two of the team members got lucky. They spotted Darius eating breakfast at one of those little outdoor bars next to a canal called Rio Novo. They tailed him to an alley that dead ends in a small courtyard not far from there."

"What's next?"

"They're still working out what apartment he's using, but they're hoping to grab him tonight. The plane will take him straight back to England."

"What do we do?"

"Watch from the sidelines."

"Do the Italian police know?"

"No."

"So, they're basically kidnapping him."

"Yes. But they don't call it kidnapping. They dress it up with legal-sounding words, like 'rendition'."

"When you snatched me, was that rendition?

"No. That was straight kidnapping." He looked at her ruefully. "And, boy, am I paying for that mistake!"

"Yes, and I'm going to make sure you keep on paying," Emma declared solemnly. She slid her hand between his legs.

They kissed.

The coffee and croissants were soon forgotten.

It should have been quick, and it should have been flawless.

But this was Darius. The man was a killer, and the killer had a sixth sense.

His bolthole was a second floor flat in a small building at the back end of an alleyway behind Campiello Basego. The flat backed on to a narrow canal, barely fifteen feet in width, crossed at intervals by short, arched bridges. The location had advantages, but they cut both ways – for the snatch team and also for their prey – because Piazzle Roma was virtually the only place in Venice that had vehicle access.

Because of the location, Boswell had elected to use an ambulance to transport Darius to the airport. How he had arranged for a completely fitted-out Ambulanza to be put at their disposal without the knowledge of the Italian authorities, Emma never knew.

The plan was supposed to be simple: grab the target, inject him with a knockout tranquillizer, load him onto a gurney, and – dressed as EMT's – roll him across a bridge to the ambulance.

"Now do you see why you needed me?" Emma said when they met in Room 9 on the night of the snatch. "What are you using?"

"Definitely not Alsik," Juneau said.

"Why not? It worked on me!"

Juneau looked embarrassed. "Can we not go there, Emma?"

Boswell intervened. "Ketamine."

Emma's brow knitted. She turned to Juneau. "How much does he weigh?"

"I'd say one-ninety, maybe two hundred."

"Show me what you've got."

Boswell handed her a small bottle. Emma studied the label, then looked at Boswell. "This is a veterinary prep. Can't you do better than this?"

"It's worked well in the past."

A team member piped in. "It sells on the black market. The street people call it 'Special K'. It's easy for us to get."

"You're MI-5! Why are you buying street drugs?"

"We don't normally," Boswell answered. "This operation is, let us say… off the books."

"How can it be 'off the books'? We flew here on a government jet. We landed at a major airport. We entered the country on our own passports." Emma saw the expression on Boswell's face. "Didn't we? You collected all our passports before we…" She looked at him suspiciously. "*You* dealt with Immigration!"

"Your real passport is in safekeeping on the plane," Boswell said quietly.

"Okay. So… What? MI-5 has gone back to pretending it doesn't exist?"

"Sometimes we have to."

"And therefore none of your usual lab rats have clearance for this little mission. Is that it?"

"Correct." He smiled. "But we do have you, M'Lady."

Amused realization dawned on Emma's face. "All that coyness at the airport in London… you wanted me to come all along, didn't you, Alan?"

"I should have choked you when I had the chance," Juneau growled.

For a fleeting second, Boswell looked afraid.

Juneau grinned

General laughter eased the tension.

"Give me the syringe and marker pen," Emma ordered.

A team member handed her both. Emma rechecked the ketamine label and then made a mark on the barrel of the syringe. "Fill it to there," she said simply, and handed them back.

"And, administration…?" Boswell asked.

"Will I be there?"

"No, M'Lady. We mustn't risk it."

Emma was thoughtful. "He'll be fighting it, and you. If you inject it in a big muscle, which is likely, be ready to hold him down for at least two minutes until the drug hits."

"We've seen that before."

"What about the neck?" one team member asked. He tapped his own throat, near his jugular.

"It's faster, but you'd have to give him less. Unless you know what you're doing, you could kill him."

"No loss." The man laughed.

Emma felt her bile rise.

"What's your name?"

Her tone wiped the grin off his face. "Uh… James… James Keeler."

Emma leaned closer. "James Keeler… what?"

He flushed. "Uh… James Keeler, My Lady."

"Listen to me, James Keeler. I'm the one he tried to kill! I'm not here for revenge and neither are you! Your job is to take him alive. The courts will do the rest."

No one said a word.

Two hours later, Juneau and Emma parked the ambulance at the south end of the bus ranks, flipped on the emergency lights, and waited.

They didn't have to wait long.

On his trip out for groceries, he'd spotted the surveillance.

Venice had its share of old beggar women. They hunched in skeletal heaps near the bridges and pathways most frequented by tourists, heads and bodies wrapped in ragged cotton, shaking paper cups, waiting and praying for the loving kindness of strangers.

This beggar's choice of location was his first clue. It was off the main foot traffic routes. He'd never seen one here.

But the hands were the giveaway. Only the beggar's fingertips were showing, but even from ten feet away, he spotted the short neatly-trimmed nails. To get a closer look, he fished a coin out of his pocket. He bent as he passed and dropped it in the cup.

The response, a rasping *Grazie*, was enough.

Not the quavering voice of an antique female skeleton.

Instead, a male voice, poorly disguised.

Fucking amateurs, he thought.

He wondered who their target was.

He strode quickly through the sinewy streets of Dorsoduro. In the final alleyway leading to the pocket-sized Corte outside his flat, he identified another watcher. The man was sweeping up bits of rubbish that had collected at the base of the red brick walls that lined the passage. But he wasn't wearing the usual colors of a Comune di Venezia worker, and there was no collection bag in sight. He was just moving the trash around.

As he turned into the Corte he encountered a third man, strolling out. This one was dressed like a tourist, in jeans and a printed shirt, with a camera dangling from his wrist.

The fool looked right at him… and blinked.

Then he knew.

I'm the target.

Each building in his Corte was stuccoed in a different color. He strolled to the yellow building at the far end on the right and pretended to use his key. He made a deliberate half-turn to glance at the observer, forcing the man to look away and continue his charade of leaving the Corte. As soon as the man was out of sight, he ducked across the corner and quickly entered the red building on the end.

He climbed the steps halfway to the next floor, and then quietly set his groceries on the landing. His hand slipped into his coat pocket. He pulled out a pistol, screwed on a silencer, and crept the rest of the way to the top floor.

The short corridor was empty.

He checked for the tiny scrap of paper he had left wedged between the bottom edge of the hinged side of the door and the jamb. It was still in place.

Just to be certain, he quietly unlocked the door, slipped through the opening and searched every room.

He went back to the landing and fetched his groceries. Then he retrieved a set of Bushnell 12x25 compact binoculars from a knapsack and mounted the circular staircase to his attic bedroom. There, standing well back from the room's roof-dormer window, he scanned every window in the adjoining five buildings.

He already knew the names, occupations and daily schedule of each of his neighbors. Every window was as it should be – every embroidered curtain undisturbed, every ornament in place.

Which meant his watchers were headquartered somewhere else.

They'll know they can't maintain ground level surveillance for long without being spotted, he thought. They may even suspect I've already made them.

Which means they're coming tonight.

The sound of a door latch echoed from below. Peering down, he watched one of his neighbors leave the Corte. Otherwise, everything was as before.

The square itself was a dead end. The only rear exit, if it could be called that, was a passage between his building and the next one to the west. The opening was less than a meter wide, narrowing further in to half a meter, and it led to the edge of the canal behind the buildings.

He knew they would station someone there.

He descended the stairs from the bedroom and moved to the sitting room at the back. It overlooked the canal. The building opposite presented a blank wall, devoid of windows.

He checked the canal below.

There was a gondola moored a hundred feet or so to his right, next to a tiny footbridge. The boat's scarlet carpeting, plush seating and ornately carved fittings marked it as one of the up-market vessels intended for the tourist trade. The gondolier sat on the seats normally occupied by passengers, picking his teeth. He appeared to be in his thirties. His dark hair was cut short, and he was dressed in the striped jersey and dark trousers traditional to his calling.

On any day in Venice, on almost any canal, a gondolier lounging on his boat would not have attracted a second look. But in dozens of visits to this apartment over the past four years, Darius had never seen a gondola moored at that spot. The footbridge led directly into a cul-de-sac and was frequented almost exclusively by local residents.

It was a dull, overcast day, but this gondolier was wearing sunglasses.

Darius stepped away from the window.

There are four of them, he thought, and probably one or two others directing the operation from a secure location.

He began to make his preparations.

The skies had cleared. The moon was in its last quarter, providing just enough light.

He secured his firearm under his coat. He re-checked the contents of his small backpack and then put it on. He stood near the bedroom window and scanned the square below.

Empty.

He was about to turn away when his peripheral vision caught movement.

A faint shadow rippled on the ground near the entrance from the alleyway.

Someone was standing there, just out of sight.

He descended and went to the kitchen. Earlier, he had disabled the electronic spark igniters in both of the top burners and in the oven. First, he opened the oven door. Then he switched on each of the three elements. Gas hissed, and the pungent stink of thiophane odorant assailed his nostrils. He set the detonator's timer for ten minutes, and quickly left the flat. He locked the door behind him.

He checked the main staircase. No movement. He drifted silently down. He checked the entrance hallway.

Clear.

He reversed course along the main floor hallway to the door leading into a rear apartment. Quickly, he picked the lock and entered. He didn't attempt to hide his presence – he knew the young single woman who lived there worked straight night shifts. He crossed to a rear window, unlocked it, and slid it silently upward.

Outside, below the window, a narrow concrete extrusion ran along the edge of the canal. It created a ledge about fifteen inches wide.

He scanned carefully to the left. Forty feet away, the ledge ended. The adjacent building's wall was sheer, plunging straight into the canal.

Unless he wanted to swim, there was no escape in that direction.

He shifted his gaze to the right.

The gondola was still in place, but the gondolier was gone.

Darius already knew where the gondolier was. Just after dark, he had watched the man slip along the ledge and disappear into the narrow passageway next to his building. He was probably positioned there right now, hovering just out of sight, ready to close off their prey's only perceived rear escape route.

Darius selected a small china ornament from a table near the window and slipped it into his coat pocket. Then he climbed out the window.

He moved silently along the ledge.

He stopped just short of the passageway entrance.

He removed the ornament from his pocket and tossed it into the canal. The surrounding walls magnified the sound of the splash.

A second passed. Another.

Then… a footstep. A shoe rattled a stone.

The gondolier appeared.

In one movement, Darius seized a handful of striped jersey with his right hand, punched the man with a hard left in the face, and threw him headlong into the canal.

Without a backward look, he dashed along the ledge to the bridge, checked that the way was clear, and then sprinted for Fondamenta del Gaffaro, the nearest main thoroughfare. When he reached it, he slowed to a walk and joined the moving throng of locals and tourists heading for the bus and taxi stands of Piazzle Roma.

It took him five minutes to reach Tre Ponti, the wood and stone bridge complex a few hundred feet from the south end of the Piazzle. As he crossed a final bridge over the Burchiele Canal, he first felt, and then heard, the explosion. He turned in time to see a brilliant tongue of flame erupt skyward from the tight nest of buildings near the far end of Rio Novo. Seconds later, a roiling column of smoke joined the flames.

Darius permitted himself a faint smile. He turned and threaded his way down the steps to the promenade next to the Risparmio Bank, unnoticed by the dozens of shocked pedestrians who were rooted in place, gazing in disbelief at the spectacle. To his right, a handful of gondoliers were standing on their moored boats and on the promenade, gawking at the column of smoke. To his left, a wide pathway, lined on one side with kiosks selling tee shirts, masks and assorted tourist bric-a-brac led straight into the Piazzle, where buses and taxis moved about restlessly. On the opposite side of the path was a small, leafy park.

He mounted a low wall, entered the park and took up a position in the shadow of its largest tree. He scanned the Piazzle, alert for any thing – or any person – that seemed out of place.

His eyes were drawn to a waiting ambulance, its emergency lights flashing.

He considered his position. A fully-lit ambulance would deter scrutiny and easily clear his way across the causeway to the mainland. He loitered under the tree while he studied the scene. There was a tall man standing near the driver's door. He had his back to Darius. The man's substantial frame was bathed in the ambulance's blue strobes. Darius's sharp eyesight focused on the reflection of the man's image in the vehicle's oversized side view mirror.

The man had one arm in a sling.

The man was speaking on a cell phone. As he finished his conversation and slipped the phone into a pocket, he bent toward the side mirror. He rubbed at one eye, as if he had something in it. Then he straightened and half-turned, showing his profile.

Darius recognized him immediately.

Dawson's security man...

The sling was puzzling. That botched shot through Dawson's salon window must have done some damage. Darius had noticed blood on the man's shirt while he was tailing him during their foot chase in London.

Suddenly it all made sense.

That ambulance is for me.

How did he find me?

Darius hesitated. He had a clear choice. Disappear now, and wait for this bastard to track him down again, or… kill him now to end the pursuit.

And take the ambulance.

He decided against using his gun. Even with a sound suppressor, there were too many people around. This called for close work.

He knew his opponent was fast on his feet. But right now he only has one working arm.

A gaggle of tourists walked past on the pathway, heading for the bus ranks. He left the park and tagged along behind them as he moved in on his quarry.

Fifteen feet…

The tourists straggled past the man.

Darius felt in his coat pocket.

Ten feet…

A lethal looking hooked knife glinted in Darius's right hand.

Three feet…

Darius raised his free hand, ready to grab the collar of the man's jacket Ready to yank him backward and slit his throat.

A single smooth movement was all that was required – he had executed it flawlessly many times before.

His fingers reached for the man's collar...

He barely felt it.

A sting on the back his neck.

A wasp?

His target swam before his eyes. He watched as the big man turned and looked at him. Not with surprise. Not with fear.

Just with... curiosity.

The man was holding a pistol. In slow motion, Darius saw him tuck the gun into his sling and reach for him with his good arm.

The man was strong. He lowered Darius carefully to the ground.

The man spoke.

His words seemed to spool out with infinite slowness.

"You cut that pretty fine, my love."

My love?

From somewhere nearby, a female voice: "Sorry. We didn't have much time to rehearse."

Another face loomed above him. A middle-aged man with a neat beard.

"Quick thinking, Alan," the security man said.

"Thank Keeler. He spotted him on the last bridge."

"How's your man?"

"A broken nose, and he coughed up a few pints of canal sewage. He'll live." Boswell stared down at Darius. "What about the dose?"

Now a third face appeared in Darius's rapidly narrowing field of view.

A young woman wearing a physician's lab coat.

She was holding a syringe.

Her!

As the woman knelt beside him, Darius heard the rattle of a gurney being wheeled closer.

He felt gentle hands check for his vital signs. Then a pair of kindly eyes looked directly into his. "I'd say he got just enough."

God, she's beautiful...

This last thing Darius saw until he woke up in a British prison van was Emma's lovely face, bathed in pulsing blue light.

44

Jan and Rita sat at the bar, nursing drinks. Jan's hand trembled as she butted a cigarette.

Twenty feet away, a sound-muted TV was tuned to local news.

"You haven't heard anything?" Jan tried not to sound anxious, but she didn't succeed.

"Nothing since she called from the hotel."

"Where the hell's she gotten to?"

"The press found out where she'd been staying. All she said was that they were hounding her, but she and her friend had a plan."

The bartender's voice interrupted them. "Hey, guys! Look!"

Lou was standing rooted in one spot, holding a half-poured drink, gaping at the TV.

Emma's face was on the screen.

"Omigod!" Rita shouted. "Sound, Lou! Sound!"

Lou set down the glass and grabbed the remote.

"–were amazed today when Queen Elizabeth's private aircraft landed at Newark's Liberty International Airport. On board was Bayonne physician Emma Parks, seen here disembarking from the Royal jet. Dr. Parks is the central figure in a constitutional crisis that has shaken the British establishment to its foundations. Dr. Parks declined interviews and left the airport in a private vehicle…

"In related news, media mogul Victor Dawson, the man who first revealed Dr. Parks' amazing family history to the world, has been formally charged with conspiring to have Dr. Parks murdered. There are unconfirmed reports that the would-be assassin, who was allegedly hired by Mr. Dawson, is in police custody in London and is cooperating with the prosecuting authorities. Ironically, many commentators are questioning why Dawson has not been charged with High Treason, for attempting to take the life of the Sovereign. Brian Pelham, the UK's Attorney General, responded by stating that such a course would be, quote, 'highly irresponsible and fraught with much uncertainty'."

As Jan and Rita gaped at the television screen, the doors behind them hissed open. Lou turned. His jaw sagged as Emma materialized behind her friends. A smiling Carl Juneau stood next to her, his arm still in a sling.

Squealing with joy, Jan and Rita smothered Emma in hugs. Lou muted the TV.

"I want you guys to meet someone special." She tugged Juneau into their midst. "This is Carl. The man who saved my life."

Juneau's good arm encircled Emma and held her tightly against him. "And this is Queen Emma," he said quietly, "the Lady who saved mine."

Juneau was immediately yanked into a melee of tearful hugging.

At exactly 4:00 p.m. on Saturday, December 6, 1997, three months to the day after Princess Diana's funeral had brought London and much of the world to a standstill, three sleek black vehicles turned into Downing Street.

The vehicles' eminent passengers were expected. Uniformed police officers hurried to open doors.

Eight white-haired men in dark suits and one elderly woman with badly dyed hair stepped out into a light rain. Officers opened umbrellas and held them above the heads of the visitors as they escorted them to the door of Number 10.

The door opened, and one by one they entered.

Ten minutes later, the Prime Minister stepped into the Cabinet Room. An aide pulled the door shut behind him, remaining outside. The Prime Minister's eyes swept along the row of silent, grim-faced figures who were seated along one side of the long boat-shaped Cabinet table. The elderly woman sat in the center position, directly opposite the Prime Minister's usual seat.

"Good afternoon." the Prime Minister said.

"Good afternoon, sir," came the nine replies.

No one rose to his feet.

The Prime Minister walked slowly to his chair in front of the marble fireplace. He sat. An inch thick binder with a red leather cover sat waiting on his blotter. His fingertips touched it warily, but he made no move to open it.

He looked directly at the woman.

"Baroness Brindle…"

"Sir."

"You are here to tell me…?"

"That we have a problem, Prime Minister. A very big problem."

**Camden, Maine
August 2001**

45

Atlantic swells washed a wide granite shelf that ramped up out of the depths. Emma sat in brilliant sunshine, watching sea birds wheel above the billows.

She was wearing a wedding band.

Nearby, a little boy played happily, singing to himself.

Behind them, Carl Juneau stepped out of a tidy bungalow. A police detective's shield hung from his belt. The little boy squealed and ran toward him. He scooped him up and swung him aloft. He carried the boy to Emma. He sat down beside her. He kissed her.

"You can't delay that forever, you know," Emma said. She nodded at the old red spruce at one corner of the property, where its gnarled trunk anchored one end of escarpment fencing. Heavy brooms of mistletoe infested every major bough, lending an alien quality to the tree's silhouette against the sky.

Juneau sighed. "I know. I'm going to call the tree guys. I just hate the idea of taking that old girl down."

"You once took this old girl down," Emma shot back, smiling.

Juneau laughed. He handed her an envelope. "The courier was on the porch when I drove up."

Emma heaved a sigh. She looked at the envelope. The return address was 10 Downing Street.

She looked at the addressee on the envelope.

H.R.H Dr. Emma A. Parks...

It had been three years, but the title still unsettled her. Juneau watched her run a fingertip over her name.

"Guess they don't know how else to address you."

"At least it's not 'Your Majesty'."

"No, but I bet it still sticks in some people's craws."

"It does. Jan called today. She'd just picked up a British paper. There was another story about me. The headline was 'Dawson's Pretender'."

"'Young Pretender' would have a nicer ring."

Emma's celebrity status had caused some problems. The worst of it – especially during that first year when Victor Dawson's criminal trials in the Old Bailey had required Emma and Carl to travel back and forth across the Atlantic to testify – was the myriad of pushy photographers, drooling tabloid reporters, and snarky bloggers who had turned scurrilous lies into a cottage industry. Added to that was the wave of autograph seekers who stopped her in the street, bothered her in restaurants, and at times even followed her into ladies restrooms. Fortunately that tide of annoyance had begun to ebb, at least locally. The townsfolk in Camden and Rockland had begun to close ranks and refuse to answer outsiders' questions about Emma. If the questioning seemed too persistent, Emma would receive a warning call at the hospital or at home, or someone would leave a message and a vehicle description at the State Police office. One of Carl's fellow officers would take it from there.

But that was only part of it. People Emma barely knew would invite her to house parties or gatherings. Politicians would drop in at the hospital, angling for a photo op. "Patients" with no discernible medical condition would appear in the ER waiting room, hoping for a glimpse of her. One woman had mutilated herself with a kitchen knife, on the chance that Emma would be the on-call assigned to sew her up. She was. The woman promptly fainted. Emma still wasn't sure if it was from loss of blood or a reaction to meeting "Queen Emma" in person.

But perhaps the most sublime – or ridiculous – exemplar of Emma's wondrous new status was her apparent effect on local property values. One beaming realtor claimed he'd received several confidential inquiries from people he mysteriously referred to as "Hollywood types", who were showing a sudden interest in owning a second – or third, or fourth – home in the Camden-Rockland area. This phenomenon was known as "the enclave factor", he'd explained weightily when he bumped into Carl in a coffee shop. "The same thing happened in Malibu back in the thirties, and in Santa Fe in the eighties." He asked Carl to pass along his deep and undying gratitude to "Her Royal Highness, your wife".

Emma opened the envelope. She extracted a single sheet of cream-laid paper. An ornate signature appeared below a single paragraph of text. Emma read it quietly. "They have more legislation for me to sign."

"When?"

"This weekend." She lifted her head. Her eyes followed her son as he romped on the grass.

"Aren't you on night shift?"

"Yeah."

"When's this going to end? For years you've been co-signing their damned Acts of Parliament! You're the Queen of Limbo Land!"

"Imagine how Her Majesty feels." Emma's eyes stayed locked on her son. She drew a deep breath. "It's been worse since Victor started giving those ridiculous interviews from prison. He's tearing that country apart, Carl! *My* country."

"Your country?"

"Carl... the House of Lords couldn't ignore Victor's evidence. How can I?"

He sighed and nodded. Emma slid her arm around him and leaned against his shoulder. "You're my life, Carl. You know that."

"And you're mine."

They watched their son play. "Along with..." Emma began.

"... our pampered Prince," Juneau finished.

They sat in silence, perfected by each other.

"Are you thinking of ending your exile?" Carl asked gently.

"No! It's crazy enough over here! It's given me a real taste of what Diana went through. *And* her boys! It's even worse for them, now that she's gone. Would we really want to expose our little guy to that?"

As if on cue, the child ran over. "Daddy...? Mommy...? Can we go riding?" Violet eyes pleaded. Sunlight glinted off tiny golden hairs on a perfect golden cheek.

Emma and Juneau exchanged a glance.

"Let's." Emma said.

Juneau stood. "I'll get changed."

He sauntered back to the house. Two bicycles leaned against the stairs, one with a child's seat mounted on the back.

Emma hugged her son. "Where do you want to go?" she asked.

"Kelley's house! I wanna play with Patches."

"Okay. We'd better phone first and see if she's home." She got up. "Let's get your jacket and helmet, Mister."

They headed for the house. The little boy skipped happily ahead of his mother.

Four hundred yards from Carl and Emma's home, a derelict panel van sat propped on blocks behind a dilapidated house. Tall weeds poked up through empty wheel wells. The windshield was opaque with years of grime; the driver and passenger windows darkly tinted.

The neighbors on either side of the abandoned property had no inkling that the rotting old van was occupied.

Inside the van's rear compartment, lights on high-tech equipment glowed and blinked as two shadowy figures, a man and a woman, sat very still, watching a sharp-color image on a glowing CCTV screen.

The man's name was David Kingston, although he sometimes went by Stanley Wisdom. He didn't know the first name of the woman sitting beside him. He only knew her as Conyers.

The audio feed was slightly distorted, but the watchers had no difficulty hearing the little boy's words.

"Maybe Patches will smile for us!"

Three thousand miles away, a man sitting at an antique desk was watching the identical image on a computer.

He was watching Emma and her son.

Deep lines of worry etched the man's face.

Alan Boswell had aged considerably over the past three years.

He watched Emma follow her boy across the lawn.

"Sure he will!" Emma called. "What does Kelley always say? 'Patches is the–"

The camera zoomed in.

"–smiling-est dog what ever was!" the child finished.

The camera locked on the little boy's face.

There was a knock on Boswell's door. He clicked his mouse. The video feed vanished from the screen.

"Come!"

A Palace servant stepped into the room. He stood stiffly just inside the door.

"Hello, Frederick."

"Evening, sir. I have a message from upstairs."

"Yes?"

"It has just been announced that Mr. Victor Dawson will be making a statement on his network."

"Another 'State of the Union" address from England's most famous prisoner, I expect."

"Yes." The man paused. "Forgive me, sir, but why is he permitted to do this?"

"Those who make these decisions have decided that muzzling the man would likely create more controversy than allowing him to rant."

"I see… Well, Her Majesty asked me to say that she intends to watch."

"That's a first," Boswell said quietly.

"She mentioned something about 'ratings', the man added.

Boswell looked genuinely surprised.

"Her Majesty asks you to join her."

46

The treatment room was small, but well equipped. The patient was a young man in his late teens, attired in a work-stained tee shirt and faded dungarees. He was alone. He sat in a straight-backed chair, his left arm extended on the examination table, staring morbidly at his mangled hand lying, palm up, on a bed of sterile dressing.

Emma entered the room. She was carrying a sheet of x-ray film.

"Jeffery…"

"Where's my Dad?"

"In the waiting room. He and a young fellow named Paul."

"Paul's the deckhand."

"He told me your mother's on her way."

"She's going to be pissed at him."

Emma smiled. "Of course she is. She's your mother."

The young man's eyes locked on the x-ray film. "Is it bad?"

Emma switched on a light box and mounted the film. She studied it.

"The good news is… only two broken bones and they're both closed fractures."

"Closed?"

"The bones aren't exposed. They didn't break through the skin. That's a good thing."

"Which bones?"

"These two…" Emma ran a finger across the back of her own hand. "You have four bones here. They're called the metacarpals." Using her pen, she pointed to the two metacarpals closest to the thumb on the film. "These two are broken, here, and here. They should heal without a problem."

"Okay. What's the bad news?"

Emma rolled a stool to the examination table and sat. She fixed the boy with a grave expression. Still using her pen to indicate, she pointed at an oozing gash across the palm of his hand. "When that hatch cover fell on your hand and broke those bones, the rim of the deck opening made this laceration. The cut went very deep." Emma paused. "You said you're left-handed."

"Yeah."

"While we were cleaning up your hand, you couldn't flex your index finger or your middle finger."

"I've been trying since the x-ray."

"And?"

The boy shook his head.

Emma's lips tightened. "Let's do this again."

She snapped on a surgical glove. She rubbed the tip of his index finger. "Can you feel that?"

"Yes."

She moved to the pulpy sections of the finger.

"Can you feel that?"

"Yes."

She repeated the exercise on each finger. The young man nodded each time.

"Okay, that's good. It means you probably don't have nerve damage. Now I want you to flex each finger, one at a time, starting with your little finger, like this…" She demonstrated.

He tried the small finger. It flexed.

Then the ring finger. It flexed.

Emma touched his middle finger. "Go ahead."

The finger didn't move. The boy's forearm bulged slightly as he tried harder.

The finger remained immobile.

"Try your index finger."

No movement.

Emma was silent, thinking. After a few seconds, she put a hand on the boy's knee and spoke to him gently.

"Jeffrey, we can't just sew you up. I'll freeze your hand and explore the wound, but I know what I'm going to find. Two of your flexor tendons have been severed. Tendon repair is a very delicate procedure. We'll have to call in a specialist."

"What kind of a specialist?"

"A micro-vascular surgeon – the one I'm thinking of specializes in hand surgery."

"Is that going to… cost a lot?"

"Yes. I'm afraid so."

"I don't know… my Dad's kinda broke, ya know… The lobster prices tanked, and I don't think he's even got medical insurance any more! I heard him and Mom arguing because they couldn't pay the premium or something… and I don't really work for my Dad, like an official employee… I was just helping out over the summer before I start college, so probably worker's comp wouldn't pay, and…" His voice trailed off. He looked at Emma with pleading eyes. "Doc, I know you're, like, a Royal Princess or something, but everyone says you stayed here 'cause you'd rather be a doctor, and they say you're really great at it… so, I mean, couldn't you do the operation?"

Emma took a breath. She was surprised… and touched.

And suddenly very sad.

"Thank you, Jeffrey. I'm grateful for your confidence. But you're young, and you have a long life ahead of you. This is your dominant hand – you're going to college and this is the hand you write with. The surgery you need takes years of special training. It just wouldn't be right for me to try to do it, and it wouldn't be fair to you."

Tears welled in the young man's eyes. "My folks… this is going to kill them–!"

He's more worried about his parents than he is about himself.

Emma swallowed. She squeezed the boy's shoulder. "We'll work something out," she said. She stood. "I promise."

Emma left the treatment room, the x-ray film in her hand.

She was heading for the waiting room, lost in thought, when a nurse headed her off.

"Two people are here to see you."

"Who?"

"A man and a woman. The man was very insistent."

"Where are they?"

"Rita took them to the exec conference room."

"Why?"

"We thought it might be important. The man sounded English… you know, like one of those upper class people." The nurse looked impressed.

"Tell them to wait. There's something I have to…" Emma stopped herself. She looked hard at the nurse. "The man… in his fifties, dress shirt with cufflinks, trimmed beard?"

The nurse nodded. "That's him."

Emma drew a breath. "Okay." She reversed course and marched to the elevator. She rode to the second floor. She headed down a corridor.

When she rounded the final corner, she stopped.

Conyers was standing outside the conference room.

Emma slowed her pace and walked toward the woman. Conyers watched her approach. Emma tried to gauge her expression. If anything, she looked more hostile than she had when they'd first met.

"Conyers." Emma said. "It's been a while."

Conyers nodded, said nothing, and opened the conference room door.

Inside, Boswell was on his feet, pacing. He turned and smiled broadly when Emma entered. Emma noticed a large red document box sitting on the table.

Behind her, Conyers pulled the door shut.

"Alan…" She offered her hand. He took it. "Don't tell me the Prime Minister sent *you* all the way over here with the statutes?"

"Yes, Your Highness."

Emma gave him a sharp look. "This is America, Alan. 'Emma' will do."

"Forgive me, but I don't think so."

Emma looked at him. His face wore a strange expression.

"I have a request from the Queen," he said quietly.

Silence settled over them.

Finally, Emma spoke.

"Before we get to that," she said, "I have a request for her." She laid the x-ray film on the table. "A charity case… in need of a patron."

The second bedroom of their bungalow was a work in progress. It was empty of furniture. Paint cans and a roller tray anchored a plastic drop cloth spread in front of a half-painted wall. Juneau stood near a ladder dressed in an old work shirt and paint-stained jeans.

Emma was still wearing her lab coat, with her stethoscope protruding from one pocket.

"Dawson is saying that every law they've passed since the Privileges Committee affirmed my claim is probably a nullity. He said if Parliament won't abolish the Monarchy, they'll have no choice but to offer me the Crown. At that point I have to either accept it or abdicate. He hired a team of lawyers to track down the next in line after me. He says if I do choose to abdicate, the Crown would go to an eighty-four year old retired railway worker who lives in Odessa."

"Odessa, as in, Texas?"

"No. As in, Russia."

"That would be interesting."

"The man has no living children. He had a son, but he died years ago."

"What about grandchildren?"

"There weren't any. The son died in a gulag."

"Great."

"But there's another group of lawyers. The English Bar Council assembled them into a Special Committee. They're supposed to be experts on genealogy and peerage law. Their report says if I abdicate, the Crown has to go to some distant cousin of mine who lives in Luxembourg. I didn't even know that branch of our family existed. Neither did Dawson. His name is Otto O'Neill Ritter."

"The Irish middle name should go down well."

"Yes, and also the fact that his father served in the SS!" Emma shuddered. "Carl, I can't believe how crazy this is getting!"

"Ease up, love. You'll end up with a migraine."

"I'm not being fair to my patients! My mind is on too many other things!" She stared out to sea. "I need to fix this!"

"Fix it?"

"I think I need to... do this."

"Emma... are you saying what I think you're saying?"

"Yeah. I guess I am." She looked away. "If I don't do something, the Monarchy will collapse."

"To quote you: Why should you care?"

"At one time, I didn't." She looked at him. "Now I do."

"You would actually give up medicine? You?"

"Not exactly. Just practice it in a different way."

Juneau didn't say anything. He tapped the skin on the back of his hand. "There's an issue. Me... and our son..."

"It's not an issue."

"Emma, you know it is! It might be the twenty-first century, but some people are still stuck in the nineteenth–!"

"The Queen is going to make a speech. A very pointed speech. It will be a big moment for the country. For the world."

"You're doing this... for that?"

"Partly, yes. It's long past time."

He looked into her eyes. "The Queen has had years to make that speech! And she can make it without abdicating! So there's something else. What is it?"

Emma's eyes filled. "I'm not sure I can put it in words. It's a kind of patriotism, but not the way that word is used in this country. It's not used as a bludgeon. It's more a sense of dedication... a feeling of awe for an ancient office. I know I sound completely ridiculous, Carl, but I can't ignore it." She was quiet for a moment. "But you're right. There is something else."

"What?"

"I can make a difference! I can make the Monarchy more hands-on. I wouldn't just be the patroness of five hundred charities, touring and making little speeches and cutting ribbons. I'd be personally engaged, like Diana tried to be. I could use the Crown to really help people! Personally."

Juneau was silent. Emma touched his cheek, her eyes wide with apprehension. "Could you handle it?"

His expression was wooden.

Emma's face fell.

Then, something – a tic? – tugged at one corner of Juneau's mouth. The tic became a smile. The smile became a grin. His eyes twinkled with sudden mischief.

"Will you let me run Palace security?"

Emma threw her arms around his neck. "That's not really a job for the Queen's husband!"

"Maybe… but who'd be more motivated?"

Emma laughed.

"That sounded nice," he said. "You haven't been laughing much lately."

Emma bit her lip. "I know. I'm sorry."

"It would be Dawson's worst nightmare…" Juneau mused, enjoying the imagined scene when his former boss got the news.

"Maybe not. An American on the throne is going to upset a lot of Brits. Victor's republican dreams might come true sooner than he or anyone else imagined."

Juneau wrapped one arm around her, inhaling the scent of her hair. "You said Boswell brought a note from the Queen."

"Yes."

"Can I see it?"

Emma fished in the pocket of her smock. She extracted a folded sheet of notepaper. She handed it to Juneau. He opened it and read.

"Dearest Emma,

Ultimately all history is tragic. Now I realize that I am responsible for making it. I have spoken to the Prime Minister. We would like you to come to London.

Elizabeth"

Purbeck's General Store sat at the junction of two country roads about three miles from their house. The store's century-old clapboard construction, wide verandas, and ornately-embellished false front had been meticulously maintained for almost a century. Inside, the wide pine floors, stacks of intriguing oddments and goodies, and barrels of old-fashioned candy had earned the store an honorable mention in several Down East travel guides.

Emma rode up on her bike with her son in the carrier behind her. She lifted him down and held his hand as they climbed the steps. He pulled away and ran to the door with a squeal of excitement. A bell rang as they entered, the boy's pattering feet trailed by Emma's quiet step.

The boy darted from barrel to barrel, eyes alight.

"Mommy... Look at those, Mommy! How many can I have?"

"As many as you can fit in one hand."

"But what about Patches? Patches wants some!"

"Now you know dogs shouldn't eat candy. What did Kelley tell you about Patches' teeth?"

"The dog doctor lady hadta pull one out!" The boy's eyes widened with sudden inspiration. "But I could brush his teeth, Mom! I could!" Encouraged by his mother's silence, he babbled on about toothpaste and brushes...

"Brushing a doggie's teeth? Now there's an interesting idea!"

Emma turned. A middle-aged woman in a rug coat stepped from the aisle behind her. She smiled at the boy, and then looked at Emma.

Her smile seemed warm, but her eyes were not.

Emma felt the hair lift on her neck. She examined the woman's expression, alert for recognition.

The woman tilted her head to one side. "Do we...?" She paused. "I'm sorry. For a second, I thought we'd met. But how could we have? I've never been to this community before."

That accent... What is that accent?

The woman turned her attention back on the boy. "What's your name, young man?"

Her voice wasn't quite as friendly as before.

The boy blinked, faltered, and went suddenly shy. He ducked behind Emma and held on to her leg.

Emma scooped a handful of candies from the barrel, led her son to the till, handed the cashier with a five-dollar bill and didn't wait for the change. She led her now very quiet son toward the door.

The woman was waiting. "I think I recognize you now," she said.

"Excuse us." Emma hoisted her son into her arms and pushed through the door.

The woman followed them out. She stood by the railing on the veranda, watching Emma strap the boy into his seat.

"What's his name?" the woman asked.

Emma straddled the bike.

"What's his name, Dr. Parks?"

Emma looked up, her remarkable eyes suddenly as cold and hard as the woman's.

"His name is Rex."

She rode away.

The woman stood watching until the bicycle disappeared from sight.

ALSO BY **DOUGLAS SCHOFIELD** - FROM **MIWK PUBLISHING**

FLIGHT RISKS

A WORLD IN TURMOIL

In the wake of al-Qaeda's catastrophic attacks, western democracies scramble to meet a deadly new threat...

A LIFE IN TURMOIL

For legal secretary Grace Palliser, the war on terror is just background noise. Twenty-four years ago, her father shot her mother and then killed himself. Today, Grace's life is a torment of nightmares, drug addiction, and custody fights over her daughter.

Being framed for murder is just about the last thing Grace Palliser needs...

But her accidental discovery of a vast international fraud triggers a cascade of terrifying events. Within days, Grace is running for her life, hunted by both the Canadian police and the American FBI. She flees across the continent in a desperate search for the evidence that will clear her.

Hot on her trail is a corrupt former cop with a simple assignment...

...to kill Grace Palliser.

ISBN 978-1-908630-18-6

RRP **£12.99**
(**£9.99** if ordered direct from **Miwk Publishing**)

PRAISE FOR **FLIGHT RISKS**

"Sadly, but completely satisfied, I finished reading *Flight Risks*. I arrived on the set of Diary of a Wimpy Kid two hours before my call time. I wanted to be alone without any interruptions and just sit down with all the characters in the novel. What a wonderful and exciting story! I just could not wait to pick up the book to continue on from where I left off. What a ride!"
- *Alf Humphreys, film and TV actor*

"My heart was racing from start to finish with no let up in sight. If I have one criticism of the author is that he is relentless in keeping me on the edge of my seat and unable to sleep."
- *Christopher Dalton, film producer & author*

"There are some pretty tough situations here, but everything is believable and real, especially the dialogue, at which, I feel, this author excels."
- *Tricia Heighway, author*

"Schofield's easy and simple style of writing brings such vividness to his characters, scenes, the action, and the suspense and does not get in the way of his story's breakneck speed. And best of all, he skilfully ties up the entire story in the final chapter with an ending that took this reader completely by surprise."
- *Tom Kovacs, film actor and musician*

"*Flight Risks* is an accomplished novel with a little bit of everything you fancy – mystery, murder, mayhem, sprinkled judiciously with a smattering of sex. Well-researched facts flavour the story instead of overpowering it, and the twist at the end will take any reader by surprise. The perfect book to take your mind off the dreary summer, it will captivate your imagination and never let go."
- *Elise Hattersley, literary editor*

ALSO FROM **MIWK PUBLISHING**

CARRY ON CONFIDENTIAL

by Andy Davidson

The Carry On films have delighted audiences around the world. Saucy yet subtle, the Carry Ons are the very best of British.

From gentle romantic comedies, through innuendo, double- (and single-) entendre to an all-too-brief dalliance with alternative comedy in the 1990s, the Carry Ons and the people who made them have become cultural icons and household names.

But how well do you really know our most beloved comedy institution?

Carry On Confidential is the thinking fan's guide to the Carry Ons, taking a fresh look at these classic British comedies. A unique spotter's guide with something new for even the most seasoned devotees, Carry On Confidential is packed with trivia, bloopers and gaffes, spin-offs and collectibles and a guide to the locations used in every film.

You'll fall in love with the Carry Ons all over again.

ISBN 978-1-908630-01-8

RRP **£19.99**
(**£12.99** if ordered direct from **Miwk Publishing**)

ALSO FROM **MIWK PUBLISHING**

PROPHETS OF DOOM

THE UNAUTHORISED HISTORY OF DOOMWATCH

by Michael Seely

In February 1970, one of the most important television drama programmes was broadcast on BBC1. Not only did it introduce a new word to the English language, it also brought to a mainstream audience the emerging idea of the scientists' moral and ethical responsibility in society. This was *Doomwatch*, a visionary series which took scientific research and technological advances and imagined where they could go disastrously wrong if greed, politics or simple ambition won over caution. This was drama with a message. And it was heard.

With contributions from the family of Dr. Kit Pedler, Darrol Blake, Jean Trend, Glyn Edwards, Martin Worth, Adele Winston, Eric Hills, and others, this book will tell the proper story of *Doomwatch* both on and off the screen, how it was made, the true story behind the stories, the controversies, the back stage bust-ups, and how the programme inspired those who looked around the world in which they had been conditioned to accept, and begin to question.

ISBN 978-1-908630-11-7

RRP **£19.99**
(**£12.99** if ordered direct from **Miwk Publishing**)

ALSO FROM **MIWK PUBLISHING**

JUSTYCE SERVED
A SMALL START WITH A BIG FINISH

by Alun Harris and Matthew West

In 1984 a group of Doctor Who fans began a project which would continue for another decade and eventually lead to much greater things.

Audio Visuals: Audio Adventures in Time & Space were a non-profit, fan endeavour creating full-cast audio *Doctor Who* drama. 27 plays later the majority of the creative team would go on to be involved with Big Finish, an officially licensed range of *Doctor Who* audio dramas.

For many fans Audio Visuals seem almost canon. Nicholas Briggs was our Doctor. We remember the Daleks' destruction of Gallifrey before it even happened on TV. We supported our Doctor through drug addiction, companion-loss and the horror of Justyce.

This book is a guide to those days.

With contributions from Nicholas Briggs, Gary Russell, Nigel Fairs, John Ainsworth, John Wadmore, Alistair Lock, Patricia Merrick, Richard Marson, Nigel Peever, Jim Mortimore, Andy Lane, Chris M Corney and many others, all wrapped up in a new cover by Tim Keable.

Celebrate *Doctor Who* fan creativity at its very best.

100% OF THE THE AUTHORS' PROFITS FROM THIS BOOK WILL BE DONATED TO AMNESTY INTERNATIONAL UK.

ISBN 978-1-908630-03-2

RRP **£19.99**
(**£12.99** if ordered direct from **Miwk Publishing**)

ALSO FROM **MIWK PUBLISHING**

THE QUEST FOR PEDLER
THE LIFE AND IDEAS OF DR KIT PEDLER

by Michael Seely

For many people, Kit Pedler is best remembered as the man who created the Cybermen for *Doctor Who*, a real life scientist who was brought in to act as an advisor and bring some science to the fiction. The Cybermen were his ultimate scientific horror: where the very nature of a man was altered by himself, by his own genius for survival, creating a monster. Pedler was a scientist with an imagination. He liked to think 'What if...?'

Together with his friend and writing partner Gerry Davis, he created the hugely successful and controversial BBC1 drama series Doomwatch, which captured this fear and frightened the adults as much as the Cybermen scared the children.

The series changed his life and launched him as a prophet of doom, whose stories uncannily predicted real life ecological accidents and disasters and became a much sought after pundit in the press and on television.

With contributions from his family, friends, colleagues and critics, this book tells the story behind a fascinating, charismatic, complicated, and demanding human being; a natural teacher who didn't just want to pontificate about the problems facing the world in a television or radio studio, but actually do something practical about them.

ISBN 978-1-908630-11-7

RRP **£19.99**
(**£12.99** if ordered direct from **Miwk Publishing**)

publishing

www.miwkpublishing.com/store/

www.facebook.com/MiwkPublishingLtd

www.twitter.com/#!/MiwkPublishing